THE
BONE
SPINDLE

THE
BONE
SPINDLE

LESLIE VEDDER

Hodder
Children's
Books

HODDER CHILDREN'S BOOKS

First published in Great Britain in 2022 by Hodder & Stoughton
First published in the United States in 2022 by Razorbill
an imprint of Penguin Random House LLC, New York

1 3 5 7 9 10 8 6 4 2

A CIP catalogue record for this book is available from the British Library.

ISBN 978 1 444 96614 5

Typeset in News Plantin MT Std

Printed and bound by Clays Ltd, Elcograf S.p.A.

The paper and board used in this book are made from wood
from responsible sources.

Hodder Children's Books
An imprint of Hachette Children's Group
Part of Hodder & Stoughton Limited
Carmelite House
50 Victoria Embankment
London EC4Y 0DZ

An Hachette UK Company
www.hachette.co.uk

www.hachettechildrens.co.uk

For my partner, Michelle,
who is everything

PROLOGUE

IN A FARAWAY time, in a great kingdom of magic, a baby was born to the last king and queen of Andar.

Their first child had been blessed with extraordinary magic; their second, with great wisdom and intellect. But the third child was sickly, hovering on the edge of death. His mother named him Briar Rose after the wildflowers that thrived in the forest hollows, which bloomed even in the darkest shadow.

At this time, the royal court was guided by four women of incredible power known as the Four Great Witches. The first was the Snake Witch, who tamed beasts and performed masterful transformations. Second, the Dream Witch, who walked effortlessly into sleeping minds. And third, the Rose Witch, a descendant of the first Witch Queen, Aurora.

The fourth Witch was ancient, said to be older than the kingdom itself. She carried a drop spindle of gleaming bone through which she worked a darker magic, manipulating the flow of life with her golden threads. It was she who approached the queen in her hour of need, offering a bargain. She would save Briar Rose, for a price: the secret spells hidden by the first Witch Queen, forbidden to all and safeguarded by the royal line for generations.

Desperate, the queen agreed. The Spindle Witch spun her wicked golden threads and saved the child, but the magic exacted a heavy toll, trading the queen's life for her son's.

The king, heartbroken by his wife's death and furious at the Spindle Witch's treachery, refused to honor the bargain. Swearing she would never have what she sought, he banished her from Andar and ordered every image of her stricken from the land.

The Spindle Witch vowed revenge, for she had waited lifetimes to obtain the secret spells. The magic that had saved Briar Rose now bound him to her. Before the court and the Great Witches, she swore that by the prince's sixteenth birthday, he would fall to darkness and belong to her forever. Once he was under her power, she would use him to find the forbidden spells—and to destroy the kingdom she loathed so deeply.

The Great Witches tried any and every means to break her hold on Briar Rose, but the dark magic was too powerful. Cursed and ill-fated, the prince was locked away in the castle, until at last, on his sixteenth birthday, he reached for a rose in his garden, only to prick his finger on the bone spindle hidden among the thorns. Before the Spindle Witch could claim him, the Dream Witch cast him into a deathless sleep, hiding him away in a white tower wreathed in protective roses.

The Spindle Witch's fury at being denied was great.

Summoning all her power, she raised an army to crush the Witches of Andar—an army conjured of hatred and malice, great storms of crows and fiendish creatures of malformed bone animated by her golden threads. The people of the kingdom fled as she advanced, leaving nothing but devastation in her wake.

At last, only the castle remained, besieged by an impenetrable Forest of Thorns. The Spindle Witch was on the cusp of victory. But the Great Witches stood against her one last time, giving their lives with three final acts. The Snake Witch became a great ivory serpent and wound through the Forest of Thorns to preserve a path to the castle. The Dream Witch spelled everyone inside to sleep, to protect them until they could be awakened alongside the prince. And the Rose Witch left behind all that she loved and fled with the broken pieces of the bone spindle, taking refuge in the neighboring kingdom of Darfell to sow the seeds for Andar's rebirth.

Among the survivors, a legend was passed down, one generation to another: One day, a girl would be drawn to the spindle—a girl who could wake Briar Rose and, in doing so, set in motion the Spindle Witch's ultimate demise.

A drop of blood, a drop of hope. The sleep of death broken with a single kiss.

1

Fi

FI PUSHED OPEN the door and stepped into the dingy tavern known as the Silver Baron. The bang of the door closing behind her raised a flock of crows pecking the dry dust outside, and the shadows of their wings against the window drew the attention of the crowded room. Suspicious faces peered at her over pewter cups of dark wine and the scraps of finished meals. Fi pulled her hat down over her eyes. She made her way through the tables and took a seat at the counter, where she could watch everyone in the room without looking like she was watching them. She had business here today, the kind that might attract unwanted attention.

"Lemon tea, if you have it," she said, catching a barmaid by the elbow. The dark-haired woman sashayed away with a clipped *milord*.

Fi was actually *Lady* Filore Nenroa, the title official since she'd turned seventeen a few months back, but that was probably not immediately obvious between her dusty brown jacket and her low-brimmed hat. It kept the sun off her face when she was traveling and also, apparently, was not terrible for keeping a low profile. So far no one in Darfell had recognized Fi, but it was only a matter of time.

She slid a creased map out of her pocket and onto the bar—then snatched it up again as the serving girl clanked down her cup so hard tea sloshed into the saucer. Carefully, she unfolded the map to reveal the torn scrap of parchment hidden inside—the real reason she had come to this tavern.

The Silver Baron hadn't changed much in the year Fi had been gone. The patrons seemed as disreputable as ever. A hard-faced woman played chicken with a quicksilver dagger, stabbing it into the scarred tabletop between her spread fingers, and a raucous game of dice was punctuated by harsh barks of laughter and the clink of money changing hands. A sallow, balding man deep into his cups eyed her from the end of the bar. Toward the back were private enclaves hidden behind thick wine-red curtains, for small gatherings of nobles and those who didn't want their faces known. No one stood out, but then, Fi didn't know who she was looking for. She slid the scrap of parchment into the cup of her palm, frowning at the messy scrawl.

Meet me at the Silver Baron at sundown. I have an offer you can't refuse. No signature.

The note had been slipped under her door at the Iron Lantern Inn, where she'd been staying the last two days. Her first instinct—probably her best instinct—had been to pack up and leave town. But every time she reached for her travel

6

bags, she found herself lifting the note instead, studying the puzzle it presented. Who knew she was back in Darfell? And what did they mean, *an offer you can't refuse?*

Fi drummed her fingers against the counter, staring at the black fingerless glove on her left hand. The crumpled map was scratched with harsh Xs, drawn in her own frustrated hand, as search after search failed to turn up what she was looking for. Following a mysterious note to a place like the Silver Baron was an act of desperation.

She pulled off her hat and set it on the bar. Her skin was tan, her cheeks dusted with freckles from hours in the sun. She ran her hand through her dark brown hair, which was just long enough to trap in a small ponytail at the nape of her neck. She wasn't keeping a low profile because she was a fugitive, nor was she up to anything shady enough to take place in the back rooms of the Silver Baron. She was just avoiding her ex.

He had been her first horrible guess as to the author of the message, but cryptic notes weren't his style. And she'd never known *him* to sign off without a telltale flourish from his silver-tipped quill. That didn't leave her with a lot of suspects.

Fi lifted the cup of tea, tipping it to study the yellow-ish liquid before taking a sip. Only years of practice at being polite kept her from spitting it out. It was supposed to be lemon tea. It tasted more like an old lemon rind steeped in a bucket of rinse water.

"Master," Fi said, signaling the tall man with the neatly trimmed beard who was wiping glasses behind the bar. "This isn't tea. I think you may have poured water in a dirty cup."

7

The man's expression said that's what she got for ordering tea in a place like the Silver Baron. "I can throw it out for you free of charge."

Fi snorted. She'd spent the last year in the coastal nation of Pisarre, where exotic teas and spices had come in from the ports every day. She let herself get lost in the memory of salt air and long afternoons in the giant library with a wall of windows that overlooked the sea, lush green lemon trees swaying in the breeze. Then she wiped the dirt from her brow and shook it away.

This wasn't Pisarre—this wasn't even the same kingdom. This was the town of Raven's Roost on the eastern edge of Darfell, nestled up in the Cragspires a stone's throw from the fallen kingdom of Andar. She was going to have to get used to border living again: harsh terrain; roughing it; and other, less pleasant things.

Her eyes slid to the posting board beside the bar. Among the Border Master's bounties on wanted criminals and merchants' calls for muscle for hire hung a scatter of notices and hand-drawn sketches of suspected Witches in the area. This time it wasn't the tea that pinched her face. The Witch Hunters were getting bolder if they'd started to hang their notices out in the open, even in a place like the Silver Baron.

The Witch Hunters were a vicious cult who believed all magic was corrupt and vowed to stop Andar from ever being restored—probably the only ones left, after a hundred years, who still believed the great kingdom of magic could be saved. They operated mostly in the scorched, lawless wastes of Andar, looting magic relics and chasing Witches out of the fallen kingdom. Raids over the border into Darfell used to be rare, but recently they'd started coming after Witches in the border towns, where the Guard was always stretched too thin. Fi's eyes lingered on the rough sketch of a man with wispy hair and a large crystal earring.

She fisted her gloved hand under the counter. There wasn't anything she could do. Witch Hunters were outlawed in Darfell, but they still operated in secret, vanishing into the hills whenever the Border Guard was dispatched. Worse, it seemed like the harder life got in Darfell, the more people were willing to look the other way. The cities on the border had once been the most prosperous in Darfell, bustling with merchants coming and going from Andar. But ever since the great kingdom of magic collapsed, the whole area had been in steady decline, leaving a lot of hard, hungry, desperate people.

The door swung open with a bang, and a figure swaggered into the tavern. A short, stocky girl headed toward her, wearing a rust-red coat that fell to her knees over a gray tunic and a scuffed pair of dark pants. Her ash-brown hair was braided and wound into a knot, and a battle-ax was slung across her back, its dull head gleaming between her shoulder blades. But what really caught Fi's attention were the heavy boots with thick soles and wedge heels. Those she would recognize anywhere. They were a custom design that gave a few extra inches of height to the young woman who went with them.

Shane—the huntsman for hire.

Fi set her teacup in its saucer and tucked the map back into her pocket as Shane elbowed her way through the tables instead of going politely around. She slung herself onto the high stool next to Fi. Her heavy canvas pack hit the floor with a thud.

Fi waved the note. "You," she said flatly. "You sent me this?"

"Yep." Shane grinned. The girl hailed from the Steelwight Islands of the north, but she'd been in the borderlands long enough to dress like all the other rugged scouts and explorers—namely, in well-worn travel clothes with a thick layer of dirt, her fair skin sunburned in the cheeks. Her sea-gray eyes studied Fi. "You're a hard one to track down."

"Clearly not hard enough," Fi muttered, pushing her tea away. It certainly wasn't fit for drinking. "How'd you find me?"

"A mutual friend told me you were back in town," Shane said, shrugging her eyebrows.

Fi's gaze darted to the wall of posters, seeking out the man with the crystal earring. Shane leaned forward over the bar, craning to see. Her face twisted into a scowl when she realized what Fi was looking at.

"Oh, no they don't!" Shane pushed up from her seat and stalked over to the Witch notices.

Conversation at a few of the tables trailed off. Shane crossed her arms, staring up at the wall before raising a hand and ripping down through the overlapping posters. She was short enough, even in the boots, that she had to jump to get the highest ones. She landed heavily and turned to glare at the room. Fi wasn't sure whether Shane was so mad because the *mutual friend* they'd been discussing featured prominently on the board, or whether she just hated Witch Hunters in general. Shane was well-known for her aggressive brand of justice—the tavern was probably lucky she hadn't buried her ax in the wall.

Shane crumpled the last scrap of paper into a ball, spinning to face the bar master. "You," she warned. "Don't let those scum post their garbage here!"

"It's a public board," the master said, not looking all that concerned—either by the notices themselves or the fact that they were now in shreds on the floor. Shane huffed.

Satisfying as it might be to make a scene, the kind of patrons who frequented the Silver Baron weren't likely to be shamed by one angry huntsman. Fi didn't tell Shane that, though. She wasn't in the mood for a fight. They'd only worked together a couple of times before, and never closely, but she hadn't forgotten the girl's temper.

Shane thumped into her seat backward so she was facing out toward the silenced room with her elbows crooked up on the bar, daring anyone to have something to say. Nobody met her eyes. "Cowards," Shane hissed.

Fi shook her head. "Isn't this a little out of your way for a social call?"

"Actually, I have a proposition for you," Shane said.

Fi rolled her eyes. *A proposition* for her and everyone else in the place, since every ear was turned toward them.

"You sure you want to be *propositioning* so publicly?"

Shane snorted out a laugh and threw up her shoulder in a shrug that said she didn't particularly care. Then again, she wasn't the one trying not to attract attention. Fi fought down a wave of irritation.

"Master, we'll take one of the back rooms." She pulled two copper coins from the pouch at her waist and slid them across the bar.

The man put down his cleaning rag to retrieve his money, then raked a disapproving gaze over Shane's ax. "No weapons in the back."

"I don't carry any." Fi lifted the edges of her jacket and spun in a circle to show her belt. Aside from her money pouch, all she carried was a rope tied off with a blunt ring, fastened in a tight curl.

"And I'm not disarming for this," Shane added.

The master was unmoved. "Ax stays out front, or you do."

"You're not going to part me from my stuff!" Shane warned hotly, clearly winding up for precisely the kind of public display Fi was trying to avoid.

"I'll do it, then." Fi ducked behind Shane, deftly sliding the ax from its straps. It was heavier than she'd expected, and the metal head lurched toward the floor before she heaved it onto the bar. Now that she was looking closer, she could see how fine the weapon was, the wooden handle worn but polished, and the single curved blade inlaid with a design of interlacing knots. She kicked Shane's overstuffed pack under a stool. "There, problem solved," she said, pushing Shane toward the back.

"I have everything in that pack memorized, down to the balls of lint!" Shane yelled over her shoulder. "And I'll know if you've so much as polished the spots off that ax!"

Fi shook her head, giving the girl an extra push into the curtains of one of the enclaves. "Stop making a scene." With the way she acted, it was hard to believe Shane was a year older than Fi.

The small enclave was thick with shadows, lit only by the flicker of tall candles in cast-iron candlesticks. A round table and chairs hunched against the wall. The heavy velvet curtain muffled the sound from the bar as it swirled closed behind them.

"You know, that guy only took my ax," Shane said, throwing herself into one of the high-backed chairs. "I could easily be killing you back here with a hidden dagger."

"But it would be much harder to destroy the furniture while you did it," Fi pointed out, sitting carefully on the edge of her seat, "which I think was his bigger concern."

Shane chuckled, tipping back in her chair. "I forgot how sharp you can be."

"Feel free to leave anytime," Fi offered blandly.

"I meant it as a compliment!" Shane protested. "And anyway, we'd both regret that. Didn't you read my note? I have an opportunity you can't refuse." Fi threw her a look, but Shane leaned over the table, suddenly serious. "I found something when I was exploring a ruin down by Haverfall. It's a map—one you're going to want a look at."

Fi clicked her tongue, refusing to be baited. "There are a lot of maps floating around, most of them for ruins long discovered. What's so special about this one?"

Shane grinned like a fiend. "It's in the Witches' Jewelry Box," she said, pulling a piece of paper out of her tunic and laying it down with a flourish.

The map looked ancient. Through the splotches and creases, Fi recognized the range of high mountains that reared up just beyond Raven's Roost. Within them lay a deep valley riddled with alpine lakes and high waterfalls, all clustered around the river that cut the gorge like a vein.

Up until a hundred years ago, the area had been part of

Andar. Treasure hunters called it the Witches' Jewelry Box because, for a thousand years before the fall, Witches had congregated there, building secret manors and hideaways, strongholds and stargazing towers tucked into switchbacks or teetering on cliffs—now a string of lost ruins studding the river canyon like jewels on a chain. They'd been abandoned when Andar fell and the Witches fled. Technically it was within Darfell's border these days. The whole valley was a crisscross of traps and counter traps, with entire buildings designed to safeguard relics and treasures of long-dead Orders of Magic.

Fi's eyes scoured the map. She frowned, peering closer. "I think someone played you for a fool. There's nothing here." Besides the geographical features, there were no marks at all—there weren't even any roads.

"Watch."

Shane held the map up to the candle, so close Fi worried there wouldn't be a map in a second. Then she saw it. Something was starting to appear—dark lines of ink revealed by the heat, bleeding across the parchment like water soaking into the page. *Invisible ink.* When the lines stopped spreading, the river in the center of the Witches' Jewelry Box was overlaid with thick curls of vines, each one hung with blossoming ochre roses.

Fi pressed her finger to the page, tracing the complex whorls and loops in astonishment. "These aren't just vines. They're words in one of the magic languages." There had been countless Orders of Magic throughout Andar's long history. Many of them crafted their own languages to keep their spells secret. "It's the Order of the Divine Rose."

"I figured that much," Shane said. "The roses were a dead giveaway."

Was it possible? The Order of the Divine Rose was the oldest and most powerful of all of them, and every Witch in the royal line had been a member. Shane was right. This wasn't just any treasure map.

"Now you can see why I brought this to you. What's it say?" Shane asked.

Fi leaned close, breathing in the scent of old paper as she studied the intricate letters. "It says, *among the roses.*"

"Well, that's not much of a hint," Shane grumbled. "There are a dozen roses on that vine. You mean the map could be pointing to any one of them?"

"No. It's none of them." Fi couldn't keep her excitement out of her voice anymore. "At the top of the vines— see how there's one rosebud that hasn't blossomed yet?" She pointed to a spot northwest of the gorge, perched on the edge of a cliff. "Sometimes the Witches of the Divine Rose used a rosebud to indicate something hidden in their scrolls—things too important to write down, in case they fell into the wrong hands."

Shane squinted at the paper. "But that cliff's less than a day's hike from here—it's not even in the canyon! How has nobody found it after all this time?"

Fi shook her head. "I guess I'll find out when I get there." A curl of anticipation teased her stomach, but she tried not to seem too eager. "How much are you selling the map for?" she asked, thinking about her slightly thin purse.

"Selling?" Shane snorted. "I'm not selling it. I'm looking for a partner. You used to be a treasure hunter—*used to be* pretty good at it, too. I can't imagine all your skills have dulled during your grand travels."

"*None* of my skills have dulled," Fi snapped back.

"Great." Shane smacked the table. "Then you're hired. Standard agreement: All treasure goes to me, all books and boring historical stuff to you, and nobody touches any magic relics."

That breakdown worked fine for Fi, unless they found only treasure—though she supposed it would be equally unfortunate for Shane if they found only books.

"Wait," Fi protested. "I haven't agreed yet."

"You will," Shane said, smug. "Your eyes haven't left this map since I pulled it out."

Fi felt her cheeks getting hot. She prided herself on having a good poker face, but Shane had seen right through her. *Way to keep your cards close to the vest,* she thought, annoyed.

"Fine." Fi reached her hand out over the table. "We do this one job, then go our separate ways."

"One job," Shane agreed, seizing her hand. It was a rough handshake, like everything else about Shane.

"Meet me at the crossroads past the old watchtower two hours before dawn," Fi said, already calculating what she'd want to bring on an expedition like this.

Shane gave a pained groan. "Two hours *before* dawn? No wonder you can't keep a partner."

Fi's chest gave an unpleasant squeeze. It was only a gibe, like the other insults they'd been trading, but it hit a little too close to home. She'd only ever had one partner, after all, and now—well, now she didn't.

Something must have shown on her face, because Shane was suddenly backpedaling.

"Sorry. Forget it, I'm just hungry. Oh, and in case you were wondering about that note—I'm actually in the room next to yours at the Iron Lantern. That's how I found you so easily." Shane snatched the priceless map, bunching it up and shoving it back into her shirt. "I'm going to go scare up some grub." She nearly got into a fight with the curtain as she made a hasty exit.

"I'd recommend a different tavern," Fi called. The aftertaste of the sour tea still curdled on her tongue. She wouldn't risk a meal here.

The curtain whispered closed, leaving Fi alone with her thoughts. She was about to have another partner, even though she'd sworn never to go down that road again. At least Shane was nothing like her former partner—now her ex in every sense of the word.

Slowly, Fi worked the fingerless glove off and set it aside. She held up her hand beside the guttering candle, looking for the thousandth time at the butterfly mark burned into her palm—a stylized swallowtail, dark as ink, with long tails that trailed over her wrist before curling in toward the sharp, angular wings. It was a curse mark, and it had been her old partner's parting gift to her a year ago, before she fled Darfell.

Fi curled her fingers into a fist. She had come back for one reason: to find a way to break the Butterfly Curse. She'd searched so many ruins, buried herself in old libraries of forgotten books, and none of them had held the answer she was seeking. Shane's map could be just another dead end. But the Witches of the Divine Rose had been masters of warding and protection magic. Maybe they'd left something behind, something that could help her. Maybe this was finally her chance to wipe the slate clean and get rid of the ugly mark.

She wasn't the same person she had been a year ago, and she wasn't going to make the same mistakes.

No more partners. It was safer that way—especially for the heart.

2

>>>——<<<

Shane

SHANE SURGED UP in bed, all her senses on high alert. She blinked away the haze of sleep. She was in her small room at the Iron Lantern. From the darkness that pressed in at the window, it was either really late or really, really early.

A noise had jerked her awake. She couldn't place it, but it set her teeth on edge. Shane listened hard. The kinds of places she usually stayed, she could hear every rat and cockroach scuttling through the rafters, but the Iron Lantern was more upscale, with stone walls and thick oak doors. The silence prickled in her ears. Then she heard it—the creak of a foot on a loose board, like someone sneaking around deep in the building. It could be nothing, but . . . Shane swore, kicking her blankets away.

She crammed her feet into socks and boots and hurried to the door, cursing when her own pack nearly took her out. Her shin throbbed from a rude collision with her ax's wooden handle. Limping, she snagged the weapon and plunged into the corridor.

The windowless hall was pitch-black. Shane hugged the wall, the metal ax head cold against her thigh. Fi's door was shut tight. Shane considered shaking her awake, but if it turned out she was stalking some terrified raccoon through the halls, her new partner didn't need to know about it.

The Iron Lantern was a sprawling inn right at the edge of Raven's Roost. It took its name from two giant lanterns that stood to either side of the main doors and burned all through the night. She was close enough now to see the sputtering red light pouring through the front windows.

Another footstep. The crackle of broken glass. Shane hefted her ax. Whoever or whatever was awake, it was in the foyer.

A shadow detached from the wall ahead, darting forward to crouch in the doorway to the foyer. Shane stiffened. Then the figure tipped her head, and Shane caught a glimpse of her new partner silhouetted in the dim glow. Fi's brown hair feathered over her shoulders, and her white nightgown was sleep-rumpled.

So Fi had beaten her there. At least Shane had thought to come armed.

She inched up until she could lay a hand on Fi's elbow. The girl nearly jumped out of her skin. Her wild eyes darted to Shane. Fi sagged in relief, then lifted a finger to her lips, scowling—as if Shane was going to do all that work sneaking down the hall and then blow it by braying out a *fancy meeting you here*. She ducked low and took up position beside Fi, peering around the doorframe.

The lantern light gave the room an eerie glow. Amid the shadows stood a figure dressed all in black, his cloak thrown over his shoulder. A shorter, balding man lurked at his elbow, wringing his hands. Glass glittered on the floor. They had broken one of the windowpanes to reach the lock. That was the sound that had startled Shane awake. She strained to make out their harsh whispering.

"You're sure she's here? The girl with the ax?"

Shane's guts lurched.

The shorter man nodded, the light sickly on his sallow skin. "Shane. I don't know who the other one was, the girl in the hat, but I heard them talking about some big score."

Now Shane recognized the snitch. He had been in the tavern, hunched over the bar when she tore the Witch notices from the wall. Fi scowled, and though she didn't say a word, Shane could just *feel* her partner chewing her out for *propositioning so publicly*.

"Find them." The cloaked man turned, and Shane caught a flash of grim eyes above a sharp, beaky nose, an amulet of yellow topaz glinting at his pale neck. Her blood ran cold as her gaze cut down to the saw-toothed longsword tucked into his belt, the iron cut with nasty-looking spines. Shane cursed. Only one type of lowlife carried a blade like that.

Witch Hunter, she mouthed to Fi.

Fi went still. For the first time, she looked worried. Shane didn't blame her. She hadn't cared much about Witch Hunters one way or the other when she'd first found herself kicking around Darfell. Now, three years later, just the thought of them turned her stomach.

There was an unspoken code among treasure hunters:

Whoever made it through a ruin first got to claim the prize. But the Witch Hunters had other ideas. Roaming the borderlands in mangy packs, they swore a claim on all magic relics and other treasures in the Witches' Jewelry Box, and they weren't above taking them by force. In their flapping black cloaks, they reminded Shane of vultures, stripping the old ruins down to the bones, looting what they wanted and often burning the rest.

She didn't know what they used the relics for, whether they sold them, or destroyed them, or locked them away somewhere for safekeeping. But she knew why they carried those ugly swords. To make people too afraid to get in their way.

Shane was wide awake now, her blood thrumming as every muscle geared up for a fight. "What do we do?" Fi whispered, so close Shane felt the words on the back of her neck.

Her hand tightened around the ax. The snitch had found the inn's ledger, where the guests and their room numbers were recorded, his fingers sliding greedily down the columns. In a second, he would have them.

She grabbed Fi's shoulder, pulling her from the doorway. "Get our packs. Then go out the back window and wait for me there."

"Why?" Fi asked. Her eyes darted to the foyer. "What are you going to do?"

"Slow them down."

Fi looked like she wanted to argue. She bit her tongue at the expression on Shane's face. "Don't get yourself killed," she murmured as she slipped away, silent on her bare feet.

Shane gave her partner a ten-second head start. Then she drew herself up from the shadows and stepped into the doorway. The blade of her ax shone molten red in the guttering light.

"Looking for me?"

The intruders whirled.

"That's her! The huntsman," the snitch from the tavern hissed. He backed toward the door, his eyes locked on her ax.

Shane had a better view of the Witch Hunter from here. Brutal and broad-shouldered, he was at least a foot taller than she was, his heavy boots jangling as he stalked toward her. He drew his sword, beating the flat against his palm.

"I heard you found something valuable in a Witch ruin, little girl. Hand it over."

"Or what?" Shane chambered her ax on her shoulder, staring him down.

The Witch Hunter's face twisted into a sneer. His eyes slid to her weapon. "Can you even use that?"

Shane smirked. She could feel him sizing her up, underestimating her. Everyone always did—ever since she'd first wrapped her fingers around this ax handle, when she was too small to lift it. She never got tired of proving them wrong.

"I can use it," she said. "But for someone like you, I won't even bother."

Inside a breath, she spun and slammed her foot into the innkeeper's stool, sending it flying into the Witch Hunter's legs. He hit the floor in a heap. Before he could scramble for his sword, Shane seized the tall candelabra and threw it down onto him, the heavy brass clanging on the stone. Then she sprinted down the hall, her ax swinging and her face split with a fierce grin.

She could hear cursing and spitting, the Witch Hunter struggling to his feet. She threw herself into her room and slammed the door, twisting the lock.

Heavy footsteps pounded after her. The Witch Hunter had given up on stealth. Just as she wrenched open the window, a body crashed into the door from the other side, determined to break it down. She leapt out into the dark and landed with a crunch in the overgrown weeds.

Fi was crouched low with the packs. Shane almost laughed at the sight of her new partner, still in her nightgown but with her worn traveling hat jammed resolutely onto her head.

Fi's eyes flashed over her. "Shane, are you—"

"Go, go!" she whispered, pushing Fi ahead of her through the bushes.

The last thing she heard was the door splintering open into the empty room as they raced into the night.

"DO YOU THINK we lost them?"

Shane leaned against the trunk of a knotty pine, watching the first shafts of sunlight pierce the forest gloom. She crunched into an apple scavenged from her pack. Between their surprise guests and running for their lives, there hadn't been time for breakfast.

"Seems like it," Shane said. "But I wouldn't let my guard down."

After their close call at the inn, they hadn't stopped running until they were well into the foothills, both of them panting and out of breath. Shane hadn't seen any sign of their pursuers, but Witch Hunters never traveled alone. They were like cockroaches—if you saw one, you knew there were more scuttling around just out of sight.

Shane glanced at the thicket where Fi had disappeared. "They might catch up if you take any longer changing, though."

"Trust me, I'll be much faster without my nightgown snagging on every thistle from here to the Witches' Jewelry Box."

Shane chuckled. "You know, if you slept in your clothes, you'd never have this problem."

"Spoken like someone with a lot of experience bailing out the window in the middle of the night," Fi said. "Something I don't plan to make a habit of."

Shane couldn't deny that.

Fi reappeared fully dressed, with a blue shirt under her brown jacket and her hair caught in a ponytail. Shane gave her partner an appraising look. Fi was attractive enough, she supposed, with sharp hazel eyes flecked with green and warm tan skin, but she wasn't Shane's type. Shane went for girls, but not bookish know-it-alls—especially if they were taller than her.

Fi had a reputation among treasure hunters as one of the best, mostly because she'd studied everything ever written about the fallen kingdom of Andar. But she also had some famous ex she was supposedly locked in eternal war with. Rumor had it they'd flamed out so badly Fi quit treasure hunting entirely and left the country, and Shane knew better than to get in the middle of something like that.

As Fi shouldered her pack, Shane pulled out the map. She scowled at the crumpled parchment, irritatingly empty of rose vines. "You hold this. I'll get out the torch so we can see where we're going. Trust a Witch to make this as complicated as possible . . ."

"No need," Fi said, digging a piece of parchment from her pocket. When she opened it, Shane could see Fi had sketched a rough version of the curling vines onto her own map and drawn a circle where the rosebud had been.

"You copied my map!" Shane accused, impressed in spite of herself. Fi had only looked at the original for a minute or two at most.

"I have a good memory," Fi offered with a shrug.

"Good enough to steal a score right out from under me," Shane grumbled.

Fi ignored her. She bent over the map and pulled out a compass, turning it a few times until she was satisfied. "This way," she said, taking off without waiting for Shane.

Though the ruin had seemed close, the hike still took most of the day. The low foothills gave way to high mountains as Shane followed her partner along narrow switchbacks cut right into the rock. The summer slopes rustled with cedar and silver-green sage. From what Shane had seen, the kingdom of Darfell was almost all mountains—it seemed like she was always trudging up a hill or tumbling down one. The hot sun glared out of a clear sky, and she could practically feel her fair skin burning.

At times like this, Shane missed the foggy Steelwight Islands, rippling with waterfalls and emerald forests and storms lashing rocky coasts. Her native kingdom was a chain of islands in a misty archipelago, each home to one of the eight clans and ruled by a War King. It would be the rainy season now, the whole island of Rockrimmon glittering with silver droplets clinging to the leaves. She imagined her grandmother sitting on the ring of mossy rocks beside the meadow marsh, singing "O Wispy Waters" in her raspy voice, a folktale about the spirit of a drowned girl who became the guardian of the willow grove.

It had been Shane's and her brother's favorite. When they were young, they would link hands and dare each other to look into the glassy water, hoping to see the ghost. All they ever saw were their own reflections staring back: nearly identical twins, distinguishable only by Shane's long, unbrushed hair.

My little wildling warrior. That's what her grandmother had called her. *So eager to take on the world, she beat her twin brother out by three and a half minutes.*

But along with those memories came all the things she'd rather forget. The bitter fights. The broken promises. The years of watching her twin's face grow distant and cold, her position as firstborn driving a wedge between them. All the reasons she'd left Steelwight and her family forever.

Shane wasn't just some warrior from the north, as she let people believe. She was the daughter of a War King, the lord of Rockrimmon, and the heir to his throne. Her birthright by three and a half minutes—one she had never wanted.

"I think we can take a shortcut through here."

Fi's voice broke into Shane's reverie. She shoved the old thoughts away, following her partner into a wall of spiny juniper.

Shane liked the idea of the shortcut in theory. In practice, it meant scrambling through a tunnel of brambles that

27

grabbed her like they had been lying in wait. By the time she tumbled out the other side, she'd made the acquaintance of everything that crawled or slithered in the whole kingdom.

When she got to her feet, she found Fi staring at a craggy rock wall. The cliff towered over them, the shadows of the pine forest thick and deep. It looked alarmingly like a dead end.

"This is it?" Shane asked.

"This is the spot on the map," Fi hedged.

Shane glanced around. "I don't see any roses." Actually, she didn't see anything. No crumbled fortress. No mysterious statues. These old maps weren't always reliable, but if someone had gone to this much trouble to hide the royal Witches' favorite picnic spot, Shane was going to be peeved.

"Among the roses," Fi murmured absently. She jerked her head up. "Roses grow in the sun. We have to get higher."

"That I can do." Shane walked along the foot of the cliff, studying the outcroppings and fissures for the best handholds. She squinted at a strange mark. "Hey! Look at this." She scrubbed away a crust of yellow lichen to reveal the whorl of a rose carved into the rock—and another, and another, a chain of roses pointing a path to the clifftop.

Excitement churned in Shane's gut as they scrambled up the slope. Finally, she was starting to feel it—the rush of taking on a ruin, each one dangerous and unpredictable. It was why she'd become a treasure hunter in the first place. She liked the payout—as someone who'd come to Darfell with nothing, she knew the value of having a big pile of money when you needed it. But she lived for the challenge, never knowing what to expect and trusting her skills to get her through one more time.

She reached the top first and turned back to watch her partner. Fi missed a step and her foot shot out from under her, but Shane caught her before she could slip, pulling her easily over the ledge.

Fi gave her a sideways glance. "You're stronger than you look," she said grudgingly, probably the closest to a compliment she could manage.

Shane tossed her head. "Looks like we made it."

Ahead of them was a tall manor, built right into the high cliff overlooking a glistening lake. The stone walls were so overgrown with ivy and wild roses that Shane could easily have walked right by it. From a distance, it would have been indistinguishable from the crags in the rock. That was the kind of thing a Witch would come up with. They were a secretive bunch in general—really, it was no surprise Fi got on so well with them. Shane thought she could make out the skeleton of a tower that had once risen above the hulking ruin, but it had long since collapsed into the body of the house. It looked like a good stiff breeze might knock the whole manor off the cliff.

Fi was making for the entrance, and Shane hurried to catch up. She helped her partner brush away the roses and ivy to reveal a wooden door. It was badly warped and blackened with decay, sitting at odd angles in the frame. A dusty half-moon window glinted above it.

Fi bent over her notebook, a stick of charcoal clutched in one hand as she copied down a line of intricate markings cut into the door. They looked a lot like the ones on the map.

Squinting over her shoulder, Shane saw the notebook was full of similar notations, clusters of old symbols scrawled all the way to the margins. "More Divine Rose squiggles, huh? What's this one say?"

Fi was entranced, running her finger over the grooves in the wood. "Give me a minute—"

"Or we could just try the door," Shane suggested, grabbing the ornate metal handle and pushing. To her surprise, the door yawned inward, creaking on rusty hinges.

Fi squawked indignantly. She stood up fast, brushing herself off. "It said *a drop of blood, a drop of hope*," she snapped, shoving her notebook into her pack.

"And now, even better, it's open." That was a pretty ominous thing to be written on a Witch's door, but far from the worst Shane had seen.

Fi gave her one last look. "Ready?"

"Born ready," Shane replied. Then they ducked through the doorway and disappeared into the narrow space beyond.

They'd gone only a few steps when Fi stopped dead. Shane forgot her grumble about *rude partners blocking the way* as the details of the house surged out of the gloom.

The sunlight spilled in through the wrecked door behind them, throwing their shadows across the stone floor of a dingy entrance hall. A crystal chandelier spun slowly on a rusty chain. On a second look, Shane realized the crystals were carved into intricate roses and the metal ring was shaped like a snarl of thorns. It might have been beautiful if it hadn't been shrouded in a thick layer of cobwebs pocked with dead flies.

"Real homey place," Shane muttered.

Fi stepped over hunks of rotted wood scattered across the floor like bones. She parted the curtain of spiderwebs stretched across the mouth of the hallway and then stopped to brush a hairy spider off her shoulder. Shane's guts clenched, and she had to remind herself that using her ax on spiders would be overkill—that's what boot heels were for. Still, she was happy to let Fi take the lead.

"So, any idea what we're dealing with here?" Shane asked.

"I'm not sure." Fi ran her hand along a rose design scratched deep into the wall. "This manor is centuries old, but there are signs someone's been here more recently."

Shane went quiet, instantly on alert. *Recent* meant there could be danger lurking in the shadows. Could the Witch Hunters have found this place without the map? Or worse, beaten them here? She squinted down the murky hallway, shoulders tensed. The stone walls were slanted with the weight of the house, and she could smell something dank rising up from between the stones, probably mold festering in the cracks.

"How recent are we talking?" she asked in a low whisper.

Fi dusted her hands off on her pants. "The writing on the door is definitely less than a hundred years old," she said, sounding almost excited. "Which means someone was here after the fall of Andar."

"Oh yeah, that's what I call *recent*," Shane muttered sarcastically. Nobody bothered lying in wait for close to a century. She resisted the urge to put her boot heel in the back of Fi's head.

It's only one job, Shane reminded herself. Then they would go their separate ways, only much richer. She imagined herself spinning a jewel-studded crown around one finger, hip-deep in a pile of gold.

A door set into the wall seemed to be the only way forward. Shane frowned. She hated being led through these ruins like a rat in a maze. As if taunting her, a wicked-looking spider slid along a thread, its jointed legs skittering before it vanished under the door.

Fi dug out her bandana and knocked the webs off the knob. She pushed the door open, leading the way cautiously into the room beyond. This one was narrower, the walls tapering toward the ceiling so the whole room felt like it might collapse on them. It was also strangely dim. Six small half-moon windows were set deep into one wall, keeping the room in a perpetual twilight.

If you were going to bother to put in windows, Shane wondered, *why not make them big enough to light the place?* The door clicked shut, making her shoulders jump up to her ears.

The room contained only one thing: a small stone table, which held four statues, each about as long as Shane's arm. An off-kilter door was tucked into the far wall.

"I'll check the door," Fi said.

"Great. I've got the creepy statues, then," Shane muttered, shuffling over to the table. Up close, she could see that the statues depicted four identical figures in long robes and flowing cloaks, hoods pulled close to their faces and obscuring their features. Each figure had its stone hands outstretched, offering a gleaming key.

"The door's locked," Fi confirmed, twisting the handle.

"Well, not for long. One of these has to be the key." Shane frowned at the statues. If one of them was right, odds were the others were very, very wrong—she didn't want to find out what nasty traps the Divine Rose might have left behind. Shane ran a finger over one of the stone hands, brushing off a grimy layer of dust to get a better look at the first key.

The instant her finger touched the cool metal, the key popped out of the divot in the statue's hand and clanged against the table. The noise was instantly lost in a much louder sound—the deafening groan of ancient mechanisms screaming to life behind the walls. Shane grabbed the table as the room shook. Iron bars rushed down from the ceiling with the screech of metal on stone.

Fi had been braced against one wall, inspecting the door. She barely threw herself out of the way before the bars slammed into the floor, right where she'd been standing. Chips of stone flew up at the impact.

All the walls were now blocked off—everything except the locked door.

"Fi!" Shane called, worried in spite of herself. The other girl was getting to her feet, breathing hard. She threw Shane a withering look.

"Watch what you're doing!" Fi snapped.

Shane laughed nervously. "I guess that was the wrong key."

"Is that a joke?" Fi bent to snatch the runaway key that had fallen to the floor. She shook it at Shane. "Why would you yank one of the keys out?"

Now, that was just unfair. "I did not *yank one of the keys out*. I barely touched it."

33

"Maybe don't touch anything at all, then," Fi advised, snippy. Shane was not sure she deserved that—she had a reputation for being a hothead, not a bonehead.

"Not a problem," Shane said. "By all means—show me how to choose between four identical statues."

Her sarcasm was lost on Fi, who now had eyes only for the ornate bronze key. She twirled it in her fingers and then turned to the table, clearly fascinated by the puzzle of the room. Shane had no idea what Fi was looking for as she examined the statues from different angles, peering into their hoods and even pulling out her spiderwebby bandana to polish the stone table. *Or maybe this is some bizarre form of revenge*, she thought, when Fi made Shane boost her up for a closer look at the small half-moon windows, her boot heel digging relentlessly into Shane's spine.

At last, Fi stood in the middle of the room, eyes closed and her fingers tugging absently on one earlobe. It was a classic *I'm-thinking* look. Shane had been hoping for more of an *I-got-it* look.

Shane tapped her foot. "Let's just guess," she suggested. "There's a one-in-three chance of getting it right now. I've always been pretty lucky."

Fi huffed. "I will not be trusting my life to your luck."

Shane wanted to accuse her of exaggerating, but she probably wasn't. There were a lot of ways for traps to kill you in places like this. Now that they were locked in, the room could be flooded with sand or water, or sliding floor tiles could dump them into a pit of spikes, or worse. Then again, Shane could also die of boredom waiting for Fi to make a decision.

"Well?" she pressed.

"Shh! I'm thinking," Fi said, eyes squeezed tight. "Andar was known for its powerful Witches. Those have to be the figures in the statues. Four statues, four Witches—"

"Skip the history lesson," Shane said. "Left, right, or center?"

"The statues have to represent the Great Witches who served the last royal family of Andar," Fi rushed out, clearly aware that Shane's patience was growing thin. "They erected statues of the Witches in the courtyard of the castle, giant statues that looked down on the main square . . . and the people looked up at them!" Her voice shot up at the end— the classic *aha* signal Shane had been waiting for. "Shane, pull out a torch," Fi said excitedly, digging into her pocket.

"Bossy," Shane grumbled, but she was grinning all the same. There was no point in partnering with someone like Fi if you weren't going to listen to her.

By the time she found a torch in her overstuffed pack, Fi already had her flint and tinder ready. Shane pulled back the heavy canvas wrapped around the torch to reveal a blunt metal stave, one end bound with tar and oil-soaked cloths so it would catch quickly. Her eyes watered at the pungent smell. Fi struck the flint with practiced ease and the torch flared to life.

"What do you want me to do with this?" Before Shane had even finished the question, Fi snatched the torch, turning back to the statues. Too curious to be offended, Shane crowded behind Fi as she thrust the torch at the first statue, the one missing its key. A face flared out of the dark beneath the cowl.

Shane hissed a breath in through her teeth. The statue's grotesque features were twisted in a cruel scowl, and the hard stone eyes seemed to look right at her. Instinctively, she pinched the nerve between her thumb and forefinger. It was a trick her grandmother had taught her in case she ever met one of the wandering mist spirits out of Steelwight legends, which were said to weave illusions to lure lost travelers toward the rocky cliffs. Shane was pretty sure mist spirits didn't exist, but she'd picked up the habit anyway. Pain grounded you like nothing else.

Fi looked pointedly at her. "It's not magic," she said. "It's a trick of the design. The features can only be seen when lit from below." She slid the torch under the second cloaked figure. Another hideous face leapt out in the firelight, wicked teeth bared. "These figures are meant to mimic the great statues in the courtyard of Andar's castle. They can only really be seen from below."

"I hate traps that are all about knowing your history," Shane mumbled, unsettled by the stone eyes that still seemed to be following her.

Fi shook her head. "Hardly. Everything about this room is a clue."

"Now, I know *that's* an exaggeration," Shane said, looking around at lots and lots of nothing.

Fi gave an exasperated sigh. "The windows are set high and deep so the room is dim enough to disguise the trick sculpture, but not so dark we'd naturally think to light a torch. And when you set off the first trap, even though everything else in the room shook, the statues remained perfectly

36

still. They're affixed so we can't lift them up." Fi shrugged. "And then there was the table."

Shane could hardly believe what she was hearing. "The table?" she repeated as Fi slid the torch under the third statue.

"Yes," Fi muttered, not paying attention anymore. This time the light revealed a woman's face, smooth and serene, her eyelashes lowered as she stared at the key in her outstretched palms. "It's made of a reflective stone to bounce the light up into the statues' faces."

Shane whistled, impressed. She'd had a lot of fleeting partnerships over the years, but this was the first time she really felt matched.

"I know. The detail in these old traps is amazing," Fi said, completely misunderstanding what had impressed her.

Shane shook her head. "So can I touch the key now?"

Fi blinked, like she had totally forgotten what they were doing and why. She passed the torch under the final statue just to be sure, revealing the curl of a demonic smirk.

"I think we have a winner," she agreed, nodding Shane toward the third statue.

Fi's reasoning was sound—flawless, in Shane's opinion. Still she held her breath as she took the key from the hand of the third statue. The metal teeth came free at the slightest touch, but this time, there was no crash of gears from another trap springing. Shane sighed in relief. Maybe they were through the worst of it.

She had to wiggle the key into the rusted lock, but once she had it in, it turned easily in its grooves. When she heard the tumblers click, Shane gave the handle a tentative push—

but the door was warped by time and damp, and the corners stuck in the frame. Shane shoved again. No luck.

"Give me a hand here?" she called over her shoulder.

Fi moved in beside Shane, both of them leaning hard against the door.

With a loud crack, the door sagged inward, and suddenly they were both stumbling into the next room. The treacherous door swung shut behind Shane, plunging them into darkness. The torch sailed out of Fi's hand and spun across the floor. Through the wild shadows, Shane saw a gleam of wire stretched taut across the room—just in time to watch it snap against Fi's ankle as they went down in a pile of flailing limbs.

A trip wire, Shane realized. And her partner had set it off.

3

Fi

FI GASPED AS she landed hard on the stone floor. She had to fight to get her bearings. The darkness and the smell of mold and rot made her light-headed.

"Trip wire! Trip wire!" Shane hollered right in her ear, having crushed Fi when they went down. She could already feel bruises forming in five or six places.

Trip wire? Fi wiggled out of her cumbersome pack, sweeping her hand frantically across the floor. She couldn't see anything in the torch's red glow.

In the chaotic moment after the door flew open, Fi got one glimpse of the room: wooden chairs with chewed-up legs, a cluster of rotting baskets, a collapsed loom, and a spinning wheel set against the wall. *A sewing room?* It seemed like if someone was going to set a trap here, it would be in the doorway.

"I can't find a trip wire," Fi said.

"You set it off already!" Shane barked, ditching her pack, too.

Fi blinked. "Then why didn't you say that? Yelling *trip wire* is just confusing."

"You want to argue about this now?" Shane demanded.

Fi struggled to her feet. Now that she was listening for it, she could hear a strange clicking sound, followed by a hiss as something shot into the darkness. Suddenly Shane tackled her from behind, dragging her back to the floor.

Clink! Something sharp pinged against the wall behind them.

Fi ducked her head down. "What was that?"

"It's either arrows or bolts!" Shane warned, as another one hissed by overhead.

Fi forced herself to concentrate, trying to guess their direction from the whistle in the air. She caught a glint of metal out of the corner of her eye—a short iron bolt streaking through the glow above the torch before it vanished in the dark. They had to be coming from the walls. "The trip wire must have set them off. If we'd been standing, we'd probably be full of holes by now. Lucky you bowled us over in the entryway."

"I didn't— You know what, never mind." Shane crawled forward on her elbows. "If we're safe down here, should we wait it out?" Even as she said it, there was another whoosh, followed by the ping of a dart landing close enough to give Fi goose bumps.

"*Safe* is relative," Fi warned. "They're coming from all over the place."

"We may have another problem," Shane said. The metal

torch had rolled into the remains of a woven basket, which had caught fire. Fi felt the heat bloom as the flames licked at an overturned chair.

"Let me think," she snapped. A bolt struck the floor next to her elbow. Shane swore, scuttling backward.

"Anytime, partner!"

Fi forced her mind clear. She could hear the crackle of the hungry flames, the hissing of the bolts, Shane's heavy breathing . . . and that strange clicking sound, disguised by the rest. It was too loud to be coming from inside the walls. *Click, click, click, click,* like the spinning of a wheel.

Fi realized what had bothered her about this room even in that first wild second. Though the furniture was all rotted away, the spinning wheel was completely intact. It couldn't be made of wood. When the trip wire snapped, it must have started the wheel moving, and the wheel was connected to the bolts. *Somehow.* She'd have to figure that part out later.

"When I say go, get ready to move." Fi got to her knees and quickly unwound the rope from her belt. The cord was smooth beneath her fingers, soft from years of handling. She wrapped her right hand around the blunt ring at one end. A bolt whizzed by her ear.

In a second, she was on her feet, spinning the heavy ring. She released low, sending it flying toward where the spinning wheel should be—*if* she remembered right. The rope sailed out with practiced ease, and Fi heard the telltale clang of metal on metal. Through the gloom, she could barely make out the end of her rope caught in the spokes of the wheel. It jerked to a halt.

Fi's heart soared with relief. She had been right—the

wheel was connected to the mechanisms in the wall. It was already pulling on her, trying to break free. She wound the rope tight around her wrist. If she relaxed her hold for even a second, bolts would start flying again. Worse, the smoke was starting to burn in her throat, threatening to choke her.

"Shane, now! Get the window open!" She tugged the girl up by her coat and pushed her toward a faint line of light, the seam of a window set into the outside wall. If the shutters hadn't been in such disrepair, it might not have been visible at all. Shane yelped as she stumbled through a broken loom.

A sudden plume of smoke enveloped Fi, making her gag. The flames were leaping between the rotted baskets, and it wouldn't be long before the fire surrounded her. Keeping the rope taut, she rushed to the growing fire, kicking chunks of wood away from the torch. She tossed aside a spindly chair and then lurched forward as the spinning wheel tugged greedily at the rope. The wheel clicked. A dart whizzed past her, clipping her sleeve.

"Shane!" she called desperately.

"I know, I know," an angry voice shot back. "But the cursed latch is stuck—"

Fi struggled against the rope as the spinning wheel dragged her forward.

"Forget it! I'm chopping it down!" Shane yelled.

A rush of air. Fi ducked. The bolt sank into the burning basket, the metal rod gleaming in the angry flames.

Fi was torn. She could let go of the rope and try to take cover, but that would leave Shane wide open. She looped the rope tighter around her wrist, gritting her teeth and holding on with both hands. This time, when the rope pulled, she yanked back with all her might, using her full weight to stop the mechanism from moving.

"Take *that*!"

She heard Shane's cry a second before the ax bashed into the wooden shutter, splitting it with a terrific crack. Shafts of sunlight pierced the room. Shane's determined face shone as she heaved the ax up again. Shutter slats crashed to the floor.

Finally, Fi could see what she was up against. Her rope had indeed tangled in the spokes of the spinning wheel. A metal bar stretched from the center of the wheel into a hole in the stone wall, no doubt triggering the mechanism every time it turned. The walls were pocked with small holes, and the tips of metal bolts gleamed in the dark pits.

The rope burned against Fi's skin. She wasn't going to be able to hold on much longer.

Her eyes fell on the metal handle of the torch. Bracing her feet, she kept the rope looped around her right hand but let go with her left, reaching for the rod. Fi strained as far as she could, the muscles in her shoulders and back screaming. She could just brush the handle with her fingertips.

A sudden turn of the spinning wheel jerked her back. Two bolts shot toward Shane, embedding in the splintered wood over the huntsman's head.

Now she was even farther from the torch, and the flames were only getting higher. Fi made a quick decision.

"Shane, duck!" she warned, then let go of the rope. The spinning wheel whipped free, unleashing a flurry of bolts. Fi dove forward. Yanking her jacket sleeve over her hand, she seized the metal torch. She could feel the heat through the heavy fabric as she scrambled up and raced for the spinning wheel. Fi surged the last few steps and shoved the metal torch into the space between the spokes and the wheel's long arm, jamming it for good.

One last bolt shot over her head. It sailed across the room and sank into her pack, which now looked like a pincushion. Fi sagged to the floor in relief. Shane was extracting herself from the broken loom, which had snagged around her foot. Without the oil-soaked torch to fuel it, the fire spent itself fast, shriveling in the last chunks of wicker and musty wood.

The stone floor felt good against her sore back. Fi stretched out as far as she could, blinking as her fingers slid over a silver embroidery hoop. She lifted it curiously. It was tiny, smaller than her fist.

"You know," she said absently, peering through the ring, "the Order of the Divine Rose was renowned for its embroidery as well as its magic. A lot of their relics are beautifully woven tapestries."

"Really?" Shane demanded, from where she'd been stomping out the last of the flames. "We almost get killed by some moldy old spinning wheel and you want to talk handicrafts?"

Fi sat up, embarrassed. "The spinning wheel's not moldy. It's actually made out of metal. That's how I—"

Shane held up a hand. "Save it. All I want to know is if this ruin is done trying to kill us yet." She prowled deeper into the room, kicking the broken chairs out of her way like they'd personally insulted her.

Fi spun the embroidery hoop again, resisting the urge to lecture her partner on the finer points of those *handicrafts*.

The Witches of the Divine Rose were famous for their binding magic, and many had the ability to embroider spells into everything from elaborate robes and tapestries to small tokens of good fortune. The curls of vines and roses woven or sewn into their textiles were often powerful spells disguised as decoration. She wondered what spell had been sewn using this tiny silver hoop, just big enough for the embroidery on a pocket or a handkerchief.

Fi set the hoop aside and got to her feet, leaning over to untangle her rope from the spokes of the wheel. She was still working the blunt ring out of a vicious snarl when Shane hollered excitedly from behind her.

"Hey, Fi, come take a look at this!"

"In a second," she called back, tugging on the rope.

"You're going to want to see this right now."

"Can't it . . ." The rope came free all at once, and Fi stumbled backward, landing on her butt in the middle of the room. *Graceful,* she chastised herself, wishing her cheeks weren't burning as hot as the smoldering basket. Luckily, Shane hadn't noticed. Fi looked up to find Shane holding back a moth-eaten velvet curtain to reveal a wall of yellow stone.

The entire wall was covered in text—line after line of the beautiful script of the Divine Rose, which glowed pink as the evening light caught in the curling runes. Fi gaped at the wall, her embarrassment forgotten. Shane yanked on the curtains until they ripped free and slumped to the floor.

Fi wound the rope around her arm, tucking the ring under the loops to hold it in place. She moved to stand before the inscription.

"Tell me it's not the world's longest riddle," Shane drawled.

"No," Fi breathed, her eyes tracing the flowing words. "It looks like a passage from a book. 'As the prince's sixteenth birthday approached, the kingdom despaired, for even the Great Witches in all their power had found no way to save him from the curse . . .'" Fi trailed off. She knew this story—could have recited it by heart. "This is the tale of Briar Rose, the sleeping prince. Or the end of it, anyway." The only question was, what was it doing here—in this ruin, on this wall? Was it some kind of test? Some kind of message?

Shane was grumbling about history lessons again, but Fi ignored her, skimming the passage. She squatted down to be at eye level with the last line of text.

"'The prince was locked away in the castle to keep him safe. But it was all in vain. Briar Rose pricked his finger on a thorn in his rose garden . . .'" Something about that line seemed off, but Fi let it go, finishing the last of it. "'And fell into an enchanted sleep, awaiting the kiss that would set him free.'" Fi frowned, resting her hands on her knees. "I think there's something missing."

"Yes," Shane agreed. "The part where, before fleeing the kingdom, some fabulously wealthy Witch of the Divine Rose hid all her treasure here for us to find."

Fi wrinkled her nose. "Not that." It was something else bothering her—something about Briar Rose. From the corner of her eye, she caught sight of the spinning wheel.

That was it. That was the part that was wrong. The story of Prince Briar Rose was one she'd first heard when she was very young—young enough to tug on her mother's nightgown and interrupt the telling to ask, *What's a spindle?* Her mother had pointed to the picture: the prince in the garden, his hand outstretched toward what looked like a shining white blade hidden among the roses. *A drop spindle is used to spin flax and wool into thread. It looks like a bobbin with a long shaft. But in the hands of the evil Witch, it was a terrible weapon.*

"This part's wrong," Fi told Shane, her finger hovering over the text. "It wasn't a thorn Briar Rose pricked his finger on. It was a spindle." Fi's finger brushed the words—and then sank into the stone like it was nothing but sand.

Fi gasped. She pulled her hand back, pressing hesitantly against a different line of the inscription. It was solid, the carved grooves of the letters unmoving beneath her hand. Shane banged a fist on the wall above with similar results.

Fi looked down to where the curling words for *rose thorn* had begun to disappear. She hesitated for a moment before brushing away the rest of the letters. They disintegrated, a few sparkling grains of sand falling to the floor. She and Shane traded wide-eyed looks.

"That's real magic, isn't it?" Shane asked, pinching the nerve in her hand again. Fi couldn't even blame her this time. She could hardly believe it herself.

"I think it is," she whispered.

Real magic in ruins was exceedingly rare. Not many spells survived their caster's death, which was why most of the traps in the Witches' Jewelry Box were mechanisms, not magic. Some of the powerful Witches of old had been able to infuse magic into objects—the greatly sought-after magic relics—but even those were few and far between.

The spot where she had brushed away the words was still soft like sand, waiting for something.

"Maybe you're supposed to fill in the blank," Shane suggested.

Fi lifted her finger, pressing the tip carefully into the sand. She braced her other hand against the wall and then froze, staring at the back of her fingerless glove. Should she really do this? She'd run afoul of powerful magic before. Even through the glove, Fi swore she could feel the butterfly mark tingling in warning on her palm.

"What's wrong?" Shane asked. "Did you forget how to write it? That language looks batty to me."

Fi resisted the urge to bicker over the notion of the beautiful script of the Divine Rose being *batty*. Her heart was banging on her ribs like a hammer. But deep down she knew she'd regret it if she turned back now, if she never found out what was beyond this wall, what the Witches of the Divine Rose were safeguarding here.

Fi finished writing the long, looping characters for *spindle*, stepping back to examine her work. For one moment, the letters seemed to grow stiffer, becoming stone engravings like the rest of the wall. Then the whole story began to shiver, turning into powdery sand and raining down to the floor. And it wasn't only the letters . . .

Fi stumbled into Shane as she backed away. The wall was disintegrating, turning to golden dust before their eyes. A brilliant cloud hung in the air, and when it settled, the entire wall was gone, revealing a room warm with sunset light.

When they stepped through the opening, it felt as if they

had entered an entirely different house. From here, they could look out over the lake, a view of the valley framed by carved archways of streaked yellow stone that led onto a crumbling balcony. The railing—constructed of a row of winding bronze roses—was badly tarnished, and Fi could see at least one patch where the wooden floorboards had fallen out altogether, leaving her peering down at the deep water below. She made a mental note to be careful where she stepped.

Fi could only imagine how beautiful this place must have been, even just a hundred years ago, before the last Witches had fled. It was the kind of building that probably could have stood another thousand years if anyone had been around to tend to it.

In the evening light, the floating specks of dust from the broken spell burned like flecks of gold, illuminating wall-to-wall bookshelves filled with all the things someone had hidden here: old vials of colored glass; fine porcelain teacups hand-painted with blushing roses; and spools of expensive fabrics dyed burgundy and cobalt, the trademark colors of the silk makers in southern Andar. Fi hadn't seen craftwork like this since the antique shops of Pisarre. Darfell was rich in ore, wood, and wine, but most of its exports were raw materials. Artifacts like this had to be from Andar. The shelves bowed under the weight of ancient books with thick cloth bookmarks spilling over the yellowed pages.

"This is more like it!"

Fi glanced over at Shane, who had gone straight for the treasure. A weathered chest on the far side of the room spilled over with gold chains and ropes of jewels. A silver crown set with pink diamonds already sat askew on the girl's head. Fi sighed. In that way, Shane was like every other treasure hunter she'd ever known.

Fi had just stepped around a hole in the creaking floorboards, making for the books, when something else caught her eye. A narrow alcove had been cut into the wall near the balcony, and inside sat a long, low table draped in black cloth. Something shone in the table's center, something that gleamed like shards of white marble. No, Fi realized as she moved toward it—*it was bone*.

She drifted closer and stared down at the shattered pieces of a bone drop spindle, smooth and pure white as if they had just been polished. She couldn't tear her eyes away. A few rust-red drops clung to the whorl, and Fi suddenly wondered whether this was the spindle from the story, the one that had been hidden in Briar Rose's garden.

Her hand seemed to move on its own. Almost against her will, she found herself reaching for the broken piece of the shaft. She hissed as something bit into her finger, making her jerk back. Only now did she notice the snapped-off end of the spindle hidden under the other pieces, sharpened to a point.

Suddenly it was hard to think. Black slanted into the edge of her vision, and all the blood in her body seemed to be rushing the wrong way, leaving her faint. Fi stumbled backward onto the sagging balcony. Her legs trembled as if the floor had begun to shake. A drop of blood welled up on the tip of her finger. Fi stared at it, captivated, the words from the ruin's door echoing in her mind.

A drop of blood, a drop of hope . . .

"Fi, watch out!"

Shane's shout brought Fi back to herself in a rush. She hadn't imagined it—the weathered boards under her feet *were* shaking and groaning. The balcony was collapsing under her weight. A great crack split the air as the support joists snapped out of the divots in the stone wall.

Fi jumped away, but she was too late. She felt a great heave in her stomach as the whole balcony collapsed, taking a large chunk of the room with it.

She threw her rope helplessly toward the carved archways. The metal ring bounced off the stone—and then she was falling, the breath crushed out of her. Shane threw herself down at the edge of the ripped-apart floor, her hand outstretched over the gap. The distance between them might as well have been a mile. All Fi could hear was the echo of Shane shouting her name as she plunged toward the lake.

At least I didn't take any of the precious books down with me.

It was her last thought before she hit the water.

4

Fi

FI SUCKED IN a breath as the icy alpine lake swirled up around her.

The crumbling balcony had hit the water first, breaking the surface tension, so at least she hadn't fractured anything when she went under. But that was the least of her problems. All around her, the lake was full of splintered stone and wood spiraling down into the black depths. A heavy brick hurtled through the water inches from her head. The cold bit into her flesh, but Fi held back the scream that tried to tear from her lungs, knowing she would need every possible second of air. She kicked with all her might toward the surface.

The golden light of the sun was watery and thin above her. She lost it in a cloud of bubbles as something dark and heavy plowed into the lake—a piece of the ornate metal railing wound with roses and thorns. It was coming straight at her. Fi wrenched herself to the side, kicking at the wicked rail to push it away. One sharp thorn ripped into her pant leg, and suddenly she was choking, swallowing mouthfuls of the frigid water. She twisted, making for the surface. Her fingertips raked the cool air for one second—then something jerked her viciously downward, back into the dark.

Fi swallowed her gasp of panic. Her leg was caught in the metal roses. She yanked at it, but it remained wedged between a metal vine and a jagged piece of rail. A tarnished thorn sank into her calf above the boot, releasing a flare of blood that spread like ink in the water. Fi's hands clawed through the red curls as she sank, the railing's horrible weight dragging her deeper and deeper.

She couldn't get free. Her chest was so tight it felt like it was being crushed. Her heart beat a hundred times a second, but every other muscle was at a dead stop.

Fi stared up at the distant shimmer of the surface. The water was hazy around her, a blur of white bubbles. In a moment, her lungs would give out and she would suck in water, and that was it. Fi closed her eyes.

They flew open again as a flash of light enveloped her and a warm hand curled around hers.

Fi blinked, trying to make sense of what she was seeing. A boy was floating next to her in the water—the most beautiful boy Fi had ever seen. His skin was soft and pale, and his short golden hair drifted around his head like a halo, one wispy curl framing his twinkling blue eyes. His dark pants and loose white blouse rippled around him, as if teased by a playful spring wind. A heavy blue velvet coat floated off his shoulders like a cape. And he was smiling—smiling right at Fi, staring back at her with such a calm expression that she found herself calming, too, her pulse feather soft in her ears.

Fi blinked again, trying to force his image out of her hazy mind. She'd heard of people having near-death hallucinations, but if that's what this was, shouldn't she see someone from her own life—her parents? Her friends? Her ex, if fate was really cruel? She was sure she had never met this boy before. Without thinking, she parted her lips to ask who he was, and then choked as the icy water rushed into her mouth. *Don't breathe in*, she begged. *Breathe in and it's all over.*

She gagged, desperate to keep the water from reaching her lungs. The boy threaded his hand through hers, his pale fingers entwined with hers, and pulled her into his arms, one gentle tug somehow freeing her from the metal rail. The breathtaking blue of his eyes was all she could see. Then he kicked upward toward the surface, and at the same moment his rose-red lips covered hers, a kiss that would have taken her breath away if she hadn't lost it long ago. His lips were soft and inviting, and even better, she found she could breathe again, her lungs heaving in her chest.

Fi dug her fingers into the shoulders of the boy's velvet coat, losing herself in the warmth and sweetness of the long kiss. He tasted of flowers, like a perfect drop of honeysuckle nectar on her tongue.

She broke the surface with a great splash. Silver droplets of water flew up around her, sparkling in the last rays of the fading sun. Fi spun in the water, searching for the boy who had saved her. The lake was empty.

Fi's mind raced. Before she could second-guess it, she dove again, the silt stinging her eyes as she peered through the murky water. There was no golden-haired figure waiting just under the surface. He was simply gone.

A shiver ran down Fi's spine. The boy couldn't have been a hallucination, because as far as she knew, hallucinations couldn't save people from drowning—or touch them. Fi's fingers rose unconsciously to her lips. If she hadn't been half frozen, her face definitely would have been burning up.

The stubborn part of her wanted to stay right where she was until she figured it out, but another shiver got her moving. Even though it was summer, it was still about to be night in the high mountains. If Fi didn't get out of this lake and get dry, fast, she was going to be in trouble. Luckily, as the child of historians, Fi had been camping out and investigating forgotten history in inhospitable places since before she could walk. Unlike most of the noble families of Darfell, the Nenroas were a Border House family through and through. Survival skills had been a basic, right alongside reading and writing.

She treaded water, assessing the cliffs around the lake before taking off toward the far bank with a silent apology to Shane. Fi was confident the girl was fine, since the floor had only fallen out on Fi's side, but climbing the sheer cliffs under the manor would be impossible. She sidestroked to the low bank instead, eyeing the jagged rocks that seemed to grin at her like a row of crooked teeth. A few long-finned fish darted away as Fi got her hands on a big ledge of granite and heaved herself out of the lake.

There was only one place she could think to go for help—somewhere Shane would likely be heading, too. They would meet up there, or not at all.

The slope wasn't that high, but it was a long, hard climb on her shaking legs. Fi grabbed for a clump of sage and jerked back as the spiny branch dug into her skin. Her mind raced with the memory of the bone spindle—the way it had glistened with a strange light, the eerie pull that had drawn her toward it against her will. Fi ran a thumb over the pad of her finger where the spindle had pricked her. Under the fiery sky, the wound almost seemed to be bleeding again, a tiny curl of red twisted around her finger like a coil of thread.

Fi shook her head, chasing away thoughts of spindles and relics and beautiful boys with rose-red lips who disappeared like ghosts. She had no time for speculation. On top of all her other problems, there were probably Witch Hunters somewhere in these hills, and Fi wouldn't stand a chance against them on her own. She considered trying out a few of the more inventive curse words she'd heard her new partner muttering, but even totally alone, she couldn't bring herself to be that vulgar.

She reached the top of the hill as the moon rose. The breeze that had been so pleasant in the hot afternoon now made her teeth chatter. She'd have to risk a fire. She worked as quickly as she could, gathering dry branches and setting up a fire ring in a small pine thicket. Then she dug in her pocket for the one set of tools she always kept with her, not in her pack, but on her person. Her flint and tinder.

Fi leaned back against a boulder, reminding herself that she'd been in worse situations before and gotten out of them. She traced the grooves of the blackened iron striker that had once been her father's. If she closed her eyes, she could imagine his big, warm hands around her small, shaking ones the first time he'd shown her how to light a fire—the time they'd gone looking for an ancient crystal chamber and ended up tumbling down the entrance shaft. They hadn't had any packs that day, either, only the contents of their pockets.

"FLINT STRIKES IRON, Filore, not the other way around," her father prompted as she hammered at the flint over and over. Filore didn't understand how he could be so calm. The slick gray stone of the shaft rose around them on all sides, deep and cold as a grave. They had no chance of climbing out—not when she was eight and short, and they had no rope, and one of her father's legs was sticking out at an odd angle. He'd tried to cover it, throwing his coat over the twisted limb, but Filore had already seen it. He'd broken it in the fall.

Dom Nenroa's stern face was usually softened by a smile, but right now he looked ashen, his thick hair a bird's nest speckled with dirt and twigs. A crack split one lens of his bent wire spectacles.

"It's not working," Filore insisted. Her hands curled into fists around the tools. They'd emptied their pockets, but all they came up with were a compass and a few bent copper coins, her father's leather-bound journal, and the smudgy stick of charcoal Filore used to make rubbings of carvings and runes. And the flint and tinder. Nothing that could save them.

Across from her stood a rusted green door etched with the blocky letters of some magic language, one she hadn't learned yet. Inside was supposed to be a chamber whose walls were studded with thousands of smoky gray crystals that shone with their own inner light. Any other time, she would have been spellbound by a find like this, inspecting the lock and demanding to know what the runes said, letter by letter. Now, she just wanted to be back at camp, surrounded by the other scholars from her parents' historical society, listening to them argue about which order of Witches had left the most powerful relics. In her heart she always rooted for her mother's favorites, the Witches with the power to walk in dreams. The thought of her mother made her eyes sting.

Filore tried again, scraping the flint and tinder together. A spark jumped from the metal, but it died before reaching the pile of dead leaves. Her throat closed up at the thought of how far they were from the ring of canvas tents hidden in the pines. No one would stumble on them here.

"We'll never get out," Filore said, swallowing back tears.

"Of course we will." Her father smiled. "We have everything we need." He opened her fist gently, revealing the curl of blackened iron in her palm.

Filore huffed. "Because you're secretly a Witch, and you can turn this into a grappling hook?"

That made him laugh. Dom gathered her hair at the back of her neck and tugged it a little, like a tail. She hated when he did that.

"What is the greatest feat of magic ever performed?" he asked, not for the first time.

Filore rolled her eyes, but answered as she'd been taught. "The invention of words."

"That's right," her father said. He took her hands again, positioning the flint against the smooth edge of her striker. "This is simply another kind of language. We're communicating through smoke. Once we get the fire going, your mother will see the smoke and come rescue us. As long as she hasn't gotten lost in her book again."

"She's not," Filore said, her voice a little stronger. "She was clicking her tongue and flipping the pages back and forth. She only does that when she doesn't like what she's reading."

"Well, she should know better than to read Rivarrcha's account of the founding of Andar," her father said with a wink. "It's a good thing Lillia was born two centuries after him, or I think they'd have come to blows."

Filore gasped as a spark caught at last, raising the tiniest breath of smoke from the leaves and twigs. Her father bent forward and blew on the pile until a bright ember burned at its heart. Filore watched the silver curls rise into the sky.

She tried to give the flint and tinder back, but he shook his head.

"I think you should keep them. You never know when they might come in handy."

FI OPENED HER eyes to the sound of dry needles crackling in her fire. She smiled to herself. Like most academics, her father had taught her many things that had no practical application whatsoever, but this skill had saved her many times. "Thanks," she murmured to the memory as she returned the flint and tinder to her pocket.

Once the flames spread to the longer branches, Fi stripped off her wet clothes, laying her jacket and pants over the rock to dry and wringing out her light underthings. She waved them over the fire until they were warm enough to put back on, even damp—she wasn't going to risk being caught out here and forced to make a run for it stark naked. For the first time, she regretted saddling Shane with the packs.

Fi wrapped her arms around her knees. She was scratched up, exhausted, hungry, and thirsty, despite the huge mouthful of lake water she'd swallowed. Every snapping twig and pop of the fire sounded like cloaked figures about to descend on her through the trees. She was still reeling from everything that had happened, not sure whether to even believe what she'd seen. An overactive imagination seemed way more plausible than the idea of a beautiful boy lurking under the lake who disappeared after a really friendly kiss.

Fi banged her forehead against her knees. She was putting that boy—that kiss—out of her head forever. *Keep your heart out of it*, she reminded herself. Still, it was a long time before she fell asleep, staring up at the crooked slice of moon through the dark frame of pine boughs.

That night she dreamed of a white stone tower thronged in roses. Thick green leaves rippled up the glistening walls. Wild pink roses swept like a sea through the tower's small curved window, climbing so high they burst through the slats of the cone-shaped roof.

The room inside the tower was equally overgrown, but here the roses were bloodred. The blossoms filled every corner, dangling like bright rubies from the walls and the ceiling. At the very center of the room, a tangle of vines surrounded a wide bed ringed by gauzy curtains, pulled open where the fabric had caught in the thorns. A gust of wind swept through the roses, making them shiver and sigh.

A boy lay sleeping in the midst of the roses—a boy with golden hair and red lips and a beautiful velvet coat. And even though his eyes were closed, peaceful and dreaming, somehow she knew they were a brilliant, breathtaking blue.

Fi shot up from sleep with a gasp.

Her savior was Briar Rose, the sleeping prince.

5

⤜⤜⤜ • ⤛⤛⤛

Shane

SHANE STALKED THROUGH the forest, one arm up to block low-hanging pine branches from whipping her face. She was covered in bumps and bruises, courtesy of all the trees, shrubs, rocks, and streams she'd bushwhacked through since the sun went down. The thick pines cut the moonlight into wisps thin as spiderwebs. She cursed as she tripped over yet *another* fallen log, making some night creature chatter in a way that sounded suspiciously like laughter.

Shane considered herself an expert woodsman. Unfortunately, the first rule of woodsmanship was pretty much *don't trek through unfamiliar mountains at night*, especially without a light, and she'd already trampled all over that one. Shane made a face as something squished suspiciously under her heels. She couldn't tell whether she'd walked through a soggy patch of mushrooms or something much more revolting.

"Whatever that was, it better not have been alive," she muttered.

She braced her hand against a trunk and readjusted her load. The strap of Fi's little rucksack kept sliding down her arm, and Shane's own overstuffed pack was working a permanent groove into her shoulder. Fi's hat bobbed on top. Shane was starting to regret keeping all the treasure. Well, not really, but she did regret having to haul it such a long way. She just couldn't bear to leave the manor empty-handed after losing the only thing she'd brought along.

"Oh, sure," she grumbled. "Be careful, Shane. Don't go yanking on things, Shane. Leave it to me. That way, when *I* yank on something, I can take half the ruin down with me."

Shane's guts lurched. Too late, she wished she hadn't called up the look of shock on Fi's face as she reached out for Shane, already plummeting toward the lake.

Shane had been about two seconds from diving in after her when a flash of light burst up from the water, so bright it left her blinking spots out of her eyes. Fi came up a moment later, gasping and coughing. Relief hit Shane so hard she felt like she'd been kicked. She had no idea what that light had been—it was too bright to be glare off the water—but as long as her partner wasn't dead, she didn't really care.

Her relief faded as Fi jerked her head around, and then dove again, and finally made for the far shore. Shane supposed that meant their partnership was over. It wasn't a good feeling. She'd broken up with a lot of partners, but she'd never lost one over a cliff before.

Most of Shane's partnerships lasted one job—if they

even made it that long. Usually, it was her fault. Her grand-mother had insisted that calling her *stubborn as a mule* was insensitive to mules, because no creature in Steelwight was as willful as Shane. But Shane couldn't help it. She knew what she wanted and she knew what was right, and she wasn't the kind to back down on either count. It was how she'd ended up with her first and oldest partner: the ax strapped between her shoulder blades.

At age seven, the children of War Kings were expected to choose the weapon they would carry for life. A warrior's choice of weapon was considered to be deeply significant and, for an heir, a harbinger of what kind of ruler they would be. On their birthday, Shane and her twin had been led to the armory, where a line of weapons waited for them—swords, bows, glaives, maces, and battle-axes—every one of the finest craftsmanship and inlaid with gleaming silver.

Shayden had waited patiently as the weapons master sized him up and made his recommendation, but Shane had eyes only for the ax, with its curved, sickle-like blade.

SHE COULD STILL remember that moment—wrapping her small hands around the carved birch handle and heaving with all her might. It was so heavy she couldn't even lift it.

Her father stood behind her, his pale face stern. "The battle-ax is far too big for a little thing like you, even to grow into. Choose again."

Shane tightened her grip. Angry fire clenched in her

stomach, but not at her father. At the weapon. "It's my choosing ceremony, and I choose the ax!"

"Shane," her father said sharply, a warning.

"I will handle this." Shane's grandmother stepped forward then. A tall woman with long silver hair, she was something of a hardened old battle-ax herself. She lifted the ax effortlessly, weighing it in her wrinkled hand. "The battle-ax—a conqueror's weapon. It is the symbol of the wild wanderer, chaotic and headstrong, one who will carry the battle flag far from home. There are better weapons for someone of your stature. Better weapons for a future War King of the Ragnall clan."

"No." Shane set her jaw. From across the room, Shayden watched her with wide gray eyes, his tiny hand wrapped around a pearl-encrusted sword: the symbol of wisdom and loyalty.

Grandmother huffed. "Fine. If you want the ax, then you will learn to use it. And first, you will learn to lift it." She moved to the wall and retrieved a smaller ax, the kind the woodcutters wore on their belts. "For the next three weeks, you will chop all the wood for my hearth with this. Only after that, if I am satisfied, will we begin your training."

"That's not a battle-ax!" Shane protested.

Grandmother's gruff laugh filled the armory. "You are not ready for a battle-ax. An old firewood ax is more than enough for you. But if you wish to choose a more suitable weapon—"

Shane snatched the firewood ax before her grandmother could take it away. It was still too heavy for her, but she forced it up onto her shoulder, matching the old woman's glare.

"Never."

SHANE STILL REMEMBERED how her small arms shook from chopping logs day after day, every nerve and muscle burning so hot she could barely sleep at night. She didn't know if that old bat was torturing her or thought she could make Shane quit. But after three weeks, her hands were thick with calluses and she could slam that ax down into the firewood stump without breaking a sweat.

By the time she was twelve, she was the best warrior in her generation. Good enough to impress even her grandmother. And through it all, Shayden was right beside her. Tossing her a waterskin from the edge of the fighting pitch. Pinching her if she snored during council sessions. Scrambling after her from the battlements to the top of the watchtower and sprawling out on the cold flagstones, correcting Shane when she made up the constellations she couldn't remember.

"THAT'S THE GIANT sea serpent, ready to crush Rockrimmon in its meaty jaws."

Shayden pushed his disheveled hair out of his face. "It's not a serpent. It's the Bow of the Shield-Maiden. The one who protected Steelwight from the onslaught of a hundred ships, whose arrows could pierce the planks of the thickest hulls."

Shane wrinkled her nose, considering the stars. "Looks more like a snake to me. Maybe she's a snake-wrangling maiden. The greatest War King of all time, with her snake belt, and her battle-ax—"

"And that must be her big fat head," Shayden said, jerking his chin at the moon hanging low over the horizon.

Shane laughed. "The best warriors always make the best War Kings."

"That's not what Father says. He says there's a lot more to being a leader than just fighting."

"Too bad I'm hopeless at those other things." Shane stuck out her tongue. "Memorizing the laws and the treaties and the names of all those stuffy diplomats."

"Maybe you'd remember if you stopped calling them Fox-Face and Badger-Breath," Shayden teased.

Shane laughed along with him. Sometimes the responsibilities of being the next War King pressed down on her like an impossible weight that grew heavier every year. But she felt better up here, with Shayden—just them and the stars and all the sounds of Rockrimmon at night, watchfires crackling and waves churning and ships rocking against their moorings in the port far below. The way he stuck out his tongue at her when he knew she was about to say something silly. She always said it anyway. Every time the doubts crept in about all the things a War King was supposed to be that she wasn't, Shane thought about Shayden, her mirror, who could do everything she couldn't do.

"Look. The Lovers," he said, pointing through the

gap in the merlons at two bright stars rising over the sea, gleaming in the far-off waves. Always side by side.

Shane snorted. "Those aren't the Lovers. Those are the Twin Stars. You and me." She rolled up on her elbows. "It doesn't matter that I'm firstborn. We're twins anyway. We should just be War Kings together. I'll do all the fun stuff, like the conquests and ceremonial battles. And you can do all the boring stuff."

"Hey!" Shayden shoved his boot into her face, and she dove on him, laughing as they went down in a heap. And Shane let herself believe—for a while, anyway—that she and Shayden were unbreakable, and nothing would ever come between them.

AN OWL'S LOW voice murmured through the trees. Shane let the memory slip away. There was a time when she'd thought Shayden was her perfect partner, the only companion she would ever need. But that was a long time ago, and she had a new partner to worry about now. If she traveled all through the night, she'd reach a tower hidden in the nearby mountains—the tower of their mutual friend. She'd have to hope Fi had the same idea.

Halfway through a clump of bushy firs, Shane stopped. Something flickered through the trees: strange red light, the glimmer of a campfire in the grove up ahead. Her nose twitched with the scent of woodsmoke and something greasy cooking. She took one step toward the grove and then froze, her fighter's instincts warning her to stay in the shadows. The night was suddenly close in her ears.

"What do you see, Tavian?"

Shane sucked in a breath. She could see him now—a tall man standing at the edge of the firelight, peering out into the dark just like she was peering in. The light caught his face, and Shane recoiled. It was the Witch Hunter from the inn, the one she and Fi had barely escaped.

Shane dropped to the ground, biting her tongue as her knee cracked against a rock. Tavian jerked toward the sound.

"There's something out there, Aris," he hissed.

Shane eased the packs off one at a time. She considered grabbing her ax, but it wasn't a stealth weapon and wouldn't be much use in the close quarters of the grove. She'd have to rely on the dagger in her belt, if it came to that. She crept forward, staying low. For once, being short wasn't such a bad thing.

"There are a hundred things out there." The first voice spoke again, a woman's smooth tone that was low and unimpressed. "Squirrels and rabbits and everything else that crawls, and none of it wants anything to do with you. Sit down and eat. I'm tired of your nagging."

Through the fringe of a twiggy scrub oak, Shane peered at the camp. Tavian rubbed at his beaky nose, shifting nervously from foot to foot while his companion, a tan, dark-haired woman, bent over the stew pot. A telltale topaz amulet swung from her neck. *Another Witch Hunter,* Shane thought, resisting the urge to spit. Their black cloaks were stained from the dust and muddy marshes of the forest, and beyond them Shane could see two horses on generous lead ropes. A pair of saw-toothed blades leaned against a tree, dull and menacing.

Tavian hunched his shoulders. "But what if it's the Witch?" Shane realized he was wringing a Witch notice in his hands, the same one that had been dead center on the board. The crumpled face of the man with a dangling crystal earring stared out of the balled-up sheet.

"The Paper Witch is no longer your biggest concern," Aris snapped. Her lip curled. "You saw that flash earlier. That was powerful magic, maybe even light magic. And it's no coincidence it happened after you lost those girls."

Magic? Shane's mind churned. She hadn't thought too much about the flash off the water, but last time she checked, Fi couldn't do any magic. So what *had* happened in the lake? And what kind of trouble was her partner in?

"I didn't know they were Witches," Tavian insisted.

"It doesn't matter what they are." Aris's eyes were merciless in the red light. "Magic corrupts—it's a poison. It caused the ruination of Andar and brought the wrath of the vile Spindle Witch down on us all. It breeds evil. If the Witches are ever allowed to rise, it will happen again—and again and again!" She kicked a log into the fire, setting the pot swinging on its chains. "We take no chances. The girls die."

That was something Shane had never wanted to hear from a Witch Hunter. She'd gotten on the wrong side of them before, but never like this.

"I said I'd find them, didn't I?" Tavian groused.

"You'd better," Aris said. "Now shut up and stop ruining the meal."

Tavian grumbled but did as he was told, dropping heavily onto the log.

Shane leaned her elbows in the dirt, weighing her options. Two on one would be tough, and Shane had never tangled with a Witch Hunter who didn't fight downright mean. On the other hand, they were already after her, and Fi. And even if she forgot that, these Witch Hunters were practically camping in the Paper Witch's backyard. Shane seriously doubted they could take him—the Paper Witch was the most powerful Witch she'd ever met—but his home was a sanctuary for animals and Witches and all the other misfits on the run from something. A few of them might not be so lucky.

Shane eyed the swords again, the firelight gleaming on the sharp sawteeth. Her gaze flicked to the horses.

Maybe this was an opportunity. Transporting her treasure would go much faster with horses. And she'd be clearing the way for Fi, too.

Decision made, Shane got to her feet, careful not to make a sound. All she had to do was creep to the packs, grab her ax, and lure the Witch Hunters into the trees one at a time—

She stopped with a jerk as something grabbed at her foot. Shane looked down and almost gave herself away with a loud curse. Her boot heel had gotten wedged between two knobby roots of the scrub oak. She pulled on the leather boot as hard as she could, but it didn't budge. Shane threw a quick glance at the fire. If the Witch Hunters noticed her now, her odds were going to be pretty grim.

She gave one more good yank. Her heart soared as she felt something come loose. But it was just her foot sliding out of the boot—a fact she realized about the time she crashed into the undergrowth, going backward through a scraggly patch of junipers with one shoe on and one shoe off. There was a clatter as the Witch Hunters jumped to their feet, dinner forgotten.

"That was not a squirrel!" Tavian snapped.

"Stay here," Aris hissed. "I'll check it out."

Shane pushed up on her hands and swept her hair out of her face. Her ax was still ten feet away. She might make it if she ran, but she'd just as likely end up with a dagger in her back. She scrambled up and into the shadow of a tree, stripping off her heavy coat and holding it by the collar. Then she pressed her back against the trunk and held her breath, listening.

The forest was dead quiet. The crickets and owls had stopped calling. She could feel sap slicking the back of her neck and some insect with too many legs crawling along her arm, but she forced herself to remain still.

Something flashed at the corner of her eye—the gleam of a polished blade. Aris was barely a foot away, stalking through the woods with her sword raised. Shane waited until the woman drew even with the tree. Then she lunged out and whipped her heavy jacket into the Witch Hunter's face.

Blinded and surprised, Aris fell back, spitting curses as she clawed at the fabric. She swung her sword wildly. Shane caught it at the hilt, seizing the woman's bony hands and shoving the pommel of the sword into her opponent's stomach. Aris crumpled with a grunt, pitching into the dirt.

One down, one to go, Shane thought with a smile, leaning down to retrieve her jacket.

That jacket probably saved her life. A sword sliced through the air where her neck had been seconds before, the wicked sawteeth of the blade sinking into the trunk of the

72

tree. Chips of bark exploded over Shane, flooding the air with the sharp smell of pine.

Tavian had been too paranoid to obey orders and wait by the campfire. He was better with the heavy longsword than she would have hoped, and his eyes had taken on that feverish look all Witch Hunters wore.

"Witch!" Tavian yelled, wrenching his blade out and stabbing at her with a two-handed thrust. "You won't get away from me again!"

Shane didn't have time to argue about the Witch thing. It was all she could do to get out of the way, abandoning her coat and stumbling as her socked foot sank into a patch of spiny needles. She yanked her dagger out of its sheath, but one dagger was no match for a sword that big. Her opponent knew it, too, judging by the way he lunged at her.

Dagger as decoy, then. Shane made as if to block and then dropped into a squat instead, swinging out a leg to trip him. Tavian dodged, but his sword caught in a tree, buying her a few seconds. She'd have to make the most of them—Aris was groaning, which meant it was about to be two on one again. If Shane could just get some distance, she could surprise Tavian with a high kick and knock the sword out of his hands.

Tavian wrenched his sword back, off balance in the backswing. *Now.* Shane ratcheted her leg for a kick, and then found herself flat in the dirt as her socked foot slid right off a fallen log slick with moss. The dagger flew from her hand.

Shane groaned. It wasn't going to be the Witch Hunters that killed her—it was going to be this vindictive forest.

The man cried out victoriously. Shane scrambled back on her elbows until she hit a thick pine. Her war with the undergrowth gave her an idea. As Tavian reared above her, Shane pulled down a thick branch and let it go. The sharp needles whipped into the man's face like a fistful of nails.

He stumbled. Shane leapt to her feet. She relished the sound of her heavy boot crunching into his face, his sword flying off into the darkness as he fell to his knees, howling and clutching his nose. She kicked him in the ribs for good measure, tremendously satisfied when his head hit the mossy log on the way down.

Shane grabbed her dagger, breathing hard. Then she smiled, flipping the weapon once and sliding it back into its sheath. She planted one foot in warning on Aris's back.

"I've got you people outmatched with one dagger and one shoe," she announced.

Aris's eyes blazed with hatred. "You'll regret siding with Witches. Magic brings nothing but destruction—"

Shane slammed her foot into the woman's stomach, and Aris broke off, coughing. "Yeah, yeah," Shane muttered, snatching the coil of rope off Aris's belt. If you'd heard one fanatical Witch Hunter speech, you'd heard them all.

She made quick work of binding the Witch Hunters and hauling her packs close to the fire. She was just lacing up her wayward boot when a lilting voice rose at her back.

"Now, this is an unexpected sight."

Shane lurched for her ax. Her fingers stilled against the handle as a figure stepped into the firelight, pushing back her hood. It was a girl, maybe Fi's age, with tan skin and a waterfall of loose dark curls that tumbled down her back. She wore a fitted red tunic that flared at her hips, cinched with a bodice that emphasized her curves. The crimson lining of her cloak flashed around her, bright like the crackle of sparks. Against the night, she was hypnotizing.

"Who are you?" Shane asked.

The girl lifted her hands. "Just someone looking for those Witch Hunters."

Shane tightened her grip on the ax handle. "You don't look like a soldier of the Border Guard. And I'm really hoping you're not one of them," she added, jerking her thumb at her captives.

"I'm not." The girl's pert lips, painted with deep red rouge, twisted into a smile. "If you want proof, just look at the reception they're giving me."

Shane glanced back. Tavian's eyes had gone wide and white with fear. He yelled something into his gag, struggling against his bonds.

The girl gave a silky laugh. "He's trying to warn you that I'm a dangerous Witch."

Shane's pulse thrummed in her ears. "And are you?"

"Dangerous?" the girl repeated cheekily. "Absolutely. But tonight, I'm only here to retrieve a certain item these two have in their possession. Something that doesn't belong to them, I assure you," she added, at Shane's look. "Unless this is a robbery I've interrupted, and you've already laid claim to their things?"

"I'm no thief!" Shane protested. She watched the girl saunter over to the saddlebags, giving the squirming Witch Hunters a wide berth. "You're pretty brave to be out here in the middle of the night, chasing down Witch Hunters . . ." Shane trailed off, hoping the captivating girl would fill in her name.

"Call me Red," she said. "And you give me too much credit. I was planning to sneak into their camp once they fell asleep, not take them on all by myself." Her cloak hissed across the ground as she knelt, digging through the saddlebags. "I'm impressed. Not many people are willing to face off with Witch Hunters. You must be pretty dangerous yourself."

"Shane," she offered. "The huntsman for hire."

"Shane," Red repeated, testing it out. "Ah—here it is!" She stood up quickly, holding a small iron box.

"What is that?" Shane asked.

"It's what the Witch Hunters use to transport magic relics."

Shane jerked back, suddenly wary. "What kind of magic relic?"

"Nothing *too* dangerous," Red promised. She cracked the box open and lifted out what looked like a piece of archaic jewelry: five onyx rings connected by tiny, glistening chains. "You wear these on each finger of the left hand, sort of like a glove," Red explained.

"But what does it do?"

Red gave her a knowing look. "Well, *if* you know how to use it, it lets you sense magic—even when it's hidden."

That didn't sound so bad. In fact, Shane could think of a dozen ways that would come in handy for a treasure hunter. But Red didn't look like a treasure hunter. She gave the girl another searching look. "What do you want it for?"

"I'll tell you what." Red stepped close, looking up at Shane through her dark lashes. They probably would have been the same height if not for Shane's thick heels. "You tell me what you're doing out here tonight, and I'll tell you what I'm doing." At Shane's silence, she laughed. "I thought so." She waved the jingling onyx rings. "A little free advice—you might want to get out of here. These woods will be crawling with Witch Hunters soon."

"How do you know that?" Shane asked suspiciously.

"Didn't you see the flash earlier? That was light magic. It's going to draw all kinds of the wrong attention."

Shane felt her guts sink. "You don't say," she mumbled, sending a sideways glare to her tied-up hostages.

Red paused, studying Shane with sudden interest. "Did *you* have anything to do with that flash?"

The truth was on the tip of her tongue, but something made Shane hesitate. "No."

"Pity." Red shook her head. "Light magic is extremely rare. Most light Witches belong to the royal line of Andar. It would be quite a feat to have found one of those." She turned for the woods.

"Wait!" Shane was speaking before she even realized it. "If you need somewhere to stay tonight, I know a place that's safe." She didn't know whether Red really was a Witch, but she was definitely an enemy of the Witch Hunters, and that was close enough.

"So sweet, but I'll be fine." Red threw a look over her shoulder. "I'm dangerous, remember?"

Her voice was playful, but there was something about her that sent a thrill down Shane's spine, her breath catching as Red's eyes locked on hers.

"Shane," the girl said again, rolling the name over her

tongue like she was tasting it. "I won't forget it." Then she sauntered away, her fiery cloak swirling as she disappeared into the trees.

"See you around, Red." The name sizzled on Shane's tongue like a spark.

Mystery and danger—everything she loved about taking on a ruin, all wrapped up in a stunningly beautiful girl. Shane wasn't going to forget her anytime soon, either.

6

Fi

FI SHRUGGED OUT of her jacket, enjoying the morning sun on her face. She'd had a fitful night and woken early, exhausted but glad to leave her dreams behind.

Shivering in the gray light before sunrise, her clothes still damp and her fire nothing but ashes, Fi had felt like she'd never get warm. A few hours' hike up the steep slopes changed that. She'd kept a close eye out for any signs of pursuit, broken branches or footprints in the dirt, but found none. Now she looked out across the wide basin of purple-tufted thistles and wildflowers, the trees so tall and thin here a light breeze made the whole forest sway. The dark shapes of birds rustled in the pines.

From her rough calculations, she should be nearly to the tower by now. The tight knot that had been sitting on the back of her neck finally relaxed. She'd be safe here.

Fi tied her jacket around her waist and pressed on, lifting a cloud of bees as she waded through a clump of sky-blue flax. In the light of day, the golden-haired boy who had saved her seemed like just another dream. She had read so many accounts of the story of Briar Rose—the great kingdom of Andar destroyed by the wicked Witch and the sleeping prince waiting for a kiss—it was no wonder that spindle gave her wild ideas. *Clearly, I'm more of a romantic than I thought*, Fi decided, scraping deer droppings off her boot with a flat stone.

She'd nearly managed to convince herself when a familiar structure rose above her, the crooked tower dwarfing even the swaying pines.

It was probably good that the Paper Witch lived so far out in the forest, because Fi had a feeling his neighbors would've complained about his aesthetic. The house was a strange combination of rustic log cabin and lofty stone tower, and the tower itself was a work of art, built wider at every level so that it looked strangely top-heavy, with a round workshop capping the third floor. A small curl of gray smoke rose from the tower's conical roof. So the Paper Witch was home.

Fi jumped over a knee-high wooden fence, startling a pair of deer munching on bean plants near the side of the house. The Paper Witch was a strict vegetarian, and the local wildlife took full advantage of his overgrown garden. Fi remembered playing here when she was a child, chasing rabbits around the yard while her parents consulted with the Witch.

At the thought of her parents, her hand clenched around the butterfly mark. Fi fought down a wave of bitterness.

Back then, she hadn't known how dangerous it was for the Paper Witch to live in the borderlands, where the Witch

80

Hunters seemed to encroach farther every year. Most Witches in Darfell stuck to the capital, far outside the Witch Hunters' territory, or moved to the bustling ports of Pisarre, where their talents were more welcome.

The oak door was carved with an inkwell and a long feathered quill. As always, it was unlocked. Fi pushed her way in. "Hello," she called into the cabin.

"Yo!" a voice called back.

Fi stepped inside. The cabin was built as one big room, so she could see everything at once: the small kitchen bright with dust motes, the colorful woven rugs laid across the stone floor, and the very familiar figure seated at the kitchen table with at least three people's worth of food spread out before her.

"The Paper Witch said you'd be coming," Shane said through a full mouth. "Or I'd have gone out looking for you." The huntsman had pulled a crate of firewood over for a footrest and looked incredibly pleased with herself. Fi's hat rested on the end of the table. "I was worried about you," Shane finished after she'd finally managed to swallow.

"I'll bet," Fi muttered, staring at a plate stacked high with melon slices and fresh strawberries. She'd been hoping to meet up with Shane, but the sight of her partner plowing through a biscuit generously slathered with jam was not the reunion she'd imagined. "How did you get here before me?" she asked. Shane had been all the way on the other side of the lake; she should have had the longer journey.

Shane licked her thumb with a grin. "I lucked into some horses."

There was a story there—one Fi probably didn't want to hear—but it would have to wait. As would her empty stomach.

She looked longingly at the table before shaking herself. "I need to see the Paper Witch. Is he here?"

Shane jerked a thumb toward the winding stairs that led to the tower. "He's burning something up there, I think," she said, before wiping one hand hastily down her shirt and picking something up off the table. "Oh, hey—he left this letter for you. It's from your parents. Why's the Paper Witch getting your mail?"

"You opened it?" Fi demanded, her stomach tight with anger. She stalked over and snatched the letter away, folding the paper over the broken seal and jamming it into her pocket.

"Don't worry. It was really boring, so I've forgotten it already," Shane said, as though that made up in the slightest for her appalling manners.

"In the future, spare yourself a dry read and don't go through my things," Fi snapped. Shane's eyebrows shot up, and Fi cursed inside her head. Getting angry revealed more than she meant to. She forced herself to take a deep breath. "Thanks for forgetting it."

She almost left it at that, but paused on her way to the staircase, laying a hand on the back of Shane's chair.

"You didn't see anyone else in the lake with me, did you?"

Shane wrinkled her nose. "That's an odd question."

Like I didn't know that already! Fi flicked the messy coil of braids on the back of Shane's head. "I'm serious."

"Okay," Shane groused, wincing. "No, I didn't see anybody. There *was* this strange burst of light, though, and then you came up and started splashing around in the water. Are you sure you're okay?" She tipped back in the chair, pinning Fi with a look.

"We'll see." Without warning, Fi let go of the back of Shane's chair. The girl flailed as she almost tipped over, cursing. Fi headed up the steep tower steps with a private smile.

She continued up the winding stairs until she stood in the doorway to the workshop on the top floor.

The circular room was filled with reams and reams of paper. Rolled bundles of thick, cream-colored sheets leaned against the walls, and there were three small writing tables covered in every kind of ink and quill imaginable, the long feathers of birds of prey tangling with shorter white feathers and the husks of dry reeds. A pewter-gray dish held stubby sticks of charcoal. Against the far wall, an ornate spiral of stairs rose to a hatch in the roof. The room's entire floor was covered in overlapping sheets of paper, some marked with strange symbols, some scrawled with flowing magic scripts that Fi recognized. Like most Witches, the Paper Witch worked magic through a medium—in his case, by writing intricate charms. *Small wishes*, he had called them when he first explained his power to Fi—a wide-eyed child in the great rustling workshop of pens and pages.

She had wanted him to do big magic, like in the old stories. The Paper Witch had knelt beside her with a smile. *Magic is in all things—plants, animals, even people,* he explained. *Witches just have a little more than most. Spells allow us to channel that natural magic for a task, but the bigger the spell, the greater the risk of unintended consequences. Which is why big magic should never be used thoughtlessly. My magic works best for small spells—a charm to keep sickness away, or to ward off dark magic, or to make a garden flourish. Small wishes.*

Fi stepped through the door, glancing up at the hand-crafted paper lanterns hung from the ceiling. The Paper Witch stood at the brazier in the center of the room, wearing his customary white robe and silver sash. A long piece of silver-blond hair hung over his shoulder, wrapped in blue thread and tinkling with a little silver bell. A folded piece of paper burned in his hands. As Fi watched, he leaned forward to blow on the curling sheets, making the embers glow as the ashes rose in a swirl. Red sparks and bits of paper flittered up to escape through the chimney with the smoke.

"Did you come to watch me from the doorway, Filore?" the Paper Witch asked. He didn't even bother to turn around.

How does he do it? Fi wondered. Despite his talk of small wishes, she'd long suspected the Paper Witch was capable of much more than he let on.

She cleared her throat awkwardly. "I didn't want to interrupt."

"I'm finished," the man said, dusting the ashes from his hand and turning toward her. His pale face was friendly, and he regarded her with a soft smile, his crystal earring glinting as it caught the light.

Fi had spent all morning trying to figure out where to start her story. In the end, she didn't have to say anything at all. As the Paper Witch approached, his eyes grew wide, and he reached out for Fi, taking a gentle hold of her wrist. He uncurled her hand carefully, revealing the tiny glimmer of red that coiled around her finger like a scarlet thread.

"Oh, this is powerful magic," he whispered. His earring trembled as he looked up at her sharply. "What have you been up to, dear?"

Fi felt numb. This was exactly what she *didn't* want to hear. As humiliating as it might have been to be laughed at by the Paper Witch and Shane, she'd hoped she was imagining the whole thing. She clamped down on the emotions that threatened to choke her. Panic wasn't going to help her right now. She had to keep a cool head.

"In a ruin, I pricked my finger on a bone spindle—"

"The spindle of Briar Rose." The Paper Witch's grip tightened.

"I think so," Fi said woodenly, meeting his searching blue eyes. "Actually, I know this is going to sound impossible, but I think I *saw* him. Is this . . . some kind of curse?"

Her left hand, the one marred by the butterfly mark, ached as she said the words. How unlucky would a person have to be to end up twice cursed?

The Paper Witch let out a long breath. "It's not a curse, Filore," he said, cupping her hand between his. "It's what all of us descendants of Andar have been hoping for all these years. It means you're destined to wake Briar Rose."

"Me? No, that can't be right." Fi backed away, pulling her hand free. "Just because I got careless with a spindle?"

"That bone spindle is the same one that pricked Briar Rose, and it was enchanted with very particular magic." The Paper Witch pursed his lips. "If you saw Briar Rose, there's no doubt. You're the one."

"I can't be," Fi protested. She rubbed her finger hard against her pants, as though she could rub the mark away. There was a time when she would have given anything for a chance like this, to become a part of the history she'd studied and see the kingdom of Andar with her own eyes. But how could she possibly save Briar Rose from a curse when she couldn't even save herself? "I don't want this."

The Paper Witch's expression was sympathetic. "I don't think that's how it works, dear," he said softly.

"So that's it? It's decided. Just like that?" Fi snapped her fingers. "And now I'm supposed to wake the sleeping prince— with true love's kiss." In all the stories, all the tapestries, all the folktales, it was always *true love's kiss*. As a skeptic, Fi had never really bought that. Even ignoring all the other ways the story had probably been exaggerated, how were you supposed to fall in love with someone who was fast asleep?

"There is no spell like that," the Paper Witch replied, amused. "Love and magic are different forces. Your heart is its own master, Filore. Sometimes a kiss is just a kiss."

Fi's racing pulse slowed, but ultimately, that didn't change anything. She wasn't a hero or adventurer. She wasn't even really a treasure hunter anymore. "You've got the wrong person," she said with finality.

"Are you sure?" the Paper Witch asked. "Perhaps being guided by a great purpose would serve you well." His gaze moved significantly to her gloved hand. "It's very easy to be consumed by a curse."

"I'm handling it," Fi ground out, fisting her hand and shoving it into her pocket. Why was everybody so determined to get into her business?

The Paper Witch shook his head. "It's been over a year since you came to me for help. I will not betray your secret or your trust, but I wish you would confide in someone. Like your parents?"

"Don't," Fi warned, her voice tight enough to snap. "Leave them out of this."

The Paper Witch's face was stern. "This is no way to live—running yourself ragged chasing every rumor about the Butterfly Curse, keeping everyone at a distance."

"I partnered with Shane, didn't I?" Fi said, looking away. She couldn't deny the rest. When she'd first ended up under the Butterfly Curse, alone and out of the treasure-hunting business, she had spent months trying to piece her life back together, followed by months and months more chasing even the faintest whispers about the curse. She wasn't ready to give up. "All of that is why I need this gone." She held up the finger with the spindle's mark. "Can you get rid of it? Please?"

The Witch sighed heavily. "The binding magic of the Divine Rose is very powerful. But I can try."

Turning to one of his worktables, the Paper Witch smoothed a wide piece of silken paper onto the dark wood. He closed his eyes, letting his fingers trail over the feathers of the quills, until he stopped on a black one that looked like it must have belonged to a crow or raven. The Paper Witch plunged the pen into a glass jar of ink, tossing the threaded bell over his shoulder as he worked. He laid the pen against the page and moved his hand in a wide arc, leaving a bloodred pattern behind. The rune was too complicated for Fi to follow, especially since he drew it without once lifting the pen from the page. The final strokes were thin as wispy threads, the hooked tip scratching a groove into the page as the pen ran dry.

"Come here," the Paper Witch said, motioning Fi to the side of the brazier. She barely had time to register the complex symbol curled in at the edges, almost like Divine Rose script, before the Paper Witch threw it into the fire. Sparks and ashes flared out of the brazier, seeming to hover in the Paper Witch's hands as he extended them over the flames.

"Hold out your hand," he instructed. Fi did as she was told, trembling.

The Paper Witch cupped the burning page in his hand and blew on it. The charred flakes of paper flared bright red and then swirled out, disintegrating around Fi's hand. She gasped at the sudden, sharp pain. The tip of her finger began to bleed again, as though she had just pricked it.

The fire roared up, turning a blinding white, and a force like a storm wind slammed into Fi, knocking her and the Paper Witch back. Fi caught herself against a chair, the carved rail digging into her side. It took a few seconds to blink the black spots from her eyes, and when she did, she found the workshop in disarray, inkwells overturned, and the beautiful quills scattered on the ground. Bits of paper and ash drifted in the air. A few of the hanging lanterns were shriveled as though burned.

The Paper Witch lay slumped against the far wall, unconscious.

"I'm afraid it won't be possible to break our bond that easily."

Fi spun around. Her breath hitched at the sight of the golden-haired figure lounging on the stairs that curved up to the tower's roof. He leaned carelessly back on his hands, his blue velvet coat draped across the stairs like a glistening pool. Five silver buttons nestled in the fabric, each engraved with a thorny rose.

"Don't worry about the Witch," the boy said with an airy wave of his hand. "He's just sleeping."

Fi was torn. She wanted to check on the Paper Witch herself, but she was mesmerized by the figure from the lake and her dream, looking very real all of a sudden.

"You're Briar Rose," she said, her voice barely a whisper. The boy's blue eyes twinkled as he nodded, golden curls falling around his face. "But—that's impossible," Fi protested. "You're supposed to be sleeping, hidden away in Andar."

"I am," the boy said, resting his chin on a hand. "That's cute, by the way, but you don't have to call me by my full name. You can just call me Briar. *Rose* is the second name given to all the Witches of the royal line."

Even with her mind spinning, Fi couldn't stop her curiosity. "And you're not a *Rose*?"

"I didn't say that." The boy lifted his hand, making a small white spark dance from one fingertip to another. "I'm a very powerful light Witch, and you're welcome to call me whatever you want, but . . ." He leaned forward, locking eyes with Fi as he caught the spark in his palm. "It's a little formal for our relationship, don't you think?"

Fi remembered the soft feel of his lips and fought against the traitorous heat creeping up her neck. "And just what *relationship* would that be?" she asked, crossing her arms.

"Do you believe in love at first sight?" Briar's smile was half teasing, half serious, and Fi felt her stomach do a little flip-flop.

"I find it highly improbable," she said, "given that you first saw me flailing and drowning."

Briar's eyes sparkled. "On the other hand, you first saw *me* bravely rescuing you from the depths."

Just her luck—she got to meet one of the legendary figures of history, and he turned out to be a total flirt. "Doesn't count," Fi told him flatly. "I never would have fallen if not for that cursed spindle, so you're the reason I was drowning to begin with."

Briar laughed. "Hard to argue with that."

He stood gracefully, sweeping down the steps to stand in front of Fi. He was tall—she hadn't been able to tell in the lake—and willowy and apparently a Witch. His smile was playful and he smelled intoxicatingly of roses. Fi bit the inside of her lip, almost as effective for dispelling illusions as Shane's nerve pinch. Unfortunately, the figure didn't disappear, and if Fi wasn't mistaken, his coat had swirled right *through* the ornately carved railing beside him when he moved.

A sudden thought struck her. "Are you a ghost?" she asked, both fascinated and slightly unnerved. Old legends weren't always reliable. Maybe the sleeping prince had actually died years ago.

"Hardly," Briar sniffed, looking a little offended.

Fi wasn't convinced. She lifted her hand and thrust it toward his chest. It went right through him. There was no change in pressure or temperature—just a strange sensation, like the charge of electricity hanging in the air after a storm. The hairs on Fi's arm stood on end, and she wiggled her fingers experimentally.

Briar looked down to where her hand disappeared into his coat. "That's very personal for someone who still hasn't told me her name."

Fi pulled her hand back fast, a little heat rising into her cheeks. "It's Fi," she said, distracted. "But I don't understand. You were real in the lake. I . . . felt you." She forced herself not to fidget while remembering.

"I told you before, I'm a powerful Witch." Briar trailed his hand absently over the Paper Witch's cluttered table. His fingers passed through papers and quills without rustling a single feather. "I'm using magic to appear to you, just like I used magic to save you in the lake. Though I'd better warn you, that took nearly everything I had. I'm afraid I won't be able to help you again until I've recovered my strength."

"Help me?" Fi repeated. "With what?"

"Breaking the sleeping curse, of course." The flames in the Paper Witch's brazier seemed to flicker as Briar took a step toward her. "You are my savior, after all."

Fi felt that uncomfortable squeezing in her chest again, the heavy weight of a responsibility she wanted nothing to do with. She had her own problems—she even had her own curse!

"Do you have any idea what you're asking?" she demanded hoarsely.

"Simply pass through the Forest of Thorns, enter the sleeping castle, and wake me." He didn't say *with a kiss*, but Fi heard it as loudly as if he'd shouted.

"Your information is woefully out of date," she shot back. "First of all, we're one kingdom over right now, in Darfell. Your kingdom, Andar, is absolutely crawling with Witch Hunters. Even *if* I got past them, the wastes around your castle are a deathtrap. Half the people who enter just disappear. And no one has ever made it through the Forest of Thorns."

When she was a treasure hunter, she'd thought about trying her luck once or twice—not with some foolhardy idea of breaking the curse, but for the books and the spectacular historical finds that had to be preserved in the lost castle of Andar. In the end, it had seemed too dangerous even back when she did dangerous things for the thrill of it.

Briar's eyebrows knotted into a frown. "Exactly how long have I been asleep?"

"A hundred years," Fi answered immediately. She wished she'd sugarcoated it a little when he squeezed his eyes shut as though she'd struck him.

"I had a sense of years passing," he whispered. "I knew it had been a long time. But a hundred years?" His lips pressed into a tight line.

"I'm sorry," Fi said weakly. It was hard to look at Briar when she recognized his expression only too well. It was the same expression she'd worn the night she trudged through sheets of rain to show up at the Paper Witch's doorstep bedraggled and soaking, curse-marked, with nothing left and nowhere to go. The same one that stared back at her from the mirror when she was wishing desperately for a way to escape the Butterfly Curse.

A girl under a curse meets a boy under a curse.

It sounded like the beginning of one of those cautionary fables where everyone ended up worse off than they started.

"I'm sorry," she repeated more forcefully, "but I'm not the right person to save you. You have to pick someone else."

Briar's blue eyes weren't teasing anymore. He looked dead serious, the firelight throwing strange shadows across his face. "Impossible. I didn't choose you—the spindle did. We're bound together by its magic."

He had moved to the other side of the brazier. As he held his hand out to the fire, she saw that a trickle of red encircled his second finger, as if he was bleeding. Then she realized it wasn't blood at all. It was the same tiny coil of red that marked her own finger. It seemed to shimmer in the unsteady light, leading away through the smoke—leading toward her.

"We're connected, Fi," he said, and Fi started, hearing her name for the first time on his lips. "The moment you pricked your finger, the sleeping curse that held me prisoner all these years weakened just a little. That's how I'm here. But that spindle originally belonged to another Witch—one who has haunted my nightmares and my kingdom. She would have felt the magic awakening in her spindle, too."

Fi's mouth had gone dry. "The Great Witch who betrayed Andar."

The flames guttered and burned low, as if smothered by a chill wind. The Spindle Witch was the villain of countless stories, the monster used to scare children at night. Those who had fled Andar had brought tales of her sinister powers—that she could control the corpses of beasts, that she could drain a Witch's life with her golden threads, that she rode on a storm of crows and used them as her spies and familiars. And above all, that she was nearly immortal. She had disappeared into the ruins of Andar a century ago, some had dared to hope for good. But what if she had been lurking in the fallen kingdom all the while, biding her time?

For the first time, Fi felt a sliver of fear. The birds in

the trees outside the Paper Witch's tower—had they been the usual jays and robins, or something bigger, more menacing, disguised by the shadows? All she could remember was the flash of dark wings beating.

"She'll be looking for me," said Briar. "So, as the girl destined to wake me, she'll be looking for you, too. Our only chance is to break the sleeping curse before she catches up with us."

"You're saying I don't have a choice." The words felt hollow in her ears. She wanted to keep arguing until she found a loophole, but she had enough experience with magic to know that, too often, there wasn't one. And if there was no way out, her only choice was to get this over with as quickly as possible. "Then I guess I'm headed to Andar."

"I'll be with you every step of the way," Briar promised.

That, Fi could do without. "Can't I just meet you there?" she asked hopefully.

"You wouldn't really rob me of the opportunity to get to know you better?" A little of the playfulness had returned to Briar's voice. "You are planning to kiss me on the other side—my first kiss, by the way." Fi shot him a flat look, thinking about that moment in the lake. Briar laughed like he was thinking the same thing. "Well, my first real kiss. Besides, this is destiny. I've been dreaming of you for years—a *hundred* years—waiting for the moment I get to fall in love with you."

"I don't believe in destiny, either," Fi said firmly, quashing the little tingle that rolled down her spine. She had already pegged the prince for a flirt; now she was annoyed with herself for letting him get to her.

Briar's lips quirked into an odd half smile. "You don't believe in destiny, you don't believe in love at first sight. What do you believe in?"

Fi bit her lip before spitting out something she might regret—not because she cared about Briar's feelings, but because she was on the cusp of revealing that she had once believed in both of those things, before her faith was shattered by a boy almost as beautiful as Prince Briar Rose. She wouldn't make that mistake again.

"Fair enough," Briar said, when she didn't answer. He tipped his head, taking a step toward her. "Then I'll have to convince you, won't I? Of the existence of love and destiny." Suddenly he was the figure from the lake again, mysterious and dazzling, close enough that the scent of roses threatened to overwhelm her. "If I'm right, and you and I *are* destiny, then we'll fall in love no matter what. I won't even say the word *love* again until you've said it first. If you're right, and destiny doesn't exist, then I guess we'll just kiss and go our separate ways."

Fi wrinkled her nose. "It doesn't sound like there's much in it for me either way."

"Well, I can't offer you anything equal to the love of a prince," Briar teased, leaning forward. "But as a reward for saving me, I will give you any treasure from the entire kingdom of Andar that your heart desires."

The possibilities were endless. Briar was probably imagining she'd choose priceless jewels or golden scepters, but Fi could ask for a rare spell book from one of the secretive Orders of Magic only hinted at in old stories, or the fabled *History of Andar*, said to fill forty leather-bound volumes. Or something even better—like a relic that could break curses and free her from the butterfly mark.

Fi still remembered the last page in her storybook, illustrated with a white castle surrounded by roses under a bright blue sky. *And on that day when the curse breaks, the Forest of Thorns will fall to dust, the wastes will be swept away like sand, and the people of the castle will rise from their enchanted sleep to restore the great kingdom of the Witches.* It was impossible to know how much of that would truly happen and how much was wishful storytelling. But if the legend of Briar Rose was true, the rest of it could be, too.

"So all I have to do is kiss you, and your entire kingdom is restored?" Fi asked.

"I'm afraid even your lovely lips don't have quite that much power," Briar said with a wink. "Only the destruction of the Spindle Witch can truly free my kingdom. But before the castle was lost, the Great Witches were working on a way to defeat her. Break the sleeping curse, and the heart of Andar will beat again—the sleeping Witches will rise and take up the battle, and the Spindle Witch's ultimate demise will be set into motion. It all starts with you, Fi."

Briar straightened and offered her a lopsided smile, hands folded behind his back. "So, do it to save a kingdom or for the treasure . . . or for the chance to prove me wrong about destiny."

Fi bit her lip. "How about all of the above?" she suggested acerbically. She'd sworn never to fall in love again. Briar might be handsome and consider himself irresistible— he might even be a powerful Witch—but Fi didn't make decisions with her heart anymore. Just her head.

"I've clearly got my work cut out for me," Briar said with a smile. "Unfortunately, I don't have the power to stay here very long. But I'll be around."

"What does that mean?" Fi asked with a sinking feeling.

Briar shrugged. "We're connected now. While you're awake, I can come to you. When you're asleep, you might end up in *my* dreams." He wiggled his fingers in a wave before disappearing in a swirl of velvet coat.

Fi shook away that thought. Whatever Briar said about destiny, she refused to believe in some invisible force moving people against their will. She made her own decisions, and all she had to do was *not* fall in love. How hard could that be?

7

❯❯❯❯──❮❮❮❮

Shane

SHANE ROCKED BACK in her chair at the Paper Witch's table, licking the last of the jam off a daisy-patterned plate. Distantly, she listened to the sounds of Fi shoving supplies into saddlebags while the Paper Witch trod on her heels, pestering her about whether she had everything she needed for her journey. Shane snorted. She was pretty sure nothing in this dilapidated old tower could prepare Fi for where she was going.

Shane was still reeling from everything her partner said after coming down the stairs. Only Filore Nenroa could keep a straight face while she rattled off a story about being haunted by an undead prince and becoming the hero that would rescue Andar from its century-long curse. Shane might have suspected it was all a joke if the Paper Witch himself hadn't been standing behind Fi, holding a cold cloth against the goose egg on his skull and nodding sagely. It sounded like a seriously dangerous quest, not to mention a very good way to wind up dead. Shane couldn't help thinking she'd gotten out of this partnership just in time.

Which was why she was definitely not listening to the thump of Fi's boots as the girl shouldered her bags, exchanging a last round of *so longs* with the Paper Witch before the door closed behind her with a click.

The silence that followed was deafening. Shane didn't have to turn around to know the Paper Witch was staring at her, his eyebrows furrowed in disapproval. She could feel his gaze blistering the back of her neck like a sunburn.

"You're really going to let her go alone?"

Shane dropped forward, the legs of her chair hitting the flagstones with a bang. "It's not my problem, and I know better than to get in the middle of it."

She reached for an apple, but the Paper Witch leaned over the table and scooped up the fruit bowl, lifting it out of her reach. Shane huffed. No one could get judgy and self-righteous like a Witch.

"She wasn't exactly looking for company," Shane pointed out. Fi's story had been light on details, and Shane had a feeling she probably would have left the whole thing a mystery if she thought she could get out of the tower without sharing. "Besides, I gave her one of the horses free of charge."

"That hardly strikes me as a fair trade." The Paper Witch set down the bowl and waved at Shane's overstuffed pack. "You came out of this job with plenty of treasure, and what did your partner get? A soaking in the lake, a secondhand horse, and a great burden—one you're going to let her carry alone."

Shane shifted uncomfortably. He'd left out the horde of Witch Hunters that now had Fi on their hit list. Her breakfast suddenly sat heavy in her stomach. "She didn't ask for my help," she grumbled.

"And I suppose you never got any help you didn't ask for," the Paper Witch said. His voice was quiet, but he fixed Shane with a pointed look.

Shane dug her fingers into her coat. Even here in the Paper Witch's sunlit kitchen, it was all too easy to imagine herself in that moment a year and a half ago: tucked into a back booth at a rowdy tavern in western Darfell, nursing a black eye and staring down at scraps on a hammered tin plate, probably the lowest she'd ever been in her life.

SHE'D PICKED HER dinner off ribs so spare she wouldn't have been surprised to find out she'd been served rat. She couldn't pay for better, though. She was down to her last two coppers. All she had was a shabby pack of patched clothes and her ax, unslung and gleaming dully at her feet. Shane knew better than to sit unarmed in a place like this.

Drunks pushed and shouted over one another, and a guy at the bar was definitely giving her the stink eye. Maybe they'd crossed paths during her last job, when she was the bodyguard for a sleazy merchant who ran gambling dens all over the capital and needed somebody to crack heads when his patrons couldn't cover their debts. Or maybe the job before that, guarding a warehouse of apples and grain while people were fighting for scraps one street over. It was hard to guess. Since coming to Darfell, she'd done a lot of things she wasn't proud of.

Shane slumped forward, enjoying the thunk of her head smacking the table. Sitting there, surrounded by the smell of spilled wine and sweaty bodies, it was hard not to dwell on how far she'd fallen.

Shane had spent fifteen long years chafing against everything it meant to be a War King's heir. Fifteen years of failing to live up to her father's expectations. Fifteen years of watching Shayden being overlooked and pushed aside, never more than a spare in her father's eyes. She was the better warrior between them, but Shayden was better at everything else—statecraft and diplomacy and governing and law—and they both knew it. But tradition said a War King's firstborn took the throne, and her father wasn't one to break with tradition. Not unless she gave him no other choice.

So that's what she'd done. She'd deserted Rockrimmon, turned her back on her birthright, snuck onto a merchant ship, and set off to make a new life somewhere else. Only it hadn't quite turned out like she'd expected.

She'd wandered through the seaside kingdom of Pisarre and then into Darfell, sure she could make her way as a mercenary for hire. But that meant something different here than it had at home. In the seedy border towns, mercenaries were just hired thugs, paid to beat one another bloody while their clients conducted shady back-alley deals. And everywhere there were rumors of Witch Hunters, who offered exorbitant sums to anyone with few enough scruples. It wasn't the life she'd come looking for.

Someone bumped her table, and the hard edge of the wood bit into her swollen cheek. Shane lifted her head, staring unseeing at her empty plate. She could never go back to Steelwight. She would have been disowned by now, a disgrace to the Ragnall clan, the mantle of heir passed to Shayden as it always should have been. And even if she was willing to admit defeat and limp home, she couldn't pay for passage.

"That's quite a miserable expression."

Shane jerked around, astonished to find a man in pristine white robes smiling down at her. Everything about him screamed that he didn't belong here, from his twinkling crystal earring to his friendly blue eyes. If his pocket hadn't been picked yet, it would happen down the next dark alley.

The Paper Witch politely shuffled out of the way as a drunk lurched for the door, holding his stomach. "Are you Shane, the mercenary?"

"If you're not here to hire me, get lost," she grumbled.

The Paper Witch laughed. "But I am here to hire you. I've been looking for someone with skills like yours."

Shane whipped around so fast she banged her elbow against the table. "Oh, to do what?" she snapped, fed up with this place and this man and this entire kingdom. "Some guy owes you money? You want me to beat somebody up, steal something, bust a few kneecaps?"

"Nothing so distasteful." The Paper Witch paled at the thought. He leaned down and lowered his voice. "I have quite a few friends. Sometimes these friends get into trouble with . . . bad elements." Shane could have sworn he snuck a glance toward the black-cloaked figures at the bar. "I'm looking for someone like you to help them get out of it."

"I'm not cheap," Shane warned, though she was mostly bluffing.

The Paper Witch's eyes crinkled, as if he could tell. "I'll pay you well," he said, "starting with a place to stay whenever you need it and a free meal—and a bath," he added as an afterthought, his nose twitching. "It may not be as exciting as some of your other jobs, but I assure you, it will be much easier on your conscience."

He extended a hand, his long sleeve trailing as if in a far-off breeze. For a fleeting moment, Shane felt like she could breathe again.

Still she held back. "Why are you offering me this?"

The blond man smiled. "Because I have it to give," he said simply, eyes bright. "What kind of a person walks away from someone in trouble?"

THOSE WERE THE words ringing in Shane's head as the memory faded and she found herself staring at Fi's dusty traveling hat, forgotten on the table. The Paper Witch was still giving her that look. Shane groaned. Then she pushed up from her chair, swinging her small travel pack onto her shoulder with a sigh.

"Fine. Fine! But this is a big favor, and you and I are completely even after this."

The Paper Witch only smiled. Shane kicked her treasure pack under the table.

"That's still mine!" she called over her shoulder, snatching the traveling hat. She threw open the door to the tower and made for the horses, tromping right through the Paper Witch's cabbages for good measure.

Fi hadn't gotten far. When Shane reached the outer fence, she was unhitching the brown gelding with big black eyes, speaking softly to the horse as she smoothed a hand down his white blaze. Her fond smile vanished as she fixed Shane with a suspicious look.

"You forgot this," Shane said, tossing Fi the hat.

"Thanks," Fi replied. She still had that pinched expression, though, her face scrunched up like she was sucking a lemon. Shane leaned against the weathered fence post, trying to look nonchalant in spite of the second, smaller horse snuffling at her hair.

"So, I've been thinking—"

"Can't have done much thinking in the five minutes since I came outside," Fi cut in.

Shane ignored the barb. "Maybe I should, you know, come along."

Fi stopped petting the horse and turned to stare at her. "Come along?" she repeated. "Did I not just explain how ridiculously dangerous this is going to be?"

"There was that bit about becoming heroes, too," Shane replied. "Andar was a pretty rich kingdom. Seems like saving it might come with a nice payout."

Fi spluttered. "One job and we'd go our separate ways— that was the deal, remember?"

"Yeah, and personally, I don't feel like that *one job* is over," Shane replied. She saddled the black horse, trading the lead rope for a bridle and strapping her small pack down. "I hate leaving things half finished, and you seem like you could use somebody to watch your back." She was beginning to suspect Fi wasn't nearly as calm and in control as she tried to appear. Shane held out a hand. "So, what do you say? Partners?"

Fi just stared at Shane for a long time, then rolled her eyes before climbing up onto her horse. "I guess I can't stop you."

"Gee, thanks, Shane," Shane grumbled as she yanked herself into the saddle. "What would I do without you? I'm so grateful that you've chosen to accompany me on this impossible quest out of the goodness of your heart."

I can't stop you wasn't the response she'd been hoping for, but Shane never did things halfway. If she was joining Fi, then they were partners all the way, and partners put up with snarky comebacks and a serious lack of gratitude.

They set off at a trot, winding down the hill along the Paper Witch's garden. Shane blinked as Fi turned them away from the midmorning sun.

"Isn't Andar in the other direction?" Shane asked, pointing vaguely east.

"The only way to get to Andar is through one of the border checkpoints, and you can't get through the checkpoints without a pass," Fi explained, not all that patiently.

"A pass?" Shane had never paid much attention to boring, official things like getting permission to do what she wanted. "Isn't that something you have to get special from the Border Guards?" That didn't sound like an adventure as much as a bunch of time wasted kissing pompous noble . . . shoes.

"Usually, yes," Fi confirmed.

Shane cracked her knuckles. "Well, we're in a hurry, right? I say we find some lousy treasure hunter or mercenary with a pass and *borrow* it. Forcefully."

"Brilliant," Fi said flatly, "except for the part where those mercenaries you *borrowed* from report us to the Border Guard, and we get arrested trying to cross back into Darfell with stolen passes. What exactly would you suggest then?"

Shane scrunched up her nose. "Beat up some Border Guards?"

"Lovely. If it's all the same to you, I'm going to go with a plan where no one gets arrested," Fi said. "As one of the Border Houses, the Nenroa family has a permanent pass. My parents used to keep it at the branch house in Raven's Roost."

Shane snorted. "You couldn't have led with that?"

Fi rolled her eyes again, picking up speed.

Shane clicked her tongue and hurried to catch up. "Whatever. You're the bossy—" She changed her mind at Fi's sharp look. "I mean, the boss."

THE PAPER WITCH'S tower was nestled in the mountains east and north of the Witches' Jewelry Box. Even with the horses, it was full night before they crested a hill and looked down over Raven's Roost. Fi didn't seem concerned about the late hour. She also hadn't consulted her partner about riding for hours without a break. Fi, Shane was remembering now, wasn't a very considerate partner, and she was already second-guessing signing up for this long term.

They dismounted at the outskirts of the city. Shane had never seen Raven's Roost so dead. Even the Silver Baron was shuttered for the night, the swinging sign creaking over their heads as they led their horses through streets choked with thick fog.

The hairs on the back of Shane's neck stood up, and she stopped short, pulling Fi back into the shadows. The watery echo of running footsteps filled the silence as a trio of dark figures appeared. Shane's whole body tensed. The mist obscured their features, but she would know those black cloaks anywhere.

"*Witch Hunters,*" she hissed, reaching for her ax. Fi caught her by the sleeve.

"Wait."

The Witch Hunters were moving furtively, clearly not looking for a fight, even if Shane was more than willing to give them one. They clustered together beneath the window of the tavern, and when they moved away, sheets of crumpled yellow paper had been tacked to the wall—new notices, hung right out in the open. They'd be ripped down by morning, but not before a few of the lowlifes in Raven's Roost got a look at them.

Shane had a bad feeling as they drew closer, squinting up at the posters. It was even worse than she could have imagined. She clenched her jaw, jabbing her finger into a sheet of paper right at eye level.

"I can't believe this!" she seethed, staring at her own face on a Witch Hunters' notice. At least, she thought it was supposed to be her face. It was her name, anyway, but the chicken-scratch picture made her look like a squat, angry troll.

"I can't either," Fi breathed. "I've never seen a reward this high for information."

Information? Shane looked at the paper again. On closer inspection, it wasn't just her they were after. It was a joint notice, offering an obscene amount of money for *the whereabouts of the Huntsman Shane and her unknown partner, a possible light Witch.* The sketch next to hers was vague, just the silhouette of a girl with short hair. Apparently, Fi's identity was still a mystery—but it wouldn't be for long, not with that much money up for grabs.

Fi looked deeply troubled. "How do they know about Briar's light magic?"

"I hate to break it to you, but everyone who was anywhere near that mountain saw light magic erupting from the lake. I'll tell you the real tragedy here." Shane ripped a poster down, waving the drawing of the furious troll in Fi's face. "This doesn't look anything like me." Some short, angry crone was going to find herself on the wrong side of the Witch Hunters, and she wouldn't even get the satisfaction of smashing Tavian's nose first.

Fi shook her head. "*That's* the worst part? Come on, fugitive. We'd better get off the street."

Shane hunched into her coat as Fi led them on, feeling a little sore about the whole thing. Still, she couldn't help a whistle when they stopped in front of a wide iron gate, tying off the horses' lead ropes on the bars.

At first glance, the house didn't look like a rich family's country estate—probably a good thing in a town full of travelers and rabble-rousers. Like its neighbors, the house was about two stories high and built of wood and stone, the narrow windows all barred to keep intruders out. It was the details that gave it away: the carefully cultivated lupine growing in the small courtyard; the polished brass of the door knocker; and the well-oiled hinges of the front gate, which didn't so much as creak when Fi pushed it open. When she looked closely, Shane realized the metal bars on the windows were all stylized, depicting artfully curled scrolls. The Nenroas had put a lot of time and money into this place.

She'd already started toward the front door when Fi grabbed the shoulder of her coat, jerking her head toward the side yard. "Not that way. It'll be easier if we go around back."

That was odd. Sure, Shane was a fugitive, but only since five minutes ago. No one was even awake yet to have seen the notices. Still, she didn't question it until they scrambled through a row of prickly shrubs at the rear of the house and stopped under a balcony jutting out from the second floor. Fi unwound the rope from her belt and whipped the metal ring on the end into a slow rotation, judging the distance for a throw.

Shane crossed her arms. "You know, by *back*, I thought you meant a back door."

Fi shrugged. "There's a door up there."

Shane cocked an eye at the door in question, carved out of glossy wood and set with three small panes of beveled glass. "You get a lot of guests coming in this way?"

"I said it'll be easier, and it will," Fi insisted, though Shane could see a hint of red on the tips of her ears. Fi released the ring, which sailed soundlessly through the narrow gap in the balcony's rails, looping three times around a post and holding when she tugged. Fi glanced at Shane. "Trust me, okay?" she said. Then she set off up the rope, winding the cord expertly around the toe of each boot and climbing hand over hand.

"Not sure we're at the trust stage yet," Shane grumbled

under her breath. But she had to leave it at that, because it took all her concentration to scale the rope with a heavy ax strapped to her back and her thick boot soles slipping against the braided fibers. Shane made a mental note to change shoes next time before visiting the Nenroas.

By the time she got to the balcony, huffing and puffing, Fi was already at the door. She jiggled the bronze handle, then let out a rare curse. "They never used to lock this," she muttered, squinting up at the house.

"Maybe they got tired of people dropping in on them from the second-floor balcony," Shane suggested, rubbing the sting out of her roughed-up hands. Fi ignored her. She spent a moment inspecting the door, frowning at the lock like it was a complex puzzle. Then she pulled back and drove her elbow into one of the beveled windows, knocking out the whole glass panel with a crash. Shane snorted.

"Oh yeah, this is definitely easier."

"Quiet," Fi whispered, as if she hadn't just broken something. She slid her hand into the dark space and fished around. With a click, the door swung open, revealing shards of the broken glass panel shimmering on a thick ornamental rug. Fi's reflection rippled in the cracked glass as she squeezed inside.

Shane had begun to wonder whether this house really belonged to the Nenroas, or whether Fi had decided to *borrow* a border pass from some other unlucky noble. Still, her partner certainly knew her way around the darkened hallway— she grabbed two candles from a narrow niche in the wall and skillfully dodged the sharp corner of an end table that took a bite out of Shane's hip. Fi lit their candles from a small glass lantern and then ducked into a doorway, her light revealing a room so cluttered Shane wasn't sure they'd both fit inside.

"This is my parents' study," Fi said.

"Study?" Shane repeated. "It looks like a junk shop." Wall-to-wall bookshelves crowded in around her, each overflowing with strange relics—from ancient daggers and urns with broken handles to a woven basket full of spiral-etched stones. Shane nearly tripped over a parasol stand stuffed with maps, each yellowed scroll as tall as she was. She had a feeling someone could be buried alive in here and no one would ever notice.

Fi had shimmied over to the battered desk, where she was yanking drawers open like she was tossing the place. She sighed. "It's not here. Check the desk in the storeroom down the hall."

"Remind me again what I'm looking for?" Shane asked. Not everybody had grown up tagging along with famous historians.

"It's a wooden token about this big," Fi explained, making a square with her hands. "It'll have the Border Master's seal burnt onto one side and the Nenroa name on the other."

With effort, Shane made it back out of the study, though she almost took a coatrack with her when it hooked her by the hair. Fi waved to the left, and Shane moved that way down the corridor, the thick rug muffling her steps. The house was silent around her. Shane wondered why Fi had insisted on breaking into her own home. She tried not to wonder who had lit the lanterns guttering in the wall niches.

She'd just found the storeroom door when something else

caught her eye. A glossy painting hung at the end of the hall, the colors seeming to run in the watery candlelight. Shane paused beneath it. A man and a woman stood in front of a garden, each resting one hand on the shoulder of a scrawny child. Darfell was a kingdom of all sorts, many of them dark-haired with warm tan skin like the Nenroas. The man in the painting wore a spindly pair of spectacles, and the woman's long curly braid was bright with pearl hairpins. *Dom and Lillia Nenroa*—Shane remembered their names from the scrawl on Fi's envelope.

Fi didn't look much like her parents, but all the figures had the same smiles, not to mention the same armfuls of dusty books. Shane was relieved to know they were stealing from the Nenroas after all.

That relief didn't last. She'd barely started rummaging in the desk when she felt something cold and sharp press up against her spine. Shane froze, recognizing only too well the tip of a crossbow in her back.

"Stop what you're doing, thief, and turn around very slowly."

Shane could have kicked herself—or Fi. Since the other girl was out of range, she did as she was told, hands up as she turned to face a fair-skinned old woman with thin gray hair. She clenched the crossbow tight in her craggy hands. Shane probably could have fought her off, but they *supposedly* weren't doing anything wrong, and she didn't want to be responsible for any broken hips. Besides, at this range, even shaky hands weren't likely to miss.

"Okay," Shane said. "I admit, this looks bad. But I'm not a thief."

"What else are you supposed to be," the caretaker demanded, "rifling through Lord Dom's things in the middle of the night?"

"Again, I was doing that, but—" Shane gave up on negotiating, her eyes shooting to the door. "Hey! A little help in here!"

It was almost the last thing she ever said. The old caretaker moved faster than she'd imagined possible, and Shane choked as a bony hand seized her collar, yanking her forward with surprising strength. "I might've known you'd have an accomplice!" she hissed.

Shane grappled with the hand. "No, it's not—"

"Nina, no!"

The hand at her neck disappeared as the caretaker whirled around, crossbow at the ready. Then the weapon clattered to the floor, the woman's eyes instantly bright.

"Lady Filore! It's been so long!"

Suddenly she was a sweet old lady, her housegown billowing as she rushed to embrace Fi. Fi put up with it well enough, patting Nina awkwardly on the back after a few seconds to let her know it was time to let go.

The woman drew back. "You startled me. I didn't hear you and your . . . friend knock." She shot Shane a mistrustful look, which Shane was more than happy to return.

"This is my partner, Shane," Fi said, moving to stand at her side. "We were in a hurry," she explained, in a way that didn't explain anything.

"If you say so," Nina said, though she didn't sound convinced.

"Look, we need the border pass," Fi rushed on. "Is it

here?"

Nina's brow furrowed. "Your parents took it to the main house weeks ago, when they moved to Idlewild for the summer. Didn't you know? Lady Lillia said she was going to write you."

"I'm a little behind on my letters," Fi admitted grudgingly. Shane rubbed at her throat, more confused than ever by what had Fi so dodgy. She had stuck her nose into one of those letters at the Paper Witch's tower—nothing but chit-chat about her mother's garden and some big expedition they were planning, with a veiled invitation for Fi to come along. Shane hadn't seen anything in there that would make someone turn tail and run.

She cleared her throat, not missing the way the caretaker's eyes darted to her crossbow. "You know, Idlewild's just down in the foothills. Not far out of our way. We could stop in."

If looks could kill, the one Fi shot her would have Shane dead and buried. Nina gasped, clutching her gown. "Oh, your parents would love to see you—"

"No!" The word was sharp, too loud in the silent house. Shane stared at Fi as she visibly got herself under control, offering Nina a strained smile. "Like I said, we're in a hurry. Besides, it's not that important."

"What do you mean it's—ow!" Shane gasped as Fi drove a very sharp elbow into her ribs. "Right," she muttered. "My mistake."

The caretaker looked between them, puzzled. At last she seemed to give up. "You'll at least stay the night, won't you? I'll go make up your room." The way the woman was looking at Fi, Shane suddenly wondered whether Nina had been caring for this house since Fi was that little girl in the painting, her face still lit by an easy smile.

Fi sighed, defeated. "We'll stay. One night."

That seemed to appease Nina, who hurried off into the house, happy to have won that small concession. Shane was pretty happy herself at the prospect of a nice soft bed—but the second Nina was gone, Fi rounded on her with a furious look.

"We are not going anywhere near my parents' house. Keep out of my business."

Shane took a step back, surprised. It didn't take her long to find her tongue. "I'm sorry. Did I just imagine the conversation where you said the border pass was our first priority, and we weren't going anywhere without it?"

"I know somewhere else we can get one," Fi ground out through her teeth. "Just stay out of it, and don't mention my parents in front of Nina again. Or this journey. Or Prince Briar Rose, or any of it. I'm going to stable the horses." Then she turned and stormed out of the room, the candle flickering madly as she passed.

"Trust goes both ways, you know!" Shane called after her. She didn't expect an answer. Clearly, with Fi for a partner, answers were going to be in short supply.

8

Fi

FI CRUMPLED THE letter in her hand and stared out the window, her eyes unfocused.

She sat on the edge of the canopy bed she had slept in so many nights growing up, the soft cream-colored curtains draped from a silver hoop and gathered around the four tall posts. It was as if the room were frozen in time. She recognized every book on the shelves and all the small souvenirs from her family travels tucked in between them. The drawers were still stuffed with her old clothes, even ones she hadn't worn in years. Her parents were always moving from place to place, chasing rumors of undiscovered ruins and great historical sites, and rarely bothered to go through their own things. Someday the Nenroa houses would be their own archaeological sites for some unlucky descendant to dig through. But it wouldn't be her.

Sorry now that she'd been rough with it, Fi uncurled the letter, trying to smooth the wrinkles against the heavy coverlet. The letter itself was like all the others Fi had received—small tidbits of news in her mother's beautiful cursive, telling her about the Idlewild squirrels that had raided the tomato patch and her father's ugly mustache he refused to shave off. She could just picture that fight. Fi smiled thinking of her parents, quick to argue, quick to make up, and half in love with whatever fantastic new location they found themselves in. The letter ended the way they always did.

When are you going to come home, Filore?
Your father and I miss you dearly.

She'd thought those words had lost the power to pierce her heart, but here—in her old bedroom, surrounded by her old life—Fi found them hard to swallow.

It had been a year since she'd last seen her parents—the longest year of her life. She'd gone from being Filore Nenroa, best treasure hunter in Darfell, to being a nobody hiding in empty barns and scrounging leftover meals from the scrap heaps of inns. In one fell swoop, she'd lost her family, her security, even her sense of who she was. And she'd learned to live with a new, gnawing fear: the possibility that this year was only the first in a long line of years she would spend alone.

A prickle rose behind her eyes. It wasn't that she didn't want to go home—she couldn't. She pressed a hand against the precious letter, remembering her mother in the garden, a thick spray of foxglove gripped in her gloved hand as she taught Fi about poisons. Her father and how excited he got when he introduced her to a new magic language, the lesson veering off into history and folklore until it turned into a field trip, the two of them scrambling through raspberry brambles to find an old well whose waters were said to bring prosperity. They'd all spent winter evenings curled up in the library with their noses buried in different books, trading looks over the tops of the pages.

Now it was all gone. That was what the Butterfly Curse meant: She no longer had a home, and never would again. Fi folded up the letter and moved to her old vanity, tucking the paper into the top drawer, where she wouldn't have to look at it. She caught her reflection in the mirror. A girl with a dark look in her eyes, her nightgown loose around her, and the fingerless glove that she never took off. Not even while she slept.

Fi had never been accused of being beautiful. She'd been accused of being smart many times, both as a compliment and an insult, but she didn't think of herself that way anymore, not since she'd let someone get the better of her.

THEY STOOD IN the very heart of the old manor, she and her partner, the first people in decades—maybe centuries!—to enter this place. Their boots left matching footprints in the layers of dust and silt. Colored light filtered down on them from the beautiful stained-glass lanterns hung from the ceiling, and her partner's skin was speckled with the image of glowing butterflies, etched with firelight glinting through leaded glass. They had found the secret study of the Lord of the Butterflies, sometimes known as the Wandering Witch, a powerful man cursed to wander to the end of his days.

"Filore—catch!"

She turned instinctively, fumbling the lantern in her right hand and reaching out with her left. Her fingers curled around the cool metal handle of a stylized letter opener, and then she screamed as it burned into her palm—and burned and burned, even after she dropped it, the letter opener clattering into the dust.

"I'm sorry it had to come to this."

Fi could only scream again, falling to her knees and gripping her wrist tightly enough to make the bones ache. She couldn't even hear her partner anymore as she stared at the mark burned into her palm—the mark of the wandering butterfly.

FI STARED AT the glove. Nothing stopped her from feeling that mark; she could be wearing a steel gauntlet and she'd still see the curling wings pressed into her skin like a brand. The Curse of the Wandering Butterfly doomed her to bring misfortune on any home where she stayed too long—any more than three days.

She'd overstayed at the house of a distant aunt once, before she'd really understood the magnitude of the curse, only to wake on the fifth night to a fire that burned through the manor, leaving nothing but rubble behind. Fi still remembered the haunted look on her aunt's face as she stood outside in the snow, staring at the wreckage with ash in her hair and her two small children cradled in her arms. That moment lingered behind Fi's eyelids sometimes when she tried to sleep, her aunt's trembling voice saying, *We're ruined*. But in her heart, what Fi heard was *You've ruined us*.

Fi learned to keep moving, because every time she stopped, it seemed the curse was right on her heels. She'd gotten sick in Pisarre and lain there, feverish, in the home of a family friend, while small incidents began to plague the household: lost keepsakes and falling beams and a bad burn from an overturned kettle. The master of the house was in a carriage accident and very nearly killed. They hadn't blamed Fi, but then, she hadn't told them about the curse, only apologized over and over through her fever. She swore to herself never to let this curse hurt anyone again.

So she was on the hunt for signs of the butterfly, trying to find out what happened to the Wandering Witch and whether he'd ever escaped the curse himself. He was an ancient figure, more of a legend really, and it was hard to find any solid information about him. In the great library of Pisarre, she finally uncovered a tantalizing reference to his underground workshop, hidden in a place of great magical power. She'd hoped that meant the Witches' Jewelry Box, but so far, she'd found nothing.

In the meantime, she could never go back to her family house. The Paper Witch had warned her that like any truly nasty curse, this one was connected to her feelings. The more she loved a place, the more dangerous and powerful the magic became. She had no idea what would happen if she returned to Idlewild, even for a single night, with its store of magic relics and shelves spilling over with spell books. She just knew she couldn't be the reason something terrible happened to her family.

And she couldn't face them. Her parents warned her about treasure hunting. They warned her not to trifle with dangerous magic relics. They warned her, most of all, to stay far away from her ex. She hadn't listened, and they'd been so disappointed in her, even before it had all gone wrong. She wasn't going home until she'd found a way to fix this. By herself.

Fi moved back to the bookcase, running a finger along the dusty spines and ruffling the little strips of paper sticking up from the pages. Absently, she slid out one of the thicker tomes: Antonia Gregoire's *The Order of the Divine Rose*, a dangerously speculative account of the founding of the royal order of Witches. She had to smile when she cracked it open and a half sheet of paper fluttered to the floor. You'd never catch a Nenroa scribbling in the margins, so notes like this were a familiar sight, though at least half the time they were in the wrong books. She picked it up to read the annotation in her mother's hand: *Utterly implausible. See Rivarrcha's driest history, p. 1280.*

Fi remembered Rivarrcha's *driest* history on the founding of Andar's Orders of Magic. It was amazing that Andar's most famous historian had managed to turn such a fascinating topic into such a dull read. Fi had spent one whole summer, the year she was twelve, huddled in the Idlewild library trying to get through the eight-volume set.

Not by coincidence, it was the same summer her mother's friends, Lord and Lady Alfieri of another Border House, had come to stay at Idlewild, bringing their two daughters. Fi had never spent much time with children her own age, and she had been awkward around them. More than once, she took refuge at the rosewood table under the library's sunny window, losing herself in the dusty old tomes.

"FILORE?"

Filore jerked up from the book, trying not to look like she'd been falling asleep over the thick yellow paper crammed with very tiny print. Her mother stood behind her, a crinkle between her eyebrows.

"Shouldn't you be outside with the girls?" Lillia asked. "Ana and Tomasina are only here for two more days."

"I'm happier here," Filore told her firmly, flipping another page. "This is more interesting than they are."

Lillia smiled, slipping into the chair next to her. "Well, that's simply impossible. Rivarrcha's fourth volume has been known to put even hardened scholars to sleep." She leaned close, searching Filore's face, but Filore refused to meet her eyes.

When Ana and Tomasina first arrived, she had tried to make friends. But even though she was already fluent in four magic languages and could recite the names of all of Andar's rulers from Aurora to Amarise, she couldn't understand the Alfieri girls. They had no interest in history or ancient Witches. All they wanted to talk about was music and politics and which heir of which noble house had done some scandalous thing, and other topics Filore knew nothing about and didn't care to learn.

That afternoon, while the girls took lunch in her mother's garden, Filore tried one more time. She showed them, cradled in her hands, a wolf tarantula she'd found crawling under the woodpile. Her father had taught her how to lift them gently, without scaring them, so they wouldn't bite. Filore found the spider fascinating. But the Alfieri girls hadn't.

"That's disgusting," Tomasina declared, glaring at Filore while her sister cowered behind her, shrieking. "What is wrong with you?"

Filore hadn't known how to answer. Right up until that moment, she hadn't thought there was anything wrong with her. She'd imagined everyone grew up this way—going on expeditions, debating history at the dinner table, learning to handle poisonous spiders and snakes. She hadn't realized that the children of other Border Houses all knew one another, took lessons together, gossiped about one another. They already had alliances, friends and enemies. And Filore was outside of it all.

Filore glanced over at her mother. Lillia wore a burgundy dress and glistening pearl earrings, and the sunlight picked out the freckles on her cheeks. She looked like a perfect noblewoman except for the frizzy hairs sticking out of her long black braid, proof she'd been rummaging in the overstuffed attic. Somehow, her mother managed to be both: a historian and a lady. Filore couldn't do that. And more than that, she didn't want to. So why had Tomasina's question stung so badly?

Her mother seemed to decide she wasn't going to speak. She brushed the dark hair out of Filore's eyes. "Well, never mind. Take a break from Rivarrcha—let's look at this one instead." She pushed the heavy book aside and slid a children's storybook into its place.

Filore gave her a flat look. "I think I'm a little old for made-up stories."

Lillia laughed, a melodic sound that echoed through the mahogany-paneled library. "You're never too old! Half of what historians do is look at old storybooks like this one." She let the book fall open. The page shimmered with an illustration in crackling paint, a Witch calling forth a great plume of water. "People make up stories to explain things—an earthquake, a plague, maybe an incredible act of magic. Every made-up story starts with a grain of truth." Her mother paused, glancing at Filore as if to check she was listening—then she smiled joyfully, flipping ahead to the start of the next story. "Besides, look at these gorgeous illuminations. Hand me that magnifying glass."

Filore had to laugh at the sight of her beautiful mother peering through the brass-handled magnifying glass, one of her eyes as big as a saucer through the bubble of the lens. She squinted down at the illumination—a bramble of carmine-red roses and golden sand encircling a white serpent, whose long body formed the first letter of the story that started "In a faraway time," the way they all did. She would recognize those three symbols anywhere. Sand, rose, and serpent: the symbols of the last Three Great Witches.

Though she'd seen it a hundred times, she couldn't help studying the oil-bright painting of three women on the facing page. First came the Snake Witch, tall and stern, who carried a silver serpent wound over her tawny arm like a cuff. Then came the Dream Witch, with brown skin and lush curls, winking as she pressed one finger to her lips like she was about to share a fantastic secret. The Dream Witch was her mother's favorite. Last came the Rose Witch, barely a teenager, with sunny features and a crown of rosebuds nestled in her golden hair.

Filore traced her finger down the page, soft and fragile from being turned so many times. When she was young, she loved the stories of the Great Witches best. They made her think that, if she was smart and brave and clever enough, she could overcome anything. But maybe that was only true in fairy tales.

She didn't realize her mother had squeezed her close until she heard Lillia's whisper in her ear: "You are exactly who you are supposed to be, Filore. And no matter what, you will always have us to come home to." Filore didn't dare look at her, afraid the prickle behind her eyes would turn into tears.

They kept turning the pages until Filore forgot everything—her awkwardness and her embarrassment and the disgust on Tomasina's face. Sometimes being different was lonely, but other times, tucked up next to her mother with the stories of the Witches spread out before her, it felt like the best thing she could ever be.

FI TUCKED THE note back into Gregoire's book and returned it to the shelf, wiping the dust away with the heel of her hand. She wondered whether she was part of the story of Andar now, and whether one day she and Briar would be small illustrations in some other children's book. Her mother would love that.

A small, square painting of Lillia hung beside the bookcase. Fi's eyes traced her mother's face, her lips turned up in a friendly smile and her eyes looking somewhere beyond the canvas.

"My mother was prettier, but she didn't smile much for paintings."

Fi spun around. Briar was leaning casually against the bedpost, his thoughtful eyes fixed on the painting.

"Don't sneak up on people!" Fi hissed, trying to calm her racing heart. Briar was unchanged, the same velvet coat swirling from his shoulders, though it looked almost black in the dim glow of the moon through the picture window.

"Sorry," he said, looking genuinely embarrassed. "I guess I'm out of the habit of announcing myself. Though I did warn you I'd be stopping by."

I want to get to know you. Briar's words from the tower echoed in Fi's head, but she shook them away, fixing the spirit with a glare. She certainly hadn't forgotten her new magical baggage, but she wasn't in the mood for visitors.

"Well, consider knocking next time," she suggested. "Or just not coming."

Briar pressed a hand to his heart, as if she'd mortally wounded him. The sparkle in his blue eyes gave him away. "I have clearly made a very bad first impression on you. If I want any chance of winning you over, I'm going to have to figure out what it is you don't like about me."

"Maybe I just don't like people who pop into my bedroom without warning and insult my mother," Fi shot back, stomping out her blush.

Briar laughed. "I wasn't insulting her. Or at least, I wasn't trying to."

He moved forward into the spill of moonlight. Fi had to fight down the urge to put her hand through him again. It was a strange feeling, to be standing next to someone who seemed so real and still be all alone.

Briar nodded at the painting. "My mother was uncommonly beautiful. I'm told that's where I get my staggering good looks." He shot Fi an audacious smile, and she rolled her eyes, even though she had a feeling it would just encourage him. "She died soon after I was born, though, so that's almost all I know about her."

"Oh. Right."

Fi wasn't sure what to say. She knew the legend well, but this was the first time she'd ever thought of it as more than a story. Briar was real, which meant the people he'd lost were real, too. And he'd lost everything. When she glanced up at him again, he seemed much younger, wistful and sad, just a sixteen-year-old boy sharing his secrets with a stranger because she was the only person he'd had to talk to in a hundred years. Lonely the way Fi was lonely.

Suddenly Fi thought she understood what Briar was doing here. Maybe it wasn't about getting to know her at all. Maybe it was about not being alone for a while.

"Briar, are you . . ." *Are you okay?* was what she'd been about to say. The words vanished when she realized Briar wasn't next to her anymore, but behind her at the bookcase, inspecting the keepsakes on her shelves. "Are you going through my stuff?" Fi demanded, arms crossed over her nightgown. Briar jerked up, rubbing the back of his neck.

"Curiosity got the best of me," he said, which wasn't even close to an apology. "I've never been out of the castle before."

"You mean, in a hundred years, right?"

Briar shook his head. "Even before that. I was a child destined to fall to dark magic. It was too dangerous for me to go anywhere."

Fi couldn't imagine that. Growing up, she'd had all the freedom she could ask for—*and plenty of rope to hang myself with*, she couldn't help thinking bitterly.

Briar had turned away again, leaning in until he was almost nose to nose with a small wooden statue. "What is this?" he asked.

Fi relented, joining Briar at the foot of the tall shelves. "It's a luck token, carved by a master artisan on the islands off the coast of Pisarre," she explained. "It's supposed to ensure good weather, but we got six weeks of rain."

"I'm sure you were lovely with mud up to your elbows," Briar teased. His eyes darted across the shelf, settling on a bone-handled knife. "This is beautiful."

"It's almost five hundred years old," Fi told him, running her finger down the handle carved with blossoms and vines. It was a family heirloom, supposedly made by one of her own ancestors.

Briar laughed. "And here I thought a hundred years was a long time."

"Compared with most of this stuff, you're relatively recent," Fi told him, relaxing in spite of herself. Somehow her heart didn't feel so heavy anymore—the room was just a room again, filled with good memories she could share.

Briar's voice was playful. "I bet that's what you don't like about me. My age. You think I'm too old for you." He craned his head over the shelf, blinking at her through the eyeholes of a painted fool's mask with a long, beaky nose.

Fi tried to smother a laugh. "If anything, you're very young for a hundred and sixteen."

Briar straightened with a cheeky smile. "And you're very worldly for seventeen, so I guess we're perfect for each other." Before she could protest, he'd turned back to the bookcase, pointing to something over her head. "And what is this contraption?"

Fi propped one foot on the lowest shelf and hoisted herself up, glad for the change of subject. She braced an elbow against a row of crooked atlases. Something made of polished metal gleamed in the moonlight.

"Oh. It's a camping lantern." Fi grabbed it and dropped back to the floor. "It folds out—see?" She straightened the little metal pieces one by one until she held a small lantern in one hand, the crisscrossed bars forming an elaborate cage. "My father invented it."

"Your father is a lantern-maker?" Briar guessed, delighted.

"A historian," Fi corrected, biting the inside of her cheek to keep hold of her smile.

"Also a noble profession," Briar assured her. "May I?"

Fi didn't get a chance to ask what he meant. Briar lifted one hand, and a spark of pure white magic flared out of the dark, crackling at the tip of his finger. Fi breathed in sharply as the spark leapt into the lantern. Suddenly she was face-to-face with Briar again, staring up at his blue eyes and the soft curve of his lips. She didn't remember when they'd gotten so close. A golden curl of hair slipped into his eyes, almost glowing in the light of her father's lantern, alive again after sitting dark for so long.

Briar tipped his head. His laugh was so quiet it was more like a vibration. "So you do have your mother's smile."

"What?" Fi asked, blinking.

Briar shrugged. "Well, I wasn't sure. You've never smiled at me before."

Fi felt that familiar flush heating up her face. She lowered the lantern so it wouldn't give her away.

The deep tolling of a bell shook her out of the moment. Fi turned to the window. The bell in the center of Raven's Roost was clanging, and she counted twelve peals before the sound died off. She hadn't realized it had gotten so late. Her chance for a few hours' sleep was slipping away. For a moment, with Briar teasing her, she had forgotten everything—the curse, the Spindle Witch, even the Witch Hunter notices tacked up through the streets.

When she turned back to the prince, his expression was wistful, like he could sense the heavy shift in the air. He curled his hand and the white spark went out, leaving them in darkness.

"You'll have to show me the rest another time," he said softly.

Fi set the lantern back in its place. Her throat felt tight, and she was careful to step around Briar as she made her way to the bed—she couldn't imagine moving through him, not when he looked so hollow. It was only as she dropped onto the bed that Briar spoke again.

"Do you want me to go?" he asked.

Fi clenched her hand in the soft white sheet. It was impossible not to hear what he was really saying. *Please don't make me go.* She took a deep breath and inhaled the familiar scents of lavender and rosemary, the sachets her mother always tucked under the pillows. "You can stay," she said finally. "Though I won't be great company while I'm sleeping."

"Still the best company I've had in a long time," Briar replied.

Fi pulled the blanket up to her chin. She'd only been under the curse for a year, and already it felt like her heart was shriveling into a husk. She knew what it was like to lie in the dark and desperately wish she could hear someone else's breath heavy with sleep, something to prove she wasn't alone. She watched as Briar moved to the window and curled onto the wide sill, his elbow braced on his knee so he could look out at the sleeping city.

"It's better not to be alone." She wasn't sure who she meant, herself or Briar. Before she could think on it too deeply, she rolled away, putting her face into the pillow.

"Then maybe I'll come around more often," she heard him whisper as she drifted off to sleep.

That night she dreamed of the gleaming white tower again, only this time it was foggy with rain, heavy droplets hanging on the petals of the roses like tears. As she stared at the sleeping boy, the room seemed to grow emptier and emptier, the color bleeding out of the roses until it was just a cage of cold walls and wicked thorns and a single window, now a wash of gray rain.

9

⫸⫸⫷⫷

Briar Rose

BRIAR LEANED CLOSE to the window, peering at the darkened world beyond the glass. The moon hung like a silver bow over the silent buildings of the city that seemed very small to Briar, wreathed in fog and bound on every side by a murky pine forest. Growing up, he had looked out on the glistening castle gardens, and beyond that the cobbled streets of Andar's prosperous capital city, Leonnese, the air ringing with the clatter of cart wheels and merchants shouting while royal-blue flags flapped from every rooftop. At night, candles burned in the windows, so many of them that the city winked beneath him like a sea of fireflies. But those were old memories. For a long time, the only view from the tower had been a labyrinth of thorns.

The rustle of sheets drew his eyes back to the girl sleeping across the room. She was curled on her side, one hand jammed under her pillow and the other wrapped around herself, her breathing slow and even as she dreamed of somewhere far away. The gossamer curtains of the bed canopy swayed around her. Briar rested his chin on his hand.

He'd spent so much time imagining her, and he'd gotten just about everything wrong.

From the time he was very small, Briar had grown up knowing what all of Andar knew: that the Spindle Witch was coming for him, and that he would lose himself to her dark magic and become a rotten, wicked thing bent to her will.

When he'd pricked his finger on the spindle, he thought that was it—the end. But the Dream Witch appeared to him one last time. As she cast him into his enchanted sleep, she told him not to despair, because the sleeping curse was a curse meant to be broken. She promised a girl would come to him, one who was destined to wake him with a kiss.

After he found himself in the white tower, the promise of that girl was what kept him alive. His sister had always told him the only thing strong enough to hold back a curse was love, and deep in his heart, he clung to the belief that his love for that girl might be able to break the Spindle Witch's hold on him once and for all. So he dreamed of the moment they would be brought together, of a love so powerful it could wipe out a hundred years of loneliness.

When he finally found himself staring into her eyes across the Witch's tower, he just blurted it all out—love, destiny, breaking the curse, every wish he'd held in his heart for a century. And Fi looked at him like he was out of his mind. It was possibly the worst love confession of all time.

Briar resisted the urge to bury his head in his hands. He wasn't sure if he'd made any headway with his grand promises to win her over, or if he'd instead given Fi an incentive not to like him. But he hadn't known what else to do. That moment in the tower, when she flatly rejected him, he'd been so desperate to be given a chance—any chance—to change her mind.

And now he hoped more than ever that he hadn't ruined it. Not because of destiny or loneliness or some half-formed dream of a girl, but because he had never met someone like Filore Nenroa.

She was sharp, and not easily impressed. He had expected to sweep her off her feet, either with his looks or his magic or his being a legendary prince. Instead Briar felt like he was the one swept away, a heady rush of warmth building in his chest as she stuck her arm through him and quibbled over love at first sight. And she was so smart, ticking off information like she'd swallowed entire encyclopedias, making Briar wish he'd spent more of the last hundred years in the castle's library. She'd left home and ventured out into the world and learned so many things that Briar never learned, seen things he desperately wanted to see. And she was jaded. Briar didn't know if someone had made her that way or if she was naturally suspicious of anything she could wave her arm through, but he couldn't wait to find out.

As the cursed prince hidden away in the castle, Briar hadn't gotten out much, but he had always assumed that when the time came, he would be naturally winsome and charming. Fi didn't seem charmed. She spent most of her time frowning at him like he was a bug she hadn't decided whether or not to squash.

In spite of that—or maybe because of it—nothing had been more gratifying than winning that first smile from her.

He was hooked. He wanted more. He was brimming with emotions he hadn't felt in a hundred years. Wild galloping glee at the thought of traveling by Fi's side. Buzzing anticipation as he imagined them bantering back and forth, Fi fixing him with that sharp, flat look because she was trying not to smile. And then there was the aching pit that sank into his stomach when he thought about the curse. Would Fi be in danger trying to save him? How had that never occurred to him before? In all his time dreaming, he had never once imagined wishing his savior didn't have to save him.

A tiny wisp of doubt curled through his mind. Briar fisted a hand in his coat, crushing one of the silver rose buttons against his palm. He was asking her to face the dark magic that had defeated the Great Witches, that had toppled Andar at the height of its power—the magic that had been gnawing at him for a hundred years, grinding away at him, searching for a way in. What if Fi couldn't save him? What if no one could? What if she died trying, and he was alone again, forever this time?

The lantern across the street flickered out, suffocated by the rising fog. The room seemed darker all of a sudden, and colder, the shadows stretching toward him like malformed fingers.

Don't think about it, Briar reminded himself. *Don't think about the curse.*

When he was little, his sister had told him that magic was like wishing. It responded to intention. Briar was bound up so deeply in the Spindle Witch's dark magic, in his most hopeless moments he wondered whether he'd ever be free. Sometimes he swore he could feel the Spindle Witch reaching out to him across the vast distance, beckoning him to give in to the curse, to let it swallow him.

He lived in fear of what would happen then—what wicked things he might be used for once he was under her control. But there was one thought that had always driven the darkness away, and now she was right in front of him, more real than she'd ever been.

He turned to look at Fi, tracing the lines of her face. She rolled over in her sleep, mumbling about being out of ink. Briar's mouth bent into a smile. She would be the one to break the curse—he was sure of it. Fi wasn't what he'd imagined, but maybe that was the best thing about her.

10

>>> <<<

Shane

SHANE LEANED AGAINST the wall under the awning of the small apothecary shop, tugging in irritation at the hood of her borrowed Nenroa cloak.

Fi had roused her hours before dawn, making them ride out from Raven's Roost under the cover of darkness. Shane was sure they hadn't been spotted because even the birds had the decency to be asleep at that hour. After riding all day, they finally stopped for supplies here in Wistbrook, the last trading outpost before they headed into the Cragspires and made for the Duchy of Bellicia.

Fi, in her usual tight-lipped way, said they would get passes in Bellicia and not much else. She also flat-out rebuffed any possibility of getting rooms with cushy beds at the local inn—apparently, that was a luxury reserved for those without bounties on their heads. Shane had been instructed to keep her head down and stay out of trouble, which in practice meant skulking around outside the shops while Fi bargained with their coin and Shane suffocated under this heavy traveling cloak.

The least her partner could do was hurry it up!

Shane peered through the dusty window into the apothecary shop where Fi had disappeared. The shelves inside were clustered with loamy vines and hundreds of bright glass bottles, everything glistening in the sun. After picking up the essentials, Fi had decided to make one extra stop for information. Twyla, the apothecary, was a friend of the Paper Witch. Fi was *supposed* to be finding out about any local Witch Hunter activity, but it looked more like she and the shopkeeper were locked in a prolonged discussion of comparative herbology. Fi's eyes lit up as the brown-skinned woman waved cheerfully at the dried herbs hanging from the ceiling.

Shane studied the streak of gray running through Twyla's thick auburn hair and wondered idly whether the woman was a Witch. It was hard to tell in Darfell, where so many Witches did all they could to blend in.

Back in Steelwight, magic was the purview of the village wisewomen and the sages of the Green Shrines. The most powerful among them were the eldest men and women, their bodies covered in tattoos of constellations and the eight islands of the Steelwight archipelago. They were teachers and healers and wanderers who spoke of the call of the ancient forests, people who always knew where to find springs of freshwater and which foul-smelling brew would break a child's fever. Even Shane's arrogant father grudgingly yielded to the power of the sages. The Paper Witch reminded her a lot of the wisewoman in her village. Probably why she'd felt such a pull to trust him when they first met.

Five more minutes, Shane decided of her errant partner. Then, fugitive or not, she was going in.

Beyond the apothecary shop, the streets widened into an open-air market, loud with haggling voices and roosters cackling from the rooftops. Most of the shoppers were giving Shane a wide berth. She had to look pretty shady, lurking in the shadows with her hood up on a perfectly sunny day. On the other hand, cutpurses were pretty common around these parts, so maybe she fit right in.

Shane tried out her most menacing scowl on the next person who eyed her suspiciously. The young man's face went pale and he hurried on, clutching his bag of fat purple figs. Shane was still holding back a laugh when a commotion broke out at one of the market stalls.

"Thief!" A man's outraged voice rose over the din, followed by a girl's shriek. Shane couldn't see what was happening through the sudden crowd as people stopped to gawk at the spectacle around the jeweler's stall.

"Let me go!" the girl's voice demanded.

Shane threw a glance at the apothecary. Fi would definitely let her have it for this, but—

She pushed off the wall, elbowing through the throng to get a better look, then froze at the sight of a familiar figure.

"Red!" she blurted out.

Red spun around, her eyes widening a fraction in surprise as her gaze met Shane's. A tall, beefy man—hired muscle, from the look—gripped Red by the wrist while the well-dressed merchant behind the table hurled accusations.

Red wore the same blouse and bodice from the woods, now matched with a dainty crimson skirt that swished around her ankles. Her dark curls were pinned up around her face, and a flicker of gems winked in her hair. In her free hand she clutched a folded parasol—one that was about to become a weapon, if Shane could read the annoyed look on the girl's face.

"Get your hands off me, brute." Red tried to yank her wrist loose, but the bruiser only twisted it high over her head, making Red hiss in pain.

Shane had seen enough. "Hey! Let her go," she growled, striding forward with the same menacing look she'd been trying out before. The guard didn't seem cowed in the slightest, but the jewelry merchant looked taken aback.

"This is none of your business," he sputtered. "The girl stole a very valuable ring from my table. Search her!" he ordered his guard.

The man leered at Red, his eyes raking her up and down. Something inside of Shane turned hard as iron. Suddenly she didn't care whether Red had stolen ten rings. Some smirking guard for hire pawing Red under the guise of searching her was on the short list of things that were not happening.

"Touch her and I'll break your fingers," she warned.

Red yanked her hand free with a noise of disgust. The look she threw Shane over her shoulder was grateful and calculating all at once, her expression defiant as she turned back to the merchant.

"Tell your man to keep his grubby hands to himself and I'll let her search me." She jerked her chin toward Shane.

"What?" Shane hissed in surprise.

"Not interested?" Red raised her eyebrows.

Shane was glad she didn't have to answer that.

"Fine. Turn out her pockets—but do it in plain view!" the merchant said testily. The bruiser backed off, peering intently at Shane's cloaked face. Hopefully he wasn't the type who paid attention to Witch notices.

Red set her parasol aside and raised her hands as Shane approached, her lips pressed into a playful smile.

"Are you sure this is a good idea?" Shane asked quietly. The last time she'd run into Red, the girl *had* been stealing something.

"Go on. Don't keep all these people waiting," Red teased.

The crowd had pressed in around them, eager to see how this would play out. Shane shot the gawkers a dirty look, then slid her hands down Red's sides and patted the puffs in her skirt, trying not to think too hard about what she was touching. Fighting down the flutter in her stomach, she wedged her fingers into Red's pockets and pulled them inside out.

The first pocket was empty. The second held a velvet drawstring pouch and a ruby-studded hairpin like the ones in Red's hair. The pouch was stuffed with enough coins to make Shane think Red was doing just fine as a thief, but no missing ring. Shane returned Red's things while the merchant fumed.

"She's clean."

"Are you sure? Maybe you should check my bodice," Red suggested, blinking her long eyelashes at Shane. "I bet I could slip something in there."

Shane's stomach swooped. She didn't know whether Red was a Witch or not, but she definitely had a wicked sense of humor.

"I don't know where you hid my ring, but I know you took

it," the merchant yelled, pounding the table. "Seize her!"

The hired man lurched forward, snatching at Red. Shane thrust herself between them and grabbed him at the elbow, twisting her smaller body to send him sailing right over her shoulder. He hit the merchant's table with a crash. Glittering bracelets and glass-beaded chokers scattered into the dust as Shane's hood flopped back, exposing her face to the entire crowd.

"Hey! It's the huntsman Shane, from the Witch notices!" someone yelled. Shane tried to twist around to see who had recognized her, but it was a sea of strange faces.

"That sounds like our cue," Red whispered. "Run!" Then she seized Shane's hand, and suddenly they were flying through the market, chaos erupting at their backs.

Shane could hear the shouts of the merchant ordering his men after them. A few others from the crowd were trying to flank them, racing down the next line of stalls and jumping barrels and bales. Red threw her a daring look. Then she veered into a hairpin turn and dragged Shane down a back alley, leaving their angry pursuers in the dust.

Shane's heart was thudding, and not just from the chase. She couldn't tear her eyes away from the look of wild delight on Red's face. Her eyes sparkled like she was savoring every second. Red was just the kind of girl Shane's grandmother would have warned her to stay away from—a warning she would have relished defying.

"This way," Red urged, dragging Shane into a narrow gap between two stone buildings. There was barely space for one person, much less two, and Shane found herself pressed up against Red, the girl's supple chest rising and falling against her own. An errant curl had escaped from the pins and hung into her heart-shaped face.

"They're veering off," Red whispered as the shouts of pursuit grew more distant. Then she tilted her chin to look up at Shane, and Shane stopped breathing, staring down at Red's flushed cheeks and her parted lips, those dark, secretive eyes blazing into hers. They were practically nose to nose. She didn't know whose heartbeat she was feeling, hers or Red's, but it was racing. Her head spun with the closeness.

"Thanks," she managed, trying to keep her voice even.

Red's laugh ghosted across her face. "I have a lot of experience running away from angry mobs."

Shane forced herself to focus, listening hard. The street beyond the mouth of the alley was quiet. "I think it's safe now."

"Maybe we should wait a few more minutes, just like this." Red's whisper fluttered across Shane's neck, but she was already slipping past Shane into the street, shaking the dust and alley cobwebs from her skirts. She snagged her parasol and rested it on her shoulder. "Come on. I'll show you a back way out of town, in case those people circle around looking for you."

"Most of them were after you," Shane pointed out, but she tugged her hood up anyway. She fell into step beside Red, eyeing the girl curiously as they hugged the edges of the buildings. "So, did I just help you fleece some guy's ring?"

"Want to search me again and find out?" Red asked, shooting Shane a cheeky look. "I wouldn't worry about it. Just for the sake of argument, that ring *could* have been a magic relic, and that merchant *could* be better off without it."

"And would that make the person who took it a relic hunter?" Shane persisted, holding aside a line of laundry so Red could duck underneath. She had always steered clear of the treasure hunters reckless enough to go after magic relics, since you usually couldn't tell if a relic had any nasty spells cast on it until you'd already picked it up. But Red seemed to know exactly what she was doing.

The girl pressed one finger to her painted lips. "I guess you could say I locate and obtain hard-to-find items."

"Sounds suspiciously like a thief."

"It does, doesn't it?" Red replied, blinking innocently at Shane. Up close, her deep brown eyes seemed wide and doe-like, but Shane had never met a deer half so cunning.

They were nearly to the edge of town. Shane had just reached down to help Red over a stack of broken crates when a streak of brown fur darted out from under the pile, spitting and snarling. Shane caught a flash of yellowed eyes as the scruffy dog bared its teeth, its ears pressed flat.

"Watch out!" Shane cried.

Red didn't even bat an eyelash. In one motion, she tossed her parasol aside and dropped to her knees in the dirt, holding out her hands.

The creature was covered with matted brown-and-sable fur and a crisscross of scars, like one of the wild dogs that lurked around the mountain settlements searching for scraps. A long silver scar glistened in the fur above its ragged ear. If that thing was as brutal as it looked, Red was about to lose a finger.

"Red," Shane murmured urgently.

"Shh, you'll scare him." Red's voice was low and soothing. The dog growled deep in its throat, the angry hairs on its ruff bristling as it watched them warily. "You won't hurt me, will you, beautiful?" Red whispered, so softly Shane barely heard her. Then she began to hum—a sweet, haunting melody like a sad lullaby. It tugged at something deep in Shane's chest, dragging up memories she thought she'd locked away.

The dog blinked slowly, sitting back on its haunches. The feral growl melted away to a plaintive whine as it pushed its nose into Red's open hand. Red's lips quirked into a smile. She stopped humming and cupped her hands under the dog's muzzle, scratching its chin as its tail thumped against the ground. Shane looked on, fascinated.

"How'd you do that?" she asked, dropping down from the crates.

Red shrugged. "I've always had a way with animals. I like them more than people."

"Should I be offended?"

"Well, if it's any consolation, *you* are the most wild, animal-like person I've ever met." Red shot a look over her shoulder.

"Hey!" Shane protested.

"It's a compliment," Red assured her before turning her attention back to the dog, working the tangles out of its fur. "Animals make sense to me. Even when they're dangerous, even when they seem vicious, they always have a reason for it. People, on the other hand, can be quite senseless and cruel."

Shane wondered what she would have seen in Red's eyes, if the girl hadn't been looking pointedly away.

"Not like you," Red cooed to the scruffy dog. "You're a

sweetheart." The dog apparently agreed, yipping and jumping up to lick her face. Red laughed as it knocked her backward, and the sound was so warm and unguarded that for a moment Shane felt like she was looking at a different girl entirely, a girl she was meeting for the very first time.

One of Red's hairpins fell out and skittered across the dirt. Shane scooped it up, then reluctantly dug into her pocket, unwrapping her handkerchief to reveal her very last piece of jerky. The good jerky—the kind she never found among the Paper Witch's vegetarian stores. It was too good for a stray dog. But . . .

"Here, boy," Shane called, throwing the treat into the grass. The dog lurched off Red and gobbled it up, his tail wagging madly.

"Softy," Red accused, but she was smiling.

The dog's ears perked up, and a second later it took off, loping away from town. Red got to her feet and retrieved her parasol. Shane swallowed, thinking it wasn't really fair that Red looked even better with her hair disheveled and her dress covered in dirty paw prints.

Shane took the lead as they slipped out of town into the woods. She tried to keep an eye out for anyone following them, but she kept finding herself looking at Red instead, studying her out of the corner of her eye. Shane was always drawn to pretty girls, and Red was dangerously pretty. But there was something else, too, something hidden and mysterious that made Shane want to know everything about her.

When they reached the clearing where she and Fi had left the horses, her partner was waiting for her with their bulging packs at her feet and her face pinched.

"There you are. What happened to keeping your head down? Can't you stay out of trouble for five minutes—oh." She stopped abruptly when she caught sight of Red.

"Ignoring the fact that you were in that shop *way* more than five minutes," Shane replied, "this is Red, the girl I told you about. Red, this inconsiderate person is my treasure-hunting partner, Fi."

"I'm afraid I'm the reason your partner got in trouble," Red said. "She came rushing to my rescue in the market and things got quite out of hand."

Fi threw Shane a look that said she was going to get all the details on that later. "Sounds like Shane."

"Hey, we got out clean." Shane cleared her throat. "This is yours, Red," she said, pulling loose the hairpin.

"Perfect." Red set aside her parasol, her fingers sliding across Shane's hand as she took the pin. Her flirty look said it was no accident. Fi was glaring a hole in the side of Shane's head, but Shane couldn't even be bothered to look at her partner, utterly transfixed by Red effortlessly capturing the curls and pinning them up at the nape of her neck.

When she leaned down to pick up her parasol, Shane noticed something peeking over the collar of her blouse—a flash of black ink on her skin. *A tattoo?* All Shane could make out was a sinuous curve and something sharp, like a fang.

A glance at Fi confirmed she was staring at the same spot, frowning hard.

Red swung back to face them. "Well, I should be off. I've got a little something to take care of, after all." She thumbed open the parasol, and Shane stared in astonishment as a small silver ring tumbled out, landing right in her palm.

"You did have it!"

"I never said I didn't," Red reminded her. "Maybe I'll see you down the road." With that she sauntered off, tossing the ring carelessly in her hand.

Fi crossed her arms, pinning Shane with a look.

"So that's your type."

"What is?" Shane said, distracted.

"Dangerous."

Shane blinked—mostly at the memory of Red telling her the exact same thing. She made a face and flicked Fi's shoulder. "Anyone but you is my type."

Fi shook her head and hefted a pack into Shane's arms, whistling for the horses. "Come on. Twyla has a cottage on the edge of town, and she said we could stay the night in her attic."

"Sure—drafty attic, comfortable inn. Close enough," Shane muttered. But she couldn't stop herself from craning her head one more time, searching for a last glimmer of scarlet through the trees.

11

⟫⟫⟫⟩—⟨⟨⟨⟨

Shane

SHANE HAD SOME experience sleeping in attics, and less hospitable places, too. As far as attics went, Twyla's was on the better side: no rats, mold, or even much dust. It was cramped, though, stacked to the sloping ceiling with bundles of drying herbs and ingredient overflow—from the apothecary shop or from her kitchen, Shane couldn't tell. Sacks of flour leaned precariously against a tower of honey jars, with a few papery onions rolling around underfoot. Shane's only real concern was turning over in her sleep and being buried in an avalanche.

"Go ahead and make up some beds for yourselves by the turnips," Twyla had advised, poking her head up through the hatch in the floor and handing Shane a pile of spare quilts. "The floor slopes a little, but the smell's better than bunking in the other corner, next to the garlic. I've had complaints."

"You seem really calm about stashing us up here," Shane said, wrestling a box of ointments out of her way.

"Well, you're not the first to spend a night or two tucked up in the attic." At Shane's surprised look, Twyla laughed, dimples standing out on her cheeks. "I've known the Paper Witch a long time. His friends seem to have a knack for getting into trouble. Just bang on the floor if you need anything."

Shane had already claimed the spot under the lone window by the time Fi clambered into the attic, negotiating the ladder with two small bundles tucked under her arm.

"I would not suspect someone that cheerful of harboring fugitives," Shane announced, bunching her cloak into a pillow.

"Arguably not a bad thing, for her or for us," Fi said. "Here. I come bearing gifts." She ducked under the bundle of yellow onions strung from the low ceiling and handed Shane something warm wrapped in a cloth napkin.

Shane opened it to find a crispy sweet roll bubbling over with apples and cinnamon. She bit into it greedily, sighing in contentment.

"I needed this," she said through a mouthful.

"Worked up an appetite running from those bounty collectors?" Fi asked drily, taking a much smaller bite of her own meal. Shane had filled her in on what happened in the market, and though Fi hadn't said much, her knitted eyebrows spoke volumes.

Shane shook the sweet roll at her. "I remain deeply offended that anyone thinks I look like that."

Fi huffed. "Meanwhile—I talked to Twyla about our Witch Hunter problem. Sounds like an entire squad was seen near the main road. We'll have to stick to the mountain trade paths. One more reason we need to be careful about being spotted."

She said *we*, but she meant Shane. "I didn't pick that fight," Shane protested.

"And yet I'm sure you waded right into it," Fi returned.

She couldn't exactly deny it. "What was I supposed to do—let Red get manhandled by some merchant's goon? You would have done the same thing, admit it."

"Probably," Fi relented with a sigh. "But, Shane, how much do you really know about Red?"

"I know she's good at getting what she wants," Shane offered, remembering Red's coy smile as the ring fell out of her parasol.

"I'm serious." Fi worried her lip, as though torn about whether to say something. Her eyes flicked to Shane's. "I saw a tattoo on her neck."

Shane remembered the mark.

"I think it might have been the edge of a sealing tattoo," Fi admitted. "I've never seen one in person, but I've heard that in Andar after the fall, when the Witch Hunters were first coming to power, sometimes they would try to seal a Witch's magic away by tattooing a symbol on the back of their neck."

"What?" Shane asked, horrified.

"It didn't work," Fi hurried on, "so they gave up the practice and started chasing Witches out of Andar instead. But supposedly it still happens sometimes, deep in the Witch Hunter strongholds." She bit her lip. "The serpentine shape— it could be part of the symbol of the twining snakes eating each other's tails." She moved her finger absently, drawing a shape like a figure eight in the dust: two snakes intertwined, their fangs bared. "To the Witch Hunters, it represents magic and evil forever connected and devouring each other. I can't be sure, but the placement would be right."

Shane sat in silence, trying to digest that. "It looked old," she said finally.

"What?"

"The tattoo, it looked old. Faded."

"Then she was probably born in Andar." Fi plucked at her bread again, but she seemed to have lost her appetite. "There are still some settlements in the northern mountains, far from the castle and the Forest of Thorns, but the Witch Hunters rule that whole area like warlords. It's not a good place to be born a Witch."

Shane felt sick and angry. She could read between the lines. Fi was saying someone had done that to Red—someone who was afraid of her powers. And from the looks of it, they'd done it when she was very young.

Suddenly she was remembering Red's soft voice as she traced her fingers over the feral dog's ragged coat. *Even when they seem vicious, animals always have a reason for it. People, on the other hand, can be quite senseless and cruel.* Had Red witnessed that senseless cruelty firsthand? Maybe she'd seen past the dog's scars because she knew what it was like to be wounded in a way that left a mark on you.

Without realizing it, Shane had ground the last of her pastry into her clenched fist. There had been something about Red from that first moment they met in the woods, something that called out to Shane. Red was like a puzzle with the edges done but the middle in shambles, and Shane didn't know how it all fit together. But the thought of someone hurting Red—when she was young, when she'd done nothing to deserve it—sliced her like a knife. And Shane had just let her walk away.

"Why didn't you tell me this earlier?" she demanded.

Fi's face heated up. "Why do you think? Whatever happened to Red, it's her business. It wasn't my place to call her out."

Of course Fi would think that. She worshipped at the altar of *never-telling-anyone-anything*. But Fi didn't understand. She had people like the Paper Witch and Shane and her parents—people who made sure she wasn't alone, even when she wanted to be. From the way Red had cradled that dog's shaggy head, Shane had a feeling she had no one.

"What if Red's in some kind of trouble and she needs help?" Shane shot back.

Fi frowned. "I don't think that's our concern."

"What if she needs *my* help?"

It wasn't until she said it that Shane realized how much she wanted it to be true. Racing through the market with Red's hand in hers and pressed close to her in the alley, just a breath apart, she'd felt something that she hadn't felt in a long time. Yearning.

Fi gave her such a flat, unimpressed look that Shane felt herself withering.

"Okay. It sounds silly. But we had a connection," she insisted. "You know, sometimes you meet somebody and it just feels like—"

"If you say love at first sight, I will cram the rest of this turnover down your throat," Fi warned hotly.

Shane blinked, surprised at the usually collected Fi losing

her composure. Then she realized they weren't talking about Red anymore. They were talking about Briar Rose and his sudden interference in Fi's life.

"Well, I *was* going to say it feels like we're meant to be." Shane rubbed the back of her neck sheepishly. "But I guess that does sound a little dramatic. Not as dramatic as the *destined savior of a fairytale prince*, though." She stretched out her foot, nudging her partner's boot.

"Tell me about it," Fi agreed, dredging up a strained smile. Then she coughed awkwardly. "I shouldn't have jumped down your throat."

The *sorry* was missing from that apology, but Shane would take it anyway. "So, has your spirit prince dropped by for a visit yet?" she asked. A terrible thought struck her. "He's not here right now, is he?" She squinted around the dingy attic, wary that some royal ghost might be lurking behind the garlic.

Fi huffed out a laugh. "No. He's only appeared once so far. But I've dreamed of him every night since I pricked my finger on that spindle." She pulled her legs up, bracing her chin on her knees. "It's still hard to believe that of all people, the bone spindle would choose *me*. I can't help thinking it's a mistake."

Fi was staring at her hand, but not the hand with the spindle mark. She was staring at her fingerless glove. Shane didn't know what that was about, but she knew how to get the complicated expression off her partner's face. Fi was easy to get a rise out of, after all.

"At least you had the good sense to beg me to come along," Shane said, slinging her arms behind her head.

Fi scoffed, but a smile tugged at her lips. "That's not quite how I remember it."

As they lapsed into a warmer silence, Shane's thoughts drifted back to Red. "If Red really is from Andar, maybe we'll run into her again."

"Maybe," Fi agreed. "If I'm recalling my Steelwight proverbs correctly, if you meet a person three times by chance, you're fated to be together. Next time, maybe you can flirt some answers out of her." Fi's voice was dry, but her one raised eyebrow told Shane her partner was laughing at her on the inside.

Shane balled up her napkin and threw it at Fi. "Don't think I haven't noticed you blushing and staring off into space. Prince Briar Rose isn't a hundred-and-sixteen-year-old hunched-over grandpa, is he? Let me guess: young, handsome, blond . . ."

Fi stood up fast, but not before Shane saw the flush staining her cheeks. That was a yes.

"I'm going to get some extra blankets from Twyla," Fi said, fumbling with the hatch and hurrying down the ladder. She poked her head up one last time. "Get some sleep. I want to leave *before* dawn tomorrow morning."

"Of course you do," Shane grumbled. But she was smiling anyway as she stretched out between the bundles of sweet-smelling fennel, content to leave it at that.

SLEEP ELUDED HER that night. Long after Fi had curled up under her blankets and drifted off, Shane found herself staring out the round attic window at the small patch of night sky. Red's strange lullaby teased the back of her mind, but she didn't know the tune, so it kept bleeding into the notes

155

of "O Wispy Waters." For the first time in ages, Shane found herself thinking about the first and only girl who had ever broken her heart.

Kara, with hair as black as a gull's wing and eyes like green sea ice in the winter sun. The girl she had been engaged to back in Rockrimmon.

As quietly as she could, she rolled over and slipped the silver dagger out of her boot, turning the engraved hilt in her fingers. On one side was Astaluna, the moon princess; on the other, Daghorn, the great warrior of the sea who brought her down to earth. It was one of the oldest love stories in Steelwight, but not exactly a happy one. Astaluna missed her home on the moon so much she raised the great glaciers on the ice peaks, calling the moonbeams down to make a pathway of rainbow lights in the sky. She spent most of her life alone, returning only in deep winter to visit Daghorn and her children, and whenever she walked the path between the moon and the earth, the aurora rippled through the sky, the moon princess's footsteps glimmering in blue and green light.

The dagger had been an engagement gift from Kara, who had been matched with Shane when they were very young. At the time, Shane had seen only the story of the lovers in the engravings, but now she wondered whether there had been a deeper meaning to Kara's choice: the moon princess who flew back to the sky. In return, Shane had given her a cloak embroidered with the traditional symbols of beauty: pink daisies and snowdrops. Pink daisies had been Kara's favorite—the only thing Shane remembered about her, when she returned to Rockrimmon to prepare for the wedding.

SHE COULD STILL remember standing next to Shayden at the front gate, her palms sweating, waiting to receive Kara, third daughter of the Icefern king—the girl she was supposed to spend the rest of her life with. Her guts were in knots. She'd spent all morning trying to persuade Shayden to dress in the heir's ceremonial kyrtill and take her place, just this first time, but they couldn't pull that off anymore now that he'd grown six inches and she hadn't.

Kara had been sent to Rockrimmon as a ward back when she was small enough to run heedlessly through the meadows, staining her dress up to the elbows looking for the perfect pink daisies to weave into flower crowns. Always three: one for herself, one for Shane, and one for Shayden. But the girl dismounting from the fur-trimmed carriage was nothing like Shane remembered. Sixteen to Shane's fifteen, she seemed impossibly poised and beautiful, with her long dress of ice-blue muslin and her black hair braided into a crown. Not a ward, but Shane's promised queen.

Shane had no idea how to act around her. Whenever she sat next to Kara at a feast, or heard her tinkling laugh from across the room, her stomach went queasy and she tripped over her suddenly enormous feet. Kara seemed like one of the mist spirits out of the old legends, so perfect she couldn't be real. In the weeks after she returned to court, Shane took refuge more than ever on the roof of the watchtower, relishing the moments when it was just her and Shayden again.

Until one night, a night like any other—she and

Shayden looking up at the stars, laughing and teasing each other—when for the first time, a soft voice called: "Can I come up?"

Kara stood on the battlements, peering up at them. For a second, Shane almost said no. She didn't want to share this; it was something that had always belonged to the two of them. But Shayden was already extending his hand, pulling Kara up over the lip of the tower.

Kara settled in between them and pulled her thick wool nightgown close around her legs. Up here, away from the court, she didn't seem so untouchable anymore, with her hair loose down her back and the watchfires picking out freckles on her rosy cheeks.

Shayden seemed to be thinking the same thing.

"I'm surprised you got away from Aunt Annor dressed like that. What did she always used to say?" Shayden pitched up his voice, shaking one stern finger. "A lady's makeup is her armor. Not one hair out of place!"

Kara burst out giggling, smothering the sound with her hand. Shane groaned and said, "Don't do that—you sound just like her!" Shrewd old Aunt Annor had come with Kara when she was a child, and the woman hadn't been above chasing the future War King of Rockrimmon down with a hairbrush, either. Shane's scalp hurt just thinking about it.

"She's still ruthless," Kara warned. "Luckily, she sleeps like the dead, especially when she's gotten into the lingonberry wine."

"Well, I like this better," Shane said, thinking of

how stiff Kara looked in her fancy, high-necked gowns.

"But you used to say you liked me better with sticks in my hair, too," Kara reminded her. "So we know you're not picky."

It was easy after that, slipping into the old rhythm, the three of them comparing notes on the old courtiers and arguing about whose fault it was Shayden had once ended up in the laundry pool. Shayden and Kara were sure it was Shane's. As the awkwardness melted away, Shane found herself grinning until her cheeks hurt and trying to show off, making up stories about the constellations like she hadn't since they were kids.

"That's the shaggy wolf stalking the moon."

Shayden rolled his eyes at Kara. "It's not a wolf. It's the silver stag who guides lost children out of the woods."

Shane snorted. "Boring. It's a wolf that took a bite out of the moon, and all the slobbery bits fell out and became extra stars."

Kara scrunched up her nose, laughing. Shayden leaned over and smacked Shane on the back of the head. "Don't say *slobbery*. You try one, Kara."

Kara tipped her head back, winding a strand of hair absently around her finger. Shane had seen her do that when she was daydreaming in court, staring across the hall to where Shane and Shayden sat next to their father's throne. For the first time, Shane wondered whether Kara had been daydreaming about her.

Kara's arm brushed hers, and Shane felt a spark that made her tingle all the way down to her toes. This wasn't simply the girl she was engaged to. This was her best childhood friend. And now, it would be the three of them again—Kara and Shane and Shayden. Just like they used to be.

A breath of autumn wind raced over the watchtower. Kara shivered.

"Cold?" Shane asked.

It wouldn't occur to her until much later to wonder why Kara hadn't brought her new cloak, Shane's engagement present, the one embroidered with pink daisies. All she knew then was that she and Shayden had moved at the same time: Shayden pulling off his heavy mantle, Shane holding hers out so Kara could tuck in close to her side.

There was a moment where they both held very still. Shane had the feeling something important was happening, something incredibly fragile hanging in the balance. Kara looked at her, and back at Shayden, and then very gingerly scooted closer to Shane and rested her cheek on her shoulder. Shayden was quiet.

"What about those two?" Kara asked, pointing at the twin bright stars hovering over the sea.

Shane's heart swelled. "Those are—"

"The Lovers," Shayden broke in before she could say the Twins. Shane tried to catch his eye. But he had rolled away, turning his back to her and staring into the blackness.

Even then, she hadn't really understood it. Shayden stopped coming to the watchtower with her, but she barely noticed. She was too wrapped up in Kara, half in love with the girl Kara had been and half in love with the girl she was now, who made Shane's heart do all kinds of strange things.

Those feelings burned inside of her for months, growing stronger with every accidental touch. And then one perfect night, when the two of them were tucked up in Shane's bedroom together with glittering snow outside and whorls of ice shining on the window, she'd leaned forward recklessly and kissed Kara. And Kara had let her, her lips soft and pliant under Shane's. But she wasn't kissing back.

Shane pulled away, stung.

"Is something wrong?" Kara asked. "Have I displeased you?"

Shane's heart sank like a stone. "You don't want to be with me," she said, each word like an ice pick in her chest, because she could see the truth suddenly, see it clear as day. "You prefer my brother."

"I like both boys and girls," Kara replied, her cool green eyes betraying nothing.

"That's not what I said. Do you love him?" A hundred tiny moments flashed through her mind—all of them like the moment on the watchtower, when Kara had looked between them and chosen Shane, not because she wanted to, but because she was supposed to.

Shane closed her eyes. She knew she should feel betrayed, but all she felt was numb.

"It doesn't matter," Kara said. Her voice was impossibly calm, like she meant every word. "It doesn't change anything between us."

"How can you say that?" Shane demanded. "Do you even love me at all? Do you think you ever could?"

Kara looked hurt. "I care deeply for you, Shane. And I will always be faithful to you."

"I don't want faithful!" She grabbed Kara's hands. "I want love—real love. I want us to be meant for each other." Shane laced their fingers together tight, searching for one speck of warmth between them. But Kara's fingers were cold, so cold Shane wondered whether the girl really was nothing but a mist spirit after all.

"We are. We're meant to rule together. Meant to lead Rockrimmon together. We're just not meant to be in love."

Shane backed away, dropping her hands. "How could that possibly be enough for you?"

"Because it's my duty," Kara said like it was nothing.

Duty. It always came back to duty—a word Shane had grown to hate more and more, as the date of her confirmation as heir drew closer and her father tried to force her into the mold of a true War King. If she married Kara, that's what she could look forward to. A life of duty. A rift between her and Shayden. A marriage to a girl who would never love her. A future where no one got what they wanted.

"Shane," Kara started, reaching for her.

Shane jerked away. "Just go."

Kara's hand hovered in the space between them and then fell. "I'm sorry," she whispered as she walked away. Shane said nothing, just clenched her jaw tight to hold back the tears.

12

Fi

FI STRETCHED HER back and looked out over the Cragspires, the high mountain breeze whistling in her ears. A few feet beyond her, the ledge dropped away into a dizzying view of the black granite peaks, sharp as spear points, which gave the Cragspire range its name. The scent of wild primrose and bluebell filled her lungs. If she closed her eyes, she could almost forget that she was tired, dusty, and sore from four hard days in the saddle.

"I'm sick of your shortcuts."

Fi rolled her eyes and glanced back at her partner. They had stopped to water the horses in a wide, shallow stream that cut across the trail—runoff from the summer snowmelt or the afternoon storms. The horses wandered through the icy water, nipping at the thin grass growing in the crevices. Shane sat hunched on a rock, one boot pinched in her hand as she scrubbed algae and pond scum from the sole.

"So far, you've dragged us over a mountain, nearly dropped us off a rickety bridge, and tried to drown me in a mosquito-infested bog." Shane shook her slimy boot like an angry fist. "For someone in a hurry, you're wasting a lot of time."

"Technically, it was a marsh," Fi said.

She carefully didn't say that they wouldn't have lost any time at all if Shane's legs were a little longer. Fi had jumped the muddy patch without trouble, but Shane had gone in up to her calf and had to fight her leg out of the muck.

Shane gave the boot one last vigorous scrub and held it up for inspection before turning to Fi. "So, I've never been to Bellicia. What's it like?"

Shane had a knack for zeroing in on exactly what Fi wanted to talk about least. Fi tried to keep her expression neutral. "It's the border checkpoint closest to the Forest of Thorns," she said, keeping it simple. "They don't get many travelers."

"But you've been there," Shane pointed out.

"I've been a lot of places."

"And you're positive we can get a pass?" Shane pressed. "Because you know, in my opinion, we left our best option down the moun—"

"I am very well acquainted with your opinion on the matter," Fi snapped. Shane continued to tenaciously stick her thumb in that sore spot since their night at the Nenroa House, subtly and not-so-subtly hinting that she wanted to know what was up with Fi and her family. "The Duke of Bellicia is the Border Master, so getting passes shouldn't be hard."

Shane let out a low whistle. "You do know people in high places."

It's not all it's cracked up to be, Fi thought. Truthfully, she didn't want anything to do with Bellicia, but between that and bringing her curse down on her family home, well, she'd made her choice.

They had left Twyla's house before dawn four days ago, angling south and east toward the Duchy of Bellicia. They'd stayed away from the well-used roads, taking old trading paths that wound through the steep mountain passes. This high up, the trails were hit-or-miss, often tapering into narrow tracks barely wide enough to lead the horses through.

Fi had a lot of experience traveling rough. Her new partner, she was still adjusting to. Shane could pick a fight with anything from a lizard to an overgrown clump of sage, and she never seemed to run out of stories about saving her bumbling former partners in all kinds of improbable ways. Fi dreaded to think how she'd feature in some future tale. Still, if even half of Shane's stories were true, Fi would be glad to have the huntsman at her back if it came to a fight with the Witch Hunters.

It was an uneasy thought. Fi craned her neck around, scanning the cliffs. She hadn't seen much of Briar since that night in Raven's Roost. Sometimes she caught a glimpse of him higher up the slope, a flicker of blue winking in and out so fast he seemed like a trick of the light. She wasn't sure if he was conserving his magic or still getting the hang of appearing to her, but she felt a bolt of anxiety every time, remembering the Witch Hunters' notice seeking a *possible light Witch*. They were closer to the truth than she wanted them to be.

Fi shook the thoughts away, pressing her hat firmly down on her head. Shane had her boot back on and was stroking the neck of the sleek black horse, offering it one of their last precious apples. Fi clicked her tongue.

"If you're done grooming, we should get back on the road—"

She was cut off by the harsh screech of a bird. Her eyes darted to the edge of the trail, where water trickled down the cliff in a dozen tiny streams. Something was moving down there. She stepped closer. Just below her, she could see a thin ledge of wet rock streaked with black feathers and rust-colored stains. At least a dozen crows perched on the ledge, pecking at a bony mass in their midst.

Fi's stomach turned at the sound of the carrion birds eating noisily. She couldn't help but think of the Spindle Witch, who used crows as her spies. The day suddenly seemed colder, the breeze raising goose bumps on her skin.

Two birds struck at each other, their wings beating madly as they feuded over some choice morsel. Through the feathers, Fi caught a glimpse of the creature at the center. It was another crow, this one enormous, its shiny beak parted and its wing splayed like a tattered rag. Its body had been picked so clean it looked like a skeletal hand. The milky dead eyes seemed to be looking right at her. Then they blinked.

Fi gasped, stumbling back. Her boot caught on a small rock and sent it hurtling down, smashing into the flock of crows. Suddenly the air was filled with them, all taking off at once and rising like a great black tide. Dark wings beat around her with a cacophony of angry shrieks. Her horse shied away, its eyes wide and frightened, and Fi snatched the reins to keep it from bolting.

"Hey, take it easy!"

Fi whirled in time to see the black horse rear up, tossing its head. Its heavy shoulder caught Shane in the chest. Fi's throat seized in horror as her partner staggered backward toward the cliff. Shane's heel hit the ledge, and she teetered precariously, every muscle in her body tightening. Then she wrenched herself forward and fell onto her knees in the stream.

"Shane!" Fi cried, running to her. She grabbed Shane's arm, pulling her up and away from the drop. "Are you okay?"

"Cursed birds!" Shane was too busy shouting to answer, shaking her fist at the flock disappearing into the sky. She shot Fi a scowl. "Like I said—rethink this shortcut."

This time, when she gave the last of their apples to the poor frightened horses, Fi had no objection.

Her heart was still thrashing at the near miss. Swallowing back bile, she craned her head over the ledge again and looked down at the dead bird, only to find it gone. She wrapped an arm over her lurching stomach. There was no way the dead bird had flown away amid the pack, was there? Or that those milky eyes had actually blinked?

Fi wanted to think she had imagined it, but she knew better. She didn't believe in coincidences. Something else had been looking out at her through those dead, milky eyes: the Witch consumed with hatred for Andar and Briar Rose—and now, for Fi, too. It was the feeling of walking through a dark alley in the dead of night, and the prickle on her skin that warned her she was no longer alone.

Fi shuddered. Tales of the Spindle Witch had never scared her, but there was a difference between hearing a tale of dark magic and living it. The feeling of those undead eyes followed her even as they rode away.

She was still thinking about it hours later, long after they had made camp in a meadow at the tree line and she'd watched the sun sink down into the Cragspires. The night was quiet except for the crickets and the soft wind and Shane's snoring like a wild boar beside the wispy fire. Fi sat tensed with her chin on her knees, staring into the darkness.

She caught a flicker of movement at the corner of her eye. Fi jerked her head up, imagining black wings, but it was only the flare of Briar's coat as he sat down next to her, slinging his arms over his knees. His skin seemed to shimmer in the firelight, translucent like fine porcelain.

"Can't sleep?"

Fi pinned him with a hard look. "No—and maybe never again, now that I remember how you like to drop by unannounced in the middle of the night."

Briar gave a helpless shrug. "I sleep all the time, so day and night don't make a difference to me. What's keeping you up?"

Fi gave a noncommittal hum, not eager to confide in someone who might disappear halfway through the first sentence.

"I'll take that as an invitation to guess." Briar sat forward, following her gaze out over the night-black canyon. "You're worried about rock slides, right? One little rock slide, and you both go straight over this cliff. Whoosh!" He swished a hand toward the sheer drop beyond the ring of firelight.

"I *wasn't* worried about that," Fi grumbled, suddenly very aware of the sound of every shifting pebble. "I have a few more immediate concerns."

"Like snakes?" Briar offered helpfully. His wide smile told her he was absolutely doing this on purpose. "I mean, you're just sleeping out here on the ground, when there were all those big snakes sunning themselves on the path this afternoon."

Fi also didn't need to be reminded of that—or to start wondering whether the crevice in the rock behind them held a nest of slithering scales.

"Ooh, how about bandits?" Briar added, excited. "I've read a lot of stories with bandits lurking on the road."

Bandits were not a concern this high up in the Cragspires, where there was no one worth robbing. Witch Hunters, on the other hand, went wherever their prey was. Fi shivered, thinking again of the Witch notices.

"This is a dangerous journey." Briar lifted a hand, ticking ideas off on his fingers. "There's a lot to be worried about. Exposure, hunger, heatstroke—"

"Yes, Briar," Fi snapped, a little louder than she meant to. "We could die at any moment. I have no idea how I ever slept before."

Briar laughed, but it was a gentle sound, one that seemed to swirl around her in a breath of wind. "I guess you'll have to tell me what's on your mind, then."

Fi fidgeted with her jacket, not looking at him. "There were crows on the road today. One of them was . . ." She trailed off, not sure how to describe what she'd seen, and less sure she even wanted to. "The Spindle Witch found me, didn't she?"

"There's no way to be sure. But if not yet, then soon." Briar's face was grim. "The crows are just spies, though. I don't think you're in danger yet. We're still a long way from Andar."

Fi gave him a flat look. "So that's something to look forward to, if I make it past the snakes and the rock slides?"

"Something tells me you're the type who's prepared for anything." Briar's blue eyes danced in the firelight. "And don't forget, I promised I'd be with you every step of the way."

"Unless you wink out again," she said pointedly.

"I don't think that's going to happen." Briar studied his hands, then grinned at her over his fingertips. "But if it does, know that even a few minutes with you is worth more—"

"Stop before you embarrass yourself." *Or me!* Fi thought desperately. But somehow she felt a little better. She definitely hadn't missed Briar—she couldn't miss someone she barely knew—but the night seemed less suffocating with him beside her.

Briar chuckled. Then his eyes widened, and he leaned toward her. Fi felt a hitch in her chest, her heartbeat jumping. "You have a little stowaway," he said.

What? Fi blinked, baffled, and then realized Briar was looking at the sleeve of her rumpled shirt, where a caterpillar was crawling through the folds.

Fi moved to brush it away, but Briar shook his head. "Let me." His brows furrowed in concentration and he lifted his hand. The fuzzy black caterpillar climbed onto his outstretched finger—and then kept walking, his finger solid instead of ghostly under the insect's many feet. Fi barely had time to be impressed before Briar blinked and the caterpillar went tumbling through him, landing on Fi's pants.

Briar shot her such a sheepish look, as the insect righted itself with an angry wriggle, that she couldn't help laughing. If a caterpillar could be irritated, that one was.

"I almost had it," he said.

"Well, I won't be trusting you to carry me anytime soon." Fi cupped the caterpillar in a leaf, leaning back until she could set it safely in a clump of high grass.

"Probably a good idea," Briar admitted. "I'll keep practicing." He shook out his hand, and tiny flecks of magic leapt from his fingers like blinding sparks.

Fi looked at him curiously. "What can you do, anyway?"

Briar cleared his throat, adopting a formal tone. "As your companion, I can provide company and conversation, and carry things very short distances." Her unimpressed look made him laugh. "You meant as a light Witch. I can make sparks, light, heat—sometimes illusions."

He caught her eye and then thrust a hand into the glowing fire. Fi's breath caught, even though she knew it couldn't hurt him. Briar twisted his hand, and as he did, the flames curled around one another until he seemed to hold a scarlet rose in his palm. The fiery petals licked his fingers.

"This isn't all, though." Briar pulled his hand back, and at once it was a normal fire again. "Those are just little tricks I can do because of my *affinity* for light magic."

Fi's eyes lingered on the afterimage of the rose. "I didn't think affinities were that powerful."

Affinities were the most natural expression of a Witch's magic. A Witch with an affinity for plants might be able to coax a sprout from a seed; an affinity for wind could bring forth a puff of air, or an affinity for fire a single curl of flame. All Witches could use the magic of their affinity without training, but anything more complicated required channeling that magic through spells. For many Witches, mastering the spells in just one spell book was the work of a lifetime. Witches who were powerful enough to do great feats of magic were few and far between, and their giant statues stood in the courtyard of Andar's castle. Fi didn't know how complex illusion magic was, but she knew Briar must have a great deal of power at his fingertips if the rose was just a little trick.

"See, I knew I could impress you," Briar said, looking pleased. "My light affinity was so strong I couldn't even control it when I was little. So when I was scared of the dark, I'd light the room like a beacon and keep the nannies awake all night."

"Now you had to go and ruin it," Fi said, her amazement swept away by the image of tiny golden-haired Briar being tucked into bed by a harried nanny with dark circles under her eyes. "I'm glad you grew out of that phase."

"You haven't seen me do any *real* spells yet." His eyes seemed to glitter in the dark, as if daring her to ask.

Real spells. Fi's mind raced.

Even without a drop of magic of her own, she had always been fascinated by the spell books left behind by Andar's Orders of Magic. Unlike an affinity you were born with, spell casting was about what you learned. Spells were much more than just chanting a few special words—some worked through intricate runes or sigils, and others were complex rituals, like a sequence of movements that had to be performed in a pool of still water that held the reflection of the moon. Fi had stubbed her toe once on a spell book where every spell was written out as a musical composition.

Many Witches used mediums to focus their magic, too. The Paper Witch's medium was ink and paper, but a medium could be almost anything, from an ancient relic to a handful of sand. Some Witches even used color as a medium. She remembered one of her first expeditions with her father, stepping into the study of a Witch whose medium was the color blue and staring in wonder at blue curtains and bells with long blue tassels and a chandelier of sapphire-bright glass. The floor was strewn with crushed cobalt and withered bluebell petals, and everywhere she walked she left small blue footprints in the dust.

That was why Fi had worked so hard to learn the magic languages. Reading a spell book was like being transported back to the golden age of magic, watching from the shadows as Witches combined rare ingredients in precisely the right amounts or channeled their magic through a crisscross of bright white stones. Her heart jumped at the thought that if Briar stuck around, she might get to see those breathtaking spells up close. That sounded much more impressive than the ability to glow in the dark.

Briar leaned suddenly close, his nose only inches from hers. Her skin tingled with the almost touch.

"Ah—I figured out why you don't like me."

This again? Fi pulled back to a safe distance, crossing her arms and waiting.

Briar sighed dramatically. "You think my station is too far above yours. I'm a powerful Witch, a prince, and you're just the daughter of a lantern-maker." Fi felt her lips curling into a smile. "You don't think they'd let me get away with it. But I assure you, I am a master of defying expectations."

"You're certainly not what I expected, from the stories," Fi admitted.

"Well, you're not what I expected either," Briar teased. Then he flashed his quick, dazzling smile. "You're so much more."

He'd caught her by surprise again. Fi turned away, flustered, brushing imaginary caterpillars from her sleeves. She cleared her throat forcibly.

"And did you deign to join an Order of Magic from your lofty station, so high above the rest of us?" Some affinities lent themselves to a specific kind of spell casting, like prophecy or healing, but a lot of them could be used in almost anything: transformation, illusion, warcraft, binding. Light magic was the rarest affinity, even at the height of Andar's golden age.

Briar tipped his head back to look up at the stars. "Actually, I was never inducted into a school of magic. Since I couldn't go outside, I was taught personally by the three most powerful Witches in the kingdom." He lifted his eyebrows, waiting for her to catch on.

Fi's mouth fell open in disbelief. "You mean the Three Great Witches?" she asked. "Your *private tutors* were the *Three Great Witches*?"

"I think you mean the Three Great Busybodies," Briar corrected, flicking a leaf into the crackling fire. "Very concerned with keeping me inside the castle."

Fi couldn't help a laugh, but she muffled it fast, throwing a glance at Shane across the fire. She had always imagined the last Great Witches as women of dignity, solemn and tragic figures who gave their lives for an ill-fated prince. But it was hard to think of them that way when she was picturing those same Witches dragging a young Briar back to his studies by the collar of his coat.

"So that's how you're able to appear to me?" she asked. "By the magic of the Great Witches?"

"It is, but not the way you're thinking." Briar's voice grew pensive, and he lifted one finger into the air, holding it out to her. "This isn't a spell I was taught. It's a spell I'm under."

In the dull glow of the firelight, she saw it again: the tiny mark around his finger like a coil of red thread.

"This is the binding magic that was cast on the spindle. The magic that holds us together. When I used to walk in my dreams, I was always trapped in the castle of Andar, but now this thread ties me to you." Briar sighed, flopping backward into the dirt and locking his hands under his head. "I'm not really here, Fi. All of this—my body, my voice, even my ability to touch things—it's all coming from my dreaming self in Andar. I'm all light magic right now. I don't even think I *could* do any real spells."

There was a long moment of silence as Fi digested that. It must be frustrating for him, to have such power at his fingertips and still be so trapped. She thought maybe she could imagine how he felt, just a little.

Briar rolled onto his side, pinning Fi with a solemn look. "I could probably glow if you wanted me to, though."

"Please don't!" Fi spluttered, annoyed with herself for taking Briar seriously for even one second.

Briar shrugged, that little twitch at the corner of his lips looking suspiciously like a victorious smile. He shifted onto his back. "I wouldn't want to ruin this view, anyway."

Fi glanced up. It was a clear night, but it didn't strike her as anything special. Still, as she climbed into her bedroll, she couldn't help stealing another glance at Briar, his eyes fixed on the velvet sky. Without meaning to, she found herself picking out constellations, tracing the invisible threads of connection that held distant stars together. Maybe she and Briar were connected like that, too—part of some larger constellation invisible to them.

That sounded an awful lot like destiny. Fi forced the thought away. She bunched her pack into a pillow and closed her eyes.

TWO DAYS LATER, Fi and Shane reached the top of the pass. From the highest point, before they turned east for good, Fi turned to look back the way they had come and stared for a long time at the cascade of mountains, the lowest peaks blue and gray in the afternoon light. Far away, the navy pine slopes softened to the deep green of aspen and cottonwoods—and there, nestled in the dark splash of the forest, was the town of Idlewild, just a glimmer of sunlight winking on distant windows.

Fi felt a stab of longing at the thought of her home. Nobody knew if the Wandering Witch had ever escaped the Butterfly Curse or if he had died as lonely as he lived, far from anyone who'd ever loved him. Fi considered confiding in Briar, telling him about the curse and asking for his help. He was a Witch, after all. Maybe he could do something. Maybe he, more than anyone, would understand what it felt like to have your home ripped away.

No. Cold gripped her at the thought. The curse mark was proof of a horrible mistake—trusting someone she shouldn't have—and Fi would never make that mistake again. She hadn't asked for help with her curse before, and she didn't intend to start now.

She turned away from the view and continued on.

The wind picked up as they made their way down the slope. Fi squinted at the thunderheads roiling over the mountains. They would be able to have a hot meal and maybe even a bath if they could reach the tiny settlement of Black Pines before dark. Black Pines hosted very few residents but there was a constant stream of travelers coming through its giant battered lodge.

As a first fat drop of rain splattered against her wide-brimmed hat, they came around a bend, and suddenly she could see the lights of Black Pines shining in the distance. The lodge towered above the twisted trees, a hulking structure of thick logs and tightly fitted stone. Four bright windows glowed like watchful eyes in its dark face, and stables and outbuildings clustered around it.

"Finally!" Shane shouted. Fi cracked a rare smile and urged her horse faster. It looked like they were going to beat the storm.

13

Fi

FI AND SHANE rode up to the Black Pines lodge just as the sun dipped behind the mountains and the wind sharpened into the whip of a cold rain. A young stable girl ran to meet them, and Fi handed off her horse, fishing out a handful of coppers and slipping them into the girl's hands with the reins. Her eyes shone gratefully, and Fi smiled as she climbed the stairs to the lodge, Shane trodding on her heels. She didn't mind overpaying for some things.

Rooms were not one of them. The hard-faced woman who managed the Black Pines lodge was a born haggler, but Fi whittled her down until the woman agreed to give them a small room with two pallets for half her initial asking price. Fi slid the money across the counter in exchange for a scrap of paper with their room number. She memorized the number, then threw the paper into the fire.

As they entered the lodge, she had scanned the bounties

tacked up on the side wall. The notice bearing Shane's troll face didn't seem to be among them. Maybe they'd outrun their Witch Hunter problems for the time being.

Shane led the way through the crowded common room, finally parking them at a table under a giant chandelier of antlers. They tucked their packs by their feet, and Fi let Shane order one of everything on the menu while she took in the atmosphere. The tavern was a swath of off-kilter tables and hard-backed chairs with huge fireplaces set into the walls. The rugged support posts were wider around than the circle of Fi's arms and scarred with hatchet marks, and the whole room had a pervasive smoky smell, like something had been left on the spit until it charred.

Fi had been to the Black Pines before, but she didn't remember seeing it so packed. Most of the tables bristled with extra chairs, each one filled with men and women in dusty jackets and plain traveling cloaks. Fi felt the prickle of eyes on the back of her head, but when she whipped around, she couldn't catch anyone looking at her.

"Jumpy much?" Shane asked.

Fi frowned. "It seems unusually crowded in here."

Her partner snorted. "Probably because it's unusually stormy out there." As though to accentuate her point, a harsh gust of wind rattled the windows, rain spitting against the glass. "I could probably scare us up another chair, though," Shane offered.

Fi stared at her partner blankly. They were both already seated.

"You know, one for your . . . guy." Shane waved her hand around vaguely.

"He's not my *guy*," Fi protested, "and he's not here right now."

"Maybe he doesn't feel welcome without a chair." Shane's tone was so purposefully bland, she could only be trying to get a rise out of Fi. Unfortunately, it was working. "I'm just saying," she went on, "if you want him to like you—"

"He already likes me too much," Fi hissed, reddening when she realized what she had accidentally admitted. She kicked at Shane's chair half-heartedly under the table. "Who are you to be giving me romantic advice, anyway?"

"I'll have you know I was betrothed to a beautiful girl back in Rockrimmon, since childhood." Shane sniffed.

"Like an arranged marriage?" Fi sat forward with sudden interest. "I didn't think they did that in Steelwight, except among . . ."

Royalty! The thought hit Fi with the weight of a blacksmith's anvil. Her eyes shot to the gleaming ax by her partner's feet—the finest weapon Fi had ever seen—inlaid with decorative silver knots interlaced across the blade and on the ax head's blunt. No doubt the mark of a ruling family. How could she have missed it?!

Fi's gaze shot back to her partner, the storm and the crowded room forgotten in her astonishment. Shane, for her part, looked like she wanted to grab the words and cram them back in her mouth.

"You're a War King's daughter!" Fi said, her mouth falling open in shock.

Shane grimaced. "Say it louder. I don't think the people at the bar heard you."

Fi braced her hands on the table and leaned close, lowering her voice. "You must have been at least a third or second princess," she rattled off, her mind churning through everything she knew about Steelwight. Shane's expression remained strangely guarded. Fi's eyes went wide. "You were an heir?!"

"Hey, stop reading me," Shane groused. The table creaked as she leaned back, bracing a knee against it. "I *was* the heir to Rockrimmon, but I've been disowned."

"Oh." Fi felt suddenly awkward. "I'm sorry."

"I'm not," Shane told her. Her gray eyes had turned flinty and serious. "I left by choice."

Though she was dying to know, Fi bit down on the impulse to fish for details. Unlike *some* partners, she didn't pry into other people's pasts. "So, what's a runaway princess from Steelwight doing working as a huntsman for hire?" she asked instead.

A grin split her partner's face. "Anything I want," she said decisively, stretching her arms over her head. "And I'm very good at it."

"So humble, too," Fi muttered, but she couldn't help her smile. That answer was so very Shane. Fi couldn't imagine her partner in a court somewhere, much less sitting on a throne, dispensing sage advice and upholding the laws of a kingdom. Shane was such a wild, free spirit, she seemed to fit best right where she was: in a loud and smoky tavern, kicked back in her chair with that fierce grin.

The arrival of the food distracted them. Shane had ordered bowls of stew and plates of venison, along with a heaping platter of roasted bread smeared with garlic and scallions. Fi carefully dished some of each onto her plate, while

Shane ate straight from the serving trays. Honestly, Fi was surprised she hadn't just unhinged her jaw like a python and swallowed the whole spread, plates and all. It was impossible to believe this person had ever been a princess.

The hairs on the back of Fi's neck rose. The sensation of being watched had returned, though Fi couldn't pinpoint the source. She tried to convince herself that she was sensing Briar, but his gaze had never felt so cold.

Shane didn't seem bothered, mopping up the last of her stew with a piece of bread. She crammed the whole thing into her mouth and then sat tipping her chair back and forth, watching Fi with far too much satisfaction. Fi wrinkled her nose, but she drew the line when her partner looked like she was about to put her feet up on the table. There was such a thing as basic decency, after all.

Fi waited until Shane had leaned all the way back, the sole of her muddy boot resting against the edge of the table. Then she very casually pushed the table forward two inches, making Shane overbalance and topple back with a crash.

There was a great whoosh above them. Fi looked up just in time to see the giant chandelier of antlers plummeting toward her. She threw herself out of her chair as it hit their table with a deafening crack, splintering the wood. Chunks of broken antlers pelted her shoulders.

A few people leapt to their feet, one man fumbling for the wrapped hilt of his sword. Fi locked eyes with Shane, still sprawled on her back on the other side of the table. If the chandelier had fallen two seconds earlier, her partner would have been crushed.

"What the—" Shane kicked her way out of the ruined

chair and stood. Her ax was already in her hand as she rounded on the room with a furious expression. "That was no accident," she ground out.

Fi was barely listening. Her gaze was fixed on the hilt of that sword, set with a tiny yellow stone that gleamed until the rough-shaven man swept the weapon back under his cloak. She narrowed her eyes at the swinging rope that had secured the chandelier to a heavy anchor set into the wall. The rope had been severed above the knot. Fi's blood went cold as all the pieces came together in crystal clarity.

Now that she was looking closer, she realized most of the patrons along the bar were wearing the exact same dark traveling cloaks. And the man who'd leapt out of his seat—his sword pommel had been wrapped to hide a yellow gem. She'd bet every coin in her purse it was topaz. There were Witch Hunters among the Black Pines' regular crowd tonight. Right now they were still trying to remain hidden, but Fi didn't plan to stick around and find out how long that would last now that the falling chandelier had failed to crush them.

Fi jammed her traveling hat back on her head and swung her pack onto one shoulder. "Shane, I need to see you upstairs," she said, keeping her voice calm. She didn't want to tip anybody off.

"What are you talking about?" Shane looked about one second from burying her ax in the nearest table. "Somebody just tried to kill me!"

"*Now*, Shane," Fi warned, shoving the big pack into the girl's stomach. She grabbed Shane's jacket and headed for the stairs, listening with half an ear for the scrape of chairs and booted feet that would signal pursuers.

"You know we left some would-be assassin back there?" Shane growled as Fi dragged her up the narrow stairs toward the second floor. She stopped abruptly, pushing Shane back into the stairwell. Two figures in heavy rain cloaks were lounging in the hallway, right in front of the door painted with their number. Fi cursed under her breath. It could be a coincidence, simply two travelers taking shelter from the rain—or it could be that the manager of the lodge had sold them out. There was one other reason for their notices to be missing from the board: if someone had taken them down deliberately to put them off guard.

I should've known we got that room too cheap.

Shane shook her off. "Okay, I know you're used to this *all-on-my-own* thing, but as your partner, my opinion is actually—"

"Shane," Fi interrupted, grabbing her by the shoulders. "We've walked into a trap. It's not just one assassin. Half the common room downstairs is filled with Witch Hunters."

"Persistent bastards," Shane muttered. "I should've guessed. Black Pines lodge is the only place to stop anywhere near this pass. It's the perfect choke point for an ambush."

"I think we've got company up here, too." Fi jerked her chin at the figures in the hall, one of them digging a tobacco pouch out of his pocket.

Shane strained to look down the other wing of the hall-way, away from the Witch Hunters, and then nudged Fi with an elbow. Fi saw at once what Shane was seeing. The door to one of the rooms had been left ajar, the bolt not quite jammed into the groove. A flash of lightning lit the window and the Witch Hunters swung around to watch it, their backs turned for a few precious seconds. Fi and Shane raced down the hall as quietly as they could, disappearing into the open room and sliding the bolt home.

The room was cold, with no fire burning in the grate, and almost pitch-black with the storm raging outside. Fi was relieved to see no one was waiting for them. Still, it wouldn't take the Witch Hunters long to figure out where they'd gone. Shane turned both small cots on their sides with a clatter and braced them across the door.

Fi fingered the rope on her belt. "Should we go out through the window? Drop onto the hillside?" It would be safer than going out the front, at least.

"We take the window," Shane agreed, "but not to go down—that's too obvious, they'll be waiting for us. We've got to climb up to the room above this one."

"How will that help?" Fi demanded. "Won't we have exactly the same problems one floor up?"

"Not if we do it fast. It's dark and rainy, so no one should spot us climbing, and once we're on the third floor, we can head for the back stairs." Shane looked serious. "If there's as many as you say, it's our best bet."

Fi bit her lip. "That many or more."

Shane nodded grimly, hitching her pack up on both shoulders and pushing Fi toward the window. Fi slid the shutter open. Cool drops of rain whipped into her face as she peered down into the courtyard. She almost tumbled off the sill when the door rattled, someone trying to force it open. *It never rains but it pours,* Fi thought sarcastically, surrendering to the storm as she turned to sit backward in the window frame and unhooked the rope from her belt. The rattling turned to banging as a body crashed into the door, the bolt shuddering from the blow.

"Hold on to my legs," Fi instructed, not even waiting for confirmation from Shane before leaning back precariously over the drop. Shane swore and grabbed her legs just in time. Fi swung the rope's blunt ring in a circle, squinting up through the rain. She could barely keep her eyes open against the wind, but she could make out a heavy rafter beam eighteen feet up, hopefully strong enough to hold her weight. She spun the rope faster, holding her breath on the release. The metal ring pinged off the roof and slid back down, almost striking her in the cheek.

The pounding on the door intensified. The hinges creaked as another body joined the first, two shoulders smashing into the wood like a battering ram.

"Anytime, Fi!" Shane growled. Fi didn't need any more incentive to hurry. She leaned back even farther, her stomach muscles aching. She was soaked to her waist in seconds, and the wind caught her wide-brimmed hat and whipped it off her head, carrying it into the night. Fi cursed. She had no time to worry about it now, but that hat was never coming back.

She swung the rope in a circle again, trying to shut out the noise of the splintering door and Shane's heavy breaths and her own pounding pulse. She aimed for the edge of the roof, a dark shadow against an even darker backdrop, and released. This time the ring caught and the rope looped twice around the rafter, settling into the notch.

Fi wasted no time pulling herself up. Her feet slid against the uneven logs of the lodge's wall, and she dug her nails into the sopping rope that threatened to slither right through her fingerless glove. The rain was an angry shriek in her ears. Fi's boot slipped, and she held on with all her might, gritting her teeth as the rope burned into her right palm. She could see Shane standing on the window frame below her, her anxious face turned up into the rain.

When Fi finally reached the window of the third-floor room, she risked letting go with one hand so she could grab the shutter, glad to find it wasn't locked. It still took all the strength in her fingertips to pry it open, and it felt like her nails would tear out of her hand as she dug them into the heavy wooden cracks. At last the little door flew free, and Fi pulled herself into the room beyond. It was empty, but a small fire had been stoked in the hearth. There was no telling when the occupant would return.

Fi threw her pack aside and turned around, hanging out the window to help pull Shane up. She could no longer hear anything but the howling of the wind and the slap of the rain hitting the lodge, but she could imagine the splintering sound as the door of the room below gave way. If they weren't both through the window before any Witch Hunters thought to look up, this would all be for nothing.

Shane's hand was wet and slippery, but her grip was strong. Fi heaved back with all her might and Shane pushed off the logs and then tumbled through the window, taking Fi down with her. Fi scrambled out of the pile of limbs to retrieve her rope, tugging until it came free. She pulled back into the room and closed the shutter, breathing hard. Shane put her back against the wall, looking at Fi through straggles of messy bangs.

"Never a dull moment, huh?" She chuckled.

"I'm glad you're enjoying yourself," Fi wheezed, swinging the pack back on.

"C'mon," Shane said, clapping Fi on the shoulder and leading them out into the hall, her ax gleaming in her hands.

Every second of the trip to the back stairs, Fi was sure they were about to come face-to-face with Witch Hunters. The third floor was a warren of blind corners and sharp turns. The only soul they encountered was a tired-eyed old man, who nearly found himself decapitated, thanks to Shane's nerves. Almost before she could believe it, they were racing down the spindly back stairs.

Fi almost tripped on the last narrow step, fumbling to unbar the door and then pushing out into the night. The rain hit her face like a slap. A bolt of lightning streaked through the sky, followed by thunder so close she could feel the hum of it on her skin.

The wide yard behind the lodge was bound by a line of weathered hitching posts, the long, low stable a little ways up the hill—and no Witch Hunters in sight. Fi felt almost giddy, taking the rickety back stairs two at a time as she hurried toward the horses and their escape. She turned to smile at Shane. But her partner didn't look relieved. In fact, she looked horrified, her hand outstretched in fear.

"Fi, look out!"

Lightning cut through the sky, flashing along the curve of an ax flying directly at Fi's chest. There was no time to do anything in the second between the lightning and the thunder. She raised her arms and turned her back, all too late.

Then the thunder burst in her eardrums, and for a moment she couldn't hear anything but her frantic heart.

The ax never hit. It sank into the wood of the stairs as something soft and warm crashed into Fi instead. It was Briar, his blue eyes wide and frightened. Briar's arms locked around her, pulling Fi tight to his chest as they hit the ground and tumbled over and over in the wet grass. She was on the bottom when they finally stopped, Briar staring down at her. Rain and mud soaked into her hair as she stared back.

Briar pushed up on his hands, chest heaving. "Are you all right?"

"I think so." Her breath was a mad flutter in her throat. She could feel Briar's arms shaking around her. "Are you?"

"Yes—but I felt that." He pressed a hand to his stomach, where the ax had gone through him, as if he'd expected a gaping wound. Fi's heart lurched. For one moment, as their bodies collided, she had been afraid for Briar—afraid that somehow, impossibly, she would lose him. "I've never saved anyone in battle before," he said, sounding a little stunned.

He sat back on his knees, and Fi followed him, aching everywhere she'd hit the ground. She was soaked down to her skin, but she could still feel the circle of heat where he'd grabbed her. *Wait!*

"You pushed me!" she said.

"Sorry." Briar scrambled back fast, looking guilty.

"No," Fi said urgently. "Briar. I meant—you touched me."

"I touched you," Briar repeated softly. Then his face broke into a smile, so bright that she almost forgot the storm. He leaned forward, lifting his hand. "I can touch you."

His fingers brushed her cheek, warm and alive. Fi's eyes flickered. Then suddenly she was choking as Shane seized her collar and hauled her up. Her gray eyes were wild with the storm.

"If you're not dead, you should be moving!" Shane shouted. Fi stumbled to her feet. When she looked over her shoulder, Briar had vanished into the blinding rain.

Heart in a jumble, she raced after Shane toward the stable. But they were no longer alone. The darkness swirled as figures in black cloaks surrounded them, all brandishing topaz amulets and jeweled swords.

The Witch Hunters had found them.

14

※※➤➤— ⧫⧫◀◀←

Shane

SHANE HONESTLY COULDN'T believe what she'd seen.
One moment she had been watching in horror as an ax hurtled
toward Fi's chest, sure she was about to see her partner split
in half, and the next Fi was tumbling through the air. But for
just one second in the middle, Shane could have sworn she saw
the transparent wisp of a blond-haired boy grabbing Fi around
the waist, tackling her out of harm's way. She didn't have time
to pinch a nerve and make sure she wasn't seeing things. She
had a feeling she knew who that boy was, and for now, she was
going to have to leave it at that.

She should have known the Witch Hunters would stake
out the stables. The second they came out the back door,
at least ten of those vultures had appeared, swinging their
weapons. In the gloom of the storm, it seemed more like a
hundred.

Shane slung her heavy pack off her shoulder and threw it into Fi's arms. Fi stumbled under its weight. "I'm gonna get us to the stables," Shane promised. "Just stay with me."

Fi hesitated, then nodded. Shane twisted the ax in her hands, ready for the onslaught.

A heavyset Witch Hunter broke from the group, rushing at Shane. He howled a battle cry, but the storm was louder and Shane was quicker—she swung the ax up over her head, letting her entire body turn with it, and brought the blunt head down on the blade of his sword, driving it deep into the mud. She cracked her boot buckles into his jaw. The Witch Hunter went down with a sickening thunk.

Two figures moved immediately to take his place, their treated cloaks rustling as they closed ranks. Shane glanced back at Fi. Another minute, and they wouldn't just be fighting back to back—she'd be nailing Fi with every backswing.

Shane didn't stop to think. She let the feel of the fight tell her body what to do. All those countless hours she'd spent training as a child under her grandmother's strict instruction, repeating the strikes over and over until the ax felt like another limb—that muscle memory was still with her, matched now by years of experience facing real opponents, and winning.

With a flick of her left hand, Shane whipped the dagger out of her belt and sent it flying at the Witch Hunters closing on Fi. She only hit cloak, but it was enough to scare them back a few steps. A woman with short hair struck out with a thin silver sword, aiming for the space between Shane's ribs, while a broad-chested man barreled right at her, a wicked hooked spear chambered on his shoulder.

Shane deflected the thin blade against her ax, then ducked

so the spear jabbed over her head and she could surge up under it, trapping the spear pole against her shoulder. She dug one heel into the wet grass and spun, yanking the spear out of the man's grip and slamming the butt end of it into the woman's cheekbone. The Witch Hunter went down in a heap.

A fist crashed into Shane's ribs. She'd let the broad-chested man get too close. She stumbled back, losing the spear and almost losing her ax, too, when she slammed into one of the hitching posts. Shane hissed through her teeth. She was going to feel that in the morning.

She pushed the ache away. The Witch Hunter's spear gleamed where it lay in the mud. They grabbed for it at the same time, but Shane knew better than to wrestle with someone twice her size. The second he tugged, she let go and drove her foot into his ribs instead. The man stumbled and then hit his knees, collapsing next to his spear.

Shane snatched up her dagger and swiped rainwater out of her eyes, peering frantically through the storm. She'd made a small opening in the circle of Witch Hunters, but it wouldn't last long.

"Fi, go!" Shane yelled. Then she turned and ran back the other way, into the thick of them, catching a glimpse of the amazed look on Fi's face as she took off up the muddy slope toward the stables.

That made Shane smile. She didn't care what Fi thought, really, but she was always glad for a little appreciation.

A jagged flash of lightning split the sky. An electric charge hung in the air as the direction of the storm changed, now whipping against Shane's back. She let it propel her forward, hefting her ax and taking a wild swing at a pair of

Witch Hunters. They dodged, but she'd been expecting that. Shane drove her ax into one of the hitching posts and spun up onto her heel, putting her boot to use dislocating someone's shoulder. If she could keep the Witch Hunters from getting past her, Fi was smart enough to ready the horses, and then hopefully the last part of the escape—where they rode off victorious—could still go to plan.

Shane wrenched her ax out of the post, trying to watch all the shifting figures at once. She almost missed the quick jerk of motion to her left as a knife flew toward her, and only an instinctual dodge saved her from a dagger to the gut. The weapon skidded harmlessly against the grass. Shane dared a glance back at the stable to see if Fi had reappeared with the horses.

What she saw instead made her heart stop. A dozen more Witch Hunters were streaming out of the Black Pines lodge. They were about to flood in behind her and cut her off.

"Fi!" Shane yelled out, not sure if it was a warning or a plea.

As if she could read her mind, Fi appeared in the stable doorway, her hair wild. She wasn't leading the horses, but she had her rope in her hands, and she whipped the ring tied to the end into a fierce circle. Fi twirled the rope up over her head and then spun it low, releasing close to the ground. It flew out toward the closest knot of Witch Hunters, tangling in their feet and bringing them down in a heap.

Shane whooped. Then she was forced to throw herself into the mud as a heavy saw-toothed sword sliced through the air with such force it seemed to part the rain. Shane rolled to her elbows and looked up into an all-too-familiar face: the

Witch Hunter with a beaky nose, now conspicuously crooked where she'd crunched it with her boot.

"This time you die!" Tavian shouted, his face wrenched with hate as he hefted his massive sword.

"Out of my way," Shane growled. She had no doubt she could beat this clown again, but maybe not when his twenty closest friends were right behind him.

"Hurry!"

Fi's sharp voice sailed over the fray. Shane threw herself away from Tavian's second strike and drove the blunt side of her ax into his ankle. It was an awkward swing, but it was good enough to take down Tavian. The man crumpled to the ground as Shane scrabbled to her feet and made for the stable. Her shoulders ached from the weight of her slippery ax.

Ahead of her, Fi had closed one side of the stable's wide double doors and held the other open just a sliver. Shane balked. She was excessively short, not excessively thin. There was no way she was getting through that gap.

Fi waved frantically. Shane didn't bother tracking the Witch Hunters—she could be overtaken in the time it took to look back. She sprinted the last few feet and then dove for the stable. At the last possible second, Fi threw the door open wide and then slammed it shut behind her. Shane hit the ground and came up spitting a mouthful of straw, watching as Fi wrestled a thick slab of wood into the braces across the door.

Something that sounded suspiciously like a broadsword thunked into the wood, but the door held. Shane let her head fall back in relief. These were heavy doors meant to withstand the Cragspire winters. A couple of angry Witch Hunters wouldn't be enough to break them down.

They did have a new problem, though. The Witch Hunters might be stuck outside, but Shane and Fi were just as stuck. At least the stable had been shut up tight against the storm, all the shutters firmly latched, so they didn't have to worry about anyone coming through the windows. Shane doubted that would stop them, though. Once the Witch Hunters got someone in their sights, they were relentless. She and Fi might as well have a pack of wild dogs at the door.

Fi seemed to have come to the same conclusion, looking around the barn with a sour expression. "We're trapped," she said dully. "There's no way out."

"Of course there is." Shane got to her feet. "There's always the way we came in."

Even as she said it, another jarring crack sounded from the other side of the wood. Shane jumped. Fi didn't say anything, but her flat look was loud and clear.

"We're not trapped," Shane said, irritated with herself for being jumpy and irritated with Fi for giving up so easily. "Just get the horses ready." She wiped the mud off her ax as best she could and fastened it onto her back.

As Fi stalked off, Shane took her first good look around. There were two long rows of stalls, half of them filled with curious horses hanging their heads over the gates to get a look at the intruders. Flames guttered in the small glass-housed lanterns hung by the door, all on the verge of going out. A loft overhead was filled with hay and barrels of oats, and a small hay wagon sat to the left of the doors, half full of twiggy straw. Shane grinned.

She gave the tongue of the wagon an experimental tug. The muscles of her back cried out in protest, but she kept at it, cheering internally when the heavy wheels began to turn.

Fi reappeared leading the two horses, both packs strapped to the saddles. She pinned Shane with a skeptical look when she found her maneuvering the hay wagon in front of the doors.

"Are we offering hayrides?" she asked.

Shane had no idea why she'd wasted time worrying about Fi. If she had the energy for snark, she was clearly fine.

"I have something a lot more impressive in mind. Mount up and be ready to go when I tell you. You're going to have to trust me."

"Well," Fi admitted, shooting Shane a small smile, "you did get us to the stable."

From the tight-lipped Filore Nenroa, that was practically a glowing tribute. Wagon in place, Shane jogged down the row of stables, unlatching and swinging open the doors to each horse's stall—just in case. Then she pulled one of the little lanterns from the wall.

With a small prayer that she wasn't about to make the biggest mistake of her life, she hurled the burning lantern into the back of the hay wagon.

The glass panels shattered. Fi gasped as the hay flared up faster than Shane had imagined, bright curls of flame licking the sides of the wagon as the hay bloomed into greasy smoke. The horses began to stamp and whinny in fear. Shane had no intention of burning down the barn. Smoke stinging her eyes, she raced for the door, wrenching the heavy piece of wood from the braces and flinging it open.

Witch Hunters poured into the opening, then sprang backward almost as fast, throwing themselves out the way as Shane put her shoulder to the wagon's baseboard and pushed with all her strength, cutting a path through the Witch Hunters with the burning wagon. The wind howled and the rain swept over it in gusts as the fire ate into the wagon below. Shane gave one last great heave, and the wagon took off as it hit the slope, barreling down the lawn into the thick of the Witch Hunters.

"Go, Fi! Go!" Shane yelled.

Fi was beside her in a second, cantering out of the stable and throwing Shane the reins to her horse as she passed. More horses streamed after her, hooves flashing. Shane grabbed the pommel and launched herself into the saddle. Then they were off, leaving the flaming wagon and the shrieking Witch Hunters behind. Shane shared a fierce grin with her partner, pleased by the tiny smile she got in return.

The rain had turned the road to mud, and the shifting silt made their horses stumble more than once. As soon as they were out of sight of the lodge, Fi pulled back on the reins until the horses were walking side by side.

"Why'd you slow down?" Shane demanded, imagining an army of Witch Hunters mounting up and coming after them.

"It's too dangerous to take these roads in the rain," Fi said, leaning close so she didn't have to shout over the storm. "The water washes out the trails, and there's danger of mudslides. We should dismount and head down the slope. I know somewhere we can get dry."

"I thought there was nothing up here but the Black Pines," Shane said.

"Nothing with people," Fi agreed. "How do you feel about ghost towns?"

NOT GOOD, AS it turned out.

It took them hours to pick their way down the steep hill, slipping and sliding in the mud. The only thing Shane was sure of was that no Witch Hunters were following them anymore, because even those fanatics wouldn't be brainless enough to leave the road in this weather.

When they arrived at Fi's ghost town, it was little more than a pile of rubble. The rain had finally let up, and in the watery moonlight Shane stared at the crumbled remnants of buildings and stone warding walls and cauldrons rusted clean through in the shells of decrepit houses. There wasn't a roof to be seen, not even over the caved-in well.

Shane was about to accuse her partner of lying in the worst kind of way when, at the far end of town, they came upon one structure suspiciously still standing: a giant manor house of glistening gray stone. It was tucked up against the cliff wall and surrounded by twisted pines where the forest was creeping back in. Wide pillars braced the door, which stood open like a gaping maw, and there was a chunk of stone missing from the outer wall where it looked like something had taken a bite out of it. Shane was sure she saw something slither under the porch as they approached.

Fi sighed. "Isn't it something?"

Oh, it was something. For once, Shane bit her tongue and let it go. This place had a roof, at least. For now, all she cared about was fixing a big fire and staying beside it for the rest of the night.

"Any port in a storm," she grumbled. They dismounted and slipped inside.

15

Fi

FI SAT IN front of the roaring fire, her gray nightgown wrapped around her knees. She and Shane had taken refuge in a large hall of gray stone. Shane had gone overboard, building a bonfire out of splintered banisters and the withered legs of old chairs, but Fi couldn't deny it felt good after hours in the rain. They'd even been lucky enough to find a few rugs—not too moldy—to replace their wet bedrolls for the night.

On the other side of the fire, Shane sat slumped against her pack with her thick braid hanging over her shoulder. The huntsman inched her socked feet close to the flames, which would be fine until she got careless and set one on fire.

Fi shook her head affectionately at her partner. "Hey," she said, rousing the girl from her doze. "You were pretty impressive back there, fighting those Witch Hunters."

"Was that a compliment?" Shane asked, wiggling her big toe at Fi through a hole in her patchy sock.

"Statement of fact," Fi corrected. "You must be hearing things."

"Well, you're welcome anyway," Shane said through a splitting yawn, already looking half asleep in the hazy warmth.

Fi, on the other hand, could hardly sit still. Maybe she was still keyed up from their encounter with the Witch Hunters, or maybe old places like this just called to her. Her eyes kept drifting to the ceiling, the carved molding and the shadow of bright paint tucked into the corners where a mural might once have stretched across the cracked plaster. The storm wind continued to sigh and moan in the eaves, like a song from some distant corner of the house.

She'd been here once before, also taking shelter from the rain. She and her ex-partner had huddled side by side next to a much smaller fire, and she'd fallen asleep on his shoulder listening to the rain. They weren't all bad memories, but somehow the good ones were even more painful.

Fi rubbed her hands over her thick socks, looking over her shoulder into the depths of the house. It had been such a long time since she let herself explore, just for fun.

She stood up, startling Shane from her doze. The huntsman blinked at Fi while she searched through their wet things, strewn around the fire to dry. The few remaining torches were damp, but Fi managed to dig out a waxy candle. She cast about until she found a long splinter of wood, then used it as a taper to light the candle without melting it in the flames. She stepped easily into her boots.

That got Shane's attention. "What are you doing?"

"I'm going to have a look around," Fi said. Anticipation

was already prickling her skin as she imagined tracing the carved heads of finials and the folds of torn paintings. This was the kind of place you could visit a hundred times without uncovering all of its secrets.

"Here?" Shane asked. "In your nightgown? Alone?"

Fi had to smile. "I'm never alone these days, remember?" she said, cupping the candle and turning toward the rear of the chamber.

Shane scoffed. "Right. I forgot. You brought your own ghost to this haunted house."

"He's not a ghost," Fi corrected, almost second nature by now. "I'll be back before morning. You were going to sleep in anyway." They'd decided to lie low an extra night to keep the Witch Hunters off their trail.

"Do what you want," Shane said. "But I'm warning you right now—I'm not leaving this fire, especially to rescue your sorry behind."

After the day they'd had, Fi was pretty sure that was a lie. She let Shane keep her delusions, nodding before she headed off.

The stone floor felt cold even through her boots, and the silence was broken by creaks and groans as the old building shifted around her. Fi kept a careful eye out for any parts of the floor or walls that might be made of wood, rotted and ready to crumble. There had been no signs of Witches or Witch Hunters anywhere in the front room, so she doubted she had to worry about traps. That didn't mean the manor was safe, though.

A whisper of air at her back told Fi that she had company. She turned to face Briar, fighting down a shiver. He stood outside of the glow of her small candle, strange shadows darkening his face.

"I'm glad you're all right," he said quietly.

Fi put one hand on her hip. "I could tell by your great big smile."

Briar let out a breath, almost a laugh, but his eyes remained unusually serious. "It's just . . . I'm the reason you were put in danger."

Fi reached up, flicking Briar's nose. Her finger went right through him, but Briar started back anyway, as Fi had suspected he would. It was a reflex, after all.

"I already knew that," she said. "Bandit attacks were on your list of ways this journey could kill us, remember? You'll have to share the responsibility with Shane, though, who's been stealing from Witch Hunters and generally antagonizing them." Fi shook her head in disbelief, wondering whether she'd ever find a line Shane wasn't willing to cross.

"I hope that terrifying look is reserved for the Witch Hunters," Briar said.

"It's all for my partner," Fi assured him.

Briar tilted his head back, looking thoughtful. "When I was growing up, there was a movement against magic users in Andar. More of a cult, really." He hesitated. "They formed right after I was born—actually, because I was born. They believed the Witches of Andar had brought the wrath of the Spindle Witch down on the whole kingdom, and that those without magic would suffer for something they had no part in. They called themselves the Topaz Knights. But they were only a fringe order, at least back then."

Topaz? No one knew why the Witch Hunters wore the

203

gems. There was a general superstition that topaz protected against magic, but maybe the Witch Hunters' amulets actually came from the anti-magic movement of Briar's time. A hundred years of fear and hatred of magic could have turned the Topaz Knights into the Witch Hunters as Fi knew them. "They're not so fringe anymore," she muttered.

Briar looked troubled. "You could have been killed," he said, the words unbearably soft.

"Then I guess you came at the perfect moment." The memory of his body wrapped around hers pulled low and warm in her stomach. Fi shifted. "Did I say thanks before, for saving my life?"

Briar's eyes twinkled. "No. In fact, we were kind of cut off in the middle of something."

"Well, thanks anyway," Fi said, purposefully ignoring the rest. Then she turned, tipping her head to indicate the hallway beyond. "Come on. I promised Shane I wouldn't explore alone."

Walking next to Briar was a strange sensation. His steps didn't make a sound, and when Fi glanced back, only her own footprints trailed behind them in the dust. As they moved down the corridor, Briar strayed ahead of her, peering behind the heavy velvet curtains and leaning back to study the broken panes in a stained-glass window.

At the corner, she stopped to examine something. A rope of iron ran like a vein between the stones in the wall, the dull metal twisted into a sequence of bulging knots. Fi frowned. "I don't think this is just decoration." She traced the symbols pressed into the grooves. Loops and swirls tripped over letters constructed of interlocking triangles. "I think it's binding magic. There are two different languages here, from the Divine Rose and the Order of the Riven Earth."

The Riven Earth had been Andar's school of great builders, referred to in the oldest texts as the Earthshakers—Witches who carved away mountains and changed the course of rivers. It made sense that a Witch with an affinity for iron would join that school, but Fi had never seen metal used in binding magic before. When she stepped back, she realized that most of the walls were braced with the same veins of pure iron, locking some ancient magic deep into the foundation. Maybe that explained why the manor was still standing.

"What does it say?" Briar asked, peering at the knots.

Fi brought the candle close. "Most of it is worn away, and it doesn't help that whoever invented the Riven Earth language didn't think they needed conjunctions. But something like, *unbreakable, hold fast.*"

Briar shot Fi a smile. "How many magic languages do you know, anyway?"

Fi's lips moved as she counted in her head. "Twelve. But I can recognize and piece together a few more."

Briar laughed. "Stop, don't tell me that," he begged, pressing a hand over his eyes. "That's too many."

"Twelve is mediocre among historians," Fi replied. In the thousand years since Queen Aurora first founded Andar, there had been hundreds of Orders of Magic that rose and fell. Some consolidated, growing large enough to support great schools of magic, while others operated almost like secret societies. There were even a few orders that existed only for the lifespan of a single Witch. It was any scholar's dream: a kingdom riddled with innumerable hidden pockets of history.

Briar was still shaking his head. "How did I not see this before? You were that kid who spent her whole childhood locked in a library. I can just picture you walled off by stacks of books. Twelve magic languages and no friends, right?" he teased.

Fi couldn't shove him, but she waved a hand through his face. When she was younger, the joke would have bothered her, but she'd long accepted that she preferred books to people.

"How many magic languages do you know?" she countered. He'd had three teachers from three different Orders of Magic, so probably at least that.

Briar hunched his shoulders, suddenly sheepish. "Two and a half?" he hedged, wiggling his hand in a way that made Fi think two was probably more accurate. "I never really saw the point. Reading about magic was boring compared with actually doing it."

Now it was Fi's turn to shake her head. Impatient little Briar Rose badgering the three greatest Witches in the kingdom to skip the book learning and go straight to the spells—she could definitely picture that.

Briar snapped his fingers. His blue coat swirled as he pivoted so that he was ahead of her, walking backward. "I have a new idea why you don't like me."

"Because of your terrible sense of humor?" she suggested drily, remembering his crack about the library.

"I have a great sense of humor," Briar insisted. "You think I'm not smart enough for you. You think I'm nothing but an empty-headed princeling." Fi raised her eyebrows, waiting for him and his two and a half magic languages to prove her wrong. Briar shot her a disarming smile. "But I say opposites attract."

They walked on in a lighter mood, twisting and turning deeper into the heart of the manor until they found themselves in a long corridor. Alcoves in the wall were adorned with statues of stone knights, taller than Fi, with empty eye slits in their helmets. Most held their swords aloft as though ready to spring from the walls, though Fi noticed one knight at rest, his sword dug into the pedestal at his feet.

She walked a few steps past the statue and then stopped, spinning in a slow circle. Something felt off.

"What is it?" Briar asked as Fi walked from one side of the hallway to the other, counting her steps. The hallway was narrower than it had been before, she was sure of it. "Did you find something?"

"Give me a second," Fi murmured. She backtracked to the knight. Absently, she reached up to tug her earlobe, standing on her tiptoes to lift the candle high. Unlike the other statues, this one wasn't pushed against the wall of his alcove. There was a small opening behind him, utterly black beyond the fissure in the stone. Briar peered over her head.

"How did you know that was there?" he asked.

"The hallway got narrower," Fi said. "I figured that space had to be used for something—like a hidden passage."

She thrust her candle as deep as she could into the tiny opening. She couldn't see anything but a dark path angling down. Fi looked back the way she had come, thinking of Shane and the fire, and then glanced over at Briar, chewing her lip.

Briar's eyes twinkled. "I'm in if you are."

"Technically, since you're stuck with me, I don't think

you have a choice," Fi told him. Then she ducked into the passageway, fighting to hold back a smile.

The space beyond was cramped and narrow. Fi was overly aware of the way Briar's sleeve kept brushing *through* her. It made her think of Briar in the rain, his chest heaving after he'd saved her from the Witch Hunters. Could he get out of breath? How did it really feel to be a spirit made of light magic? Did he feel anything at all when he touched her? Heat on the back of her neck made Fi reconsider asking.

Something bright winked ahead of them. Fi stumbled as the passageway suddenly opened into a circular room, every wall lined with mirrors in silver frames. Almost immediately, she lost track of the little opening she and Briar had come through. The bobbing light of the candle glowed from every surface, her reflection moving dizzily around the room. Briar didn't appear in any of the mirrors. Everywhere she looked, Fi stood alone in the dark with her small candle, reflected over and over until it looked like she was surrounded by a hundred flames.

"Stunning," Fi breathed, turning unconsciously to look at Briar.

"That's one word for it." Briar gave a low laugh. He reached out to brush his fingers across one of Fi's reflections in fascination, and her breath hitched at the imagined touch. "Why hide this room?"

Fi's mind whirred with the possibilities. "It could be a place where spells were performed. Some spells are done on the reflection of a person instead of their physical body. But in this case . . ." Fi drifted closer, inspecting her own image. "I think it's hiding another passage."

The slick surface was cold under her hand. The light from her candle darted around as she began a slow circuit of the room, dragging her finger against the glass.

"What makes you think that?" Briar asked.

"I've explored a lot of old ruins like this. You get a feel for these things." Her hand slipped through the opening of the passage they had come through.

She didn't realize until she turned her head that Briar was right beside her, delight shining on his face. It had to be her imagination, but she almost felt warm, as if another person were pressed close to her. "Is this what treasure hunting is like?" he asked, right into her ear. "It's fun."

Fi cleared her throat. "When it's going well." She didn't have the heart to tell him that there was usually more running for your life, or worse, the dreaded dead ends.

Briar had her so off balance she almost missed the clue she was looking for.

"Wait, stop," Briar said. His hand shot out, a flick of his finger making Fi's candle burn brighter as he guided it back to one of the mirrors. "Your reflection looks different in this one."

He was right. Her reflection was dimmer here, the candle a blurry circle instead of a crisp flame. Fi leaned in to press her forehead against the surface. She could see something there, underneath her own reflection.

"This isn't a mirror at all," she said, excited. "It's just a piece of glass without silver backing. That's why the reflection looks different."

Fi looked around the room for a loose rock. She bit the inside of her cheek. Why hadn't she thought to bring anything, like her rope? She studied the glass again. It didn't look very thick. Fi stepped back into the center of the room and then hopped on one foot, pulling off her boot. She hefted the heavy shoe in one hand.

"Here goes nothing," she said. Then she wrenched her arm back and threw her boot as hard as she could. It sailed through the thin sheet of glass with a crash. Fi's reflection shattered and fell to the ground, the floor of the room glittering with tiny shards. Another passage stood before her.

"Good hunch," Briar said.

Fi hopped awkwardly, trying not to let her socked foot touch the ground. She hadn't really thought out her next move, now that her boot was on the other side of the broken glass.

"Need a hand?" Briar asked.

"Do you think you could get my shoe?" He'd been real enough to touch her at the lodge, and the shoe wasn't that far.

"I can do you one better," Briar said. He knelt down in front of Fi, gesturing to his back. "I'll carry you to your shoe."

Fi scoffed. "That sounds like a recipe for me ending up on the floor. Didn't you just wear yourself out saving me again?"

Briar laughed. "I would never let you suffer the same fate as that caterpillar," he promised. "Besides, my magic feels stronger now. Maybe we should test it out. In case you get in trouble again."

"All right," Fi said reluctantly. She'd much rather be dumped on the floor of this old manor than in the middle of a fight.

The smile Briar shot her was blinding. "Hop on," he urged.

Fi wasn't usually clumsy, but it wasn't easy to climb onto

Briar's back with the candle squeezed in her fist, especially since she kept expecting her hands to go right through him. They didn't, though; Briar's back was solid and warm, and his crushed velvet coat was soft as Fi wrapped her free arm around his shoulder. The smell of roses swept over her. Briar stood up all at once and Fi clutched him tightly, the candle waving madly in one hand.

"You're lucky I didn't set your hair on fire!"

"And even luckier you didn't go tumbling through me." Briar looked just as surprised as Fi that she was still on his back.

"Briar, if you drop me . . . ," Fi said warningly.

"Don't worry," Briar said. "I have absolute confidence that I can get you to your shoe—but maybe no farther than that, so let's not drag this out. Hold on!"

"Wait—"

The word wasn't even all the way out of Fi's mouth before Briar took off, racing for the passage. Fi yelped. Briar's arms were locked around her knees, and for one dizzy second it felt like she was flying, the candle a mad shimmer in the sea of glass. "Briar!" she cried, but it came out as a laugh, and he was laughing, too, the sound vaulting ahead of them into the dark. It was sudden and exhilarating, like everything Briar did. Fi's cheeks hurt from smiling as she bounced around on his back, choking him with her tight grip. He leapt over the jagged frame and stopped inside the passage.

"Your shoe awaits!" he declared with a grin.

"You're ridiculous," Fi said, shaking her head. Somehow it came out fondly.

"I didn't drop you once!"

His shoulder suddenly disappeared. Fi pitched forward, dragging the lit candle through Briar, who was thankfully completely insubstantial again. She got her feet down but lurched into the wall, banging her elbow and barely catching herself before going down in a heap. She shot Briar a look.

"What was that last bit?" Fi asked, cradling her elbow.

Briar rubbed the back of his neck. If Fi wasn't mistaken, there was a hint of red dusting his cheeks. "Well, you don't really bulk up practicing magic."

"I thought this wasn't your real body anyway," Fi pointed out.

Briar looked intrigued. "That's true. Maybe I could imagine myself some muscles."

"Please don't," Fi begged with a laugh. She couldn't imagine Briar as a prince with bulging muscles and a chiseled jaw. His long, willowy look suited him best. Not that Fi had a particular preference, really. In fact, she stamped out that whole thought, reaching down for her boot. She balanced one foot on top of the other to shake out any loose glass shards before pulling it on.

Fi bit her lip against the warm feeling rising in her chest. She hadn't meant to flirt with Briar, but he had a way of drawing her out. It had been a long time since she'd laughed so much, or felt so light.

It's just the mystery, Fi told herself, *the ruin.* She could probably start thinking she had feelings for anyone surrounded by secret passages and old architecture. *That's how it started last time, too,* she reminded herself. That wiped the smile off her face.

The corridor sloped downward, a gleaming passage of

gray stone cut with the rope of iron knots. Only the layers of dust and the occasional curtain of spiderwebs betrayed its age. Fi wondered what someone had gone to so much trouble to hide. At last they reached a small set of stairs leading to an iron door. Fi could see those same overlapping symbols traced over one another in deep grooves, the Riven Earth and the Divine Rose side by side. The door had three different locks on it, all of them on the outside.

A breath of cold rose to meet them as Fi and Briar stopped in front of the door. The icy metal of the bolt bit into Fi's fingers as she slid the first lock open. Briar's voice stopped her when she reached for the second.

"Are you sure?" he asked. "That's a lot of locks."

Fi looked at him, and then at the door. But she already knew her answer. The kind of person who could walk away from a door without knowing what was behind it never became a treasure hunter in the first place.

"Whatever was locked in here, it was a long time ago," she said. "And most magic relics aren't dangerous unless you touch them. As long as we're careful, we should be fine." She turned the second lock, and then pulled a thick metal chain from a hook driven into the stone. Slowly, she pulled the door open. A cold gust of air whipped past her, as though it had been waiting to escape.

Fi ventured forward, lifting her candle high. The stone walls of the silent chamber rose into a vaulted ceiling, and the sound of her footsteps echoed a thousand times over. The room was full of artwork—statues and paintings and intricate tapestries, half-rotted carvings and etchings on wooden trunks and tarnished shields—every one of them depicting the same woman. Fi moved deeper into the room, fascinated.

She held the candle up to a painted statue. The figure wore a long black dress, and her face was obscured by a matching black veil, the fabric depicted so carefully that the lace patterns seemed to shiver in the light of the sputtering flame. The veil changed with each work of art—in some pictures, it was a long bolt of black cloth, in others a wispy shroud that revealed a hint of curved lips and a sharp, pale chin. One statue had been draped with a veil of gauzy silk, but over the years it had decayed against the woman's stone face, masking her with moth-eaten scraps. The statue cradled a sewing basket, winding some kind of thread.

Fi caught her breath. The veiled figure must be the Spindle Witch who had cursed Briar and all of Andar. The Witch who wanted Fi dead. She spun around to look at a thousand veiled faces.

"What is this place?" she whispered, inspecting a silver mirror etched with glinting spindles and unspooled thread.

"It's a tomb, of sorts," Briar said. She jumped at his voice so close to her ear, as though he didn't dare speak any louder. "After the Spindle Witch was banished from Andar, my father ordered every image of her removed from the kingdom."

"Why didn't he just have them destroyed?"

"The Spindle Witch was the most powerful of the Great Witches," Briar said softly, looking up into the dark space beneath the statue's veil. "Even before she was exiled, she never once showed her face. Superstitions swirled that anyone who destroyed her image would bring her wrath down upon them. So my father ordered them locked away far from Andar, where no one would ever find them."

Until now, anyway. Fi felt a chill run up her spine. She tried to tell herself it was just from the room—cold and lifeless for a hundred years—but she was thinking about the words embedded into the iron knots in the wall. *Hold fast.* That's why the entire house was reinforced with such strong magic. The silence seemed to whisper with the rustle of wings. Fi flinched under the stone gaze of a crow perched on the Witch's shoulder.

"How is she still alive after all this time?" she breathed.

Briar shook his head. "She was already ancient when she *came* to Andar."

Now that she looked closer, Fi could see that some of the artwork featured other women, too—the last three Great Witches.

Briar had moved toward the sculpture at the very center of the room, and Fi followed, studying the life-size piece that depicted all four Witches together. The Snake Witch stood at one end, holding aloft a serpent with glowing ruby eyes. The Dream Witch reclined with her head in the Rose Witch's lap, cradling an hourglass—it looked like it had once been made of real glass and sand, but only jagged pieces remained. The Rose Witch tucked a blossom of pink crystal into the Dream Witch's hair, a sweet smile frozen on her lips. The Spindle Witch stood alone. The piece of thread dangling from her pale hands was made of gold, and her drop spindle had been carved so precisely it seemed to be spinning even now.

Briar reached out to lay a hand against the cheek of the young Rose Witch. Fi shifted, suddenly feeling like she was intruding on something personal.

Briar noticed her hesitating. He offered her a sad smile.

"The Rose Witch was my older sister. Camellia. She was one of the few who escaped the curse."

Fi hadn't known that. Like the Paper Witch, powerful Witches gave up their names and their birthrights when they took a title, something that made tracing the genealogies of famous Witches almost impossible. But now that she was looking for it, she felt like she should have put it together long ago. Camellia was a member of the Order of the Divine Rose, the magic order of the royal line, and she had Briar's golden hair and laughing blue eyes. Maybe it was even Camellia herself who had carried the bone spindle away from Andar and hidden it deep in the mountains, praying for her brother's awakening while she carved her inscription on the ruin's door.

A drop of blood, a drop of hope.

Fi considered the statue, doing some mental calculations. "She must have been quite a bit older than you."

"Almost fifteen years," Briar confirmed, "and she never let me forget it."

There was a little sparkle in his eyes again. Fi was glad to see it—that wistful expression had reminded her of the cold white tower and the sleeping prince in her dreams.

"It was the Great Witches who saved me," Briar went on. "When I pricked my finger, I was supposed to belong to the Spindle Witch forever. Instead, I was put to sleep. I wasn't even awake at the end, when . . ." Briar trailed off.

When the Great Witches had given their lives.

Fi had read various incomplete firsthand accounts of the

fall of Andar and so many more fabricated tales. But for the first time, the story felt impossibly, unbelievably sad.

Though all seemed lost, the Great Witches stood against the Spindle Witch one final time, giving their lives to alter the kingdom's fate with three final acts of great magic:

The Snake Witch swore to safeguard a path, becoming a great ivory serpent and winding through the Forest of Thorns.

The Dream Witch promised to protect those inside the castle, spelling them to sleep alongside their prince.

And the Rose Witch vowed to shield Briar Rose from the Spindle Witch's power, wreathing his tower in roses and protective spells.

Fi watched the candlelight dance over Briar's face. He was a prince and a powerful Witch, but he and Fi were the same in many ways: both torn from their families by curses, both longing to reclaim what they'd lost. Maybe that was why the bone spindle had chosen her.

Something shimmered amid the broken pieces of the Dream Witch's hourglass. Fi bent down to get a better look. The dust that had spilled out of the hourglass was so bright she wondered if it was actually gold—but when she lifted a glittering piece of glass out of the way, the rest of the dust spilled to the floor, the little flecks swirling around her like a storm. Fi stood up fast, but not fast enough to avoid sneezing.

"Maybe it was real dream dust," Briar said, offering a cheeky smile. "Some people are allergic, you know."

Fi rubbed her itchy nose. "I think it was just regular old dust." She sneezed again, and the candle guttered dangerously.

For the first time, she noticed how low it had burned. A hot drip of wax slid down onto her palm, and Fi hissed, dropping the candle. It rolled across the cold floor, throwing shadows over the images of the Spindle Witch. Fi knelt to grab it before it could go out.

Her hand met Briar's as the spirit bent down beside her. Then, amazingly, he picked up the candle. Fi stared.

"Your magic's recovered already?" She thought that piggyback ride would have taken more out of him.

"I'm getting stronger as we get closer to Andar. Watch."

Briar lifted the candle, blowing gently until the flame went out. For a moment, they were plunged into blackness, the cold air pressing in around Fi like the Spindle Witch's hundred eyes. Then a different kind of light sprang from Briar's fingers, as if he were holding a bit of pure-white flame in the hollow of his hand. Sparks danced through the air like enchanted fireflies.

"Wow. That's so . . . useful," Fi breathed, imagining all the ruins and the wonderful hidden places of the world that could shine if Briar was with her.

Briar laughed, a sweet, warm sound that chased the shadows away. "Aha. *Useful.* I finally found the way to your pragmatist's heart." He leaned toward Fi, smiling. "Admit it—you're falling for me, just a little bit."

Fi swallowed too hard, staring into Briar's eyes that spar-kled like a midnight sky. "Of course not," she whispered, but it was harder to convince herself it was true when Briar could do such beautiful magic.

16

---·›››»—‹‹‹·---

Briar Rose

BRIAR PERCHED ON the edge of the four-poster bed in the white tower, cradling a deep red rose. It was the symbol of Andar's first queen, the symbol of the binding magic that protected him here—the symbol of his sister, Camellia.

Her memory was everywhere in this room, from the heady perfume of roses to the sea of flowers, wreathing him like offerings in a tomb. Briar had lost so many people to the curse, but he missed her more than anyone. He'd known she must be dead, after all this time. But seeing her face set in cold stone made him ache, as if someone had reached inside of him and ripped something out. Camellia was gone, and the roses in this tower might be the very last of her magic—the most precious magic he had ever known.

Briar turned the rose in his hand, careful of the thorns. Camellia's affinity was for plants. The rose wasn't only her symbol; it was her medium, too. For her, braiding a flower crown was like weaving a spell of living magic, the tiny blossoms erupting into bloom before she even finished. With binding magic, she could cast spells that lasted lifetimes, creating an unbreakable oath or sealing a cursed relic into a cage of tree roots. And yet nothing made her smile like granting Briar's small wishes.

To the people of Andar, she had been the head of the Order of the Divine Rose and a prodigy even among those of the royal line, named one of the Great Witches when she was only eleven. But to Briar, she had been so much more. A sister. A mother. A best friend. The arms that comforted him when he woke from his nightmares choking on tears, imagining the Spindle Witch looming out of the shadows. It was Camellia who promised that she would find a way to save him. Camellia who had loved him, in spite of the curse. And he had lost her forever.

The rose shivered under Briar's touch. Then he realized the curtains were swaying, too, the gauzy fabric shuddering as though caught in a soft breeze.

Briar stared at the curtains, mystified. It didn't make sense. This place hadn't changed in a hundred years. But with the next gust, he could suddenly hear voices filtering up from below.

That was impossible. He was alone. He had always been alone.

Briar ran for the spiral stairs, taking them two at a time. Was this a dream within a dream? Was it because of Fi? Was he finally waking up? Even the stairway looked different, the normally dull stone now bright and glittering.

Briar braced on the wall to launch himself down the last

few steps. His hand slid against the stone, raising a cloud of golden sand. The tiny flecks winked like shining dust motes. Briar stopped. Where he'd touched it, the stone no longer shimmered. A patch of cold, dull marble had taken its place, as though he had scraped away a layer of paint to reveal the bare canvas beneath.

Briar's heart sank. That was the real tower. The rest of this was just magic, fragile enough to be broken with a single touch. Dream magic.

The voices were right up ahead. Almost against his will, Briar found himself pulled toward the sound, every footprint leaving a gray shadow on the brilliant blue carpet. He already knew what he would find. It was one of his own memories, after all.

A younger version of himself—twelve, if he was remembering right—stood in front of a tall three-arch window, looking down at the courtyard and the front gate. One hand was pressed against the glass, his fingers tensed as if he might break through it.

Close behind him stood Camellia, her hands folded into her blue gown. Nestled in her hair was a crown of pink roses, the buds bursting open as though she were the sun. Even with the worried expression marring her face, Briar drank in the sight of her. This wasn't a memory he would have chosen to revisit, but he couldn't pass up any chance to see her again.

"Briar, come away," Camellia beckoned, her voice soft.

The boy whirled around. Briar flinched at the venomous expression on his young face.

"They're taking her away, and you're not even trying to stop it!"

Briar hung back in the doorway. If he stepped close to the window, he knew what he would see: a girl with thick black curls and a lavender frock being led to a line of carriages laden with baggage strapped to the roof.

"No one's being taken away, Briar," Camellia said evenly. "Ysabel's family has simply decided to leave court and live at their estate in the west for a while."

"You're wrong." Even watching from the doorway, Briar could feel the cold glass under his fingertips, the desperation and helplessness that had risen in his chest, higher and higher, until he thought he'd choke on it. "Ysabel's my friend. She wouldn't just leave without talking to me. She wouldn't!" Young Briar swung back to the window, trying to will the girl to turn around, to shake off her mother's hand and run back to the castle.

Camellia sighed. "It's complicated," she began. The start to a speech he had heard so many times, he could recite it by heart.

"It's not complicated. It's because of me."

Briar had heard the whispers that followed him through the castle. He knew what the members of court called him behind his back—the ill-luck prince, fated to be Andar's ruin. Ysabel's parents weren't the first nobles to want their child far away from Briar Rose. It was just the first time it had cut so deep.

Ysabel stopped at the threshold of the carriage, looking back over her shoulder, but she was too far away to see Briar in the window. She disappeared as the carriage door snapped shut, and all Briar could do was watch. That was all he could ever do.

Briar had spent his life watching the children of the palace run off to play among the river willows, watching his brother and sister ride across the cobblestone bridge and into a kingdom he had never seen and couldn't imagine. Only *his* world ended at the castle walls.

"Briar." Camellia laid a comforting hand on her brother's shoulder.

Briar—the real Briar in the doorway—felt his heart shriveling with guilt. Because he knew what came next, and he would give anything to change it. To feel that comforting hand on his shoulder one more time.

"Just leave me alone!" Young Briar threw off his sister's hand, backing against the glass. "You can't help me. You're useless. Even though you're supposed to be this powerful Great Witch, you can't save anyone!"

Camellia turned away, her eyes closed as if in exquisite pain. Briar braced his hand against the wall. Had he known how sad she was then? Or could he only see it now, the worry and grief already lining her young face? He wanted to go to her, to put his arms around her and apologize, but he couldn't bear to feel her disintegrate into golden dust.

Young Briar's face was pitiless, twisted with grief and rage. "Ride off and leave me here in this cage. You always do." Then quieter, to the window: "Everyone does."

As Camellia strode out into the hall, rose petals falling from her crown like a gentle rain, Briar closed his eyes and begged for a different memory—a single glimpse of happiness to carry with him into a world without her.

Please.

Laughter rang out from somewhere beyond the walls.

Briar opened his eyes. His younger self was gone. The light had changed, as if he were standing now in a different time, the windows thrown open to let in the birdsong. Briar found himself drawn toward the sound of laughter, following it through the glistening halls.

A shower of golden sand fell away as he pushed open the door to the courtyard. At first the sunlight was so bright that he could hardly see anything, just the shaggy willow tree and the cosmos waving on their wispy stalks. Then he blinked and the figures came into focus.

There was a picnic taking place. A golden-haired boy sat at the center of a large blanket covered in pies and pastries and cream and strawberries—not a healthy thing in sight. Every dish had been requested by five-year-old Briar. The little boy sat beside the Dream Witch, her black curls tied up in a yellow scarf that matched her golden robes. Even as he watched, she tipped her head back and laughed—a rich, beautiful laugh that Briar remembered being infectious enough to get all three of the respectable "Great" Witches rolling on their sides.

To one side stood the tall Snake Witch. She had her arms crossed over her white tunic, but Briar could see her lips quirked in a smile. An empty teacup dangled from the crook of one finger.

A laugh that tinkled like a bell rang in his ears. Briar inhaled sharply as a younger Camellia, barely twenty in this memory, plopped down on the blanket next to the prince. He watched himself give Camellia his half-eaten piece of cake, but not before grabbing the juiciest-looking raspberry right off the top with his grubby little hand. Maybe his older

224

brother, Sage, had been right when he'd called Briar an incorrigible imp.

As if summoned by his thoughts, a young man's voice floated over the garden.

"Making trouble again?"

Briar whipped his head up. Sage leaned out over the windowsill, his arms crossed and a crown winking on his head. A lanky young man with golden-brown hair, at seventeen he was already Andar's king, after grief drove their father into an early grave. Briar remembered Sage best in the audience chamber, listening to blue-robed advisors with one elbow propped on the arm of his rosewood throne—then catching Briar's eye through the stuffy crowd and winking, too quick for anyone else to catch.

Briar watched his younger self run beneath the window, holding out the squashed raspberry. "Sage! Come out!"

Sage shook his head. "Dignified kings don't go out windows, Briar."

Little Briar's face scrunched up. "But yesterday—"

"A king doesn't concern himself with what happened yesterday," Sage interrupted with a theatrical toss of his cape, though Briar could see his eyes twinkling. "And if I remember right, you were sworn to secrecy about that."

"You'll tell me, won't you, Briar?" Camellia laughed, seizing Briar around the shoulders and squeezing him as he squirmed to get free. Briar had to turn away, the grief and the loneliness twisting his stomach in knots.

He should end this. He shouldn't look back at everything he'd lost.

Then Briar realized he was no longer alone. A pair of

brilliant hazel-green eyes met his across the garden, Fi's expression awed. Briar flinched. He hadn't meant to bring her here.

Fi made her way to him, staring at the lush gardens and the rope swing dangling from a gnarled willow bough. "What is this?"

"It's just a dream," Briar said. He wished the words hadn't come out so bitter. "I said you might find yourself here from time to time."

"But we're not in the tower," Fi said. "And that's you, right?" She pointed to the little Witch boy, who was showing off now, making the teapot glow with a sparking finger.

"It is," Briar confirmed. "Remember the dust you were sneezing at? There must have been real dream dust in the hourglass. That seems like something she would do," he added, watching the Dream Witch sip her glowing tea. "She loved to hide things in unexpected places. When she was asleep, she could walk inside of dreams, or whisper in people's minds and influence what they saw. That gold dust is what created all this. Here, watch."

Briar leaned over a flower box bursting with buttercups. He swept his hand through them, and the buttercups crumbled, replaced by withered husks. Briar reached for another clump of flowers.

"Don't." Fi's hand grazed his wrist. When he looked up, her expression was soft, almost wistful. "It's your family, right? Don't you want to watch for a little while?"

More than anything, Briar wanted to lose himself in this memory. He wanted to listen to Camellia's laugh and live this life again. But none of this was real—it was a vision in fool's gold, luring him in with the things he had lost forever.

Fi turned at the sound of glass breaking. Briar winced, remembering his decision to carry the plates balanced on top of cups. A laugh escaped Fi's mouth, somewhere between an exhale and a snort. Watching a smile break over her face, the loneliness that had been gnawing at Briar eased back to a dull ache. The rest of this might be a dream, but she was real. She was something he could hold on to.

Fi looked lovely in the garden. She wore a cream-white shirt and a pair of pants with suspenders, the cuffs rolled up to her knees. Her belt was laden with all kinds of tools—brushes in three sizes, what looked like a chisel, and a set of small silver picks. A magnifying glass hung from a chain in her pocket. Was this how Fi thought of herself? The dream dust had captured Briar's memory, but a little of Fi had slipped in, too. This was some younger version of the Fi he knew, one who seemed less guarded. She wasn't even wearing the glove that seemed like a permanent fixture on her hand.

Now that he was looking, he could see something there, a swirl of black lines marring her skin—a mark he had never seen before. It flashed on her palm as she pushed the hair away from her eyes. Briar started to ask about it when Fi gasped.

"What is that?"

Briar spun back in time to see a white snake as thick as a tree trunk encircle the entire picnic blanket before resting its head on its tail. Its round, translucent scales rippled in the sunlight.

"That's the Snake Witch," Briar said. "Sometimes she would guard me when I was outside the castle."

"Amazing," Fi breathed. "I knew some Witches could

transform, but the detailing, the scales—and she's so massive."

"I called her that once, and she wasn't that flattered," Briar warned.

Fi rolled her eyes fondly. Then she bit her lip. "Tell me more about them."

Briar's chest squeezed. But the thought of sharing this with Fi didn't hurt as much as he'd expected. Her interest was flattering, even though he was positive she didn't want to hear about the spoiled little prince so much as the Great Witches. If there was anyone he could entrust this memory to, it was Fi, who squirreled away fables and folktales and loved so many old forgotten things.

Soon Briar found himself seated next to Fi on the castle steps, telling her about his life in Andar and the Witches and Sage. But mostly, he told her about Camellia. Camellia's warm hand clasped around his as they raced through a midnight garden, sparks of his magic whizzing past them like fireflies. Camellia, who restored a crumbling bridge by weaving ropes of wildflowers through the fissures in the stones—and then, when Briar begged her, strung a vine bridge between the towers of the castle and let him walk in the air. Camellia forever embroidering little roses into everything he wore—protective spells bound with thread in the shape of the most powerful symbol of Andar. Fi listened with a soft smile, her eyes bright as if she were remembering it along with him.

By the time the golden dust began to fall away, Fi's hand had slipped into his. The courtyard walls crumbled, followed by the willows, darkness creeping into the edges of the memory. The laughter died away, and then little Briar and Camellia and Sage and the Snake Witch, each of them winking out like a shower of falling stars. Only the Dream Witch remained, a knowing smile on her face, almost as if she were looking at them.

Then she vanished, too, and the last of her glittering magic poured through the darkness like sand through an hourglass, the symbol of all dream magic. Briar gripped Fi's hand tightly, the only real thing he had left.

Looking down at their entwined fingers, he saw it again, the black shape seared into her palm. Briar searched her eyes.

"Fi. What is this mark?"

Before he'd even finished the question, she disappeared, and he was back in the tower, everything gray and dim except the bloodred roses.

17

⤜⤛⤛ ⤚⤚⤜

Shane

SHANE SLAPPED A hand against her neck, trying to catch the fly that had been buzzing around her for the last ten minutes. It was after her horse, too, judging by the irritated way the animal kept flicking its tail. She was tempted to uncoil her braid and let it hang down so she could shoo the fly off like her horse did, but the thought of a thick carpet of hair on the back of her neck killed the impulse.

Though Shane had been freezing every night they spent camping, that didn't stop her from sweating under the hot midday sun. The long, dusty road had her parched, and a drop of sweat trickling down her back was driving her to distraction. Shane bent around in her saddle, scratching at her spine until Fi gave her a funny look. Shane chose not to take it personally. Her partner had been acting funny for days.

Fi's bizarre detour to the ghostly manor had turned into something of a shortcut. When they crawled out of the undergrowth two days later, they found themselves once more on a wide merchant road, and had a much easier time riding down the eastern slopes of the mountains as the drop-offs and rocky cliffs gave way to wide fields dotted with flowers and grapes growing long on the vine.

Two days later, they crossed into the Duchy of Bellicia under a big blue sky.

That's when Fi started acting funny—or funnier than usual, anyway. Fi had spent hours the night before staring into the fire and folding and unfolding the same handkerchief, until Shane was tempted to grab the little cloth square and burn it just to get some peace. She was getting snippier, too, practically biting Shane's head off if she asked *anything* about where they were headed. Shane didn't get it. Her partner's mood should have been improving. Bellicia was the hub of the Border Guards. Unlike the little mountain towns that relied on infrequent patrols, Bellicia had a permanent garrison, which meant no more Witch Hunters skulking around putting bounties on their heads.

Maybe the traveling was getting to Fi, or maybe it was that invisible spirit. Shane hadn't seen Briar Rose since the lodge, but she wouldn't be surprised if being haunted by an undead prince was like having a bad rash—it just made you twitchy and irritable.

Shane looked over at her partner, sitting ramrod straight in her saddle as though she were riding to her own execution instead of some rich old man's duchy. Fi wore her familiar loose blue shirt trapped under a dark vest, her brown jacket flaring out across the back of the saddle, and she'd finger-combed her hair so it looked neater than usual. Even clearly half out of her mind with some secret, she still managed to look more put together than Shane, who smelled like a stable boy and couldn't stop bothering her nose where a sunburn was peeling. Her hair was so tangled a family of birds could probably nest in there without her even noticing. Shane had a feeling no duke was going to be thrilled to see them.

Almost before she realized it, the landscape changed from fields and forests to manicured lawns. A hulking iron gate rose up in front of them, taller than Shane on horseback. She peered through the thick bars to study the sculpted gardens and carefully trimmed hedges, a few marble fountains glistening in the sun. It was excessive, and wasteful, and had to take an army of gardeners to maintain. Not to mention the wrought-iron gate was probably a whole mile from the actual estate, which was only a gleam of sandy buildings beyond the thick hedges.

A man in a gold-and-white uniform rode up on the other side of the gate, looking them over critically through the bars. As far as Shane was concerned, they were the ones who should be critical—gold and white was a tacky color match even for a noble house.

"The duke will be receiving no visitors today," the steward said in a clipped tone clearly intended to be a dismissal. Shane bristled, but Fi was unfazed.

"I'm here to see the duke's son," she said coldly. "Lord Armand Bellicia."

The man looked surprised, probably not expecting two dirt-stained travelers to know anyone inside the estate by name. Shane was a little taken aback herself. That name sounded really familiar. *Armand*. Where had she heard that before?

The man shifted and his horse did, too, stamping its polished hooves. "The estate is receiving no visitors today, for any reason," he amended. "The young master is preparing for a party and asked not to be disturbed."

"He'll see me," Fi said, sounding absolutely certain. "Tell him it's Filore Nenroa."

"I'll tell him." The man snorted derisively, turning for the mansion. His horse gave a snooty flick of its tail.

Shane hated this place already. She had no problem with nobles in general, as long as she didn't have to be one anymore. But she absolutely despised people who clambered to the top of the pile just so they could spit on everyone below them. If the gatekeeper was already this uppity, how bad was the stuffy old duke going to be, or worse, his spoiled son?

That thought finally shook loose the memory. *Armand*. A while back, she'd heard rumors about a rich duke's kid running around playing treasure hunter in the Witches' Jewelry Box with . . .

"Wait a minute!" Shane whipped around in the saddle. "This is the guy? Your ex? *That's* who we came all this way to see?"

Fi's posture was so rigid she might have been carved of stone—or a block of ice, maybe, if she really had the guts to be doing this.

"We didn't come here to *see* anyone," Fi bit out, not meeting Shane's eyes. "We came here to get passes. Don't make me explain about the Border Master again."

That was her tricky partner, trying to brush her off. Shane was not having it.

"And your *ex* is going to do us this big favor? What makes you think we're not going to be sent packing?"

Fi and Armand's partnership breaking up had been big news on the treasure-hunting circuit, because as a team, they had beaten at least a dozen other hunters to a handful of big scores. One of those treasure hunters had been Shane herself, and she was still sore about it. Her partner at the time was a tall girl with unruly rooster-comb hair and a bad habit of following false leads. They'd taken a trapdoor to the basement of a ruin, where they'd both nearly been decapitated by a swinging ax, then wasted hours navigating a floor of trick tiles only to find themselves in an empty vault with the back door hanging wide open. Fi and Armand had beaten them there by more than a month and already made off with a fortune in silver.

Shane wasn't the only treasure hunter with a story like that. People still talked about the Azure Manor. The labyrinthine stone ruin had been considered unsolvable until Fi and Armand figured out how to move the stone walls and change the shape of the labyrinth within. They'd uncovered proof of some mysterious undiscovered magic order and, more important, bulging chests of priceless lapis lazuli artifacts.

Fi didn't look like she was counting on warm memories to get them through this gate. "Armand won't refuse me," she promised coldly.

That tone of certainty was back. Shane was sure she was missing something. Yes, they needed passes, but in what world did it make more sense to go to your hateful ex than to drop in on your parents? Shane had seen the wistful expression on Fi's face at the mention of the Nenroas. Whatever the source of this black cloud that hung around Fi all the time, Shane was more and more sure it had something to do with her infamous ex on the other side of the gate.

The man in the gold-and-white uniform came riding back at top speed, his whole affect changed as he quickly unlatched the gate. The hinges creaked as it swung open. The man bowed so low over the front of his horse Shane was surprised he didn't topple off.

"If you'll follow me, Lady Nenroa," he said with a sweep of his hand. "The young master will see you in the glasshouse."

Fi didn't bother to acknowledge the man, just followed along behind as he led them into the gardens. Before they turned onto a side path, Shane caught a glimpse of the mansion between the boughs of the plum trees, a great sprawl of curved archways, spiraling balconies, and wide picture windows. Shane snorted. If buildings had personalities, that one was looking down on them.

A couple of guards walked the grounds in stiffly pressed new uniforms. Shane's guts knotted. They could be loyal soldiers who had pledged their service to the duke, or they could be mercenaries dressed up for the party, there to do the dirty jobs—hustling less reputable guests in and out of side doors and paying off partygoers who had too good a time before tossing them into the street, while some noble sat inside gobbling truffles and slurping wine out of a crystal goblet cupped in his squeaky-clean hands. Looking at them was like looking at herself from a few years ago, before she met the Paper Witch, and Shane did not like the view.

The gardens were even more lavish up close, with alabaster

pergolas covered in bougainvillea and arched gazebos tucked between sculpted trees. They rode through a sea of marigolds in every color from pale golden to rust red, growing darker and darker until they reached a pristine glasshouse.

The man bowed to Fi one more time. "The young master awaits."

Shane dismounted slowly, giving the glasshouse a suspicious look. Most nobles held meetings in tearooms or offices. Or entryways, if they were eager to get rid of you. Either the *young master* got ready for parties by lounging in his garden, or he had chosen this place specifically to meet with Fi. They left their horses with the steward and pushed open the door.

The garden inside the glasshouse was stiflingly humid. Dew dripped from plants Shane had never seen before with leaves the size of dinner plates, and every breath was like getting a lungful of perfume. A single path of circular stepping-stones wound through the chaos of beautiful flowers. But what really caught Shane's attention were the butterflies. Gossamer-thin butterflies reclined on thick stems, slowly opening and closing their wings, while tiny blue butterflies fluttered around one another in an intricate dance. Shane brushed too close to a lavender bush and raised a whole swarm of yellow butterflies that probably had some fancy name but that Shane knew as skippers. No doubt about it: Fi's ex had weird taste.

One stone from the end of the path, Fi stopped so suddenly Shane almost ran into her. "Let me do the talking," Fi warned, not even glancing back. "Don't say *anything*."

Shane didn't like the sound of that, but Fi moved on before she had a chance to protest.

At the heart of the glasshouse, they found themselves on

a small patio of red flagstones accented with a wrought-iron table and a fine porcelain tea set. A man stood with his back to them, framed against the foliage. He wore a white blouse under a rich golden tunic, and the air around him was bright with monarch butterflies, the mottled orange insects hanging from every stem like withered flowers. White butterflies with the same dark markings fluttered through the air. The man wore at least a dozen rings on his fingers, some of them thick bands of twisted silver while others glittered with jewels. A ruby the size of a robin's egg sat on his thumb.

Armand Bellicia turned away from his butterflies to greet them with a smile. He was good-looking, Shane supposed, if you liked handsome men with chiseled features and broad shoulders. His brunet hair fell to his shoulders, feathering around his face, and his skin was a shade lighter than Fi's. When he smiled, he showed no teeth at all, his thin lips pressed together in a smug line. And he had eyes only for Fi.

Fi tugged at her coat uncomfortably. Shane could tell she felt underdressed. Well, luckily she had Shane standing right next to her, looking far worse.

"Filore," the man said in a melodic voice. "It's been too long."

Fi cringed. "Armand," she said simply.

The man looked far too delighted for just trading pleasantries. Shane's fingers itched for her ax.

"Have you been enjoying your travels?" Armand asked silkily. "It's been difficult to keep track of you. And how are your parents?"

Shane couldn't tell what was going on or why her partner looked like an overtightened harp string about to snap, but even she had caught the nasty edge in those seemingly innocent questions.

"I need passes to cross the border," Fi said, somehow managing to sound calm. "Will you get them for me?"

Armand's fingers curled into a fist. He clicked his rings together in irritation. "No small talk. I'm hurt," he said. "You didn't even compliment me on my beautiful glasshouse and all the treasures I've been collecting. Do you like them? My butterflies? I have almost a hundred white monarchs now." He smiled, gesturing to the white-and-black butterflies swirling through the air above them.

Fi took a deep breath. "Two passes, by tomorrow. Can you do that?" Her voice was still icy, but Shane could see the fingernails digging into her palm, leaving deep grooves.

"Two?" Armand asked, glancing at Shane for the first time. "Is one of them for your charming little maidservant?"

"Actually, I'm her partner," Shane corrected. She wouldn't try to get in the middle of whatever complicated dance Fi and Armand were doing, but she was not about to stand there and be insulted—not when the insult was that obvious.

Armand's eyes flashed strangely. "So you've taken a new partner," he said, his voice almost a purr. "How comforting. Still, I wonder how much she really knows about you, Filore. How dangerous it can be to travel with you."

"If you can't get me the passes, I have no reason to be here," Fi warned, finally showing a little temper.

"Always so hasty." He shook his head. "I'm sure we can come to an arrangement."

Shane wanted to grab Fi by the collar and haul her back

to Idlewild before any *arrangements* were made. But Fi wasn't even looking at her, or at Armand. She was looking at something on the floor.

Shane bent down. A praying mantis was slowly devouring one of the white monarch butterflies, its hooked arms ripping into the delicate wings. The butterfly was long dead.

Armand made a disgusted sound. "Damaging my collection," he muttered. He lifted his heavy gold-buckled boot to crush it.

"Don't," Fi said, darting forward to lay a hand against Armand's shoulder. Though it was only a brush, the man backed off at once, clearly startled by the light touch. Shane filed that away with the rest of the mysteries.

With a strange gentleness Shane wasn't sure she'd ever seen from her partner, Fi picked one of the giant leaves off a shivering palm and rolled it into a cone, scooping up the praying mantis and its sinister meal with one deft stroke.

"Here," she said, pressing the leaf cone into Shane's hands. "Let it go in the garden. It'll give me and Armand time to come to an agreement."

Shane caught her partner's wrist, pulling her close enough to whisper. "You don't have to do this." She wasn't entirely sure what was going on, but she knew she didn't like it. "We can find another way to get passes, or we can climb over the damn wall for all I care."

A small smile flitted across Fi's face at the suggestion, but she pulled away, dropping her gaze. "That solution is very *you*, but it won't be necessary. I have this under control."

Shane wondered whether Fi really believed herself this time.

She snuck one last glance at the pair over her shoulder as she headed out of the glasshouse. Fi stood stock-still while Armand moved slowly toward her, like a predator stalking through the trees.

Shane wasn't feeling very charitable to the praying mantis. She took the first small garden path and dumped it into a patch of marigolds under a plum tree.

"See if you can catch any butterflies when they're free," she challenged.

A harsh cry made her jump. Shane jerked her head up, realizing only now that the tree was thick with crows—dozens of them perched on the branches above her, feasting on the split-open bodies of ripe plums. That would have been unnerving enough without them staring at her. But they were. All of them. Even the one in the middle with the milky, unblinking eyes.

Crows at the Silver Baron. Crows in the Cragspires. Shane had worn out two good pairs of boots traveling all over Darfell, and she'd never seen so many crows.

"I don't know which one of you is the spy for the Spindle Witch, but you can flap off and get lost! All of you!"

She slammed her foot into the trunk hard enough to make the whole tree shudder. The crows took off shrieking, wheeling overhead before fleeing over the garden walls.

Shane rubbed her arms. Five minutes in, and she already hated this place—and whatever bad deal Fi was making behind her back.

18

Fi

FI SCRUBBED HER soapy fingers through her hair, sighing as they came away slick with grime. She tipped her head back into the hot water, going boneless. For the most part, Fi didn't mind being on the road, but she always missed the luxury of a long bath. Dunking herself in a freezing alpine river or a pounding waterfall wasn't the same. At the other end of the giant bath, Shane seemed to be doing more splashing than washing, her mussed brown hair still half lathered as she pawed through the array of expensive oils and soaps.

A woman in Bellicia's gold-and-white livery had shown them to a lavish set of rooms. A steaming bath was already waiting. The huge porcelain tub would have taken a long time to heat—long enough that Armand must have ordered these rooms prepared before Fi had even spoken to him. She hated that he'd known he could persuade her to stay, and she hated herself for coming here in the first place. Through the bubbles and the milky water, Fi stared at the emblem of the butterfly seared into her left hand. She'd stripped off her fingerless glove before the bath, but was careful to keep the curse mark submerged and out of sight. Not that Shane was paying her much attention. Apparently, Fi really *wasn't* her type.

Her partner was the only thing keeping Fi sane right now. Even though they'd been given the premium guest suite, with canopied beds under silk coverlets and wide-thrown windows looking out over the garden, Shane wasn't intimidated or impressed by anything. And she had no qualms about hopping into the bath right alongside Fi instead of properly waiting her turn behind the privacy screen. But Fi wasn't complaining. The bath was big enough that she couldn't reach Shane even when she stretched out her feet. And she didn't want to be alone here.

"So he's going to give you the passes for free? No strings?"

"Like I said," Fi huffed, "we just have to go to his party tonight. It's a masquerade ball."

"See, that sounds like a string." Shane pulled the glass stopper from a bottle and gave it a curious sniff. "I bet you have to dance with him all night or wait on him hand and foot."

As if Armand would ever be so straightforward. Fi almost wished he had asked for something demeaning and unreasonable. Then at least she'd know where they stood. "Nope," she said, swishing her hands and sending ripples through the swirls of soap. "We go to the party, and then in the morning he'll escort us through the checkpoint. That's the deal."

Shane didn't look happy. "You know that moment in a ruin, when you've just set off a trap but you don't know what it is yet, and anything—*anything at all*—could happen, but it's going to be bad? This feels like that moment."

Fi couldn't disagree. She felt the exact same way. Out loud, she said again, "I have this under control." She had to. She had already lost her family and home to a curse. She wasn't going to leave Briar in the same position.

"If you say so." Shane rummaged through the bottles, yanking out the stoppers and adding random dashes of oil and powder to the bath. Fi felt light-headed from the clashing floral scents.

"Go easy on those," she suggested. "Or better yet, just pick one and use that."

"Use it?" Shane snorted, hanging over the side and setting the bottle down. "What are you talking about? I'm stealing these." She opened another bottle, brought it up under her nose, and then gagged. "Not this one."

Even from all the way across the bath, Fi recognized the pungent aroma of oils and strong herbs. "It's for removing warts," she said, unable to stop a chuckle.

"Huh." Shane corked the bottle, shooting it a sideways look. "Might be worth stealing after all." Apparently bored with her perfumery, she dunked her head under the water and came up spitting, finally working the lather through her thick hair. "I don't see why we have to get all dolled up for this guy," she complained. "We should've gone to his party dirty and stinking like pigs. He deserves that."

"Yes, but I don't." Fi ducked her chin into the water to hide a small, pleased smile. It felt good to have someone on her side, even if her companion didn't know the whole story and was preoccupied with burgling the bath soaps.

Fi decided she'd better get out before the hot water made

243

her too relaxed. She needed to stay sharp. With a sigh, she dragged herself up, pulling a towel from the wooden stand. She wrapped it around herself tightly, tucking the ends together so that it would hold as she headed into the other room.

A servant had been in at some point during their bath, taking away their pile of dirty clothes and leaving a tray set with square cakes and a steaming teapot. Something else was draped across the white-and-gold coverlet—a rustle of skirts and rich fabrics, tiny gems winking out of the collar. It was a costume. Armand had said he would send something *appropriate* for the party.

All the warmth of the bath evaporated, replaced by dread. Fi forced herself to look at the outfit strewn on Shane's cot first. Armand had sent a black tailcoat and pants, paired with a porcelain skull mask painted so convincingly Fi might have thought it was actual bone if she hadn't seen the costume before. His guards wore the skull costumes at his masquerade parties so that they didn't stand out in the crowd. Clearly, he didn't think much of her new partner.

Then she looked down at the dress on her bed.

It was a monarch butterfly costume.

The fitted black bodice flowed into a layered skirt of deep red and orange, with black stripes sewn in along the seams. From the back of the bodice jutted a small pair of wings, gauzy burnt-orange cloth wound carefully around a frame of wires. The delicate tips were crafted of copper so fine they seemed to flicker, like the gown might fly away at the slightest touch. A porcelain mask painted orange and black lay on her pillow.

Fi's fingers curled around the butterfly mark, her whole

body trembling. Armand had done this to torment her. His snide little remarks in the glasshouse about *enjoying her travels* and *seeing her parents* had shaken her, but she'd refused to break down in front of him. Not again.

As tears filled her eyes and the costume blurred, she wasn't sure she could keep it back anymore. Fi sat down hard, crumpling the gown in her fists.

Maybe she hadn't changed as much as she thought. She'd come here to use Armand, but she'd still come. She hated him—hated him with a fury that shook her all the way to the bone—and she had refused to bend to his will even after he burned the butterfly into her hand. But maybe he'd still gotten exactly what he wanted. Because as much as she hated him, she had nowhere else to go.

No matter how much she wanted to, even if she longed to bring the whole manor crashing down, this was the only place in the world where Fi didn't have to worry about the Butterfly Curse. That had been part of Armand's plan all along. Her eyes swam with the memory of that day.

FILORE AND ARMAND stood before a great door in the heart of the old house. They'd finally found it—the hidden study they'd been searching for. The door had once been set with three diamond-shaped panels of glass in a starburst pattern, but they were all broken now. Shards of glass cracked under Fi's feet as she held her lantern aloft to get a look inside.

Through the jagged hole, she could see the outline of a desk and a set of shelves, the latter bowing with the weight of ancient books. There would be no jewels or riches in the room beyond. That was the reason this house had been overlooked so many times, and why they weren't racing any other treasure hunters to the prize. But what was in that room was worth ten times any treasure to Filore—the books and notes of one of the most brilliant and infamous scholars of magic who ever lived.

She caught her reflection in a large sliver of glass, her rich black coat flaring over her close-fitted white blouse. Armand was nothing but a shadow behind her, the light glinting off his richly embroidered vest. Filore bounced on the balls of her feet with excitement. The door was locked, but that wouldn't be a problem with the glass panels broken. She reached forward, only to have Armand shoulder her gently out of the way.

"Let me go first," he said, using the hilt of his dagger to knock the last jagged pieces of glass out of the frame. "If we're right about who this study belonged to, it could be dangerous for you."

Filore wanted to argue that it would be dangerous for both of them, but she knew he was right. The bloodline of the dukes of Bellicia had always had a strong resistance to magic and curses. It was why they had been given the lands on the border of Andar and the duties of the Border Master, long ago when the kingdom of Andar was a powerful center of magic.

When he was finished with the glass, Armand threw his monogrammed pocket square over the frame and then reached in to unlock the door. It came free with a snap. Filore bit down on the urge to rush past Armand into the room. Being resistant to magic was certainly a useful skill, especially for a treasure hunter, but Filore had learned by now that most traps weren't magic anyway. This might be the exception, though. If they were right about whose study this had been, it was as old as the kingdom of Andar itself.

As she followed Armand in, the first thing Filore noticed was the strange stone groove carved deep into the wall. She stood on her tiptoes to run a finger through the trench. It came away covered in grease and pale yellow dust.

"Armand—your torch," Filore said, setting her own glass-housed lantern aside. He passed it off to her with a bemused look. Filore tipped the torch into the groove and then backed away. Bright blue fire sprang up, racing around the room in the trench that spiraled up the wall. The fire went out again in seconds, except where it caught a bed of oily rags behind panes of stained glass set high in the wall, throwing the image of orange-and-black butterflies down into the room. A few books were strewn across the desk in the corner, with bookmarks sticking out from between the pages at odd angles, as though they had just been closed moments, rather than centuries, ago. The books were so old she would have to be careful about opening them so they didn't crumble in her hands.

"This could be our greatest find," Filore murmured, staring at the delicate glass butterflies dancing with flames. "It's beautiful."

"It is," Armand agreed, though he wasn't looking at the butterflies. He was looking at her. Filore's breath caught as she turned to find Armand had moved in close. "It's the perfect place for me to ask you this one last time. Filore Nenroa, marry me. Come back to Bellicia with me and be my bride."

His eyes were intense, unwavering in the low light. Filore looked away. "I don't want to have this conversation again," she said. It wasn't the first time he'd asked, or the first time she had turned him down.

"And I don't want to live my life without you," Armand persisted, ducking around her until she had to look at him. "I will give you anything. Access to every ruin in Bellicia, the run of my entire estate. I will finance every expedition, find every book, every ancient map— provide you with everything you could ever want."

Filore bit her lip, almost feeling sorry for him. Her parents had told her to keep clear of treasure hunters, but Armand had been exciting, intoxicating, and when they'd paired up to scour the ancient ruins in the borderlands, every day had been a new high. She'd fallen in love with him and with their wild rides through the dangerous Witches' Jewelry Box, late nights poring over ancient books, and passionate kisses in the secret passages of dusty manors. But that wasn't enough for Armand. He always wanted more. He wanted promises. He wanted to show off his riches—show off Filore at his lavish parties. He wanted someone he could take home to Bellicia when he took over as the Border Master. She'd fallen for Armand, hard, but she had never wanted that life. They had fit together perfectly for just one moment, but that moment was over. So was their partnership. She'd already told him this was their last venture.

"What I want is for you to let me go," Filore said. She pushed past him to get to the desk, running her fingers over the pages curled with age.

She could feel Armand's gaze on her back. He let out a heavy sigh and tossed his bangs out of his face with a gloved hand. "Well, I had to try one last time, didn't I?" He sounded calm, his voice cold.

Filore felt her shoulders relax. In the past, he had insisted he would keep asking until she said yes. Maybe he was finally ready to move on, too.

When she picked up the stack of papers, she could see they were marked with the imprint of a wax seal. She retrieved her lantern, holding it close to the wood and tracing the pattern with her fingertip.

"This is it. I recognize this symbol. It's—"

"The mark of the Wandering Witch," Armand filled in smoothly. "The Lord of the Butterflies."

Filore frowned. How had Armand known that? The symbol was so faded she could barely make it out. Maybe he had found something more obvious? She straightened, marveling once more at the stained-glass butterflies. "Then this is the lost study. We could do it—we could solve the mystery of what happened to the Wandering Witch after he disappeared."

"If only we had the time," Armand murmured. Then he called out, "Filore—catch!"

Why had she turned toward him then? Why hadn't she heard the malice and spite in his voice until it was too late? In the nights that followed, tossing and turning and feverish from the pain, she had relived that moment so many times—the flash of silver, the crackle of fire in the wall, the blistering agony as her fingers closed around the letter opener carved with a stylized swallowtail.

Fi screamed. The curse magic burned into her palm—and burned and burned. Long after she'd dropped it. Long after she'd fallen to her knees. Long after her eyes blurred with tears and the world narrowed to shadows and pain and the wavering shape of Armand looming over her.

"I'm sorry it had to come to this."

"What have you done?" Fi hissed. She was so dizzy the butterfly projections almost looked real, a thousand butterflies dancing across Armand's mocking face.

"You know what that mark means better than anyone."

She did. The letter opener was the dangerous magic relic she had warned Armand to watch out for—the cursed object that had turned the great Lord of the Butterflies into the Wandering Witch. The flesh of her left hand was seared and raw, but that was nothing compared to the agony in her heart. She looked up at Armand through her tears.

"How could you do this to me?" she sobbed, rocking back and forth on her knees.

"I did it for us," Armand said, kneeling down as though he wanted to draw Filore into his arms. She flinched back in horror. "You'll see that one day," he promised, rising and looking down at her with a sneer.

"Bellicia is the only place that curse will have no power. I don't expect you to understand right away, but when you're ready to come home, I'll be waiting for you, Filore. As long as it takes."

THERE WAS A sound in Fi's ears that she didn't recognize. Then she realized she was screaming, screaming out in anger and frustration and hate. Her eardrums were ringing with it. She grabbed handfuls of the butterfly dress and ripped the skirt with all her might, tearing the gauzy fabric right down the seam.

A second later, Shane appeared, wrapped hastily in a towel. She rushed to Fi, grabbing her shoulders and spinning her so they were face-to-face.

"Fi, hey! What happened? Are you all right?" Shane shook her by the shoulders, and Fi choked, pressing a hand over her eyes to hold back tears. Shane swiped at the gob of soap stuck to her ear. "We sure got from *everything's under control* to total breakdown pretty quick."

Fi didn't know if she wanted to laugh hysterically or throw herself into the other girl's arms. She sank to her knees. "I'm sorry, Shane, I . . ."

"Don't apologize," Shane said. She glanced at the dress, then moved to sit next to Fi on the floor, leaning back against the bed. "I have a feeling that whatever I learn about your ex is going to make me so mad that you apologizing will be the last straw and I'll have to kill him."

Shane didn't sound like she was joking. Fi let the savaged dress fall from her fingers as she leaned back, shoulder to shoulder with Shane, not caring that they were both wet and Shane was soapy and she was almost crying.

"That guy gave me a slimy feeling the second we met," Shane went on. "You don't have to tell me everything—I don't expect that. Just tell me: What is it with him and these butterflies?"

Fi didn't know who to trust. Not Armand, certainly, but she didn't trust herself anymore, either. And then there was Briar. She almost wished he were here right now, trying to make her laugh—dropping tea cakes all over Armand's pristine rugs or bemoaning the fact that he hadn't had a nice bath in a hundred years. Or maybe he'd be so flustered, popping in on her in a towel, that he'd be the one blushing for a change. She didn't know if he could appear in Bellicia at all. Briar had said he was all light magic now. Maybe Fi was alone in a way she wasn't used to anymore.

No—*not alone*, she reminded herself. Shane was probably the most trustworthy of them all. If Fi could rely on anyone, it was the brash, hotheaded huntsman for hire.

Slowly, Fi uncurled her left hand, lifting her palm to show Shane the butterfly burned into her skin. The wings seemed to ripple with the movement of her fingers. "It's a curse mark," she said, not sure what else she wanted to reveal. She could just imagine the look of pity in the other girl's eyes. Fi never wanted to be looked at like that, like she was someone to be rescued.

Shane's face swam with a million questions. She fixed Fi with a long look. "He did that to you?" she demanded, her voice tight with rage.

Fi nodded. "So that I'd always have to come back to him.

Since then, the butterfly sort of became his emblem." She gestured helplessly to the butterfly costume on the bed, now crumpled and torn. "I thought I could handle being here, but I can't wear this," she said, wrapping an arm around her knees. Suddenly she felt so cold.

Armand kept his butterflies in cages.

"I won't *let* you wear it," Shane promised. "Luckily, I don't see your name anywhere on this costume, and his little lordship didn't think to send a note, so I guess that makes it mine." Shane stood up fast, seizing the butterfly outfit and shaking it out. "I doubt Armand will get nearly as much pleasure from seeing me in it," she said with a grin. "And you don't have to worry, because I will wear the hell out of this dress. I am going face-first into the refreshments, and I am going to work up a hell of a sweat. When I'm through, no one will ever be able to wear this dress again."

Fi sniffled, giving a watery chuckle. "You know I ripped the skirt."

Shane shrugged. "Just means it'll have a sexy slit up the side."

Fi could do this. She gathered herself, looking up at Shane and clutching at the part of herself that used to be that confident, that unbreakable. She wasn't here because Armand had won. She was here because she had something important to do, and nothing was going to stand in her way.

Closing her eyes, she pictured the white tower of her dreams. She wasn't a captive butterfly. She was the hero on her way to save a prince and a kingdom. Shane would wear the monarch costume, and Fi would wear skull mask and tail-coat, and play the undead. That suited her much better.

19

Fi

ARMAND'S PARTIES WERE exactly as Fi remembered them. If anything, the young lord's tastes had only gotten more extravagant since they'd gone their separate ways.

The grand ballroom, wide as a courtyard, gleamed with polished floors and sweet-smelling peonies in painted vases, the whole room lit by a flourish of alabaster candles in gold chandeliers. Heavy velvet curtains framed balconies that overlooked the gardens, and the heady scent of flowers trailed in with the breeze, mixing with the smell of garlic-roasted eggplant and zucchini blossoms. Heavy casks of fine burgundy wine had been brought up from the cellars and were decanting in wide-mouthed pitchers. One wall was covered in mirrors. Fi watched the dancers spin in the glass. Their reflections made it seem like the room stretched on forever.

Armand had clearly spared no expense for this party, and neither had his guests, who looked to be from all over Darfell and farther. Not a single person was out of costume, though some had pushed their masks up into their hair, while others looked coyly out of thin eyeholes, holding masks on delicate sticks. Women with rubies and pearls braided through their hair danced with men in finely tailored coats, bowing to each other at the waist as the flutes ended each movement. The dance floor was a sea of swirling gowns and slim sheath dresses, most of them in dusky colors. Fi felt like she was staring into an oil painting, watching the colors begin to run as the deep-bodied violins took up the next tune.

Against the dark crowd, Armand stood out like a beacon. Fi had no doubt it was intentional. Her ex wore a white coat and pants trimmed in gold, and the half mask over his face was decorated with a diamond set into the forehead, long plumes of white feathers flashing over his dark hair. All his rings were gold, too. The young lord stood among a flock of admirers, mostly girls. Some looked Fi's age, others a few years older. She watched a girl in a vibrant peacock costume, her curly hair radiant with rhinestones that shone against her brown skin, giggling behind a fan of glistening blue feathers. Armand leaned down to whisper something that made her flush, while a blond girl in a black-and-gold dress offered him a drink from her goblet.

Fi looked away. She had been those girls once, taken with Armand's looks and his charm, unable to see the cruelty that lurked beneath his elegant façade. She could see it now, in a way she hadn't been able to when they were together. The way he preferred to be waited on by his admirers instead of his staff. The way he took pleasure ordering them around and threw out compliments and insults in equal measure to set them at one another's throats. Looking at him, Fi didn't recognize much of the adventurous young man who had been her partner. Maybe he had changed, or maybe he'd always been this way and she just hadn't looked closely enough to see the rot under the gold plating.

Fi forced her gaze elsewhere, seeking out her new partner instead.

Shane was not hard to spot. Armand's party had started late, so he hadn't served a formal meal, only finger foods, but Shane was making the best of it anyway, staked out in front of the serving table and loyally stuffing herself as she'd promised. On the stocky, muscular huntsman, the delicate butterfly dress looked more like a pirate costume, especially with the skirt yanked up and tied off to hide where Fi had ripped it. The gauzy wings were already torn and sagging from the bodice, and the butterfly mask was snarled up in Shane's coiled hair, out of the way as she gulped down another glass of wine. In her other hand, she guarded four skewers of pearl onions and soft white mushrooms, and she was taking bites from two sticks at once. Most of the partygoers were giving her a wide berth.

Fi smiled. She had found a spot against one of the brocade curtains, barely a shadow in her black tailcoat and skull mask. From the way the partygoers moved right past her, she could have been invisible. Still, that was much better than being the center of attention, as she would have been in Armand's handpicked dress. She caught him looking over at her every so often, probably to gauge how well he was humiliating her. She thought about making for the wine, but the sight of Armand and his entourage had soured her stomach.

When the next song ended, the musicians lowered their bows and flutes, taking a brief recess. Armand pushed his goblet into some poor girl's hands and strode over to Fi, an arrogant smile on his lips.

"It's a shame, Filore," he said with mock sadness. "You could have been the envy of every girl at this party, if you'd simply worn what I picked out for you."

"It didn't suit me," Fi said, her jaw tight.

"Are you sure?" Armand asked, tossing his head. The long white feathers rippled. "You might have found you were enjoying yourself, if you'd just give in."

You are not a butterfly, Fi reminded herself. She gave Armand a cold look through the skull mask. "Your line of dance partners is waiting."

"Jealous?" Armand slid the mask up to sit on his forehead, fixing Fi with a stare. "I would send them all away for you. All you have to do is ask."

Fi left her mask in place. "Don't forget about my passes."

Armand's eyes narrowed dangerously. He looked Fi up and down with a sneer, then slid his mask down and sauntered off to his group of admirers. If Fi had been closer to the wall, she would have sagged gratefully against it.

She didn't want to be here. She didn't like playing these games with Armand. Shane had said this felt like a trap about to snap shut around them, but that was wrong. The mechanisms in traps engaged for a reason, and they could be stopped if you figured out how they worked, what made them turn, what set them off.

There was no figuring out Armand.

He hated her or he loved her. He'd done what he had

out of spite or out of some kind of twisted obsession. There was no one answer. Armand could think he loved her and still destroy her. That scared Fi more than anything. Because somewhere, buried deep within her hate and her bitterness, there was still a drop of envy as she watched him stride off with a girl on each arm. That was the part of herself she couldn't trust. Maybe her heart was just as selfish and unreliable as his—maybe all hearts were.

A red cape swirled into her line of vision, blocking Armand completely. Fi looked up as a figure stopped in front of her, a young man in the deep red costume of the infamous thief, the Red Baron. He had a tricornered red hat with a single long feather, and under his high-collared mantle everything he wore was the same deep red, even the gloved hand he held out to her. Like Fi, he wore a mask that covered his entire face, though his was smooth and white, with no features except for the eyeholes. The legendary thief had never been unmasked, after all, disappearing and reappearing in old fables like a ghost. In most of the stories, he was the son of a disgraced house, who made a game of robbing the nobles who had brought his family to ruin.

"May I have the honor?" the young man asked.

"I'm not here to dance," Fi said, looking away.

"Even with me?"

Fi wheeled in surprise at the familiar voice. The figure had lowered his mask just enough to wink at her, a mischievous sparkle in his blue eyes.

It was Briar.

Fi's gaze shot to the row of mirrors. The red figure's reflection stood right next to hers, looking as real as the rest of the guests. Fi grabbed his outstretched hand, pulling him close enough to hiss, "How is this possible? Are you really here?"

She couldn't see Briar's expression under the mask, but she could hear the amusement in his voice. "It's just a little magic. I'm disappointed, Fi—what do you think I was doing all that practicing for?"

"Not for dancing at a party," Fi replied. "Are you okay here? I should warn you, this estate is special—"

Briar held up a red-gloved hand. "I know. That's why it took me so long to get here. And also why I've had to borrow this lovely costume. Only you can see me, Fi," he said, leaning in conspiratorially before stepping back with a flourish. "But everyone can see the clothes!" Briar turned a quick circle, the cape swirling at his heels. "So, come on—dance with the mysterious Red Baron."

"It's incredible," Fi admitted.

Briar looked pleased. "I was going for *dashing*, but I'll take *incredible*."

Fi shook her head. "No. I mean, it's incredible that you know the story of the Red Baron, too. The legend must be well over a hundred years old."

Briar laughed. "That's the part of my daring appearance that intrigues you the most? Placing it historically?"

Fi's cheeks burned, but at least he couldn't tell through the mask. "That shouldn't surprise you by now," she said flatly. "And if being here uses up so much magic, maybe you should disappear and save it for something more important."

"This is important," Briar insisted. His eyes were serious for a second before he tipped his head, and she could imagine his wide smile. "Besides, I've always wanted to be the mysterious stranger at a masked ball. You wouldn't really rob me of the chance to live out one of my fantasies?" He held out his hand again. "Dance with me."

Fi bit her lip, holding back a smile. He was ridiculous—using his magic so frivolously—but was she really any less ridiculous, tucked away in the shadows, letting Armand get to her?

"This is a one-time thing," she told him, laying her hand in Briar's.

Briar winked. "Let's hope not."

His fingers closed over Fi's, and he stepped back onto the dance floor, pulling her along as the music swirled into a crescendo. He kissed the backs of his fingers before entwining them with hers, and it took Fi a second to remember that it was merely a custom, one of the court dance gestures that had fallen out of favor in the last century. It was unexpectedly charming, like dancing with a history book.

Briar kept them at the edge of the dancers, near the long line of mirrors. Fi could barely hear the music over the pounding of her heart as they began to spin.

All of a sudden she could breathe again. Armand's party and the weight of his gaze fell away. In this moment, how could she think about anything except Briar—Briar whose hand was warm through his red glove, Briar whose eyes never left hers as he guided her under the curve of his arms, spinning her in close and out again too fast for the stately music. Briar who didn't know the steps of this dance any better than she did, Fi realized with a start, when he pulled her in again and their feet got tangled, both of them moving left instead of circling in opposite directions. She almost ended up in a backbend when Briar tried to spin her while keeping hold of both hands. Fi came up spluttering, fighting not to laugh.

"Usually when someone asks for a dance, brimming with confidence, they're a little better at it," she said.

Briar shrugged. "Seems like we're evenly matched. Though I admit, I don't have much experience. I was always running off from my dance lessons to get into the spell books." Her heart gave a funny little squeeze as he pulled her close enough to whisper, "Besides, I've always thought some moves were more fun than others."

His grip on Fi's hand changed, and he spun her once and then twice, faster and faster until she was dizzy. She had to steady herself against his chest. As she caught her breath, Briar took his turn, walking a slow circle with her at the center, the tips of their fingers just brushing. The reflection of the skeleton and the Red Baron followed them in the mirrors, Briar's long red cloak swirling in the glass. Fi was so light she couldn't believe she was still standing on the floor instead of floating a few inches above it.

She had danced with Armand at parties like this one—following along with each impeccable step, Armand spinning her in perfect time as all eyes followed them through the hall. It had never left her breathless and glowing. She had to laugh out loud as Briar spun himself under her arm, crunched almost in half to slip through the gap.

There was a time when it would have bothered her that Briar was a bad dancer, when she had this image of love and what it meant, what it looked like, and that image would have been moving gracefully across the floor. But that was never who she had been. She would skip a party in favor of a ruin, she would pass on a dress for something more practical, and she would give up a thousand perfect dances with Armand for the chance to fall all over Briar's feet.

"You really are nothing like a typical prince," Fi said.

"Would you like me better if I were?" Briar asked.

"No," she said. "Not one bit."

Fi could tell he was smiling. As the song began to wind down, Briar pulled her close once more, so close she could feel his heart beating as fast as hers. "I think we deserve a big finish," he said. "I've never dipped anyone, though, so I take no responsibility for what happens."

Fi clutched the shoulders of his coat as she tossed her head back, letting Briar dip her over his arm. The song had simply tapered off—there was no call for a big finish, and yet it felt like the perfect end to their dance. She caught a glimpse of their reflection and had to laugh at the image of the elegant Red Baron dipping a skeleton in a tailcoat.

Briar was laughing, too, so hard that Fi almost did tumble out of his arms. She managed to pull herself up with Briar's help and some clenching stomach muscles. Even after she was upright, Briar kept hold of her hand. They'd drawn a few curious eyes, probably wondering who would dare make a spectacle at one of Armand's glitzy parties. Luckily, no one seemed to have noticed Fi was dancing with a pile of empty clothes. Still, she decided they probably shouldn't draw any more attention. Briar seemed to have the same idea, tugging her toward one of the balconies.

Outside, Fi pushed the skull mask up, enjoying the cool air on her face. The stars seemed especially bright, the way they always were in the mountains. She rested her hands on the metal rail. With Briar beside her, she could almost forget that she was looking out over Bellicia. It had sprinkled early in the evening, and all the trees and flowering bushes glimmered under the hanging lanterns. Even Armand's glasshouse looked like a diamond plucked from a jeweled necklace, bright under the newly risen moon. Fi imagined the butterflies trapped behind those glass walls, their wings closed tight as rosebuds.

White monarchs were rare, an accident of coloring that couldn't be bred on purpose. Which meant every one of them had been captured wild and brought to his glasshouse, some of them probably from these very mountains.

She gripped the railing tighter. She knew she should go back inside—Armand would be looking for her—but she didn't want to. She glanced over at Briar, both his arms folded over the rail. He still wore the red costume but had removed his mask to watch the sky.

"Look," he said, pointing up. "A falling star." The bright tail of light streaked across the darkness, and Fi's breath caught as Briar leaned close. "Now you have to make a wish," he said. "Whatever you want."

He lifted a hand, and the tips of his fingers sparkled like he'd caught the fallen star in his palm. Fi knew what that meant. He was offering to do magic. He still had his playful smile, but there was a dark gleam in his eyes that she'd never seen before. She wondered what Briar's light magic was truly capable of. Could he drop the chandeliers and break all the mirrors, bring Armand's party crashing down around them? Would he burn himself out trying to reduce the manor to rubble and ash? She didn't know, but she had a feeling he would throw caution to the wind and risk it all—his magic and maybe even his life—if she wanted him to. Fi's heart thudded as she looked at the sparkles of white light reflected in Briar's eyes.

She didn't want any of those things.

Small wishes, she could almost hear the Paper Witch's voice whispering. *That's what magic is best for.* Fi turned away, looking out at the shining glasshouse.

"I want to free Armand's butterflies."

"Such a small wish," Briar whispered, but he didn't sound disappointed. The white light disappeared from his fingers as he shot her a smile. "Well, what are we waiting for?"

One moment he was right there, and the next the red cloak whipped around her, the empty costume sagging against the metal rail. The hat landed on the pile with a soft plop.

"Fi!" Briar's voice called from somewhere below her. "Jump!"

Fi leaned out over the balcony to find Briar waiting in the wet grass, dressed in his blue velvet coat once more. His golden hair glowed in the moonlight. He held out his arms.

Fi glanced back toward the party. Then she ripped off the skull mask, dropping it beside the Red Baron costume. She pulled herself over the railing until she was balanced on her toes, leaning back over the drop. It was only the second-story balcony, but it was still high enough to make her hesitate.

"If you drop me . . ."

Briar laughed. "After all our practice?"

Fi squeezed her eyes shut and let go of the railing before she could overthink it. Air rushed around her, and her stomach lurched at the sudden drop.

Then she was in Briar's arms, his body soft and giving under hers. He spun her around to absorb the force before letting her slide to the ground. It wasn't graceful—Fi had a feeling it was never going to be between them—but it was exhilarating.

"Now, to make your wish come true," Briar said.

Fi could hardly believe what she was doing. She felt mesmerized, the same way she had when entranced by the bone spindle, except this time it was all Briar. Side by side, they raced toward the glasshouse. Part of her tried to insist this was a bad idea. But Fi was tired of the games with Armand, tired of trying to anticipate his next ten moves, tired of thinking altogether. She wanted to lose herself in this feeling and give in to this fragile thing—whatever it was—that was blossoming between her and Briar. At least for one night.

They reached the glasshouse breathless and panting. Fi turned the knob and found it unlocked. Who would rob a glasshouse, after all?

She traded a last, giddy look with Briar and then threw the door open. Nothing happened. Fi knew she shouldn't have expected anything more, but her heart lurched just the same. The butterflies probably didn't even realize they were captive. Maybe hers wasn't such a small wish after all.

Then Briar was all around her, his velvet coat flaring as he encircled her with his arms. He wasn't solid anymore, but she could still feel him there, whisper-close and electric on her skin. He lifted a hand, drawing a complex whorl with the tip of his finger, and as he moved, he left a trail of shining golden flecks. The air was suddenly thick with the heady scent of roses.

With a great shimmer of wings, the butterflies streamed out of the glasshouse, following trails of light that Briar painted into the sky. Fi gasped, and Briar laughed in her ear as he raised both hands, conducting a symphony of butterflies all around them. The orange and white-winged monarchs swirled among tiny blue butterflies and yellow ones with rounded wings and so many others. Wingbeats fluttered around her like the heartbeat in her chest, and Fi looked up at Briar, blinded by his radiant smile.

"Like I said, a small wish," Briar whispered.

The butterflies took off all at once, fluttering away in every direction, to leave, to escape, to be free. She hoped they would fly far enough to avoid being caught by Armand again, living instead on the summer wildflowers that carpeted the mountainsides in white and purple blooms. The monarchs might even join the great swarms that migrated to distant countries Fi had never seen. And Fi realized something, as the world swirled with the colors of the swarm.

Maybe she was starting to believe in destiny, just a little.

20

⫸⫷

Shane

SHANE COULDN'T BELIEVE Fi had run off and ditched her at this snob-fest. And with what she deeply suspected was a haunted set of clothes, no less!

The party still whirled around her, but as far as Shane was concerned, the main event was over. She'd basked in the heat of Armand's death glare as his eyes raked over the ruined butterfly costume, she'd scandalized his guests with her appalling manners, and she'd plowed through every dish laid out on the long refreshment table.

Shane tugged off the butterfly mask, grimacing as a few strands of her hair came out with it. She tossed it onto an empty platter sticky from broiled figs. Hopefully, Armand would find it at the end of his stuffy party and be outraged all over again.

A fluttery laugh made Shane's head shoot up. A girl stood beside the wall of mirrors, one hand resting against the glass, her ruby lips curving as her eyes met Shane's across the dance floor. Shane's mouth fell open. It was Red.

Shane thought Red was stunning in her traveler's cloak and well-worn boots, but that was nothing compared with how she looked tonight. Her layered crimson dress bloomed around her like a rose, the silk petals dusted with crushed mica that shimmered every time she moved. A glinting silver mask was pushed up into her waterfall curls. Red raised her eyebrows, as if in a dare, and then spun on her heel, her dress flaring as she disappeared through an arched doorway.

Shane was already moving. She'd thought of Red so many times since their last encounter, there was no chance she'd let the girl slip away from her. She elbowed her way across the room, ignoring the indignant squawk of a woman in a bejeweled headdress. Then she ducked through the archway into a narrow alcove and found a wrought-iron staircase spiraling up into the gloom—and Red, waiting for her.

Red stood with one hand on the iron railing. Unlike the glittering party at her back, the stairway was lit only by a few lanterns hung from molded bronze hooks. There was barely enough light to make out the outline of her silver mask: the sharp, angular face of a wolf.

"Red," Shane breathed. "What are you doing here?" She'd been hoping to run into Red, but the last place she'd expected to see her was hanging around some pompous, puffed-up duke's son.

Red gave her a saucy smile. "Well, for starters, escaping a tragically dull party. Care to join me?"

There was nothing Shane wanted more. She followed Red up the narrow stairs, leaving the music and laughter behind. "So, does the Duke of Bellicia have some price-less magic relic you're planning to take off his hands?" she asked. Fi's niggling aside, she would flirt some answers out of Red if she could.

Red leaned toward her, batting her long eyelashes. "If I say yes, will you turn me in?"

"To Armand Bellicia?" Shane snorted. She'd go ten more rounds with the Witch Hunters before she'd do that guy any favors.

Red laughed like she knew what Shane was thinking. "No need to worry. It's a person I'm looking for this time. He's a hard one to pin down, but I think I know who he's been traveling with." She gave a playful shrug. "Still, it's good to know that if I did find something I wanted, you'd look the other way."

"Not sure I said that," Shane muttered. But she might as well have. Red was intoxicating, and Shane was dangerously sure she'd let her get away with almost anything. She had a feeling Red knew it, too.

As they wound up the spiral stairs, Shane studied the girl in front of her, her sparkling dress hissing over the iron steps. There were a hundred questions she wanted to ask Red—about the tattoo on her neck, about her home in Andar and where she'd learned that sad, beautiful lullaby, the one that still haunted Shane sometimes in the darkest hours of the night. But she had a feeling Red wouldn't appreciate being cornered and interrogated.

Red seemed to glimmer in the wash of light from the low-burning lanterns, her cheeks flushed and her cascade of hair rippling over her bare back. Shane's eyes traced the whorls of darker crimson embroidery sewn into the bodice of Red's dress, which fit her in a way that made Shane conscious of every inch and sliver of air between them.

"It's rude to stare," Red teased her.

Shane swallowed, dragging her gaze up to the girl's face. "Just admiring your costume. You don't see many red wolves."

Red looked delighted. "You don't see many wolves like this at all." She turned away from Shane, pulling the silver mask down over her face before whirling around. "Boo!"

Shane almost slipped off the stair. The mask was more monster than wolf, with ragged chewed ears and a snarling jaw full of crooked teeth. In the unsteady light, Red's brown eyes looked golden, gleaming fiercely out of the cavernous eyeholes.

"I'm surprised you didn't scare people at the party," Shane said.

"Me?" Red reached around Shane's back and wiggled one of the butterfly wings, now horribly bent. "You're one to talk. What's this monstrosity supposed to be?"

Shane grinned, perversely proud of her torn and stained costume. "I'm a party crasher out to destroy a very expensive dress."

Red pushed the mask up into her hair with a smile. "Well, in that case, it's perfect."

The doorway ahead glowed with candlelight. Shane stepped out of the narrow stairwell and found herself on a private balcony overlooking the ballroom. The massive gold chandeliers, each over seven feet high, swung from the ceiling barely an arm's length away. In the wall of gilt mirrors at her back, they became a forest of golden branches, Red's reflection and hers surrounded by guttering candles and gleaming chains. A polished mahogany railing separated them from the long fall to the dance floor.

"Now, this is a much better view."

Shane turned. Red had hopped up to perch on the railing, her feet swinging carelessly as she teetered over the drop.

"Hey, careful!" Shane grabbed Red's elbow, holding her steady. Her skin ignited with the touch, every nerve tingling as Red's fingers slid in between hers.

"I'm perfectly fine," she assured her. "Besides, you look like you could catch me." Her eyes lingered on the muscles of Shane's bare arms, and Shane had to work hard to stop herself from flexing.

She tipped her chin toward Red, feeling suddenly bold. "You know, there's a saying where I come from, that if you meet someone three times by chance, you're fated to be together."

"But then, it was never really chance, was it?" Red said, wrinkling her nose cutely. "It was just fate all along."

"I never thought of it that way," Shane admitted. Red's eyes were still on her, though, so she kept talking, just to see if the girl would keep listening. "It comes from the story of two great warriors, Sigren and Alavar. They were champions of two clans on the brink of war, but the men never met face-to-face until they visited the same Green Shrine, looking for a blessing from the soothsayer. Months later, they went to the same hot spring to prepare their bodies for battle."

"Steamy," Red said, giggling.

"Finally, on the very eve of the battle, they were both

drawn to a hemlock grove. In the starlight, they recognized each other's warrior spirit, and fell in love."

"So what happened then?" Red asked. She had slipped down from the railing, practically into Shane's arms. This close, Shane could have counted the eyelashes brushing her warm cheeks.

"They refused to fight each other and their love stopped the war."

Red scoffed. "Well, now I know it's a fable. No one in real life ever gets off that easy." She tossed the curls off her neck, and at last Shane saw it: the twining snakes inked into her skin. The sealing tattoo, exactly as Fi had described it.

Shane wetted her lips. "Red. That tattoo on your neck—" she began.

Red's hand flew up to cover the mark. "What do you know about it?"

"Nothing," Shane blurted out. "I mean, nothing except what it is. You're a Witch, right? Born in the fallen kingdom?"

Red's eyes flashed in warning. "So what if I am?"

"Then I'd ask if you were in trouble," Shane said. "If you needed help."

"Oh. You're *that* type." Red's laugh was biting. "You think I need someone to sweep in and rescue me from my miserable life, is that it? How very predictable of you." She looked at Shane with something like pity, her face twisted into a scornful smile. "Sorry to disappoint, but I don't need saving. And you don't know anything about me."

Cat quick, she slipped under Shane's arm, retreating— but Shane caught her, fastening her hand around Red's wrist before she could disappear.

"I know you have a beautiful voice," Shane persisted. "I know you're kind—even though you try to hide it. I know red's your favorite color. Okay, that one's more of a guess. But it's my favorite, too," she admitted, thinking not of the dusty coat thrown over her bed, but of the girl right in front of her: a splash of crimson against the dark mirror. She took a step toward Red, slowly as though she were an easily spooked doe. "And I know every time I've run into you, you were traveling alone."

Red shrugged, putting on a smile that didn't reach her eyes. "I find that other people just slow me down. I'm better off on my own." Shane wondered if Red could hear the bitter undercurrent of her own words.

"You know who says that?" Shane squeezed her hand. "Someone who doesn't think they have any other choice."

It was what she'd told herself, over and over, after she fled Steelwight. She'd left on her own, but she'd still been hurt, reeling from the loss of her first love and the even more devastating loss of Shayden—her other half, her lifelong best friend. For the first time, Shane had been truly alone. Wandering through the ports and border towns, navigating the life of a mercenary for hire, she'd pushed the hurt down deep and let it make her hard, until she no longer felt it. But that hardness made it too easy to do things she couldn't justify otherwise.

That was what she saw when she looked at Red. Someone who lived behind a mask because she'd done something she couldn't face. Shane didn't know what it was, but she knew that feeling—that gut-deep, heartsick certainty that nothing you did mattered, because you were too far down a bad road to turn back anyway.

"I was a mercenary when I first came to Darfell. I did a lot of things I regret."

"You?" Red's eyes glittered like chips of ice. "That's hard to believe. I'm sure there are some lines you never crossed."

"Maybe," Shane agreed. "But I know that sometimes, after you make one bad decision, it's easier to make the next one. And soon you don't even think about it anymore, what you're doing. But every bad decision is killing you a little, even if you don't feel it."

Red shook her off and swung around to face the stairs. Shane stared at the silver mask snarled in her hair: a wolf with its head thrown back, howling through ragged jaws. "You really have no idea who you're talking to. Or what I've done."

"But I want to," Shane said. The words felt like lightning on her tongue, leaving her whole body humming. She hadn't meant to blurt it all out like this, but now she couldn't stop. "Tell me anything, Red. Tell me *everything*. Nothing you say will scare me off."

Red shook her head. "What an incredibly naïve thing to say." But her face was soft, the words almost a whisper—like she didn't believe it, but wanted to.

The moment stretched out between them. Red's lips parted, and for one second Shane wondered whether she really was going to tell her everything. Then Red was moving toward her again, one slow step at a time, her skirt slithering over the floor.

"If you really want to help me, there is one thing you can do." Red laid her hand against Shane's shoulder, her fingertips brushing bare skin. "Dance with me. Just for a minute. Like we're the only ones in the world. And then forget about chance and fate and any silly notion of saving me and let this go." Her eyes burned with the light of the candles, guttering out one by one. "Don't fall in love with me, Shane. You'll only get hurt."

If that was true, why was Red the one who looked like she was about to cry?

"Red—"

"Shh." Red pressed a finger to Shane's lips. "Hear that? It's the last song."

The violins were rising, the dancers moving in a dizzy whirl far below them. Shane didn't know the dance, but she didn't know how to say no, either. She reached out and rested her hand on Red's waist, and Red did the same. Then they began to spin, slowly, so close—almost cheek to cheek—that Shane could feel the tingle of their noses barely brushing. Red's eyes never left hers. But she kept her other hand braced over Shane's heart, as if to hold her there—*this close, no closer*. Red breathed out and Shane breathed in and the whole world hung on that moment, the tiny schism of that held breath.

Shane closed her eyes, trying to remember everything, but she knew she was already forgetting. All she'd have left was a blur of scarlet, the feeling of wanting something that was so close, and losing it again.

Shane didn't know how she'd fallen for Red so fast. But she couldn't help it. She'd never felt this pull before, not even toward Kara. With Kara, everything was breathless and sweet and full of potential. Falling for Red was like being caught in a riptide, powerful, irresistible, already dragging her under. But even if Shane was going to drown in this, she couldn't bring herself to pull away.

Far too fast, it was over. Below them, the dancers took their final bows, the musicians rising to applause. Somewhere, a clock was chiming midnight.

"Thanks for the dance." Red lifted her head and brushed a kiss against Shane's cheek, at the corner of her mouth. "Don't follow me."

By the time Shane opened her eyes, Red was already disappearing down the dark stairs, leaving Shane stranded on the balcony with her heart in flames.

Kara had never refused Shane, but she had never loved her, either. Red seemed to feel something for her, but refused her anyway. She reached up to touch the spot where Red's lips had set fire to her cheek.

Don't fall in love with me.

"Too late," Shane murmured, watching the chandeliers go dark.

21

--->>> ---<<<---

Briar Rose

BRIAR MADE HIS way through the darkened room, the only sign of his passage the candles that guttered in his wake. He stopped next to a scroll-crowned bed made up with silk sheets and feather pillows and looked down at the sleeping face of Armand Bellicia.

Briar didn't know what he was doing here, not really. He should go back to Fi, or return to his long sleep in the white tower and work on rebuilding his magic reserves. He'd been using his power recklessly all night, and he was nearly drained again. He hadn't been able to stop himself, though, and the reason was lying in this lavish bed.

For as smart as she was, there were some things about this man that Fi simply could not see—but Briar had been able to tell everything from one look at Armand Bellicia and the way his eyes followed her around the party. He had put on a show for Fi, darting looks at her across the room, trying to lure her, cajole her, even insult her into paying attention to him. Every gesture and cold word and cruel smile was calculated to drive Fi back into his arms. She would stand alone and he would be beloved. She would wear what he had chosen, obey his whims. Though that hadn't turned out the way Armand wanted.

Briar hoped nothing had. He'd never had a chance to play the gallant hero before, but he'd felt like one when he'd taken Fi's hand and spun her across the floor. Not because he'd saved her from Armand, but because Armand didn't matter anymore. He'd made her smile—he'd even made her laugh. Watching Fi's face as she stared up at the night sky, the constellations rearranged in her hazel-green eyes, Briar caught himself thinking that maybe he'd been wrong about love all along. Maybe falling in love wasn't something you dreamed about, or something you left to destiny. Maybe it was something that happened when you were having too much fun to notice.

Like when Fi was busy rolling her eyes and *not* being impressed by Briar's abysmal skill with magic languages.

Or when she flushed and ducked her head under the brim of her wide hat—as though he couldn't see the red all the way to her ears.

Or when she threw him a daring look before plunging into the secret passage at the old manor, giving him a glimpse of her former life as a treasure hunter. He hadn't been able to resist showing off, making sparks fly around them just so he could see what amazement looked like on her face.

Or maybe it was when she leaned back in his arms on the dance floor and laughed, following and leading at the same time. He'd been laughing, too, everything else forgotten, his heart too full for a single wasteful thought. He had been transfixed by her, every moment of the dance and after.

How many times could one person fall in love with another, Briar wondered. And would Fi ever fall for him in return?

The figure in the bed shifted, groaning in his sleep and drawing Briar's attention. Fi didn't want revenge on Armand, she had made that clear. But still he found himself drifting here long after Fi had gone to sleep, slumped into Shane, who'd crawled into her bed by mistake.

Something was burning in him—a rage he couldn't seem to snuff out.

Fi was a private person, and the trust between them was so tenuous. Briar would never risk it by asking what Armand had done. But he had to know. There was one other person who could tell him, and Briar was going to get his answers, even if he had to reach inside of Armand's mind to do it. Walking in dreams was easy, after all this time.

Briar leaned over the bed, gathering magic in his palm. Materializing in the estate was harder than it had been anywhere else, and it had taken him a while to work out that the members of the Bellicia line were themselves resistant to magic. Even now, the closer Briar brought his hand to Armand, the more he could feel something pulling at him like a fierce wind, trying to banish him. He fought the pull, dragging his magic out. Briar's sparking fingertips hovered over Armand's face. He reached down to lay a hand over the man's forehead and then hissed as his magic was sucked away, the sparks vanishing the second he touched him. It left Briar feeling dizzy and hollow, his hand nearly invisible in the dark.

Armand began to toss and moan. "Filore!" he called out in his sleep.

Fury scorched through Briar at that name. Before he even realized what he was doing, he had reached deeper, called on another power, one he had sworn never to use. It was the dark power that flowed into him through his connection to the Spindle Witch. It came to him effortlessly, rising like a seething tide and settling over him like a second skin. Sparks crackled along his fingertips—not pale white anymore, but the deep crimson of roses and blood. Raw power coursed through him, an ocean of dark magic just waiting for his command.

Briar reached down, smoothing his fingers over Armand's face like he was closing the eyes of the dead. A breath of cold wind slithered into the room, and Armand cried out as he was thrust into a nightmare. He would suffer, at least for one night. It was so much less than he deserved.

"Filore!" he called again.

Briar's eyes hardened. Even from the depths of his nightmare, in spite of everything he'd done, he was still dreaming of her. Fi's memory was trapped in Armand Bellicia's mind like a butterfly pinned under glass, and Briar had no way of setting her free. His fingers closed around the man's throat, tight enough to feel him struggle to breathe. He hated hearing her name on Armand's lips.

Then Briar realized his hand had begun to change. His nails had elongated, sharpening to glistening bone claws. He stared at the place where the razor tips rested against the flesh of Armand's throat. He could end Armand Bellicia right here if he wanted to.

And he wanted to.

But it wasn't what Fi wanted.

Hazel eyes flashed through Briar's mind. The memory of Fi surrounded by his light magic, her face bright with wonder. The memory of Fi, offered the chance to do anything, asking for one small wish.

Briar came back to himself at once, horrified by what he'd been contemplating. He stumbled away from the bed, breathing hard.

The Spindle Witch's dark magic was always inside him now, a velvet-soft whisper in the back of his mind. If he let his guard down, that darkness would consume him. He thought he'd gotten his powers under control, but in this moment, looking down on the man who'd tormented Fi, he'd lost it all too easily. He hadn't felt this angry, this sad, this *anything* in a very long time.

Briar shook out his claws until they were fingers again. He could still feel the pull of that dark magic, low and seductive, promising him the power to do anything. But if he used it, he would become a monster far worse than Armand Bellicia. Then he wouldn't deserve Fi's love, even if she offered it to him.

Briar felt himself fading, all of his power exhausted. His gaze fell to the figure in the bed. "I'll never be like you," he promised the sleeping form.

Then he disappeared into the dark, the candle dying in a curl of smoke.

22

Fi

THE LITTLE TOWN at the checkpoint was very different from Armand's estate. By the time they reached the settlement on the border, headquarters for the Border Master and his legions of guards, the mountains were at their backs, the distant peaks gray and ominous under low-hanging clouds. All the buildings were squat except for a few soaring watchtowers, spindly overlooks with long ladders and curious soldiers peering down from the platforms. Fi felt more than a few eyes on them as they rode toward the checkpoint, Armand in the lead.

The border between Andar and Darfell was marked by a high wall, three times as tall as Fi and built of rough-hewn logs wedged between dull blocks of ancient stone. Along the top, it was set with spiked posts and patrolled by soldiers in gray coats trimmed in Bellicia gold. The only entry was a narrow gate flanked by a dozen men wearing the Border Patrol crest, a shield cut into four quadrants by crossed pikes. The iron portcullis, now closed, was sharpened to cruel-looking points. The bars of the gate cut across the landscape beyond, leaving the hulking Forest of Thorns only a black smudge in the distance.

The party was silent as they rode into town. Fi glanced at Armand, who had been tired and out of sorts since coming down for breakfast. Probably up too late entertaining some beautiful girl, Fi decided with a nasty taste in her mouth. Still, he'd insisted on accompanying them to the checkpoint personally, and seemed to be brooding over something the whole ride, barely saying a word. It all gave Fi a bad feeling.

That bad feeling got worse when Armand stopped short of the gate, dismounting and handing off his horse to an attendant. He made no move to reach into his saddlebags or to pull the wooden passes from his pocket. A low roll of thunder made the horses stamp. Fi and Shane dismounted, and Fi handed her reins to her partner, watching Armand warily. He continued to draw out the moment, tossing his short hair with a click of his rings.

"What are we waiting for?" Fi asked finally.

Armand tipped his head, fixing her with a smile. "I thought I'd give you a chance to say goodbye."

Fi steeled herself for whatever game this was. "I have nothing to say to you."

Her biting words had no effect. If anything, Armand only seemed more pleased. "I hope you won't regret that," he said. Then he turned, addressing the Border Guard at the gate. "I have two passes. One for her"—he pointed to Fi—"and one for myself. We'll be crossing into Andar."

A wave of disbelief crashed over Fi. She felt like her

heart had stopped beating, or maybe it was beating too fast. Her pulse was a rush of white noise in her ears.

"What?" Shane roared.

"You gave me your word!" Fi protested.

"And I've kept it," Armand said carelessly. "You asked for two passes, and I've arranged them. I simply decided *I* should be the one to accompany you. You'll be better off, and I'm sure your maidservant can find other employment."

"Listen to me, you slimy, underhanded, double-crossing snake—"

Shane went on, but Fi barely heard her. It was like the world had shrunk down until it was just her and Armand. More than a year had passed. She was no longer the inexperienced girl in the expensive black coat, and he wasn't the partner she trusted with her back. But somehow, Armand had brought her right back to that moment and betrayed her all over again.

"You can't do this," she said.

"Can't I?" Armand asked.

He could, she realized, and she didn't know why she'd expected anything different.

Her temper snapped. Fi shot forward and clenched her hands into his high lace collar. "You're a monster," she spat. "I don't know what I ever saw in you."

Armand laughed. "Don't be dramatic, Filore." He brushed her hands away. "I'm not going to stand here and be insulted. I'm positively famished; breakfast didn't agree with me, but I seem to have worked up an appetite. Enjoy your little tantrum. When you've come to your senses, you can find me in the tavern."

As Armand turned away, Fi realized that in his eyes she might as well be sobbing on her knees. The butterfly mark burned like a live coal on her skin. She'd been a fool then, and she was a fool now. She thought she was using him—that she had it all under control. Maybe that was the biggest lie of all, that she had ever had *any* control.

Fi turned and ran. She couldn't think, couldn't breathe, didn't even care where she was going, as long she got away from here. She could hear Shane calling after her, but she didn't stop. Not when she reached the last cluster of rickety buildings. Not when a low rumble of thunder crackled in the dark clouds.

Fi didn't stop running until she reached the outskirts of town. She threw herself down against the stone wall that ran along the edge of the settlement, the mountain rocks rough against her back as she slid into the grass. Fi locked her arms over her knees.

Something wet touched her cheek. At first she thought she must be crying, even though she felt too numb. Then more drops followed, hitting her arms and the shoulders of her brown jacket. It was raining, just a little, gentle drops falling from the sky like tears. Fi worked the fingerless glove off her hand. She sat with her knees pulled up and stared between her hands.

On her left hand was the butterfly mark, the black lines of the swallowtail seared into her skin. The mark Armand had put there to trap her.

On her right hand was the line of crimson that twisted around her finger like a thread. The mark from the spindle that tied her to Briar.

Are they really any different? Fi wondered.

She wanted to think she had chosen to save Prince Briar Rose, but maybe that wasn't true. Maybe she didn't have any real choices, and she was just being dragged around by curses and magic—like a leaf in a storm, blown one way and then the other. Cold despair curled around her heart as she stared vacantly at her hands.

Suddenly Fi realized the rain wasn't hitting her anymore. She tipped her head back to find Briar had appeared above her, his hands pressed to the wall as he blocked the rain with his body. His coat sagged around him and his hair was slicked to his forehead. He looked down at her sadly, those brilliant blue eyes muted to gray.

"I understand now," he said softly. "Why you don't like me."

Fi's heart flagged. She couldn't do this with him, not now. "Briar, please—"

"I'm serious this time, Fi." His voice hitched on her name, as if he could barely bring himself to say it. All traces of his usual playfulness had vanished. "It's because you had to come with me. I remind you of *him*."

Fi wondered whether it was a tear that splashed onto her palm or whether an errant raindrop had gotten through. She didn't know what Briar understood from her two upturned hands, but she supposed it wasn't hard to guess what she was thinking. He reached down, taking her right hand in his.

"This bond between us," he said, squeezing her fingers tightly. "I know it's not what you were looking for. But it's not a curse—it's destiny."

"You don't know that, Briar," Fi said sharply, jerking her hand away. "You think love is some beautiful dream, but love can make people do terrible things." It felt like the words had been ripped out of her, and they took a chunk of her heart with them.

Briar looked stricken. He drew back and stared at his hands for a long moment. Fi wasn't sure what he saw there, but she had never seen him looking so grim.

"Maybe you're right," he admitted. "I was so sure of everything when we started—that you breaking the sleeping curse meant we were destined to be together. But now . . ." He trailed off and lowered his hands, locking eyes with Fi. Briar breathed out slowly. "I don't want to force this."

Fi blinked. "What?"

Briar dropped to his knees in the dirt and reached for her, brushing a raindrop from her face with the back of his knuckles. "I don't want you to fall in love with me because we're connected by the bone spindle. I believe we're meant for each other, but I know what it's like to have everything in your life decided for you." Briar's pale hand trembled against her cheek, and another image of him flashed through her mind—the lonely prince, entombed in roses. "I don't want that for you."

Fi couldn't move. She couldn't feel the rain anymore, either, the storm barely a distant blur. This pain in her chest—was it because of Briar or Armand? Something was burning inside her, something bright and gentle like a spark of Briar's magic. But it was at war with this cold, numb feeling, Armand's iron grip slowly crushing her heart. It was all mixed up inside of her. She was only sure of two things: the warmth of Briar's touch and the look in his beautiful eyes, so serious and sad.

It felt like the whole world was holding its breath along with her as Briar leaned in, close enough to bump their foreheads together. "I want this, Fi," he whispered. "I want us to happen. I don't want to kiss and go our separate ways. I want you to stay with me in Andar. You mean more to me than I ever could have imagined. You're my hope—the hope of an entire kingdom. But . . ." He swallowed hard, his voice growing hoarse. "If I'm a monster to you, if I make you feel the way *he* does, then . . ."

Briar's hand slid away, leaving her cheek aching. He leaned back on his heels and raked his wet hair out of his eyes.

"Then turn around. Forget Andar—forget this whole thing. We'll go back to the Paper Witch, and I'll use everything I ever learned about Divine Rose magic to find a way to sever our connection."

Fi's mouth fell open in shock. "What about your people?" she stammered. Briar wasn't the only one who was supposed to wake up with that kiss.

Briar shook his head. "It's my kingdom. My problem. I'll find another way."

Fi choked on something lodged in her throat. Briar's eyes were clear and determined. Even if it meant giving up his best chance of saving himself and Andar, he was ready to help her run.

Was that what she wanted?

Part of her was tempted to throw it all away. But that meant throwing him away, too. He wasn't just a prince under a curse. He was Briar—Briar who had a terrible sense of humor, who asked her to dance and then stepped on her feet, who raced through the garden with her, heart wild and unsteady, and set all those butterflies free. Briar who had come to her so many nights, teasing her about bandits and rock slides and caterpillars until he made her smile. Briar who sometimes looked at her like she was the only pinprick of light shining down on him from a very dark sky.

Briar didn't want to possess her like Armand had. He didn't want power over her. He *needed* her.

She had begun to feel something for Briar—something too fragile to put into words, as though if she dared say anything or even hope too loudly in her heart, whatever it was would shatter. But even without putting a name to it, she knew she could never leave him like this, looking so lost.

Fi wasn't sure of so many things. She wasn't sure she'd really chosen to be the hero of Andar. She wasn't sure a heart—any heart at all—could be trusted. But she was sure that Briar was nothing like Armand. He had given her a choice. Now, in this moment, the decision was hers.

Fi took a deep, steadying breath. "You know," she began, lifting one hand to pinch his cheek. It was cool and soft under her fingers. "That's a very irresponsible thing for a prince to say. I thought the fate of your whole kingdom was in my hands."

Briar smiled, relief breaking over his face. "Well, as you may have guessed, I was the youngest and nobody's first choice for the throne."

Fi chuckled. "Let's just say I'm not surprised."

There was one more thing hanging in the air between them: Briar's confession. Fi swallowed.

"Briar, I . . . ," she began, feeling torn.

"Hey. I said I *didn't* want to force this. So don't make that face." Briar gave her a lopsided smile. The pain had vanished from his eyes—he was just Briar again, his voice bright with its usual teasing lilt. "I just wanted you to know how I feel, no expectations. I've sprung this on you, and I know how you feel about surprises. I don't think I'd get the response I want right now."

That made her laugh. She tipped her head back against the cold stone wall, watching Briar as he got to his feet. The sky was bright as a painting behind him, the rainstorm all but blown away.

Briar held out a hand. "You're a pragmatist. So turn it over in your head, look at it from every angle, and then tell me what *you* want. When you're ready."

Fi nodded, not trusting herself to reply. But there was one thing she had to clear up. She put the fingerless glove back on and then grabbed Briar's outstretched hand.

As he pulled her up, she said, "You don't remind me of him. And I never said I don't like you."

Briar's eyes widened. His hand slipped through hers, suddenly insubstantial, and Fi squawked as she was dumped back into the wet dirt, mud splattering all over her arms. She gaped up at Briar in shock. Briar gaped back, a little horrified.

"You're going to take it back now, aren't you?" he said, wincing.

"I should," Fi grumbled. "You'd deserve it." But she was smiling anyway as she held out her hand again, offering him a second chance.

After he pulled her up, Briar held on to her for a long

moment, searching her face. "It will get more dangerous from here," he warned. "As soon as you enter Andar, every step will bring you closer to the cursed castle and the Spindle Witch's power. Last chance to turn around."

"Not going to happen," Fi promised, and felt that spark of magic flicker in her chest when Briar smiled.

She had made her decision. She wanted to be the hero Briar thought she was. Now if she could only get to Andar without giving Armand everything he wanted.

23

❯❯❯—❮❮❮

Shane

SHANE BURST INTO the tavern, throwing the door open so hard it bounced off the wall. She had one mission: Track down that snaky bastard Armand. What she was going to do when she found him, Shane was less sure, but whatever it was, the slimy reptile had it coming.

The room she'd stormed into was nearly empty, except for a handful of travelers with stuffed packs and a few men and women of the Border Guard who turned around to study her. The group playing cards at a back table didn't bother looking up. Shane squinted through the dim afternoon light. The place wasn't exactly spit and polish, but it was a lot cleaner than most taverns she'd been in.

There was no sign of Armand. There was, however, a hard-eyed woman with a longsword in her belt standing guard beside a steep staircase, which was cordoned off with a gold rope. Shane clicked her tongue. She should have known Armand wouldn't be skulking in the common areas of the tavern with the rabble. For the moment, he had managed to slither away.

And she was fresh out of ideas.

Shane bypassed the bar and the craggy bartender—an ex–Border Guard, if her guess was right—and headed for a table in the corner where she could glare a hole into those stairs. Chasing Armand down and beating the passes out of him probably hadn't been a solid plan anyway. They were on his turf, and he knew it, judging by that little show at the gate.

One day, when we cross paths alone in a dark alley, Shane promised, cracking her knuckles.

But that only left her frustrated. She didn't need to beat Armand *one day*—she needed to beat him right now if she wanted to help Fi. Her partner had run off somewhere, and Shane had no idea what she was thinking. Would Fi go with him? Would she leave Shane behind, just like that? They were partners, sure—Shane wouldn't have worn that ridiculous dress for anyone else—but they'd never made any kind of promise. Maybe this was as far as they went. Maybe that *one job* ended here.

Only that felt awful. Shane pressed her forehead down against her knuckles. She hated problems her ax couldn't solve. She thought she'd left this feeling of helplessness behind in Steelwight: the feeling that no matter what she wanted, an ugly future was barreling toward her, and she was powerless to stop it.

SHANE BURST THROUGH the door and out onto the castle wall, the wind lashing her in swirls of snow. The cold bit right through her thin tunic, but she was too angry to feel it.

Shayden stood at the battlements, where she knew he'd be. His thick wool kyrtill whipped around him, the long coat and his lash-tied boots glowing in the red morning light as he stared out at the churning winter sea. His cheeks were flushed with the bite of the wind. Below him, the high cliffs plunged down into the black water roiling with mist. He barely glanced at her.

"How could you do that to me?" Shane demanded. "How could you leave me to face Father alone?"

Shayden kept his eyes fixed on the horizon. "I told you nothing would change his mind. But you wouldn't listen. You never do."

How could she? Ever since she had kissed Kara and realized how empty and hollow the rest of her life was going to be, Shane felt like she was a pot that had been slowly coming to heat and was now boiling over. She'd spent all last night pacing at her window, staring at the two bright stars—the Twins, the Lovers—shining through the barren wych elm trees. At dawn, she'd confronted their father.

Standing before him in the Hall of the War Kings, she'd begged him to make Shayden the heir—to let him take her place at the head of the Ragnall clan and marry Kara.

"Shayden cannot be king." Her father looked as

stern as the statues of their ancestors lining the hall, staring out at Shane from eyeless helmets with their weapons held ever at the ready, an army of silent sentinels.

"But why not, Father? You know it should be him!"

"The line of succession has never been broken," her father said coldly. "The title of War King passes to the oldest child without exception. That is the tradition that has kept Rockrimmon strong."

"But I'm not good at it!" Shane ground her fists against her pants, trying to keep her voice below a shout. "Shayden knows the history of every clan, he remembers all the treaties and trading agreements, and he never insults the ambassadors at the feasts—"

Her father flicked a dismissive hand. "He'll make an excellent first minister."

"He would be a better king," Shane growled. "My whole life, you've tried to make me more like him, patient and serious and wise. But Shayden's already those things. You could have your perfect heir if you would just bend one little rule—but you're too stubborn to do it."

"Well, at least we know where you get it from." Her father rose from his knotted oak throne, a clear sign that the conversation was over. But Shane couldn't let it go—not when the ocean was inside of her, this vast angry thing pounding at her breastbone. Not when she remembered Kara's horrible blank expression as Shane's kiss cooled on her lips.

"Shayden is the better choice, for Kara, for all of Rockrimmon! They could even have an heir together," she'd thrown out desperately.

That had been the last straw. "You will carry the next heir, Shane!" her father thundered, slamming his hand down on the arm of the throne. "And Kara will choose a boy from Icefern of the proper bloodline. That is how it has always been done. Do not invent problems where there are none."

He took a slow, ragged breath, pulling himself back from a brink that only Shane ever pushed him to.

"Your mother died bringing you into this world. I will not let you dishonor that sacrifice with your self-ishness." Her father had transformed into a king again, hard and unyielding. "You were born to be a War King, Shane. If you're not that, you're nothing."

Those were the words that had driven her out of the hall, into the snow, so angry she had to fight to get a breath.

Maybe she'd known it was useless. But she'd expected Shayden to be right beside her, shoulder to shoulder. Not standing alone on the wall beneath the watchtower, staring out at the harbor like he'd already given up.

Shane moved toward him, her footsteps crunching in the hard crust of snow. "You have to talk to him. You and Kara together. With pressure from Icefern, maybe Father would change the line of succession—"

"It'll never happen," Shayden said. So sure, so resigned. Shane wanted to punch that solemn, brooding look off his face.

"And you're okay with that?" Shane grabbed his coat and yanked him around to face her. "Damn it, Shayden—fight for something, for once in your life. I'm doing this for you."

"And I'm doing it for you!" Shayden shouted back. The words echoed off the cliffs and the icy walls, repeating a thousandfold. Shayden squeezed his eyes shut, his breath coming too fast. "You're the heir, Shane. You were born for the throne—and for Kara. What I want doesn't change anything."

Shane's hand fell away. "You're wrong, Shayden. It changes *everything*," she insisted, her voice raw. "Because I can't live with this—not when I know how you feel."

"You won't have to," Shayden promised, bowing his head. "At least not for much longer." For a moment, he didn't say anything else, silent as the statues of the old kings in the hall. Then he let out a breath. "Father's received a betrothal offer for me—from Nika, second daughter of the War King of Blacksquall. I'm leaving after the solstice festival."

"What?" Shane's mind whirled. Shayden, leaving Rockrimmon? It didn't make sense. "That's impossible. Blacksquall is tiny, and Nika's not even the heir. Father would never accept—"

"I asked him to. It'll be better. For all of us."

Shayden raised his head. At last Shane could see all the things he'd been hiding—the hurt and the longing, and the deep-down secret wish he would never speak out loud: that he had been born three and a half minutes ahead of her.

Three and a half minutes. That was the difference between a world where Shane was forced to take the throne, trapped in a loveless match with Kara, and one where Shayden inherited the crown he seemed born to wear and ruled with the girl he loved at his side. How could that possibly be the right path? How could the roles they were meant for be so wrong for them? And why couldn't her father see it?

Three and a half minutes. That was the difference between a world where everyone got what they wanted, and one where no one did.

"You can't leave."

Her throat felt tight and thick. It hurt to be Kara's second choice, but she'd only started to love Kara. She had loved Shayden forever. Just the thought of a life without him made her feel ripped open and raw.

Shane shook her head. "We promised to rule together, remember? Twin War Kings. What happened to that?"

Shayden's eyes had turned as cold as the gray sea. "We were children," he said simply. "Grow up, Shane."

The words rang in her head as he walked away. She didn't know yet that they were the last words he would ever say to her. All she knew was how helpless she felt, standing there with her teeth clenched against the howling wind—angry, and guilty, and useless. She leaned into the wall, her reddened fingers clenched in the snow.

Maybe it was time to grow up. Shane had always told herself she and Shayden were meant to rule side by side, but the truth was, Shane wasn't meant to be king at all. Maybe if these were different times, when the War Kings still led their armies into great battles like in the old stories. But the eight clans of Steelwight had been at peace for generations.

Shayden was the king Rockrimmon deserved. He had earned the crown every day—devoting himself to the study of the laws, taking Shane's place at the council meetings even though their father always reprimanded him for it, and doing it all without asking for anything in return. But he would never fight for it. Senseless, loyal, self-sacrificing Shayden—he was going to give it all up and disappear. Worse, he was going to do it for her sake.

She wouldn't let it happen. Not over three and a half minutes. She watched the boats plowing through the icy water until they vanished into the mist and wished she could vanish with them.

Maybe she could.

The idea came so fast, it was like it had been inside of her all along, waiting for the right moment to surface. Shane jerked her head up and stared after the boats, remembering something her grandmother had told her long ago, when her hands were still chapped and raw from the firewood ax.

My wildling warrior. The weapon chooses the War King, not the other way around. The ax proves you have the spirit of a wanderer—one who knows the right road and takes it, no matter what they have to leave behind.

Shayden had said there was nothing she could do. But he was wrong. She could leave—first, right now, tonight— before the solstice festival. Her father would be forced to disown her, and Shayden would become the heir. With that one choice, she could set everything right.

A great weight seemed to fall away from her. Suddenly the world came alive again—the salt and sea air, the wild winter wind that seemed to sing of places unseen, beyond what she had ever imagined. A place where she could be herself.

It hurt to think of leaving her family. It would hurt Shayden, too. But she knew, all the way down in her bones, that it was right. Shayden would get the crown and Kara. And Shane would get something she wanted, too: her freedom.

Her father had said she was nothing if she wasn't a War King. But her father was wrong about a lot of things, and Shane was willing to bet this was one of them.

SO SHE'D SAILED away from Steelwight, set out to forge her own path. She hadn't given up then, and she wouldn't give up now.

Loud laughter from the card players made Shane's head jerk up. Whoever was winning the game sounded like a jackal with a throat cold. Shane grimaced. There was always some jerk having a good time when you were trying to wallow. The stairs remained irritatingly empty.

Another bark of laughter bounced through the tavern, hoarse and gravelly, almost familiar.

Wait.

Shane shot out of her seat, pounding over to the card table. She took in the game at a glance—poker. A pair of scarred hands swept a pile of money to one side of the table. Shane recognized the winner's pale, leathery face only too well. She ignored the Bellicia guardswoman and the merchant cursing their losses, focusing on the grizzled man with silver hair and an ugly sneer.

"Stoleroy," Shane ground out, glaring into his jackal eyes.

Stoleroy was a treasure hunter—one of the oldest and most successful still alive to brag about it. He sold the magic relics he picked up to the highest bidder, usually Witch Hunters. He and Shane had gotten into it a few times over him selling out information on suspected Witches along with his relics.

"Shane," Stoleroy returned, stacking his silver and copper coins into a precarious tower. It was clearly a low-stakes game, if there was no gold on the table.

"Figures I'd run into scum like you out here in the sticks," Shane said. "Still doing business with those filthy Witch Hunters?"

"Hey, you know I don't pay attention to labels," the man said smoothly. He flicked a silver coin so it spun across the table. "Everybody's money speaks the same language." He brought a hand down, smashing the coin under his palm. "How've you been, Shane? I saw your ugly mug on a wanted poster—or at least, I think it was you."

Shane scowled. "So what? You looking to cash in?" Stoleroy was a shady, money-grubbing bottom-feeder who spent so much time over the border in Witch Hunter territory that Shane was surprised he hadn't been inducted yet. She banged her hip against the edge of the table, relishing the look of annoyance on Stoleroy's face as his piles toppled over.

"Move along. You're ruining my fun," the grizzled man said, shuffling his cards.

Shane licked her lips, an idea slowly forming. Usually, she

put as much space between herself and Stoleroy as possible, but for once, he might be good for something. "One thing first. Do you still have those border passes that keep you so chummy with the Witch Hunters?"

Permanent border passes were rarer than gold, and Stoleroy was one of the few treasure hunters known to have a pair. Shane suspected he'd paid a small fortune in bribes to get his hands on them.

"Just came back from the other side," Stoleroy said by way of an answer. He kicked at his pack under the table. A few fat oranges bulged from the front pouch.

Shane forced herself not to sound too eager. "I see you're still a degenerate gambler, too. Why don't you quit this two-bit ante stuff and make a few wagers with me?"

Stoleroy looked her up and down. "Got any money? You're notoriously broke."

"Flush with treasure, actually," Shane shot back.

She hadn't brought much, of course. She usually left her earnings with the Paper Witch, even though a lot of it seemed to disappear into the pockets of needy Witches and other charity cases while she was out of town. The little pouch of gold in her pack wouldn't last long. She'd have to play at the top of her game.

Stoleroy's look said he knew what she was after. His eyes searched hers as he flicked the cards with a callused thumb, considering. But Shane knew Stoleroy wasn't the type to turn down easy money, especially if he could humiliate someone to get it.

"All right," the man agreed. "I could go another round. Let's see if your game has improved since last time."

Shane made a face. Cards weren't her strong suit and she couldn't bluff worth a damn. She was counting on getting lucky.

"Beat it," she warned the other two players. Then she thumped down onto the woman's empty stool, leaning her elbows on the table. "Now deal."

Two hands in, Shane realized this might not have been a good idea.

Though she broke even on the first round, her second draw had been a whole lot of nothing, while Stoleroy picked up an easy two pair. Half her money was gone with one sweep of his hand. Her whole plan depended on stripping Stoleroy of his gold so she could lure him into gambling with his prized border passes. Another hand like that, and she'd be finished.

She dealt the next hand too roughly and had to reshuffle when the seven of diamonds flipped faceup on the table. The card drew her thoughts to the hidden pocket of her jacket, and the item she'd tucked away in there what felt like ages ago. It wasn't the kind of thing you gambled with, but she might have no choice.

Shane checked her cards. This time she was looking at a pair of queens, spades and hearts, but the other three cards were hearts, too. Should she keep the pair, or go for the flush? She looked over at Stoleroy, who was calmly arranging his cards, his expression carefully bored. A pair might not be enough to beat him.

"Wisdom says you never let go of a lady once you have her," a soft voice breathed in Shane's ear. She jumped an inch off her stool, shocked when she looked up to find a very familiar figure leaning over her.

"Red," she blurted out, surprised. The girl wore another crimson dress, the skirt high enough to reveal heavy black boots with soles almost as thick as Shane's. "I didn't expect to see you again so soon."

Shane honestly hadn't expected to see Red again *at all*, ever. And yet here she was, her perfect smile back in place, acting like nothing had happened between them. Shane wouldn't mind knowing how she pulled that off—all her organs had squeezed up into her throat, which made it a little hard to swallow.

"Well, I didn't expect to see you either, especially not losing your shirt at cards in a place like this." Red's voice was light and amused. "You should listen to me." She nodded down at Shane's hand, adding in a whisper just for her: "Something tells me ladies are your lucky cards."

Shane's stomach flipped, remembering Red's kiss seared into her cheek like a brand. Had she read too much into that moment on the balcony? Maybe that was just Red's idea of a good party—a quick dance, a soul-wrenching conversation, break a few hearts, and call it a night. But even if Shane wanted to be angry, she couldn't forget Red's bittersweet smile as she stood framed against the chandeliers, lying to herself as much as to Shane when she said: *I'm better off on my own.*

Stoleroy cleared his throat loudly, shooting them an impatient look. "I'll take one card," he said. "Unless you've found something better to do. You can forfeit anytime."

Shane turned back to the game, though she let Red stay where she was, draped over her shoulder. For luck. It never hurt to have a beautiful girl on your side, after all—even one you had complicated feelings about. Shane tossed her three random hearts, passing Stoleroy a single card and taking three of her own.

When she flipped up her cards, she could have kissed Red—for a lot of reasons not related to the game at all, but mostly because one more queen had come into her hand. She could feel Red smirking as they placed final bets. Shane pushed the rest of her gold into the pot.

"Three of a kind," she declared, throwing down the queens.

Stoleroy chuckled, shaking his head. "You have a good eye for women, Shane," he said, "but no eye at all for cards. Full house." He laid his jacks over fours on the table.

Shane cursed. Luck wasn't supposed to desert people at times like this! Then again, her luck only ever seemed to get good at the last possible moment, and she wasn't down to her pocket lint yet.

"Too bad," Red cooed.

"Tough luck, upstart," Stoleroy said. He pulled her gold across the table.

"Wait!" Shane's hand shot out. "One last bet."

They had an audience now, a few of the other patrons peering at them with interest. Stoleroy looked smug. "I don't know if it would be fair to take any more of your gold."

Shane scoffed. "Well, good—because I've got something more valuable than gold, and I want something of equal value from you."

Shane dug into her coat pocket. Then she pulled out her ace in the hole: a crown of pink diamonds set in a delicate silver frame. The same crown she'd picked up seconds before Fi touched the bone spindle and everything went downhill.

It was the one piece of treasure she couldn't bring herself to leave behind.

A gasp went up from the bar. Even Red seemed surprised, her arms suddenly tense against Shane's shoulders.

"Last hand, winner takes all," Shane said. "My crown for your border passes and all my gold back."

It was a desperate move. So what? She was desperate. She'd seen the horror on Fi's face in the moment Armand turned on them, and she wasn't much of a partner if she couldn't do something about it.

Stoleroy balked, one hand pressed to his pocket. "These passes are worth a fortune!"

"So's this crown, and you know it."

"One treasure, no matter how priceless, isn't worth giving up my whole business," Stoleroy grumbled. Then his greedy eyes slid to the crown. "But why not?" he said finally, reaching for the cards. "I'm feeling lucky."

Shane watched Stoleroy shuffle and then flick the cards out until they each had five. Shane studied her hand, feeling a shiver of excitement. She had two pair already, kings over jacks. It was the kind of hand that was going to get her those border passes.

"Just one," Shane said confidently, pushing a six across the table.

"You must have finally got some cards worth keeping," Stoleroy said, looking obnoxiously confident for someone who had declared he was going to take three cards.

Without warning, Red dropped into Shane's lap, perching on her knee and winding an arm around her neck to speak directly in her ear.

"He's not lucky, you know. He's cheating."

"What?" Shane snapped. Surely even Stoleroy wouldn't be so brazen as to cheat in the Border Guards' local tavern.

Red's laugh was warm against her neck. "He's got cards up his sleeve. Watch."

Sure enough, as Shane watched, Stoleroy carefully dealt himself three cards from the top of the deck and then surreptitiously slipped them into his lap, trading them for the three cards that had been up his sleeve. He was disgustingly good at it, smooth as a pickpocket who could take the rings off your fingers without you even noticing.

"Liars and thieves can always spot other liars and thieves," Red whispered.

Shane was barely listening. She lunged all at once, surging across the table and grabbing Stoleroy's arm. Red spilled to the floor, squeaking in surprise. The part of Shane that couldn't seem to keep her eyes off Red thought she looked cute like that, spluttering and flustered. The rest of her was too furious to appreciate it.

"Cheating?" she demanded, yanking Stoleroy up so that the hidden cards fell out of his lap. "I oughta wring your neck."

"Hey, hey," Stoleroy said, trying to pull away. "It's just a game."

"You've got some nerve, cheating me in a room full of Border Guards," Shane snarled. "I could get you locked up until the rest of your teeth fall out."

Stoleroy scoffed. "You wouldn't do that. It's not your style."

Shane squeezed his arm. "You're right. It's not."

She let him go. A look of satisfaction slithered onto Stoleroy's face. Before he could blink, Shane flipped the table out of her way, gold and cards clattering to the floor. Then she cranked back and punched Stoleroy in the face. His head snapped back as he stumbled over his stool. It left her knuckles smarting like she'd hit a stone wall, but she'd never forget the image of his face twisted out of shape, blood flying from his nose.

Chair legs squealed as the Border Guards jumped to their feet, including the bartender, who came at them armed with a twiggy broom. Shane ducked forward, heaving Stoleroy up over her shoulder and forcing him to stand.

"My good friend here is just a little drunk," she told the bartender. "He smashed his face on the table when he slipped."

The bartender didn't look like he bought it. "Is that what happened?"

Shane threw Stoleroy a glare, but she needn't have bothered. The old treasure hunter didn't want the border authorities in his business any more than Shane did.

"More or less," the man said, dabbing at his nose. He let Shane take the rest of his weight as he reached into his pocket and fished out a wineskin, very expensive-looking and at least half full of what smelled of strong spirits. "I over-indulged, but I know when I've had enough." He shot Shane a significant look.

The bartender glanced between them, then retreated to the bar, the other patrons settling down with low murmurs.

Shane let Stoleroy go before his blood stained her coat. The man backed off at once, pinching his nose with a sour expression. "Take your gold," he groused, gesturing at the coins scattered across the floor.

"And the passes," Shane reminded him, holding out her hand.

Stoleroy eyed Shane and the door as though weighing his odds of a getaway. At last he untied the pouch at his waist, pulling out two wooden tokens burned with the Border Master's seal.

"Take it, you crook," he growled, shoving the tokens into Shane's chest.

Shane pushed him back twice as hard. "See, I was gonna let you go, but that was just rude. Leave that wineskin, too—and those oranges!" she added, pointing to the round globes of fruit sticking out of his pack. Stoleroy shot her a disbelieving look, but eventually did as she'd demanded. Shane righted the table and scooped up the gold before any could conveniently end up stuck in his boot.

"If you've finished robbing me blind," Stoleroy muttered, his ugly grin turned into a grimace.

"For today," Shane said, moving in close enough to see the stubble on his face. "But I'm gonna keep tabs on you, Stoleroy, and if I don't like what I find, we're gonna take it behind the tavern next time."

Stoleroy chuckled humorlessly. "You always were a mean one." She almost thought she heard an undercurrent of respect in the words, though, and that made up for the fact that she couldn't look down her nose at someone over a foot taller than she was. Stoleroy nodded sharply before making his way out of the tavern, limping from the wound to his pride.

Shane swept all the gold into her bag, clicking the passes

excitedly before she realized she had forgotten the crown. The only thing left on the ground was the scattered deck of cards. She whirled around in panic.

"Looking for this?" Red asked, spinning the crown around one finger. "It's beautiful—far too precious to be wasted here."

"Then I guess it's a good thing I won."

Red laughed, probably at Shane's definition of *won*—but she had everything she wanted and Stoleroy had left with nothing. She was counting that as a victory.

"Like I said," Red murmured, "always bet on the lady." She held out the crown.

Shane reached out slowly, hesitating as her fingers brushed Red's. There was that same heat, that same pull that drew her in even though she'd been burned so badly the night before. If Shane took the crown, Red would disappear again. She was sure of it.

But Shane wasn't ready to let her go.

Red didn't want her help. Fi didn't believe Red *could* be helped. So why was something inside Shane still refusing to give up on her? Even if Red was a thief. Even if Shane was only going to get hurt.

Then just like that, the answer came to her. She saw herself ungrateful and angry and hurt—tucked into a seedy bar, barely able to believe she deserved help at all after everything she'd done. And the Paper Witch reaching out his hand, his eyes crinkled in a soft smile.

What kind of person walks away from someone in trouble?

Maybe Red had rejected her feelings, but she still needed help—and Shane had it to give.

310

"I have an offer for you," Shane said, locking eyes with Red over the crown. "You really are from Andar, right? So you've been through the wastes."

Red's nose scrunched, like she couldn't quite decide whether she was being tricked into giving something away. "I know the wastes," she said finally.

"Fi and I are trying to reach the Forest of Thorns."

"I figured." Red shrugged, looking unimpressed. "What else would two treasure hunters be doing this close to the border?"

Shane licked her lips. Fi was going to kill her—no, scratch that, Fi was going to absolutely *murder* her for this, but . . . "Could you get us there? Be our guide?"

Red scoffed out a laugh. Then she blinked, her expression morphing. "You're serious?"

Shane didn't think she'd ever been so serious about anything. Every time she cornered Red, the girl lashed out and retreated. She wasn't ready to show Shane her scars, so there was no way for Shane to heal them. Pursuing Red was only going to drive her away. If Shane really wanted to help her— and she did—she needed to give Red what the Paper Witch had given her. A chance for something easier on the conscience. A chance to live her life on her own terms. Wasn't that what had really freed Shane, in the end?

"Come with us," Shane begged.

Emotions Shane couldn't read warred across Red's face. "What's in it for me?"

Shane lifted the crown in Red's hand, holding it between them. "Something too precious to be wasted here."

Red's throat bobbed as she swallowed. Her eyes lingered

on the crown. Shane could tell she was trying to decide something—something much bigger than what the journey through the wastes was worth to her. Her eyes snapped to Shane's.

"I'll get you to the Forest of Thorns," Red said at last. "But it doesn't change anything I said last night."

"I didn't expect it to," Shane agreed, tucking the crown back into her coat. "I'll hold on to this until then."

It wasn't exactly what her heart wanted. But it was the right thing to do, and for now, that would have to be enough.

Shane was distracted by the sound of boots thudding down the stairs. A moment later, her least favorite noble stumbled into the tavern, nearly tripping over his own golden cord.

"What is going on down here?" Armand demanded, his eyes sweeping the tavern and then locking on Shane.

Shane stared back, undaunted. "Nothing. Just taking what I'm owed." She held up the passes, watching as understanding dawned on Armand's face. "I guess Fi doesn't need you after all." Then she grabbed Red's hand, tugging her out the door.

She had a partner to find and a great reversal of fortunes to brag about. At last, her luck was kicking in.

24

Fi

FI DIDN'T KNOW whether she wanted to throw her arms around her partner or strangle her. Maybe a little bit of both.

She had walked back into town resigned to making the rest of the journey alone, only to find Shane waiting for her, triumphantly waving two wooden tokens and grinning wildly. Her partner had managed to procure border passes—by slightly less than upstanding means, from the sound of it, but she'd done it. Unfortunately, Shane had also run into the thief she'd been playing cat and mouse with since Wistbrook, and she'd invited Red along to be their guide. Without even consulting her partner first.

"Shane, what were you thinking?" Fi demanded. She and Shane had made arrangements to stable their horses and now stood leaning against the dusty wall of the inn, waiting for their newest companion to pack up her things and join them. Fi scrubbed a hand over her face. "How could you tell Red about us?"

"I didn't tell her anything she didn't already know," Shane protested. "She just thinks we're treasure hunters heading for the Forest of Thorns."

"And there's nothing suspicious at all about that destination," Fi said sarcastically, her frustration rising. "What if she finds out about Briar? How could you invite some stranger along?"

Shane pushed off the wall, her eyes flinty. "Red is not *some stranger*. She's someone in trouble. Someone who's been through a lot, who just needs somebody to take a chance on her. I needed the same thing once."

"You don't know the first thing about her—" Fi started.

"I know everything I need to."

Shane's eyes were dead serious, making Fi wonder whether more had happened between them at Armand's party than her partner had let on.

"Fine. Say you're right. You really think the best way to help Red is by dragging her through the wastes of Andar with us?" Fi threw up her hands at Shane's stubborn look. "You said she doesn't even want your help!"

"The way I remember it, *you* didn't want my help either," Shane replied.

Fi pulled back, surprised. She'd almost forgotten that. But she wasn't deterred. "This is reckless, even for you. What we're doing is too important to jeopardize over some *crush*. Briar's entire kingdom is on the line—not to mention his life, and ours."

Shane clenched her jaw. "You know, I keep waiting for

this partnership to be a two-way street, but that's not going to happen, is it? It's all about you and Briar, and there's no room for anyone else."

The words felt like a slap. Fi's mouth fell open. "What? No, I—"

"I get it," Shane broke in, her voice tight. "You keep seeing that prince, and you want to save him. But what you have to understand is that I feel the same way about Red." Her eyes sought out Fi's. "I can't walk away from her. I can't."

Whatever anger Fi had still been holding on to drained out of her all at once. She sagged against the wall next to Shane, tipping her head back.

"You're right," she admitted. "I do know what it's like to need help even when you don't want it. And I wouldn't have made it this far without you." They'd come a long way from that moment, at the Paper Witch's tower, when she'd grudgingly agreed she couldn't stop Shane from coming along. "If you think Red should be our guide, then so do I." Fi sighed. "Just keep an eye on her, please."

"I was planning to," Shane promised, bumping their shoulders together. "Thanks, partner."

A few minutes later, Red emerged from the inn. She had traded her dress for a pair of trousers and a long-sleeved tunic, and her hair was pinned up tight. A bandana much like Fi's own hung from her neck. She certainly looked like someone used to traveling in Andar.

"My least favorite thing about the wastes," Red huffed, wrinkling her nose. "It's no place for pretty clothes—unless you like a lot of sand blowing up your skirt."

Fi pushed off the wall, studying her new companion.

"Shane tells me you can guide us through the wastes. You do have a pass, right?"

Shane threw Fi a warning look, which she ignored.

Red didn't seem bothered. "Right here." The girl pulled a wooden token out of her pocket and gave it a little wave. It was a twin to the ones Shane carried, except for one detail. On the back, opposite the Border Master's seal, it was marked not by a house sigil or a trader's mark but by the deep grooves of an X burned into the wood.

That X marked her as no citizen of Darfell at all, but an outsider from the fallen kingdom. A pass like that allowed Red to return to Andar at any time, but not necessarily to come back. Fi found herself thinking again of the tattoo on Red's neck and what kind of a life she must have lived. Maybe Shane was right, and it was Fi who was being selfish, turning her back on someone in trouble. It wasn't a good feeling. As they headed for the gate, Fi resolved to give Red a chance.

When they reached the checkpoint, they showed their passes to the guard, who clicked his polished boots and signaled for the gates to be opened.

Fi shoved her last doubts away as the iron portcullis rose, the Border Guards at the top of the wall straining to turn the winch. No matter what happened from here, she was crossing the border with Shane—her partner—at her side.

Armand stood on the wall with a few of the Border Guards. His narrowed eyes, hard as obsidian, promised this wasn't over—but it was, at least for Fi. She would never go back to Bellicia. She would rescue Briar, and then maybe, if Andar's castle held all the relics and ancient magic she hoped it did, she would even be able to rescue herself. She didn't spare Armand another glance.

The gate finally creaked to a stop. Fi smiled and Shane shoved the wooden tokens into her pocket. Then all three of them walked through the archway, side by side.

Fi shaded her eyes as they got their first good look at the kingdom of Andar.

She had seen it once before, from the back of her mother's horse when she was barely knee high, her wide eyes taking in the dark landscape. She'd asked her mother why they were riding into a nightmare. Ahead, the last steep hills of the mountains dropped into dizzying cliffs and gave way to a great wasteland of black dust, which stretched from the border all the way to the Forest of Thorns. Old histories described Andar as having once been lush and green, the valley glistening with fields of golden grain and meadows of wildflowers. Now, it was a desolate expanse of jagged rocks and bare earth and screaming sandstorms whipped up by the fierce winds.

"Real cheery stuff, this dark magic," Shane muttered.

Red shoved an extra bandana into Shane's chest. "Here."

"What's this for? It's hot enough out here without smothering my neck, too."

"You'll want it later," Red promised.

Fi found herself trading a knowing look with Red as Shane grumbled through fastening the bandana around her neck. Fi was blistering hot in her short brown jacket and her own bandana, but she'd be glad for both if they ended up in one of the dust storms.

"We should head this way first," Red said, pointing northeast into the dunes.

"Are you sure?" Fi squinted into the haze. "I thought the Forest of Thorns was due east."

"It is, but the direct route goes through some of the most dangerous parts of the waste—sinking sand and traps hidden under the dust. I know a safer way." Fi bit her lip, unsure. Red shot her a look. "Isn't the whole point of having a guide to let them lead?"

"It is," Fi relented. "After you, Red."

Traveling the expanse was slow going. Fi's calves ached from hiking through the shifting sands, and she got tired of the view fast: endless fields of ash and the distant specter of the Forest of Thorns, which didn't seem to grow any closer no matter how far they walked. Red altered course a few times, but to Fi's relief, they never seemed to be headed too far in the wrong direction.

They crossed paths with no one. The few traders and treasure hunters who traveled into Andar tended to stick to the cliffs, where the ruins were almost intact, or head north toward the settlements in the mountains. No one had a reason to brave the wasteland anymore. The black dust was even thicker than Fi had expected, forcing her to squint through red, pained eyes. It wasn't long before Shane was holding her bandana desperately to her face.

A few hours in, they passed through the rubble of a long-forgotten town. Skeletal structures rose up suddenly out of the black clouds—remains of half-buried walls and the columns of a walkway with its roof ripped off. Red called a brief halt, resting in the shade and digging out her precious waterskin. Shane yanked off her bandana and slid down a wall.

Fi was tempted to do the same, but she might never

get a chance to see this place again. She wandered into the ruins instead and stopped to gape at a statue of a great marble snake nearly twice her height, its sinuous coils winding upward as though it were climbing into the sky. The snake's head was cleaved down to a stump, but all at once Fi knew exactly where they were: the ruins of the Order of the Rising Rain, a school of Witches devoted to the magic of transformation. Where they hadn't been worn away, the snake's scales were round as pebbles, exactly like the white serpent from Briar's dream. The Snake Witch had wielded the most powerful transformation magic ever known, which was why her statue stood at the heart of the school.

Fi peered around, trying to match the collapsed buildings with what she'd read in history books. Instead of being surrounded by ash and dust, she should have been standing in a courtyard loud with insects and birds and other creatures, some of them Witches in altered form. What Fi had first taken for a vast marble bowl must have been the innermost basin of the enormous fountain that had surrounded the white snake statue. Wider basins, now destroyed, circled the statue in concentric rings, like ripples in a pond. According to old accounts, acolytes of the Rising Rain practiced their magic in the fountain, since water was the medium most closely linked to transformation: ice to water, water to mist, mist to rain. Every Witch of the order started with those basic principles, but from there, they learned to do fantastic things. In winter, it was said they constructed massive towers of pure ice, each one carved with rooms and stairs and tolling ice bells under blinding white cupolas, only to let them melt into roaring waterfalls under the spring sun.

Something cracked under her boot. Fi yanked her foot back, recoiling. It was a length of bone, maybe a rib. Here and there, more dusty-white bones stuck up from the black ash. Some were human, but others looked like the remains of massive beasts—a curved rib as high as an archway and a skull with eye sockets she could have crawled through. They must have been from Witches who died in their altered forms. The larger the transformation, the more magic it took; just trying to assume a giant shape would be enough to burn some Witches out. Fi could only imagine the battle that had taken place here, between the Spindle Witch's army and the Witches of Andar.

As she turned back, Fi thought she caught a glimpse of Briar. He ran his hand sadly along the curve of the stone snake's tail. Then he bowed his head and disappeared.

Fi wrapped her coat tight against the wind. Briar told her he'd never left the castle. This was probably the first time he had ever seen his kingdom, and this was all that was left. It made Fi think of walking through the ashes of her aunt's house, destroyed by the Butterfly Curse.

WHEN NIGHT STARTED to fall, Red led them to another small ghost town to make camp. In the shelter of a stone building that shielded them from the worst of the whipping wind, they took turns coughing up mouthfuls of dust and tending a wispy campfire. Fi had to admit it was handy to have a guide. She had been prepared to navigate the wastes herself, but they would probably have spent their nights huddled under blankets and half buried in the dunes.

Shane dug something out of her pack. "Here," she said, tossing Fi an orange. A second one followed, slipping through Red's surprised hands and plopping into her lap. "Something I picked up in town."

"Give a person a little warning next time," Red protested. Fi got the sense if she wasn't so keen to eat it, the orange would have flown right back into Shane's nose.

"Thanks," Fi said gratefully. She'd forced down some hard jerky and smashed rolls earlier, but hadn't enjoyed it much through the coating of sand in her mouth. The first sliver of orange was sweet and cool on her parched tongue.

Shane fumbled her own orange, glaring up at the sky when her thumb slipped into the belly of the fruit and juice squirted over her hands. "You know, it's supposed to be a full moon tonight—if we could see anything through this dust."

Fi tried to spot the outline of the moon through the clouds. "In Andar, the full moon was known as the Eye of the Witch," she said absently.

"Creepy bunch," Shane muttered.

"The story predates the curse," Fi explained, leaning back on one hand. "There's an old folktale about a Witch locked away in a tower so high it became part of the sky. She looked down on Andar through her one small round window, which she kept lit all through the night."

"I know that story," Red piped up, sitting forward and swallowing a juicy slice of orange. "The way my father told it, it was her parents who locked her up. The girl was born with a wicked power and a cruel heart, and her parents tricked her into the tower and sealed her away. They say if you listen to the wind howling through the eastern canyons, you can still hear her shrieking to get out."

"That's terrible," Shane said through the dripping fruit she'd shoved into her mouth. "What parent would do that?"

Red sniffed. "One doing whatever they had to, to survive, I'd imagine."

Fi watched her closely. She wondered if Red, as a Witch born in Andar, had personal experience with doing what it took to survive.

"There are a lot of versions of that particular story," Fi said. "There's one where the Witch girl learns to suck the magic out of the earth, and eventually her body turns rigid and becomes a black spire. In that version, the moon is her real eye roving over the kingdom."

"Ew!" Shane tossed an orange peel at her.

Fi couldn't help but smile. "In another, she's a little girl who gets tricked into letting a monster inside of her."

"Does *any* version of this story have a happy ending?" Shane wanted to know.

Fi tipped her head back, looking at the hazy miasma where the moon should be. Even though the legend was old enough to have many different ends, the Witch wasn't saved in any of them. "No," she admitted.

"Then your turn is over," Shane said. "Pipe down, both of you, and I'll show you how to tell a real story—with a good ending!" She sat forward, lowering her voice. "Ages ago, in the northern islands, there was a thief who swore he'd steal the moon from the sky, plunging the night into eternal darkness. So he got the longest fishing pole in the village and rowed his rickety boat out into the black sea . . ."

Shane's story was fanciful, full of improbable twists and turns, and she even made Red laugh out loud when the thief tried to use a big round of cheese as bait to fish down the moon. While Fi would usually have been fascinated to hear a folktale from Shane's home kingdom—even a wildly exaggerated one—she couldn't focus. She kept thinking about the Witch in the tower, never saved no matter how many times the story was retold.

Her thoughts slid to Briar, trapped in a tower of his own. She'd never really thought about why he called her his hope, but looking around at this dismal waste, maybe she finally understood. She shuddered at the idea of being trapped here for a hundred years. His story wouldn't end like the Witch in the tower—she'd make sure of it.

Shane's tale wound down with the thief stumbling into a fortune as a great fisherman and maybe marrying a girl melted out of the ice by a moonbeam—Fi really hadn't been paying attention. Then her partner flopped down, punching her pack into a pillow, while Red curled up against the stone wall. Fi slipped into her own blankets and resolved to try to get a little sleep.

THAT NIGHT, BRIAR didn't return to her. Every time she woke, shaken by the howling wind, she saw him sitting on the broken edge of the wall, his gaze fixed on the thorns in the distance.

She wanted to go to him, to sit beside him and lean in until she could rest her shoulder against his—if he was solid and if he would let her. But even if she did, what could she say? She recognized the soul-wrenching grief on his face. Andar was a tomb of dust and waste and bones, and Briar was sitting beside a grave, mourning. She couldn't even imagine a loss of that magnitude. It was the kind of loss she'd spent a year running from.

Fi clenched her hand around the butterfly mark, squeezing until her joints ached. Briar had made his feelings clear and told her to take as long as she needed to decide on her answer. But Fi was afraid no amount of time would be enough. As long as she carried the Butterfly Curse, hers would be a life of loneliness, constantly on the move, unable to call anyplace home. And that would be true of anybody she chose to share it with. How could she even think of bringing that kind of torment down on Briar?

When she finally slept, her dreams were filled with the shadowy specter of the Spindle Witch, her red lips curling behind the black lace of her veil. The drop spindle twisted and whirled, spinning the tangle between her fingers into shimmering golden thread. Briar's normally beautiful white tower was surrounded by black thorns wending up through the roses, like a blight trying to snuff them out. And instead of lying serenely in his bed, Briar was snarled in a web of golden threads, his head tipped back and his limbs held at jarring angles like a twisted marionette.

25

⟫⟫⟫—⟪⟪⟪

Shane

TREKKING THROUGH THE waste didn't get any better the second day. Or the three days after that. In fact, Shane decided, mopping the sweat out of her face, this cursed desert was quickly topping the list of her least favorite places to travel—and that was a long list.

It was hot. It was dusty. The ground was riddled with treacherous sand pits, waiting to send her sliding down the dunes to be buried alive. Worst of all were the dust storms, which forced them to hunker down for hours and wait it out.

And then there was Red.

Traveling with Red was frustrating and wonderful and, at times, pure torture. Her sense of humor was sharp enough to keep up with even Fi, and Shane quickly decided it may have been a mistake to bring the two of them together, since they seemed to spend most of their time laughing at her. But Shane couldn't deny she loved the sound of Red's laugh, and

325

the way Red looked in the light of the low fire, her face rapt with fascination as they traded stories. Shane had told every folktale she could remember and resorted to making up new ones, just so she could keep those beautiful drowsy eyes fixed on her a little longer.

Unlike their fleeting encounters, where Red had seemed mysterious and untouchable, traveling together gave Shane the chance to catch Red in her unguarded moments. Like the first hazy seconds after she woke, rubbing the sleep out of her eyes, or her petulant frustration as she yanked the knots out of her tousled hair. And then there was the way Red stared at her when she thought Shane wasn't looking, her expression full of an emotion Shane couldn't quite read—regret or wistfulness or longing. A feeling that inherently held something back.

In those moments, Shane wanted nothing more than to pull her close and ask Red to trust her one more time. But she'd promised herself she wouldn't cross that line again unless Red invited her over.

Shane shot a quick glance at Red, and then let her gaze slide to Fi, marching along on her right. Her partner looked disgustingly put together, as if it didn't bother her at all to be trekking through the world's largest sand pit. Shane didn't know how Fi managed it. Every time Red shook out her curls, half a desert of sand fell out of her hair. Shane suspected the other half was in her own pants.

Shane hopped on one foot, trying to shake her pant leg out. Only a few maddening grains trickled free. Then her boot crunched into something under the surface of the sand.

Shane yanked her foot up with a yelp. Something hung off her boot—a half-caved-in skull, the teeth of the mangled jaw clamped around her heel. She really hoped it had been an animal.

Red and Fi had stopped to stare at her. Fi's eyebrows were pinched in concern, probably about whether Shane was destroying any precious artifacts. Red looked like she was smothering a laugh.

"I hate this place!" Shane growled, kicking her leg hard. The skull flew off and shattered against a hunk of stone. "I wish I was on the beach in Pisarre. The only place this much sand belongs is right up against an ocean."

Red's eyes sparkled with interest. "I've never seen the ocean," she admitted.

"Really?" Shane shook her head. "Compared to this, it's paradise." She swept out her arm. "Picture this whole waste— but instead of sand, it's deep blue-green water, stretching out as far as you can see. The air is breezy and cool, and the sun is so bright on the water it's like someone threw a fortune in gold and jewels into the waves."

"Of course that's how you'd describe it." Fi's voice was muffled behind her bandana, but her eye roll was crystal clear. Shane ignored her.

"Water as far as you can see?" Red repeated, glancing at Fi for confirmation.

"Hey! What are you looking at her for?" Shane protested. "She doesn't know everything."

"She also didn't tell me a tall tale about people fishing for the moon," Red pointed out. Shane couldn't see her partner's expression, but she suspected it was smug.

"Anyway," Shane ground out. "You can go for a swim or sprawl out in the sand and take a nap. And if you step on something, it's just a starfish or a sand dollar or a seashell—not a bunch of nasty skeletons and dead things!"

Fi cleared her throat and pulled her bandana down. "Technically, those are all the remains of dead sea creatures."

"Whose side are you on?" Shane demanded. Red giggled.

"I just thought—" Fi began. Shane reached out and tugged her partner's bandana firmly back over her mouth.

"Don't listen to her," she told Red. "The ocean is glorious. You have to see it for yourself someday."

"Are you offering to take me?" Red teased.

"Would you let me?" The words were rolling off Shane's tongue before she'd really thought about them.

Red's eyes were suddenly cool, her perfect smile back in place. "Let you take me away, or let you make a promise you can't keep?" she threw back. Then she marched off and left Shane gaping after her.

"She's right," Fi said, clapping a hand on Shane's shoulder. "You have a bad habit of making promises without thinking them through."

Shane snorted. "Says the person benefiting from the last promise I made."

Fi's expression grew troubled. "Listen, Shane. If you want out of our partnership, I'd let you go in a heartbeat."

That was the Fi she knew so well—forever trying to leave her behind for her own good. "Don't make me shove that bandana down your throat," Shane told her with a grin. "You're not getting rid of me that easily."

Fi chuckled. Then they hurried to catch up with Red.

The girl had stopped at the top of a high slope, her gaze fixed on the eastern horizon. The Forest of Thorns loomed before them. Somehow, in the hours they'd been weaving in and out of the dunes, it had gotten a lot closer, the dark mass sharpening to a labyrinth of branches snarled with wicked barbs.

Fi pushed her hair out of her face. "We're closer than I thought."

"We'll be there by nightfall." Red's lips were pressed so tightly together Shane wondered if she'd swallowed a mouthful of bitter dust. "I'll take you to the edge of the forest. After that, you're on your own." Her eyes flicked to Shane, and Shane desperately wished she could read the emotion there. She wondered if, like her, Red wasn't ready for this to end.

"That's more than enough," Fi said. "Thank you, Red. Whatever Shane offered to pay, you more than earned it."

Shane doubted Fi would still feel that way if she knew it was a priceless crown she'd filched from a Witch's ruin. But what Fi didn't know, Shane wouldn't have to get lectured about.

"Come on," she said. "Let's put this waste behind us."

RED WAS RIGHT on the mark. The sun had barely begun to sink when they reached the Forest of Thorns. It towered over them, miles thick and menacing, the massive branches rearing up against the red sky. It reminded Shane of a nest of black snakes with thorns for fangs. As ugly as it was, she found herself looking at it again and again—maybe because she couldn't shake the feeling it was looking back.

They were all on edge, jumping at every scuffed footstep

as they set up camp, their weak fire the only point of light against the rapidly falling dark. Shane wrapped herself in her blanket, and her companions did the same.

Fi's eyes were fixed on the fire. "It's said the survivors of Andar tried to burn the Forest of Thorns many times," she murmured. "But the branches were hard as calcified bone. They blackened, but never caught flame."

"Figures it wouldn't be that easy." Shane craned her head back. In the gloom, the forest was nothing but an ominous smear, but she could see the jagged branches jutting upward, as though they could rip the stars out of the sky.

Red didn't say a word. She just sat hunched over her knees, stirring the embers.

Shane fell asleep clutching her ax and staring into the darkness beneath the thorns.

"PSST. HEY, YOU."

Shane surged awake, grabbing her ax. Red jerked back from where she had been crouched over Shane, one hand shaking her shoulder.

"Red?" Shane asked hoarsely, blinking sleep and dust from her eyes.

"Yes, me." Red extended a single finger and pushed the ax back down into Shane's lap. "And hacking me apart with *that* would make for a terrible goodbye."

Shane's eyes narrowed as she took in Red's pinned-up hair and the pack slung over her shoulder. Her red-lined cloak swirled around her, buffeted by the wind.

"Slinking off in the middle of the night? Aren't you even going to wait for your payment?"

"I wouldn't have woken you if I was *slinking off*." Red put her hands on her hips. "And I already helped myself to my payment." Shane's eyes drifted to her coat, which now lay discarded across her pack, the pockets turned inside out.

"Thief," Shane accused, but she was smiling.

Red didn't smile back. She stood and wrapped her arms around herself, warding off the wind. "I told you this is as far as I go," she said. "But I wanted to give you a chance to turn back before it's too late. Don't go in there." Her gaze cut over to the seething mass of thorns, the firelight glinting in her serious eyes.

"What are you talking about?" Shane got slowly to her feet. The night air seemed to cut right through her.

"Curses are powerful things." Red's voice was low, barely a whisper. Suddenly she reminded Shane of their night in the Bellicia manor, Red's eyes glowing from behind the gruesome wolf mask. "Your partner may have to go in there, but you don't. It's a death sentence."

Shane reeled around, searching out Fi's curled form. Her partner's back was turned, but Shane could see her wispy hair and the gloved hand she'd wrapped around herself. Did Red know something about Fi and the curse mark she carried? Or was the girl just talking about the ancient curse on Andar's prince?

Shane's first instinct was to go on the defensive—put herself between her partner and the threat. But Red didn't look threatening. She looked desperate.

"You're telling me to leave my partner to a death sentence," Shane bit out. "And then what?"

"You could come with me."

Those words knocked the breath out of her. Shane stared at the girl standing before her in the dark. The sparks of the dying fire shone in Red's eyes as she lifted her hand and curled it into Shane's shirt, rearranging Shane's heartbeat with that tiny whisper of a touch.

"Maybe I *am* tired of being alone." Red shook her head, her stray curls blowing across her face. "Maybe you could show me a different way."

Shane was speechless. Red's expression was more vulnerable than she had ever seen it, hopeful and pleading all at once. She got the sense Red hadn't asked anyone for anything in a long time.

Shane didn't want to break it, whatever fragile piece of herself Red was offering. But that didn't change what she had to say.

"Red, I can't go with you." She hated watching those beautiful brown eyes turn dark and guarded again, something inside of Red slamming shut. "Look, after this is over, I'll come find you. I promise."

"You and your promises."

Red stepped forward until the tips of their boots touched, pushed up slightly on her toes, and kissed Shane. It was soft and fleeting, only the lightest brush of her lips, and even as she kissed back, Shane wanted so much more.

It wasn't enough. It would never be enough. Red started to pull away, and Shane seized her arms, taking control and deepening the kiss. She felt Red gasp against her lips, but she held on, kissing Red until she was senseless with it, her skin catching fire everywhere they touched. If this was it—the only kiss they were going to get—Shane would make sure Red never forgot it.

She slid her hand up Red's back, relishing her shiver and pulling her breathlessly close. Red melted into her touch. Her lips parted against Shane's, and then Shane couldn't think at all, her whole body dizzy with the inferno. For a moment there was nothing between them—no secrets, no masks—just Red's lips on hers, one point of blistering heat in a very cold night.

Then Red pulled away. The cold rushed into Shane's suddenly empty arms, and all she could feel was the ache and the longing.

"There is no *after*—not for us," Red whispered.

It hurt to hear the bitterness in Red's voice and to know there was a good chance she was right. If they parted now, Shane might never see Red again, never get to find out what they could have been.

"Last chance," Red offered.

Part of Shane wanted to go with her. But that would mean leaving Fi to face the rest alone, and that, she'd never do.

Somewhere along the way, their partnership had become more than just a favor she was doing for the Paper Witch. Fi was a friend, maybe the first true friend she'd had in a long time. She hadn't come all this way—invited herself along, earned her partner's trust, become the Witch Hunters' most wanted, and made a permanent enemy out of Armand Bellicia—just to walk away now.

"I'm sorry." She took a step back. "But Fi's my partner. I'm not leaving her."

Red clicked her tongue. "I was afraid you'd say that. You're too—"

"Loyal?" Shane filled in, finding a smile. "Brave? Heroic?"

"I was going to say *stubborn* and *pigheaded*." Red turned away. "Goodbye, Shane."

"Take care of yourself, Red."

The girl pinned Shane with a last look over her shoulder. Her red cloak whipped madly in the wind, and for one second it looked like she was framed against gnashing black teeth, the storm already devouring her.

"I always do," Red promised. Then she headed off, swallowed up by the night.

Shane didn't get much sleep after that, tossing and turning until the red light of dawn broke over the horizon. She sat up into the frigid morning air and found Fi already awake, kicking out the ashes of the fire.

"Red left last night," Shane said, rubbing her stiff neck.

"I figured." Fi dug out cold bread and their last orange. She tossed it to Shane. "It's a shame—she was starting to grow on me." She sent Shane a half-apologetic smile, and Shane took it for the olive branch it was.

It didn't take long to choke down their breakfast and pack up. Almost too soon, they stood before the twisted forest.

"You ready?" Fi asked.

It's a death sentence. Red's words rang in her head, but Shane shook them away. She'd made her decision.

"Bring it on," she said, hefting her ax. Then she ducked under the tortured branches and followed Fi into the Forest of Thorns.

26

Fi

THE FOREST OF Thorns was a nightmare. There was nothing green in sight, not one blade of grass or hint of leaves—just the twisting, slithering, spiraling, tearing branches covered in wicked thorns, their roots sunk deep into the black dirt. The whole forest reminded Fi of a fortress, with thick walls and narrow passages and swooping staircases all built of the snarled vines. Here and there, she could see remnants of the original forest, the skeletons of long-dead trees choked by the thorny branches. Elsewhere, the clusters of vines had knotted together into huge, twisted trees of their own, creating a cage of thorns so dense in places it blotted out the sun.

At first the wind whistled eerily at their backs, but farther in, it grew deathly silent. There were no animals or birds calling through the trees, not even any insects crawling along the branches. Fi shivered as she climbed carefully over a branch as thick as an oak tree. The smallest slip could drive one of the spikes through her hand, or her boot.

The thorny branches themselves were dark and hard as granite, unable to be cut even by Shane's ax. They'd tried that only once. Shane had slammed her ax against a vine that blocked their path, but all she managed to do was chip off one brutal thorn, which flew up and scratched her spitefully across the cheek, leaving a jagged red line. After that, they'd given up on cutting their way through.

Fi had pulled out her worn compass, but even with that it was impossible to navigate. They would start off headed in the right direction, the needle pointing sure and steady to the east, only to find their path blocked by walls of thorns. Trying to push through led them into areas as cramped as caves, where the sharp thorns seemed to leap out of the dark and the passages turned around and around until they were hopelessly lost. Fi knew it wasn't rational, but the thorns themselves seemed malicious, and the tips gleamed wickedly when they drew blood.

Briar's body, pulled and twisted like the marionette in her dream, flashed through Fi's mind, along with his warning. *Every step will bring you closer to the cursed castle and the Spindle Witch's power.* Fi felt a little sick.

"I think I've seen this thorn arch before," Shane muttered, looking up at a curve of black spikes. A second later, they came to a crisscross of their own footprints.

"Okay, that's it," Shane declared, flopping down under the arch and kicking up a dark cloud of soil. "Time to call your invisible prince."

"What?" Fi asked.

Shane gave her a look. "Well, we're clearly not getting anywhere on our own. I don't expect a ghost to pull his weight, but he's supposed to be native to these parts, right? So get him out here and make him navigate."

Fi had never actually tried calling for Briar before. She wasn't sure why the thought made her nervous. "Briar?" Fi called, feeling a little foolish. "Briar Rose?"

For a moment nothing happened, and Fi wondered whether she was talking to the empty air. Then there was a great flurry as Shane scrambled out of the dust, swearing herself blue.

"What the—I can see him!" Shane jabbed a finger. "That's him, right? That's the guy?"

Briar had appeared right behind Fi. He popped his head over her shoulder to smile at Shane. "I am indeed the guy," Briar said, waving. "And you can see me because the closer we get to where my body sleeps, the stronger I get. I'm almost at full power now. It's nice to meet you, Fi's partner, Shane."

"Likewise, I think." Shane raked Briar up and down with her gaze. Whatever she found seemed to pass muster. "So . . ." She waved around at the towering thorns. "How do we get through?"

"I don't know," Briar admitted. He drifted closer to one of the coiling branches, running a hand along the trunk. "This whole forest grew after I went to sleep, part of the Spindle Witch's attack on Andar. I don't know the pathways—all I know is that there's definitely a way through."

"Very helpful," Shane grumbled.

Fi shot her partner a look. She moved to stand beside Briar as he rested his finger on the tip of one of the thorns.

"There has to be something we're overlooking," she said. "Can you tell us anything else about this forest? Anything at all?"

Briar squinted up at the branches, his eyes growing distant as though he were picturing the forest from above. "There's a river," he said finally. "I've seen it from my tower window. I think I could point you in the right direction."

"And this river cuts straight to the castle?" Shane asked hopefully.

"Now, that would be handy, wouldn't it?" Briar agreed. "The river winds through the forest, I'm afraid, though it does eventually dead end in a lake in the castle courtyard."

"It's a start," Fi said. "Lead the way."

She set out after Briar, following him through the twisting passages of thorns with her mind whirling. There was no cutting their way through, no navigating by compass; there wasn't even a method of trial and error they could follow like they were in a maze, because there was no guarantee of a direct route. Doubt crept into Fi's heart like a rising chill. The high cage of thorns seemed to be pressing in on her from all sides. She wasn't even sure she could get them back out.

What is the only thing more powerful than magic, Filore?

She could suddenly hear the whisper of her mother's voice, and with it dozens of overlapping memories. Her mother with her long braid tumbling over her shoulder, smiling as Fi puzzled through a spell book written in ink that shifted on the page. Her mother armed with a battered hat and a carefully traced map, standing at the edge of the gorge called the Witches' Jewelry Box. Her mother's voice, clear and sure in the dark, after all their torches guttered and died, snuffed out in the skeletal remains of a crumbling manor. *What is the only thing more powerful than magic?*

But most of all, it was the moment, as a child, when she'd come to her mother clutching her Three Witches storybook and begged to be given magic powers.

"I'll give you something better," her mother promised, kneeling beside her. Filore's eyes widened, the book she'd held out falling to her side. Better than magic?

Lillia smiled. "There is only one thing more powerful than magic, Filore," she said, leaning in like she was imparting some great secret. "This right here." She tapped one soft finger against Filore's forehead. "Knowledge."

Fi's forehead tingled with that phantom touch. Maybe she'd been thinking about this place all wrong. Just because it was magic didn't mean that it didn't follow any rules. She'd almost forgotten that there was a clue to getting to the castle, threaded into the stories of Andar's fall: *The Snake Witch swore to safeguard a path, becoming a great ivory serpent and winding through the Forest of Thorns.*

She needed to approach this place like she would any other ruin. What were the clues? What were the pieces that didn't fit?

Fi tried to remember every tiny scrap she'd ever read about the Snake Witch. She had been able to speak to and command snakes and other beasts, but that was her natural affinity, and there were no creatures here to guide them to the castle. She'd belonged to the school of transformation magic. The bleached body of a dead tree reminded Fi of the massive bones in the wasteland, but she shook the thought away. Transformed or not, there was nothing left alive here. So what had the Snake Witch done?

The river was part of the answer, she was sure, because the river was the piece that didn't fit. As far as she knew, there was only one great river in this part of Andar. It ran from the high mountains past the castle, and all the way to the southern glass lakes. Even if that river had branched off over the years into smaller brooks and streams, they wouldn't be twisted through the Forest of Thorns. This place was dead, as dead as the expanse of black dust. The bone-like branches around her didn't need any water. So what could have cut a channel deep enough to form a river—and for what purpose?

"Fi."

Briar's voice brought her out of her thoughts. She looked up to find him smiling expectantly at her. Fi smiled back, not sure what he wanted.

"Yes?" she asked.

"I'm not holding this forever!" Shane warned.

With a start, Fi realized that her partner had yanked back a vicious tangle of vines and was holding it open so Fi could pass without getting gored. Fi flushed and hurried through the gap. When Shane let go, the branch sprang back with brutal force, and only Shane's lightning reflexes kept her from being sliced across the stomach.

Briar ducked under a last curtain of thorns, and suddenly Fi could breathe again, the spiky walls peeling back as they stepped into a small clearing. Immediately, she could tell what was different. Until now, the forest had been quiet, but the sound of rushing water was all around them here, loud under the thorn canopy. A gully with sharp banks cut through the clearing, roiling with fast-moving water. Something ghostly and white dangled in the branches above her, swaying in a breath of wind. It almost looked like ragged strips of fabric, but she couldn't get a good look at it.

Fi moved to study the river. There was a drop between the sheer bank and the water, about three feet down. She could hear Shane interrogating Briar again, demanding more clues, but Fi ignored them. She set her pack aside and lay down on her stomach, dangling over the edge.

She plunged her hand into the water. Fi had expected it to be ice-cold, like most mountain runoff, but it was as warm as a pool of rainwater. The current was fast, too—so fast Fi had to snatch her hand back or risk being dragged in. She stared down the river as far as she could, until it bent sharply and disappeared into the forest.

The obvious answer was to follow the river. No matter how long it took, if the river eventually arrived at the castle, then so would they. But Fi could already see how impossible that was. There were too many thick brambles along the bank to stick to the shore, and the forest was so dense she hadn't heard the river until they practically stepped into it, so there would be no following it by sound.

Fi briefly wondered if they could build some kind of raft and ride to the castle, but that would probably get them killed faster than anything. Even here in the clearing, the river bristled with thick ropes of thorny vines, some hanging so low that the water licked the dark spikes. A particularly dense and gruesome patch waited just a few feet down the river. Anyone bobbing along in the current would be ripped to pieces.

And yet, the river had to be the answer. Fi sat back on

her heels, tugging at her ear and letting her gaze wander over the thorns. She narrowed her eyes at another cluster of the stringy white threads.

Now that she was looking, there were a lot more of them than she'd first thought, woven through the thorn wall along the riverbank all the way up to the canopy. What was it? Some kind of moss? Unlikely, given how thick it was. It looked more like ropes strung between the vines, each strand speckled with dust.

"I think I see something moving out there," Shane said, pointing. She tossed her pack aside and grabbed her ax.

Fi pushed up to her feet, peering into the shadows. She didn't see anything except a thick knot of thorns. But there was something odd about the shape—the way the branches clustered around something bulbous and round. For a second, she could have sworn the forest was creeping toward them, the long black vines uprooting from the dirt.

Fi put it together at the same moment as eight vines— no, they were legs—thrashed, a creature unfolding from where it had been tucked into a crevice between the thorns. It was a giant spider—which made the white dangling threads around them webbing. The creature oozed out of the shadows, deadly graceful and silent. Its brown-banded legs were spindly, but only compared to the rest of its body. It easily dwarfed all three of them, with sharp pincers clicking under eight beady eyes. Fi's mouth went as dry as the waste.

"What is that thing?" Shane yelled.

"A cave spider," Fi breathed. "I've never seen one before." The giant arachnids mostly inhabited deep caves and crumbled rock fissures in the highest mountains—but they had been found occasionally in ruins that had been undisturbed for decades. And what place had been undisturbed longer than the castle of Andar? "These could be the oldest giant spiders ever discovered," she realized aloud.

Shane shot her a wild-eyed look. "Priorities, Fi!"

The spider's many eyes roved the clearing. Then all at once it flung itself at them, moving faster than Fi ever imagined. Luckily, its target was Briar. The prince threw up his arms, as a reflex, and the spider sailed harmlessly through him, lashing at him with its flailing legs. Its segmented body lurched as it wheeled around, catching itself on the strings of web.

Fi scrambled for the rope at her waist, cursing herself for not having it out already. She had only gotten hold of the metal ring, the rest still caught in her belt, when the spider turned from Briar, launching itself at her instead.

"Watch out!" Shane yelled, shoving her out of the way.

Fi saw a flash of pincers slick with venom as Shane caught those thrashing legs against her ax and flung the creature aside. Fi took a horrified step back, still struggling with her rope.

Her boot met empty air. Time seemed to slow as she stared into Briar's wide blue eyes. Then the sound of the water rushed into her ears as she pitched backward off the bank, straight toward the river and the waiting thorns.

"Fi! No!"

"Fi!"

She could hear Shane and Briar calling her name, but they were too far away to help. Fi had only a second. The moment she hit water and the current rammed her against the thorns, she was dead.

Fi bent back as far as she could, stretching her arms up to turn the fall into a dive. She flung the metal ring on the end of her rope. Half of the cord was still tangled around her belt, but she was counting on that. Fi sucked in a deep breath before she hit the water, and then she dove fast and deep under the thorns. There was a clear patch in the center of the river—if she could just reach it.

She kicked madly as the current snatched her body, the river dragging her along the bottom. Her eyes flew open as her hands slid across the smooth white pebbles that lined the riverbed. The stones were warm, just like the water. Then something yanked on her waist, hard enough to force the air out of her lungs. Her metal ring had caught in one of the thorny branches above, jerking her to a halt as the rope pulled taut.

Fi would have cheered, but she didn't have any breath to spare. She pushed off from the bottom of the river, gripping the rope and dragging herself up. The current was still strong enough to toss her like a twig, and she was nearly smashed against a bristling snarl of thorns as she surfaced. She fumbled with her belt, freeing an extra foot of rope so the current could pull her clear.

It wasn't quite enough. A scream ripped from her lungs as one of the thorns dug into her arm, leaving a jagged gash below the shoulder.

Fi gasped for breath, twisting in the water. She didn't dare try to grab for the any of the dangling vines, and a glance farther down the river showed nothing but more thorns waiting to rip her apart as soon as she let go of the rope. She'd never be able to dive deep enough or hold her breath long enough to get past them. There was no way out—nothing in sight but the thorns and the straining rope and a flash of white under the water, the smooth pebbles glinting at the bottom of the river.

No, not pebbles. *Scales*. Scales she had seen before, etched into the statue of the white snake and shimmering on the serpent in Briar's dream memory.

Just like that, the answer came to her. She knew how to get them through the Forest of Thorns. Everything they needed was right here, in the final resting place of the Snake Witch, who had indeed given her life to make this path.

But how would she tell Shane—if her partner was even still alive? Fi couldn't see anything over the edge of the bank, and the rushing of the river drowned out any sounds of a fight. Shane couldn't be far. If Fi could get out of the water, she'd be able to see her, help her, explain how they could escape . . .

Fi went under again as the current dragged her down. She burst up, sucking in air and giving up any idea of pulling herself to shore. Alone, she was no match for the river. For now, she would have to believe in Shane, and hold on.

27

❯❯❯⟫ ⟪❮❮❮

Shane

SHANE WATCHED IN horror as Fi lost her footing and slipped off the bank, plunging into the river channel. She had one second to pray the thorns wouldn't turn her partner into mulch before the giant spider she had flung off wriggled to its feet, and then Shane only had time for her own problems.

The spider was on top of her in a second. It was brutally fast for something so massive. Shane took a wild swing for the abdomen, but the beast scuttled back against a thorny trunk, clinging to it and striking at Shane with its hairy legs like they were pickaxes.

Beady eyes raked over her. Then its body jerked, and suddenly a rope of strange, pale ooze was flying at her. Webbing—like the stuff in the trees.

Shane threw herself to the side but she wasn't fast enough. The sticky rope caught on her boot, yanking her feet out from under her. The spider shook her like a rag doll as it whipped its torso back and forth and then, with a sickening twist, began drawing its web back in, pulling Shane along with it.

There was a brief flash of blue. Briar appeared next to her, grabbing for her coat. His hand went right through her, confirming that a spirit prince was exactly as useless as Shane had imagined.

Shane's yell was less a battle cry than a string of expletives as she was dragged across the clearing, hurtling toward snapping pincers and rolling black eyes. Her ax tore a groove into the dirt as she slid, until she was close enough to feel the prickly brown hairs of the spider's leg against her neck—and that was *way* too close. Shane drove her boot heel between its fangs.

The creature's head snapped back. She wrestled out of its grip, heaving her ax into the exposed underbelly, and then leapt away as inky blood gushed into the dirt. The spider collapsed onto its back, its legs shriveling up against its abdomen. Shane kicked her way out of the last of the webs, cursing that spider and every other spider that had ever scuttled over the earth. She didn't know how her partner could stand those ugly eight-legged creepy crawlers.

Fi. The thought was like adrenaline straight to her veins. Shane turned and raced for the river, her ax bouncing against her shoulder.

"Fi!" she shouted. She pulled up short of the bank, scrambling backward as loose dirt slipped away from under her feet. Her heart was so far up her throat she was choking on it. Her eyes flashed across the river, searching for anything in the churning water—then she caught sight of the figure clinging to her rope a short distance downstream, bobbing between two patches of thorns. Alive. Shane was so relieved she laughed out loud.

"Fi! Hang on!"

She wasn't sure her partner even heard her over the rush of the current.

"Shane!"

It took her a second to recognize that voice: Briar's voice. Shane turned to find the spirit prince standing in the center of the clearing. Another spider was sliding down a long thread from the canopy, poised above them like a rotting hand. If Briar hadn't shouted, it would have dropped on her without warning.

As much as she wanted Fi out of the water, in truth she was probably safer than Shane right now. Shane studied the spider, her guts churning. For the first time in her life, she was really wishing she carried a pike or a bow—anything that meant she didn't have to get so up close and personal.

"I hope you're better in a fight than you look," she called to Briar.

The prince shook his head. "Not really. Light magic isn't exactly battle magic, but I'll do what I can."

"Comforting."

The spider hit the ground and darted for the river. Almost too late, Shane realized it wasn't after her—it was after Fi, easy prey as she struggled in the water. No way was Shane letting that happen.

As the spider swerved around her, she swung with all her might and cleaved her ax right through its leg, shearing off one hairy segment. The spider whipped around, writhing in fury, and one of its squirming legs caught her in the stomach. Suddenly she was airborne, her ax flying from her hands as she landed hard in the dirt.

Shane hadn't expected something so spindly to hit her that hard. Her ribs ached like someone had put a fist-size hole through her chest. Her ax was halfway across the clearing, stuck fast in the earth.

She definitely had the spider's attention now. It came after her with demonic speed, its movements disjointed from the leg she had hacked away. She scrambled up and raced for the thorns. Without a weapon, she wouldn't last seconds in the clearing.

The spider was almost on her, so close she could taste the venom in the air. The thorns were dead ahead. At the last second, Shane threw herself down and slid under one of the low branches. The cruel points tore at her skin and her red coat, but all she cared about was the spider—legs thrashing, eyes roiling as it loomed over her, its greedy fangs wriggling. Shane rolled onto her back and smashed her foot into the branch, driving the thorns into the spider's head. It lurched back, blinded and squirming. If only she had her ax—

And then suddenly she did, the weapon thrust into her hands by the wispy form of Briar. Shane hadn't known he could do that, but she wasn't questioning it. She wrenched herself up and whipped the ax over her shoulder. Then she brought it down with the full force of her weight, driving the blade deep into the groove between the spider's head and abdomen.

The spider crumpled into a heap, its long hairs quivering with viscous dark blood. The acrid stench of the poison burned in Shane's eyes. She braced herself against the thorns, breathing hard.

Her ribs throbbed under her skin, definitely bruised. Drawing on years of discipline, she pushed the pain into the back of her mind and clambered out of the thicket.

Briar waited outside the thorns. Shane gave him a look. "Fine. Maybe you're not completely useless."

Briar made a face. "Thanks, I think."

There was a splash from the river, followed by a yelp. Shane slung her ax into the braces on her back and ran for the bank with Briar close behind her.

Fi was still in the river, clutching the rope and kicking to keep her head above water. Shane could see what had made the girl cry out. When she first went in, her rope had caught around a thick branch that hung low over the water, but the rope was slowly unraveling, one loop at a time. Shane's heart stopped as the metal ring slipped off one thorn and then caught on a lower one. It wasn't going to hold forever.

"Fi!" Shane yelled. A wall of thorns blocked the bank. Fi was still a good five feet farther down the stream, but her eyes were fixed on Shane, relief clear on her face.

"You're all right!" she shouted.

"You think I'd let some overgrown bug stop me? Hold on, I'm going to get you out of there," Shane finished, though she had no idea how she was going to do that. Except for some nasty webs, this forest was just thorns, thorns, and more killer thorns, and Fi's rope was already spoken for. Maybe the next giant spider could fish her out right before it devoured them.

Briar didn't hesitate, leaping from the bank to a snarled branch and picking his way toward Fi. But Fi was shaking her head, shouting to make herself heard above the roar.

"You don't need to get me out. This is the path to the castle!"

"What are you talking about?"

Fi was soaked and a trickle of blood slithered down one shoulder, but she had that glint in her eyes—the one Shane had come to recognize meant Fi had solved a riddle. "It's the Snake Witch," Fi shouted. *"The river is the Snake Witch!"*

"None of the words you just said make any sense," Shane shot back. Fi's rope was rattling on the thorn, the braided cord fraying fast. It looked like one good shake would yank it free. "Briar, get her out of there!"

"Shane, shut up and listen!" Fi shouted.

They were almost her last words. The vine heaved and the rope snapped free, the silver ring glinting in the air. Fi shrieked and went under. Then a hand shot out and seized the rope—it was Briar, braced on one of the branches, his face twisted with the effort of fighting the current. Shane's heart plunged into her stomach as Fi came up spluttering, blinking water out of her eyes.

"Briar!" Fi called gratefully.

Shane threw herself down on the edge of the high bank, not caring about the dust or the smell of rot or the churning river below her as she locked eyes with her partner.

"Tell me what to do."

Another time, Shane had a feeling Fi would be outright gloating. Luckily, she had other things on her mind. "Load our packs with something heavy," she called.

"And why am I doing this?" Shane asked, but she had already turned away, snatching up their packs. Fi's weighed nothing compared with hers, so she grabbed the sack of gold she had taken off Stoleroy, switching it over.

Fi choked on a mouthful of water as she explained. "You've heard the stories, how the Great Witches gave their lives for Andar? The Snake Witch was said to have turned into a serpent and wound through the Forest of Thorns to make a path. She literally became this river—it just doesn't look like a serpent anymore after a hundred years. You have to believe me!"

The worst part was that Shane did believe her, because Fi didn't sound like somebody whose brain was waterlogged—she sounded like classic, brilliant Fi. Still, her partner had forgotten one little detail.

"Even if you're right, anyone going down this river is going to be shredded by the thorns."

"We don't have forever to debate this," Briar called out. He sounded winded, and Shane suddenly wondered how long he could stay solid before that rope went right through him.

"That's what the packs are for!" Fi explained, talking so fast Shane could barely follow. "The thorns are only on the surface. As long as we stay close to the riverbed, the current will carry us to the castle. You can use that wineskin to breathe. Trust me, Shane!"

"And we're back to trust," Shane groused, digging out the wineskin. It was a shame to have to pour expensive liquor out on the ground, but hey—desperate times. With the liquid gone, the treated leather pouch was sad and deflated. Shane blew into the mouth, filling the wineskin with as much air as she could before corking it. It would give her a few breaths, but that was all.

"Not to rush you, but . . ." Briar's face was ashen with the strain.

"Ready?" Shane called, lifting Fi's pack.

Briar had leaned down so Fi could whisper something in his ear. He nodded.

"Ready," Fi shouted.

Shane swung the bag and released. The heavy pack sailed through the air, slamming into Fi. Her rope ripped out of Briar's hand, and he dove with Fi as she tumbled beneath the surface of the water, disappearing, pack and all. Shane panicked, realizing too late she'd forgotten something important.

She had the wineskin, but how was Fi going to breathe? She was going to have to hope Fi's *trust me* meant she'd figured that part out for herself.

Shane got a good grip on the wineskin and held it to her lips. Then she leapt into the river. The weight of the pack and the current dragged her under in seconds. It was all she could do to keep the wineskin clenched against her mouth as she was buffeted around, slamming against the river channel.

This had better be a really short ride, or she'd have more to worry about than running out of air.

28

~~»»»—◄◄◄~~

Briar Rose

BRIAR WRAPPED HIS arms around Fi, holding her tight as they plunged into the rushing river. The thorns were all around them, malicious spikes tearing into the water. Fi's eyes were squeezed shut, her dark hair a whirl as the current swept them downstream.

He could still hear her frantic words in his ear, seconds before they went under. *Briar, can you breathe for me? Like you did in the lake?*

Briar felt like he was right back in the first moment they met. Fi had been drowning then, too, her arms limp and her eyes closed. In the soft underwater light, she'd looked almost peaceful, beautiful. Briar hadn't hesitated for a moment, kissing her cold lips and breathing into them as they swam toward the surface. His heart had pounded in his ears, because after a hundred years of waiting, he'd finally found her—the girl who would set him free.

He'd known Fi would save him from the sleeping curse, but he hadn't realized all the other ways she would save him. He'd been going mad, all alone in that tower, with nothing to do but practice his magic until it came fast and strong. Even once he was powerful enough to walk outside of his dreams, he was still alone, wandering among the sleeping bodies strewn like corpses through the castle. Camellia was gone, but he knew these other faces—the arms master who had tried to teach him how to use a sword, the scullery maid who was banned from the kitchen for breaking too many dishes, the ancient magistrate who talked as slowly as he moved. Sage, slumped in his throne.

He'd gotten so lonely and desperate he'd even tried to break the sleeping curse himself. It hadn't worked, but a monstrous power had flooded into him for the first time, the same dark magic he'd called on when he'd tried to reach into Armand Bellicia's sleeping mind.

It had nearly destroyed him. If he hadn't been under the protective sleep of the Great Witches, Briar had no doubt that was the moment he would have lost himself to the Spindle Witch forever. Instead, trapped in a dream, he'd just haunted the castle like a terrifying specter. He shied away from every mirror, unable to bear seeing the skeletal claws that had replaced his hands, his whole body turned to disjointed bits of bone and nightmare, becoming less and less human with every drop of dark magic.

It had taken him years to find his way back that first time, and Briar had vowed to never let it go that far again. He'd told himself stories instead, lived on the good memories, and dreamed of a love so bright and strong it could redeem even the darkest parts of him.

A sharp turn dragged them down, raking them across the white pebble scales. Briar's stomach clenched with fear as his magic shuddered and he almost lost his grip on Fi. He locked his arms around her, holding them together with every scrap of power he had. She'd put her life in his hands. What if she was wrong about this river and he couldn't save her? What if he lost her forever? What would stop him from losing himself then?

A snarl of thorns jutted into the river. Briar saw it just in time, pulling Fi in and rolling them so he could take the thorns in the back. He felt the pain for only a moment before they rushed past. He could still feel Fi, though, warm and solid against his chest. They rolled over and over in the water, and Briar closed his eyes, letting himself pretend that they were back on the dance floor, the whole world fading away as they laughed together, breathless from spinning.

A hand tugged at his shoulder. Briar blinked and found Fi looking up at him. Her hazel-green eyes were blinding, the only stable thing in a swirl of white water, blue velvet, dark hair, black thorns. She tugged again, and Briar realized what she needed. Air.

He leaned forward and sealed his lips over Fi's. He tried to put all of himself into the kiss, not only to give her air but to make her understand how important, how precious she had become to him. How much he needed her.

Fi melted into him, meeting his desperation with her

own. He could feel her lips quaking, her fingers in his collar holding on tight.

This was who Briar wanted to be—a light Witch, a boy in a blue velvet coat who could save Fi just like she'd saved him. Fi was his hope, and he would never let her drown.

29

Fi

FI CRAWLED UP on the shore and collapsed into the dirt. She slung the heavy pack aside, sucking in one breath and then another. The river had carried them through the entire Forest of Thorns, whipping them around twists and turns until it spit them out into a small lake. Next to her, she could hear Shane coughing and hacking. Fi had to fight the urge to run her fingers across her lips. Lack of air wasn't the only reason she came up light-headed.

Maybe it had been a trick of the river, but the way Briar had kissed her seemed different. This hadn't just been a soft brush of his rose-petal lips—this time it was desperate and passionate, and deep enough to make her shiver.

It was life or death, Fi reminded herself sternly. *Of course it was intense.*

She sat up from the shallows, searching out Briar. He stood a short distance up the bank with his head tipped back. Fi gasped when she realized what he was looking at.

The castle of Andar rose before them in gleaming white stone, with soaring towers and frosted windows that sparkled like crystal ice. But it was a castle under siege.

The dark brambles from the Forest of Thorns crept over the walls, twisting through the balustrades and coiling around towers. The thorns hadn't grown all the way over the castle spires yet, but they had risen at least that high on all sides, the branches reaching out like skeletal hands that would one day clasp together and complete the cage of thorns. A white haze shimmered around the castle, and black specks circled in the sky far above them. *Crows,* she thought with a twinge.

Unlike the forest, everything wasn't dead here. The soil under Fi's hands was soft and brown. Whip-thin reeds lined the shore of the lake, and she could see scrubby grasses growing between the wide paving stones.

Fi felt like she was looking at two castles at the same time. One was a beautiful white stone structure covered in wildflowers and ringed with climbing roses, shining like it would have under a clear sky. That was the Andar of old—the one described with awe in the travelogues. *Spires so high they touched the clouds and kissed the stars in the night sky. A breathtaking place of learning and laughter and magic.*

And right next to it, like a reflection in a dark mirror, she could see what it would soon become under the curse: a silent castle in a broken kingdom, nothing but a tomb for those trapped in living death within.

Shane grunted, heaving herself out of the water. She dragged her pack and Fi's up the hill, and then came back to haul her partner, too. Once they were on dry land, Shane slumped down next to the packs, clutching her stomach.

"Are you okay?" Fi asked, worried.

Shane scowled. "Fine. Just groaning over my spacey partner, who would sit in the water staring at an old castle until she bled out."

As if it had been waiting for her full attention, a jolt of pain shot down Fi's arm. She had almost forgotten being gored by a thorn. Shane dug into her pack, tossing aside soggy bread and blankets and the old map that had gotten them into this, now thoroughly waterlogged.

Fi gathered her rope and bound it into a tight coil. She hissed as she stripped off the coat and looked down at her bare shoulder. The wound was like a jagged mouth, raw and red. She looked away, slightly sick.

Shane had found what she was looking for: a small glass jar of honey. She removed the top and gave it an experimental sniff.

"I can't believe you're thinking about eating right now," Fi said. All she wanted was to keep her breakfast down.

"Eating honey straight out of the jar? I'm not an animal, you know—I need butter and rolls," Shane muttered, yanking the bandana off her neck. "You can close wounds with honey in a pinch. The only thing we're missing is alcohol." She looked mournfully at her empty wineskin lying among the reeds.

"I thought you said you could use honey on the wound," Fi said.

"The alcohol was for you, so it hurt less."

"That's ridiculous," Fi said, trying to ignore the lurch in her stomach. "I wouldn't want to finish this thing drunk."

"Really?" Shane asked. "I think it sounds perfect for a quest that's supposed to end with a kiss."

Fi chuckled, and then hissed in pain as Shane started in on the wound.

"Hey, you!" Shane barked at Briar, still staring up at the castle. "Make yourself useful. Distract her or something." Before Fi could stop her, she snatched up a small rock and flung it at the prince. It whizzed harmlessly through his insubstantial shoulder.

Briar pressed a hand to his coat. "I guess that was a good moment to be out of magic," he said, a little startled.

Fi forgot the pain in her arm. "You're out of magic already?"

"I may have overtaxed myself a little in the river," Briar admitted. "This close to the castle, I should recover quickly." The playful glimmer returned to his eye as he added, "But rest assured, there's nothing I would rather have spent my magic on."

Fi looked away, wishing he wasn't so good at making her smile.

Shane tied off the bandana, sending one last spike of agony up Fi's arm and sitting back to admire her handiwork. "There. Now your arm won't fall off," she told Fi, scrubbing the honey off her fingers.

"I can see how that might seem funny from your perspective." Fi's shoulder throbbed as she pushed up to her feet, following Shane and Briar up the bank and binding her rope to her belt. They left all their other belongings spread out on the shore. There'd be plenty of time to pick them up later.

"Gee, thanks, Shane," her partner grumbled under her breath. "I really like this arm, and I'm so grateful I'll get to keep it, thanks to your quick thinking."

In spite of everything, Fi felt a smile tugging at her lips. "That doesn't sound like me at all," she said. "And thank you."

Shane looked at her in surprise. "Ah, shut it," she grunted, pushing past Fi, but not before Fi caught a glimpse of her smile.

Fi glanced back to share a knowing look with Briar, but his troubled gaze was still fixed on the castle. Fi bumped his elbow gently, though she knew she would go through him.

"She's kidding, you know. About my arm falling off."

Briar dredged up a smile. "I know. I was just thinking about the horrible, jagged scar you're going to have."

"Thanks for that," Fi said. She really didn't need that image when her stomach was already queasy.

Briar's eyes were teasing again. "I meant it as a compliment. The battle-scarred savior of Andar makes for a good story. If you didn't have at least one scar, what would you brag about?"

"I think I'll leave the bragging to Shane."

As they headed for the castle, they passed under the shadow of the white towers, so close that looking up at them made Fi dizzy. A gentle breeze teased at her hair, and she shivered, glad for the sunshine beating down to dry them off. They picked their way past overgrown gardens and carriage houses draped with ivy. She gazed around in wonder at what must once have been the grand courtyard, an expanse of polished flagstones wide enough to hold a hundred carriages. Around her lay the broken statues of the Three Great

Witches, which had been torn down from their pedestals. A crack ran through the middle of Camellia's serene face.

A great arc of stairs led up to the main door. As they reached the top of the steps, Fi realized that the strange haze that seemed to cover the castle was actually layers of webbing like she'd seen in the forest. The giant spiders had made their nests all over the silent castle, covering it like a shroud. A gauzy curtain of web hung from the awning above the double doors, glittering with thousands of tiny threads strung by spiders of a more usual size.

"I see why Andar's tired of having this Witch on their doorstep," Shane muttered, testing one of the giant ropes of web between her fingers. "Not too sticky, so at least it's not fresh."

A sharp caw made Fi jump. A crow swooped low over their heads, settling in a spindly tree at their backs. Fi fought down a shiver, staring at the creature as it hopped from foot to foot impatiently.

The Spindle Witch had to know they were here, but she hadn't made a move against them, and Fi couldn't figure out why. Unease churned in her stomach. It felt like she was missing something—something important. Had this been too easy, or was she just overthinking it?

"A little help here?" Shane called.

Fi turned away from the crow, helping Shane tear down the curtain of webbing between them and the castle door. The white threads were coarse and tacky, and small brown spiders swarmed over her hands and arms. She felt one crawling up her chin and barely managed to seal her lips before it ended up in her mouth. Fi tossed her head, crushing it against her shoulder. Even Briar looked a little sick, watching the creatures crawl through his insubstantial form.

Shane made a disgusted noise in the back of her throat, flinging spiders left and right. "This is by far the worst thing that's happened to us yet!"

Fi chuckled. "Way to keep it all in perspective," she said, flicking a particularly unfriendly-looking spider off the back of Shane's neck.

Shane jabbed a webby finger at Briar. "Pest control inside this place better be a lot better than outside!" she warned. Then she grabbed one iron handle, and Fi grabbed the other, and together they pushed open the double doors and stepped into the castle.

30

※≫≫──≪≪──

Shane

THE CASTLE OF Andar was as grand as promised. It dwarfed the solid, square-towered castles of Steelwight, all of them fortresses first, with thick walls and arrow slits. Every inch of Andar's castle had been built to impress, from the soaring windows to the rich blue pennants rippling on the walls. Shane squinted up at a gilt ceiling glinting with gold, and Fi let out a little gasp as she turned a slow circle, trying to look at everything at once. The tiny sound echoed a thousandfold in the cavernous entrance hall.

A line of arched windows filled with stained glass threw a tapestry of color across the staircase leading into the heart of the castle. A painting of a blue-eyed woman with long blond hair and a rose crown looked down at them from a golden frame. Shane didn't need Fi to tell her who that was. Even she had heard of Aurora Rose, the first Witch Queen of

Andar, though admittedly Shane had been more interested in the giant ruby set into her crown.

Thankfully, in spite of what they'd had to muck through to get inside, there wasn't a spiderweb or a rat's nest or a speck of dust in sight. The whole place seemed surreal, like a castle out of a dream. Shane rubbed her eyes, fighting a wave of exhaustion. The battle in the Forest of Thorns had really taken it out of her—or maybe it was being tossed around in the river like a rag doll. Or all those spiders.

Shane shuddered. The memory alone made her skin crawl.

Briar was already at the foot of the stairs. He looked more real than ever as he waved to them, excitement dancing in his eyes. "The tower's this way. Follow me."

Shane lagged behind as Briar led them through the branching corridors, under carved archways and past velvet curtains that were still as soft as if they'd been cut yesterday. Fi looked on with wide eyes, clearly fascinated by every tapestry and soupspoon and doorknob in the place. It was all Shane could do to keep up. Her ribs throbbed under her skin. She had felt fine when they first entered the castle, but now her feet were so heavy she could barely lift them.

Which was probably why she almost tripped over the man sleeping outside the banquet hall. The figure wore a blue guardsman's livery and a feathered cap that listed on his head. In one hand, he gripped the hilt of a sword. Shane swore and dodged his outstretched legs, backing into a pillar and nearly taking a blue glass vase down with her.

"Are you okay?" Fi asked, frowning in concern as she steadied the priceless antique.

"Yeah," Shane responded. "Just wasn't watching for other people's feet."

She threw one last look at the peaceful expression on the guard's face as they moved on. He didn't look like a corpse, more like a man who'd been up too late at the tavern and dozed off on his shift, his chest rising and falling in slow breaths. His sword was still polished and sharp. The people in the castle hadn't simply fallen asleep—they'd been frozen in time, the years passing without leaving a mark.

Shane shook herself, stifling a yawn. Fi and Briar had gotten ahead of her again. She could see them at the end of the hallway, Briar walking backward in front of Fi and promising to show her everything, the gardens and the ballroom and especially the library. Another time Shane would have demanded the treasure vault be added to that list. As it was, she could barely keep her eyes open. She knew why Briar wasn't tired—he was technically asleep right now—but why wasn't Fi in equally bad shape?

As they drew closer to the tower, they passed more and more people: guards asleep against their spears, men and women in fine court robes, a scullery maid with a sweet face who was drowsing against a pillar with a tray clutched in her arms. Briar navigated around the sleeping forms without even looking at them.

Shane wasn't a quitter. She forced herself to keep moving, walking blind and starting awake whenever she bumped into corners. But when they reached the base of the tower, she took one look at the long spiral staircase and knew she'd never make it to the top. Her gaze settled on the form of a gray-haired woman sleeping under a window, her head sloped gently against her chest. She looked peaceful and serene.

"It's right up ahead," Briar was saying. His footsteps sounded very far away. Shane put all she had into one last step—then her knees buckled and she went down, sagging back against the wall. She turned her cheek against the cool stone in relief.

"Shane! Shane, get up!"

She could hear Fi calling her, those insistent hands shaking her shoulders—but Shane was tapped out, and no amount of cajoling or bargaining or needling was going to stop the blackness overtaking her vision.

"Sorry, partner. Guess you're going to have to finish this thing without me," Shane slurred, relishing how easy it was to close her eyes. Fi's worried face swam and disappeared.

Her last thought was that maybe this wasn't normal after all, and maybe she should have thought twice before entering a castle under a sleeping curse.

31

Fi

FI TOOK THE steps two at a time, racing up the winding stairs of the white tower. Briar's words rang in her ears, making her climb faster: *It's the sleeping curse.* The sleeping curse had taken Shane, and there was only one way to wake her up.

The pinprick of the spindle had begun to burn on Fi's finger, as though she really were being drawn forward by an invisible thread. It felt like her feet were flying over the stairs. She only slowed down as she neared the top. She could see the shimmering roses through the gap of the doorway, and her heart thudded in her chest.

She'd been so worried about Shane she hadn't stopped to think about what was waiting for her in this tower. Or rather, who.

The door swung open with a creak, and Fi stepped into the scene she'd visited so many times in her dreams. Except this time it was real. Roses curled from every corner of the tower, a jumble of green vines spilling in the arched window and climbing the white walls. A tiny writing desk stood in the corner, brilliant red rose blossoms twining around the wooden legs. The scent of the flowers hung in the air as though it had just rained. Fi turned to the bed. A gauzy canopy of curtains was snagged in the rose thorns, and through the wispy layers of fabric she could just see the figure lying in the center of the white sheets. The same figure that stood beside her.

Prince Briar Rose lay sprawled across the bed in his velvet coat—not rigidly arranged with his hands over his chest, but peaceful, one hand resting beside his cheek as though he'd simply drifted off. His golden hair splayed across the pillow. His cheeks weren't pale, but pink and alive, and she could see his chest rising and falling with each breath. Fi found herself frozen, looking at the sleeping prince of Andar. If she reached out for him, he would stay solid and real, real in a way the Briar who winked in and out of her life couldn't be.

Fi turned to look up at the boy she had come to know, but Briar was already beyond her, his velvet coat flaring as he moved to the bedside. Fi followed more slowly, pushing aside the gently swaying curtains that Briar passed right through. Everything had been leading to this moment, and yet suddenly she was so far from ready. The sleeping figure didn't stir.

Briar turned to look at her. There was something sad about his smile, but she could see the hopefulness there, too, a tiny, fragile hope as tenuous as a held breath. "This is it."

"Yes." Fi swallowed, steeling herself for what she had to do. "And I've made my decision. We kiss . . . and then we go our separate ways." She'd wanted the words to come out cold and sure, but they were barely a whisper.

Briar's eyes widened. A thousand moments flashed across his face, the same moments she was remembering—every time he'd made her laugh, every time his warm hand had caught hers, every time he'd leaned close and she'd felt a shiver on her skin. Briar exhaled slowly, and she watched the heartbreak in his beautiful blue eyes.

"You don't have to do this, Fi," he begged. "I already promised I wouldn't force it. Even if you stay, it doesn't have to be for me. Stay as anything you want—the royal librarian, the official treasure hunter, a friend of the crown. Just *stay*."

Fi shook her head, holding back the stinging feeling at the corner of her eyes. "It's just not meant to be, Briar," she said quietly. Every word cracked her heart, but Fi felt more determined than ever, because she knew she was doing the right thing. She clenched her gloved hand at her side, looking away. "I'm sorry. I know it's not what you wanted to hear."

"Forget that." Briar grabbed her shoulders, turning her to look at him. "Forget everything I've ever said, everything I've ever asked. Look me in the eye and tell me what you really want. Don't turn away from me. Please." He pulled Fi into the hardest, most desperate hug she had ever felt. "I love you," he whispered into her hair. "Stay."

Fi squeezed her eyes shut against the tears. *I love you.* Those words were sweeter and more painful than she'd ever thought they could be. That small spark in her chest that felt like a flicker of Briar's magic ignited into a wildfire, a surge of warmth that rushed through her until she was tingling, until she was sure she must be glowing. She wrapped her arms around his neck so this could be her whole world for a second—Briar's embrace and those words in her ears. She tried to engrave every single detail into her mind: the softness of his coat, the scent of roses, the fast beat of his heart. She already missed him so much, but no matter what, staying was the one thing she could never do.

Somehow, impossibly, Briar had found his way into her heart, past every defense and wall, past every bitter thought and poisoned memory, and he had done it all while making her laugh. She didn't like just one thing about him. She liked everything—that he was hopeless at his magic languages, that he couldn't dance any better than she could, that he still smiled like he was sixteen instead of a hundred and sixteen, and that more than anything he wanted to make her smile, too.

She loved him.

Maybe destiny was real after all, because somehow, as Briar had predicted in the Paper Witch's tower, she'd fallen in love. But that didn't change the fact that she couldn't stay here with him, in this beautiful castle. As long as she was cursed, she'd only burn it to the ground. He'd seen the butterfly mark in the rain. He had to know she was under a curse, but he couldn't know the awful truth of what it did—what it had cost Fi, and what it could cost him.

So many times, Fi had been on the edge of telling Briar everything. But she was a pragmatist. She'd looked at this from every angle, like he'd told her to, and she already knew how it would end.

Even in the best possible scenario, where all the Witches were revived and they were able to restore the kingdom of magic, there was no guarantee that removing the Butterfly Curse would be simple—or quick. It was one of the most powerful curses ever cast, one that had banished a Witch of legendary power. Fi might still have quite a journey ahead of her.

Telling Briar about the curse was asking him to choose between her and everything he loved. She already knew he would sacrifice it all to come with her—his family and his life here in Andar, everything he was about to get back. She couldn't let him do it. Fi knew how precious those things were and what it meant to walk away. She had lived that. It was a sacrifice she'd never let him make.

She squeezed her arms around Briar's neck. The wispy curtains trailed around them, the red rosebuds unfurling into blooms. She would find a way to break the Butterfly Curse, and then she would come back, and Briar—the real Briar, the one who would wake from this bed, the one with a loving family around him and a whole kingdom to care for—if *that* Briar loved her, if they were truly meant to be, then they would end up together, no matter how long it took. That was a kind of destiny Fi could believe in.

Until then, she had to let him go.

She knew she'd never be able to make Briar understand. She stood up on her tiptoes to whisper in his ear. "Thanks for the adventure."

Then she threw herself from his arms and leaned over the figure of Prince Briar Rose on the bed, pressing their lips together. The prince's lips were soft, but she felt nothing at first, this kiss empty and cold compared with the one they'd shared in the river. Then gradually Fi could feel heat flowing back into his body, and a warm hand settled against her neck, holding her close. Fi shut her eyes and fisted her hands in his velvet coat. The kiss was everything soft, everything light and good between them, everything that had made Fi into the savior of Briar Rose. Their best kiss yet, probably because Fi had finally put her whole heart into it.

Impossibly bright blue eyes blinked at her as she pulled back, looking down at the figure on the bed. She wasn't sure what to say. Was it really still Briar? The same Briar who had said he loved her a moment ago? Then a familiar lopsided smile stretched across his lips. Fi's heart ached with relief. Briar's hand slipped from her cheek to tangle in her hair, winding the soft strands between his fingers.

"Fi . . . ," Briar began, his bell-soft voice ringing in her ears.

If she stayed, if she listened to whatever Briar was about to say, Fi knew she would lose her resolve. "I have to find Shane," she said. She pulled away, practically fleeing for the door.

Halfway down the stairs, she almost slammed right into Shane, who was on her way up. Relief washed over her.

"Shane!" Fi cried, clutching her partner's shoulders. "You're awake—it worked."

"Not as well as you think." Shane's expression was grim. "Something's wrong. Come quick—you too, Briar," she added, eyes flicking behind Fi to where Briar had followed her onto the stairs. His eyes were hooded and serious, but Fi wasn't sure if it was because of what had just happened between them or because of whatever was waiting for them below.

Fi realized what Shane meant the second she reached the base of the stairs. The castle was too quiet. With the sleeping curse broken, everyone should be waking up, getting to their feet, and shaking off their century-long dreams. But none of the figures even stirred. The uneasiness that had been plaguing Fi since they reached the castle returned with a vengeance, twisting her stomach into knots. Something was very, very wrong here.

Briar pushed past her. He crouched at the side of a gray-haired woman in a sweeping blue robe, calling her name and shaking her gently. Her collar was embroidered with an ivory snake, and some tiny corner of Fi's mind wondered if she were a Witch of the Order of the Rising Rain. The woman's head lolled against the wall.

Briar looked up at Fi and Shane, pale with disbelief. "I don't understand. They should be awake."

"I'm guessing it's got something to do with this." Shane squatted down next to Briar, tugging gingerly on an almost-invisible thread wrapped tightly around the woman's neck. Pulled away from the flesh, it glinted yellow in the sunlight.

Golden thread. Fi's blood ran cold.

"When I first woke up, they were glowing," Shane explained. "And not just on her. On all of them." She jerked her head toward the hallway.

Fi followed her gaze, horrified. Now that she knew what she was looking for, she could see them: Tiny golden threads twisted around the necks of every figure strewn along the hall, tight as piano wire and invisible until the light hit them.

"The Spindle Witch," Briar whispered, sinking to his knees. His hand trembled against the sleeping woman's shoulder. "She did this. She's bound them so they can't wake up."

"We'll see about that." Shane yanked a silver dagger out of her boot, pressing the blade to the golden thread.

Fi could have told her it wouldn't work. But she felt

frozen, as if she were watching from very far away. Blood rushed in her ears, drowning every thought but one.

She was right. It *had* been too easy.

Shane's knife slid off the thread and sliced deep into her thumb. She hissed. "I don't get it," she said, jamming the thumb in her mouth. "Why would the Spindle Witch bother with all this? If she wanted them gone, wouldn't it be easier to just kill them all?"

The silence hung for a long moment before Briar answered.

"Because she isn't finished with them yet." He had bowed his head, his eyebrows drawn together as if in pain. "The Spindle Witch always drains Witches of their magic before she kills them. But she can't do that while they're protected by the Dream Witch's spell."

So she had bound them instead. Saving them for later, Fi realized—like a spider entombing her prey in suffocating thread before devouring it at her leisure. Now they couldn't help Briar, but they still belonged to her.

The world felt like it was tilting on its axis. Fi's brain whirled, trying to catch up. She prided herself on considering every variable, on always having a backup plan. This time, she had nothing. They were alone in the castle, in the Forest of Thorns, with no powerful Witch allies and no escape plan. They'd walked right into the Spindle Witch's trap, and Fi had a feeling the worst was yet to come.

"What do we do now?" Shane asked, voicing what they were all thinking.

Fi looked at Briar. But Briar wasn't looking at her, or at Shane. He was looking at the Witch sleeping beneath the window, watching her face frantically for any sign of waking.

Fi swallowed. "Briar . . ."

"I don't know," Briar croaked. He curled forward on his knees, his fingers clenched into his hair. "I don't know," he repeated desperately. "It wasn't supposed to be like this. Saving the kingdom, defeating the Spindle Witch—that was all part of the Great Witches' plan. I don't know how to finish it by myself."

Briar's breath was ragged as he bent over the sleeping Witch.

"You have to wake up," he begged, ripping at the golden threads around her neck until his fingers bled. "Please! I'm not supposed to be alone anymore!"

That snapped Fi back to herself. She dropped to her knees next to Briar, pulling him back and wrapping her hands around his.

"You're *not* alone!" Fi forced him to look at her, the blood slick against her palm as she entwined their fingers. "I'm still here, Briar, and we'll figure this out together. I promise."

The desperate look he shot her almost broke Fi's heart.

"Whatever we're going to do, we better make it fast. Look." Shane stood braced against the window, staring out over the Forest of Thorns.

Fi stepped behind her. At first she thought it was a storm cloud over her partner's shoulder—a giant thunderhead billowing across the sky. Then she realized it was a mass of crows, all flying together like a great storm.

Unbidden, the accounts of the fall of Andar rose through Fi's mind: *Witches fled and fell to their knees in despair as the sky was blotted out by beating black wings, the fury of the storm of crows eclipsed only by the power and cruelty of the Witch that rode in their midst. The wrathful tempest. The harbinger of Andar's ruin.*

The Spindle Witch was coming.

Shane wheeled back from the window. "I'm pretty sure we don't want to be here when *that* shows up. What's the fastest way out of here? Briar!" she snapped when he didn't answer, still lost in a daze.

Briar shook himself. "The rose vines in my tower reach all the way to the ground. We could climb out that way, but . . ." He looked out over the sleeping figures. "We can't leave them here. We have to save them. My brother, Sage, is in the throne room—"

"We'll never make it that far," Shane cut in. "And even if we did, you think the three of us could carry him out of here?"

Fi knew her partner was right. Even if they could somehow get Briar's brother out, they'd never be able to drag him through the spiders and the Forest of Thorns and the wastes beyond. Fi had serious doubts the three of them were going to make it.

Briar seemed to know it, too. He stared down at his hands like he wasn't sure what they were even for.

Shane hauled Briar up by his coat. "You save your brother—you save all of them—by living to fight another day. Now get moving."

Emotions warred across Briar's face—anger, despair, worry, agony. In the end, he looked determined. "Right," he said, pressing his lips into a line. "One battle at a time. First we escape together."

Shane nodded, satisfied, and then took off, leading them up the tower. Fi followed Briar, staring at her partner's back and wondering whether she'd caught a glimpse of the Shane who could have been War King in another life.

When they reached the top of the stairs, Fi dashed to the windowsill. The tower was high enough to give her vertigo, but the roses that had protected Briar grew thick and lush down the wall, trailing all the way to the ground.

"Princes first," Shane said, pushing Briar toward the window. "This is still a rescue."

"She's right. Go, Briar," Fi insisted.

Briar clambered over the sill and then hesitated for a moment, his hand covering Fi's in the roses. She couldn't even imagine everything he was thinking as he looked up at her. But all he said was, "Don't fall."

I'm not the one a hundred years out of practice, Fi thought.

The storm of crows had almost reached the Forest of Thorns. Fi could see the birds in the courtyard taking off to join the fray, their wings beating in a frenzy.

"Go! Go! Go!" Shane yelled, practically shoving Fi out the window.

Fi got one dizzying glimpse of the ground far below and then almost plummeted to meet it, barely managing to stop herself from falling to her death thanks to Shane's *helpful* push. Shane threw herself after them, yelping as she grabbed a handful of vines to break her fall.

They raced down the tower hand over hand, scrambling through the roses toward the black thorns below. Under the dense branches, they'd be hidden from the crows, but once again at the mercy of the Forest of Thorns.

32

>>> ——— <<<

Shane

SHANE HAD SEEN enough of these thorns to last a life-time. She led the way through the forest at a dead sprint, letting her instincts guide her through the twists and turns. There was no way to chart a straight path, but getting out had to be easier than getting in. After all, it didn't matter where they made their escape as long as they didn't end up back at the castle.

Fi's grim face said she believed otherwise, but Fi was a pessimist. For all her brilliance, her partner had a bad habit of giving up too easily, as though if she couldn't see the answer, it didn't exist. That's where Shane came in. She'd learned from experience that as long as you didn't give up, you always had a chance to turn things around.

Shane leapt over a spiky branch lying in her path and spared a glance at the sky. She couldn't see the crows anymore, and she'd only spotted a few strands of frayed spiderweb strung between the branches, but she knew better than to let her guard down.

They broke through into a clearing. Shane slowed, considering her next move. A dark hollow, deep and long as a tunnel, stretched away into the woods on the far side of the glade, but she could see at least three more places where the thorns veered into branching pathways. Any one of them could lead them out—or farther in.

Fi was bent over, breathing hard, and Briar Rose looked ready to pass out on his feet. She didn't have time to be wrong. They'd turned and turned, but somewhere deep in her body, Shane still knew what direction they'd come from. She had to trust her gut. Her gaze fixed on the dark tunnel.

An eerie howl broke the silence of the forest. Shane swore under her breath. The call echoed through the pillars of thorns, followed by another and another, and then the whole cage of brambles was shaking as something moved toward them, crunching through the bone-like branches. She couldn't see what it was, but she thought she caught a flicker of movement to her left, a shadow stalking through the trees.

Spiders didn't howl. This was a new threat—something that had been lurking in the Forest of Thorns, waiting for them.

"Get behind me," she warned Fi and Briar, unslinging her ax.

Another howl rose above the rest, long and haunting. It reminded her of the wolf calls back in Steelwight that echoed through the deep snows and the valleys of ice. When the wild howl broke off, all the rest did, too. Shane's stomach lurched in the sudden silence.

"Do you think they're moving off?" Fi whispered.

"No," Shane said, tightening her grip on the ax. Most things got quiet when they were about to strike.

Sticks and branches exploded as the first of the creatures burst through the thick brambles. Another followed, then another. In seconds, they were surrounded.

Shane sucked in a breath through her teeth. She'd been wrong. These weren't wolves—these were *monsters*.

Shane had spent enough time in the deep forests to see wolves up close. They were majestic animals with soft fur in muted colors, striking and intelligent. The gray wolves of Icefern were even revered as omens of good luck. These were more like the grotesque monsters in her grandmother's ghost stories, hulking beasts bristling with coarse, matted fur. They were at least twice the size of normal wolves, and their backs were marred by bony juts of thick, rotting spines. An enormous white creature, clearly the leader, gnashed a spiky branch to splinters in its jaws.

Shane hadn't been able to make a dent in those thorns, but the monsters snapped them like so much kindling. These were creatures of the Forest of Thorns—creatures of the Spindle Witch.

Fi had gotten her rope out, her knuckles clenched around the frayed cord. Briar leaned forward. "Should we run?" he muttered.

Shane gritted her teeth. "Can't. They'll kill us in the trees." Four of the beasts prowled around the clearing, but she could see other shapes moving in the thorns, cutting off their escape.

She knew they'd gotten away from the castle too easily.

They'd gone right where the Spindle Witch wanted them to go—into the teeth of her monsters.

She exchanged stares with the white wolf as they sized each other up. The others slunk along the edges of the glade, and Shane jerked her head around, trying to keep track of them all at once. She caught Fi's eye over her shoulder.

"We'll have to fight our way out," she said, voice low. "I'll keep them off you and Briar as much as I can. Just—stay alive, okay? I didn't come all this way to lose a partner now."

Fi's eyes widened. "Shane—"

"Look out!" Briar shouted.

One of the beasts lunged at Fi. Its jaws snapped over empty air as Briar grabbed her elbow, both of them stumbling out of the way. Shane swung hard and fast, clubbing it right in the ribs and knocking it back into the thorns. Then the white wolf was on her, seizing her moment of distraction and lunging for her neck.

Shane ducked—barely. Her braid tumbled down her back, ripped out of its knot by those vicious teeth. She wouldn't be surprised if she'd lost a few inches of hair on that, too. Clenching her ax in both hands, she heaved the blade into the creature's neck. Her arms juddered like she'd slammed it into a tree. The monstrous head lurched to the side, spittle flying—but then it was on top of her again, snarling and snapping, smashing into Shane with its burly shoulder and knocking her clean off her feet.

Shane gasped as she hit the dirt. Her ax had left a gash in the wolf's thick ruff, but it wasn't even bleeding. Not so much as a trickle darkened its rancid fur.

The beast pivoted, racing for her. Shane wrenched her ax

up just in time to jam the handle between its jaws. But she'd seen those teeth bite clean through one of the indestructible thorns, and she knew her ax handle would only last seconds. She had to act fast.

Ribs screaming, arms shaking, Shane twisted until she could drive one of her boots right into the monster's throat. The force of her kick threw it into the dirt, and it backed away, shaking off the blow. Shane forced herself to her feet. Her bruised ribs gave a painful jolt, warning her not to do that again.

"Briar!" Fi cried.

Shane whipped around. One of the wolves had latched its jaws around the prince's boot and was dragging him toward the thorns. In seconds, he'd be gone. Gasping for breath, Shane threw herself bodily at the wolf. The bones in her shoulder creaked as she smashed into its cavernous flank, both of them tumbling end over end through the dirt. Briar scrambled back, panting.

"Shane, behind you!"

Shane caught a flash of yellowed teeth headed right for her, all flying spit and rippling fur. Then something jerked it back—Fi's rope, wrapped around the wolf's hind leg as she strained to drag it away. Shane appreciated her partner's determination, but holding on to that rope was about to go from really brave to really foolish. The wolf snarled, its mouth frothing, as it rounded on Fi.

"Cover your eyes!"

Shane took a wild guess Briar wasn't talking to the wolf. She threw her arm up over her face. A flash of brilliant light burst around her, so bright she saw stars even with her eyes closed. She could hear the monsters yelping. Her blind hand stumbled on her ax handle—then she wrenched her body around and swung hard, nailing the closest wolf in its belly. A howl rippled through its rotted throat. Fi's rope fell away as it darted into the trees, its narrowed yellow eyes watching her through the thorns.

Shane's ribs were on fire under her skin. She rolled up to her elbows, summoning the strength to stand—then Fi was right there, extending a hand to pull her up.

"Nice assist," Shane panted.

Fi shoved her hair out of her face. "I'm not looking to lose a partner either," she admitted, allowing a rare smile.

Shane wished she had a second to enjoy that. But the wolves were already regrouping, and there were just too many of them. Any second, they were going to be overrun. She wiped a hand across her mouth, chest heaving. Her arms shook from the weight of the ax. She wouldn't last much longer at this rate—and neither would Fi or Briar.

Shane was not giving up, but she was short on ideas. How were you supposed to fight something that didn't bleed?

A whistle sounded from deep in the brush. The wolves' ears flicked up, alert and listening. The whistle came twice more, high and shrill. Then a figure appeared in the opening where the massive white wolf had broken through the thorns, her bright cloak a crimson stain against the dark forest.

Shane's mouth fell open as Red strolled into the clearing. What was she doing here?

Her dress this time was simple, floating around her arms

and hugging her chest before falling into a skirt of long, tattered layers. Sharp brown eyes found Shane's as Red lowered her hand from her lips.

"Look out!" Shane yelled, her heart squeezing as the giant white wolf loped toward the girl. She threw her hand out desperately—and then froze as the creature skidded to a stop and lowered its head, pushing its snout into Red's open hand. Red gave a coy smile.

"You," Shane breathed, her insides churning with horror and disbelief.

"Oh yes. Me," Red agreed, scratching the deformed wolf behind the ears. Its tongue lolled out of its bony jaw.

"These monsters—" Shane choked out. In her heart, she knew what was going on—what it meant for Red to be standing there beside the wolf. But every fiber of her being begged for it not to be true.

"My little pets," Red crooned. "You don't have to be afraid of them. They're very well trained."

Shane's heartbeat thudded in her head. She could feel Fi and Briar hovering behind her, uncertain. Then something touched her shoulder—Fi's hand, pressed to her back in some combination of *I got you* and *I told you so*. Shane wasn't sure which one hurt worse.

"Why are you attacking us?" she demanded.

Red pursed her lips. "I'm not attacking *you*, Shane. I have nothing against you at all. In fact, I tried to give you a way out." Shane's heart stuttered, remembering Red's plea for them to leave together.

There is no after—not for us.

Red had known—in that moment, she had known

exactly what was going to happen. Maybe that was why Red had looked so devastated, like leaving ripped her heart out. Shane knew the feeling. It was happening to her right now, remembering a hundred tiny moments between them— Red's daring smile as they ran together through the market, her sweet, unguarded song, the softness of her body against Shane's as they danced, the heat of her goodbye kiss. Had it all been a lie?

Red seemed to read all that on her face. She tipped her head, giving a mocking smile.

"There's no need to look so hurt. This isn't personal. I'm just following orders."

Briar stiffened. "You work for the Spindle Witch."

Red gave a little shrug, but she didn't deny it.

Shane's last hopes crumbled. "But you helped us get here," she protested. "If she was trying to stop us—"

"Stop you?" Red looked amused. "If the Spindle Witch wanted to stop you, you would have been dead long before you ever reached this castle. She wanted Briar Rose to wake up, more than anyone." Her eyes flicked to the prince. "She has such plans for you, Your Highness," Red promised, before turning to Fi. "That's why she sent me to watch you lot, to follow and report back, and above all else, to make sure the prince got his little kiss."

Fi's expression morphed with horror and understanding. "Because she couldn't reach Briar in the dream. She needed me to wake him up."

"Very clever," Red agreed. "Probably why she wants you dead, Fi. The Spindle Witch was very explicit on that point. Kill you, then bring Briar Rose back alive."

"And what about me?" Shane asked. She pushed Fi behind her, hoping her partner would have the good sense to stay there.

Red walked her fingers down the white wolf's spine. "I don't think the Spindle Witch knows you exist, Shane. Probably for the best, don't you think?" she asked, arching one eyebrow.

Shane couldn't stand that expression. It was familiar and strange all at once—Red's teasing smile, but sharper now, brittle as broken glass. How could this be the same girl who had danced with her in Bellicia, who had begged Shane not to fall in love because she'd only get hurt? That was the girl she needed to reach.

"This isn't the real you, Red," Shane pleaded. "I know it, and deep down I think you know it, too."

"The real me." Red laughed hollowly. "I wouldn't even know who that was. The Spindle Witch took me in when no one else would and did me a favor I can never repay. I'm her relic hunter. That's who I am, Shane." Her eyes burned in the low light. "But you're right about one thing. I did want things to end differently between us."

For a second, Shane thought she saw a glimmer of the real Red, her façade breaking as the girl stretched out her hand, palm upturned.

"I'll give you one last chance. Walk away now, and I'll spare your life."

There it was again—the same desperation, the same crack in her perfect mask that Shane had seen the night before.

"I already told you, I'm staying," Shane growled softly. "Now it's your turn to make a choice." She hefted her ax up onto her shoulder. "I don't know what happened to you. I don't know what you owe the Spindle Witch. But I do know it's not too late. I could still help you."

Red scoffed. "Please. You can't even help yourself." All the warmth had drained from her face.

Shane held her eyes, trying to put everything she felt into that one look. "If I could do it all again—even if I'd known everything from the beginning—I'd still try to save you."

"I know," Red murmured. "That's what made it so easy." She lifted her fingers to her mouth, preparing to whistle.

"You'll regret working for the Spindle Witch," Briar said. Shane couldn't tell if it was a threat or a warning.

Red's fingers paused just shy of her lips. A shadow of fear flickered across her face. "I think I'd regret crossing her more." Then her mouth quirked up, her smile cruel. "Besides, I only have to kill one of you." Her eyes flicked to Fi, and she gave a sharp whistle.

Another wolf exploded out of the brambles, right behind Fi. It must have been creeping around behind them while Red spoke.

Shane cursed. She should have seen that coming!

Splinters of the broken thorns hurtled in all directions. Fi threw up her arms. A chunk of wood slammed into the side of her head, and Shane watched helplessly as Fi crumpled to the ground, her eyes widening in shock before fluttering closed. The massive wolf stood over her, its lips pulled back in a triumphant snarl.

"No!" Shane yelled.

She didn't make it one step. The entire glade plunged into shadow, as though something had ripped the sun out of the sky. The thorn trees seemed to writhe in the strange light.

Briar moved faster than Shane's eyes could follow. One second he was behind her, and the next his hand was closing around Red's throat. The girl gasped, the sound choked off as his grip tightened.

Shane could only stare. The ends of Briar's fingers had stretched and elongated, tapering off into bone-like claws. His golden hair was swept back, and power seethed all around him. Shane shivered as she caught sight of his expression. His lips had twisted into a smile, and his eyes smoldered, dripping with disdain as he considered Red's astonished face. A single drop of blood ran down her throat where the curved tip of his claw dug into her soft skin.

The shadows were coming from Briar. Even the monsters cowered before him, whining and crawling on their bellies in the dirt.

"Call them off," Briar warned, pushing Red back toward the thorns.

Shane's pulse roared in her ears. This was Briar Rose, Fi's prince, and he had just saved her life. But everything inside Shane was screaming this was wrong.

Red coughed weakly. She gave two quick whistles. Her creatures got cautiously to their feet and slunk away into the forest. The giant white wolf was the last to leave, whining from the edge of the trees as he looked back at Red.

"I've done what you asked," Red began, lifting her hands to grab Briar's fingers where they gripped her neck. "Let me go, or—"

"Or?" Briar repeated, voice silky and dangerous. He forced her backward, and Red gasped as she was pushed against the wicked thorns, farther and farther until she was a breath from being impaled. Her chest heaved.

"Please," she begged through tears. But she wasn't looking at Briar. Her gaze was fixed on Shane.

Shane could see what was about to happen, almost in slow motion. Briar's lips curled as his muscles tensed. He was going to slam her against the razor thorns. Red was going to die, and only Shane could stop it.

If she chose to. Wasn't that a kind of fate?

Shane wasn't sure when she had started running. She was acting on pure instinct. She didn't know if it was because of Red's terrified expression, or because Fi wouldn't want Briar to lose himself to darkness, or if despite the betrayal, despite everything, some part of her was still in love with Red. All she knew was that she couldn't let this happen.

"Stop!" Shane swung her ax high, bringing the blunt side down toward Briar's hands. She didn't care if she broke both of his wrists.

Briar let go, leaping back and letting Red's body sag to the ground. His blazing eyes snapped to Shane.

"Get out of here!" Shane told Red, putting herself between them.

Red stared up at Shane in surprise. Then she turned and ran, her red cloak streaming after her as she disappeared into the dark after her wolves. Shane really, really hoped she wouldn't regret sparing Red's life. At the moment, though, she had bigger problems.

She turned back to Briar, not sure what to expect. His expression was furious. Shane had the sick feeling he could rip her apart right now, and his only regret would be getting blood on his coat. She tightened her grip on her ax, bracing herself.

A groan broke the stalemate—Fi was stirring, slowly coming to. Briar's gaze shot to her, and the murderous look melted away, replaced by one of shock. He held his clawed hands up in front of his face, backing away as though he could escape what he had almost done.

Briar shook his hands, and Shane watched as the shadows and the bone claws disappeared, leaving only the regular Briar in his blue coat, his fingers trembling. Shane didn't lower her ax.

Briar gave her a thin smile, one that didn't reach his eyes. "You don't need that," he said. "I'm myself again."

It was that *again* Shane didn't like. "What just happened?" she demanded.

"I lost control of my magic for a moment," Briar said. "But it's over. It won't happen again." He said it firmly, like a promise to himself, but if Briar's *in control* was anything like Fi's, that wasn't saying much.

Shane could understand that Fi's life had been threatened. She could even understand the idea of Briar losing control of his magic. What she couldn't shake was the image of his lips curling into a smile as he prepared to slam Red into the thorns, reveling in the act.

"Briar? Shane?" Fi sat up slowly, clutching her head.

Briar started toward her, but Shane stepped in front of him, resting the gleaming head of her ax against his chest. "If you're a danger to her—"

"I'm not," Briar said desperately. "I would never do anything to hurt Fi. You haven't known me long, but you have to believe me. Please. The longer we stand here, the more time the Spindle Witch has to stop us."

And by *stop us*, he meant *kill us*. Or at least her and Fi. Reluctantly, Shane lowered her ax. "Fine. But you and I are going to have a long talk later."

Briar nodded, shaking her off and rushing to Fi's side. Her partner seemed a little worse for wear, with a sluggish trickle of blood matted over her ear and slicking down the side of her face. It looked gruesome, but Shane knew from personal experience that head wounds came with a lot of blood.

The boy helping Fi to her feet looked nothing like the nightmare specter who had nearly smashed Red into the thorns. But appearances could be deceiving.

Shane looked back at the splintered grove, imagining Red somewhere in the dark woods, surrounded by her monsters. She wasn't sure she'd done the right thing, letting Red go. But now more than ever, she was sure it wasn't over between them.

33

Fi

FI WIPED THE blood out of her eye, branches flashing over her head as they ran. A dark tunnel of thorns stretched out before them, but Fi could barely see it through the throbbing in her head, the pain pounding like a mallet inside her skull. Her legs felt rubbery and weak, her knees threatening to give out any second.

The fog in her brain was finally starting to clear, but she must have hit her head harder than she realized, because when she first came to, she thought she'd seen Shane facing off with Briar. But that was impossible. Right?

The shadows were growing thicker, the tunnel of twisted brambles closing around them like a snare. Fi tried not to imagine monstrous wolves bursting through the thorns. She couldn't see a way forward—only more darkness, stretching out forever. Maybe this was another dead end. Her feet slowed, and Briar pulled up short beside her. Shane almost skidded into them from behind.

"We're close, I can feel it," Shane promised, though her partner absolutely had no proof of that.

A cool breeze touched her face like a soft hand, darting through the space between branches. Fi closed her eyes, trying to place the familiar feeling. Then her eyes sprang open. Little bits of curling paper, some of them burned to ash while others still glowed like tiny embers, were swirling all around her, darting and moving together like a school of fish.

Paper. Fi's eyes widened. Of course she knew this magic. It was the first magic she'd ever been shown—the power that granted small wishes.

Shane laughed out loud, snatching at the scraps. "Unbelievable! That Witch has come to show us the way out!"

Fi's heart swelled until it was so full it hurt. The paper seemed to shiver in the air before darting away, lighting a path through the dark.

"Come on!" Shane said, urging them forward. Fi summoned the last of her energy and chased the tiny scraps that glowed like a trail of stars.

At some point, without thinking, she had grabbed Briar's hand. His grip was tight around hers, sweaty and even a little sticky with blood, but it was solid, real in a way Briar had never been before. Fi wasn't sure what it would mean to him—she wasn't even sure what it meant to *her*—except that in spite of everything that had happened, he was still right beside her.

The paper scraps dwindled until a single spark floated through the air ahead of her. Fi pushed forward, the thorns biting into her skin. Then a flare of light struck her eyes—a bright circle of sunlight in the distance, and beyond it, the Paper Witch all in white, glowing like a beacon.

With a gasp, Fi and Briar burst through the last row of thorns. The Paper Witch caught Fi's shoulder, holding her up.

"You're here," she rasped out. He seemed unreal, his wispy blond hair and tinkling bell and pristine robe untouched by the waste.

"Filore." Blue eyes crinkled as the Paper Witch squeezed her shoulders. "I am so relieved to see you."

"And what about me?" Shane demanded, practically doubled over with her hands on her knees.

The man chuckled. "Surely you don't mean I should have been worried about *you*." Then he turned, favoring the last member of their party with a gentle smile. "And Prince Briar Rose." The Paper Witch bowed low, his eyes shining. "Allow me to be the first of your people to welcome you back."

"Thank you," Briar said. His voice sounded a little thick.

Fi could see how much the moment meant to both of them. She could still hear the Paper Witch's voice in her head when he'd first examined the spindle's mark on her finger: *the moment all the descendants of Andar have been hoping for all these years*. She took a step back and left them to it, turning to find her partner.

Shane stood a few feet away with her arms crossed. Sweat glistened on her fair face, the wind whipping through the wild snarl of her ash-brown hair. Fi moved to join her. Together they looked out over the hulking forest, searching for the white glimmer of the castle lost in the thorns. The giant storm of crows had settled over it like a shroud, some circling the high towers while others perched on the walls and ramparts.

"This is definitely one for the books," Shane said, shaking her head.

Fi knew what she meant. But for just a second, she imagined their story written into one of her childhood folktales, a dazzling illumination of her and Shane and Briar against a sea of carmine-red roses. From the grin on her partner's face, she had a feeling Shane was imagining a different retelling, preferably in a tavern, to a beautiful girl.

"We almost died," Fi reminded her.

"And yet, we didn't die," Shane countered, not sounding particularly concerned about it.

Fi crossed her arms, fighting a smile. "We didn't get any treasure."

"We got a prince. They're worth a lot."

For ransom? Because that was how Shane made it sound. Fi chuckled in spite of herself. "The Spindle Witch is still out there."

Shane winced. "Yeah, that's going to be a problem."

"Any way you look at it, this job was a failure."

Shane shrugged. "Only if it ends here. I don't like leaving things unfinished. Besides, we made it all the way through the Forest of Thorns—which everyone said was impossible—broke the curse on Andar's prince, escaped the most powerful evil Witch of all time, and even dragged the Paper Witch out of his house for once. I'd say that's a good start, partner."

Well, when she put it that way. Fi grinned back at the huntsman. "Still just the one job though, right, *partner*?"

Shane's expression was pure gold. "You know it."

EPILOGUE

>>> <<<

Briar Rose

BRIAR LEANED INTO the shelter of the broken tower where they'd made camp, staring up at the stars that winked in and out through the swirl of black dust. Night had settled like a cloak over the kingdom of Andar. For the first time in his life, Briar had watched the sun set from outside the castle walls.

He stretched his feet out toward their small fire, wincing as his knees popped. Briar had spent a hundred years dreaming of being back in his real body, but there was a lot he'd forgotten, or never known in the first place. His arms throbbed with the crisscross of angry red scratches from their flight through the forest. His legs creaked like they were made of wood, and he was pretty sure he couldn't run another step if his life depended on it. He kept sneezing when the dust got up his nose. But there was something satisfying about every sting and bruise and sneeze and ache—because he could feel it. He could feel everything.

Briar looked down at his fingers, remembering the bite of the golden threads slicing into his hands. He couldn't see the cuts anymore—his hands were bandaged in thin strips of white paper, each inked with the long, curling letters of the Divine Rose script. That one, he could read. The second those bandages closed over his wounds, the pain had vanished.

The Paper Witch sat across from him, scratching the same symbols onto more paper bandages. Fi and Shane had fallen asleep hours ago. Fi was curled on her side close to the fire with her partner sprawled next to her, and if Shane stretched out any farther, her fist was going in Fi's face.

The Paper Witch shook his head fondly. Briar's chest squeezed, imagining that same little half smile on another face. It was the expression his sister, Camellia, had worn whenever he brought her a flower with dirt still trailing from the roots or slipped a nonsense poem into one of the Great Witches' spell books, just to see if they'd notice. They always did.

Now that he was looking for the similarities, it was unmistakable—the willowy figure, the long silver-blond hair, the knowing sparkle in his blue eyes, and his elaborate crystal earring, carved with a hint of red deep within. Only up close was it clear it was a rose. Briar let his head fall back against the stone wall.

"I should have known you were Camellia's great-grandson."

The Paper Witch shook his head. "You weren't meant to know. Spells that break curses are very particular—I couldn't interfere without the risk of changing the outcome."

Briar blew out a breath. "I wouldn't mind if you had

changed it. At least a little." He closed his eyes for a second, trying not to imagine his brother slumped on his throne with golden threads twisted around his neck. Sage and all the people of the castle were still asleep, and he'd just left them there.

The Paper Witch reached out, laying a hand against his elbow. "There was nothing else you could have done for them. Not yet, anyway." Briar's head jerked up, and the Paper Witch laughed softly at his look of surprise. "This is not the end," he said. "It is only the very beginning."

Briar swallowed hard. It was exactly what Camellia would have said if she were sitting beside him, flowers instead of paper scraps crumpled in her lap. The ache of missing her was still there, but it eased a little, now that he knew a sliver of her magic lived on in the Paper Witch—and maybe in other Witches, a whole line of royal descendants with blue eyes and knowing smiles. Maybe one day he'd even get to meet them, now that he was free of the sleeping curse.

The fire flickered like it would go out. Automatically, Briar lifted his hand, reaching for the familiar magic to summon sparks to his fingers. The Paper Witch caught his wrist, his serene face suddenly serious.

"I'd be careful about calling on that power too much," he warned.

Briar jerked his hand away. "Why?"

The Paper Witch tipped his head. "Magic can be unpredictable," he said at last. "You've been connected to the Spindle Witch for a very long time. I'm afraid using your power makes you more susceptible to losing yourself. Remember, Briar, the Great Witches stopped the Spindle Witch from claiming you on your sixteenth birthday, but until she is gone, you will never be completely free of her."

Briar swallowed, looking down at his hands. Under the white bandages, they were soft and human, tender where the threads had cut into him. But he could still remember the sensation of losing himself to his power, the way his bony claws had clenched around Red's throat. He never wanted to become that again.

The Paper Witch nodded gravely. "I see you have some idea of what's at stake." He watched Briar for another moment, and then rose to retrieve more firewood, his hand alighting briefly on the prince's shoulder. "Try to remember. Magic—especially *your* magic, Briar Rose—is best for small wishes."

Briar remembered that phrase. *Small wishes* were what Camellia believed magic was meant for—a philosophy she must have passed down to her descendants.

The Paper Witch stood, moving away. Briar's hand trembled as he grabbed the stick and poked at the little bits of wood in the fire, weathered chunks of floorboards and railing posts they'd scavenged from the half-buried buildings around the tower. He had believed his sister's philosophy of magic without question as a child, but now he couldn't help wondering if small wishes weren't enough.

Hazel eyes blinked open, catching him in the act of leaning over her—the same way they'd looked at each other in the tower, with their positions reversed.

Briar sat up fast. "It's the middle of the night," he said. "You should go back to sleep."

"You're not sleeping," Fi pointed out. She pushed herself

up onto an elbow. Briar's coat slid off her shoulder and she reached out to catch it.

Briar laughed under his breath. "I've had enough beauty sleep for a lifetime. Several lifetimes, actually. If I keep sleeping, I'll get too pretty and you won't like me anymore."

The joke was out before Briar really had time to think about it. He breathed in too fast and the hurt caught up with him, aching like a fist in his chest. Sitting beside her in the dark, with the firelight glowing in her eyes, he'd almost forgotten that she'd rejected him only a few hours ago. Her words echoed in his head. *It's just not meant to be.*

"Fi . . . I . . ." Briar hesitated, not sure how to take it back.

"No," Fi said, shaking her head. "You're right. I don't think I'd want to travel with someone who was *that* pretty."

Her mouth quirked up at the corners, and Briar laughed in relief, a knot of tension uncoiling inside of him. He had lost his bid for Fi's heart—but even if he couldn't have that, he hadn't wanted to give up on the hope of being her friend. There was one thing he needed to tell her, though.

"You don't have to travel with me anymore," he said, and then winced, watching Fi blink in surprise. "That didn't come out right. I only meant that the bond the spindle made between us is broken."

Slowly, he unwound the bandages and held up his hand to the fire. No wisp of red curled around his finger anymore, no shimmering thread tying her to him. Fi's spindle mark had disappeared, too.

"If you leave Andar, the Spindle Witch will have no

reason to come after you. I'll find a way to save my kingdom and defeat her once and for all. But—"

"You mean *we*," Fi interrupted. She said it so easily, with so much certainty, that Briar's heart skipped a couple beats. "We're going to do those things."

"You're sure?" he asked hesitantly, though the last thing he wanted was to push her into leaving.

Fi shot him a flat look. "Just try to get rid of me—or Shane, for that matter. She's already decided you're her best shot for unimaginable riches and glory." Her face softened as she nudged her elbow against his, and Briar jumped at the small touch. Fi smiled. "I promised we'd figure this out together, remember?" She held out her hand to Briar. "We keep going—until the Spindle Witch is defeated and Andar is free."

"Until Andar is free," he agreed, already feeling lighter.

He could hardly breathe for fear this might be a dream, that he would wake up and be alone. But her hand was real and warm—the same hand that had gripped his as she led him out of the Forest of Thorns, into the light. Someone had told him once that a girl would save him, and she had. The rest, they could do together.

ACKNOWLEDGMENTS

BRINGING OUT A book is a challenging, wonderful, amazing, terrifying journey. There are so many people who helped this dream become a reality, and I am so grateful for each and every one of them!

Thank you to my wonderful agents, Carrie Hannigan and Ellen Goff, who saw the potential in this book and worked tirelessly to find it the perfect home. I couldn't ask for better partners and champions on this journey! Also a big thanks to Rhea Lyons, Soumeya B. Roberts, and all the wonderful folks at HG Literary.

Thank you to Arianne Lewin, the very best editor a debut author could ask for. Your insight and advice was absolutely spot-on. You pushed me and this book far past where I thought we could go, and I'm so amazed by who Fi and Shane became under your guidance!

Thanks to my amazing team at Penguin: Elise LeMassena, Ruta Rimas, Anne Heausler, Jessica Jenkins, and everyone who made this book possible. Also thanks to Leo Nickolls for the gorgeous cover art! Big thank you to Rachel Boden, Aliyana Hirji, and the entire amazing Hachette UK team.

Thanks to Chris Lupo and Verve. You blew me away with your enthusiasm, and I remain blown away.

Thanks to Rosaria Munda and Akshaya Raman, amazing authors who reached out to me in those first wild days after I got my book deal when I was so lost. Adrienne Tooley and Alexandra Overy: You are so kind and gave me so much advice and also wrote phenomenally inspiring books! Thanks to Emily Thiede, Meg Long, Lillie Lainoff, and all of the amazing 22Debuts. Being part of such a wonderful group of authors makes all the difference—you taught me so much!

Big thanks to Kyle, Christie, Sarah, Jennica, Natalie, Claire, and all the early readers whose enthusiasm was a bright spot just when I needed it most. Your feedback and encouragement meant the world to me.

Thanks to my whole family—my parents, who instilled in me a love of reading and fantasy; my sister, who stayed up watching anime with me until the middle of the night; and my grandmother, who read every one of my books even though she's a mystery fan! Also a big thank-you to the Dotters, especially my father-in-law, who is one of my first readers and has been such an amazing support.

Thanks to my two spoiled house cats. A lot of takeout. No small amount of coffee. And the Broken Shovels Farm Sanctuary, which was always there when my heart needed a little break.

Finally, thank you to my partner, Michelle, to whom this book is dedicated. You suffered through a million different drafts. You walked around and around the park with me until we came up with dialogue that made us both laugh. You were there for me when I wrote myself into corners and when I stayed up into the middle of the night figuring my way out. You are my first reader, my biggest fan, my editor, and my fellow writer. Like Alinor, you are a rock!